MORE THAN FRIENDS

I0703808

NEW YORK TIMES & USA TODAY BESTSELLING AUTHOR

NICOLE BLANCHARD

More Than Friends
Copyright © 2024 by Nicole Blanchard

All rights reserved. No part of this publication may be reproduced, distributed or transmitted in any form or by any means, including photocopying, recording, or other electronic or mechanical methods, without the prior written permission of the publisher, except in the case of brief quotations embodied in critical reviews and certain other noncommercial uses permitted by copyright law.

Publisher's Note: This is a work of fiction. Names, characters, places, and incidents are a product of the author's imagination. Locales and public names are sometimes used for atmospheric purposes. Any resemblance to actual people, living or dead, or to businesses, companies, events, institutions, or locales is completely coincidental.

DEDICATION

To your book bestie who got you into reading spicy romance, may they always have a face to sit on

CONTENTS

FRIEND ZONE

NEW YORK TIMES & USA TODAY BESTSELLING AUTHOR

NICOLE BLANCHARD

CHAPTER 1
CHARLIE

There was no way to escape.

Trust me, I'd checked. The small half-bath had no secret doorways, and the window was so minuscule I couldn't fit through it even if I lost the pesky freshman fifteen I'd packed on two years ago. I opened it despite my misgivings and despaired at the slow progression. The air filtered in, clammy and thick, but my desperate lungs drew it in greedily. My fingers dug into the windowsill and I prayed for the first time in ten years. *Please, God, don't let me faint.*

The knock at the door made me screech, and I clapped a hand over my mouth.

"Charlie," came a familiar voice. "You okay in there?"

"Liam, how many times do I have to tell you not to interrupt me when I'm on a date?" I washed my hands and gave a quick look in the mirror. I frowned at my reflection. Limp dirty blonde hair that fell rain-straight to my shoulders, plain brown eyes opened so wide I nearly scared myself.

Get it together, Charlie.

I opened the door and peered beneath Liam's raised arm. "Andrew didn't follow you, did he?"

"Why?" He sounded amused. I narrowed my eyes at him as I straightened. How could he be amused at a time like this? "What? I thought you got off on this part."

"What part? I don't get off on anything!" The screeching continued, and it was definitely coming from me. There must be something in the water. It wasn't like me to be so frantic and… unhinged.

Liam merely smiled that one-sided smile that made me want to sucker punch him. It made the dimple in his right cheek peek out to say hello. It was a tease, that dimple. It made most girls swoon, but it made me want to deck him because he only shared it with me when he was trying to piss me off, which he did with infuriating regularity. "Now, Charlie, you should know better than to keep breaking it off with these puppies if you aren't getting laid on the regular. Maybe that's why you're so uptight."

I looked to the ceiling. Maybe I'd find patience there. But there was no spiritual aid to be found, unless you counted the water stain that kind of looked like Jesus if I squinted just right. I'd grown sick of water stains. My dorm had them. My first apartment had them. What was it with college haunts and water-stained ceilings? One day I'd own my own home and there wouldn't be a water stain in sight.

"Focus."

I glared at him. "I am focused. Focused on not planting my fist in your face." I shoved around him, which wasn't easy considering how bulky he was. For a bartender-slash-veterinary student, he sure packed on the muscle. I guess it was hauling around all those kegs and delivering…I don't know calves or whatever it was he did at his family's farm that made him want to be a vet.

"Don't let your anger out on me because you aren't getting any." Liam followed close behind as I squeezed through the packed hallway of girls in skimpy dresses trying to get to the bathroom. Most of them side-eyed me until they caught onto the fact that Liam was much more interested in checking out their racks than paying any attention to me. After a lifetime of friendship, I was used to their reaction.

"I'm not angry."

"If I weren't getting laid, *I'd* be angry. Andrew must not be doing it right."

I spotted Andrew at the standing table where I left him, but paused instead of going to his side. I really hated this part. As I weighed my options, I said distractedly, "Then how do you explain the fact that you're a dick to me 24/7 if you're always getting laid? And Andrew is perfectly…nice."

"I'm not a dick," he said. My snort caused him to smile again, dimple twinkling. "Okay, well not all the time. Besides, I'm only like that with you because, you know, we're friends. The only time you should *really* worry is when I turn on the charm."

"You, charm? I doubt there's anything you could do that would ever make me forget what you were like at twelve with all your acne and that high-pitched voice. Sorry, buddy, there's no coming back from that."

Liam coughed and eyed a bombshell redhead who was giving him a sympathetic look. He leaned closer to me. "You promised me you'd never mention that again."

"And *you* promised you'd never interrupt another date."

"You can't be calling this a date," he replied, disbelief coloring his voice and expression. "Especially not if the sex is only *nice.*"

My thoughts ground to a halt and I reached up to tug at my hair. "What do you mean by that?"

Redhead forgotten, Liam reclined against the wall next to me and jerked his head to where Andrew stood checking his watch. "You only bring a guy here when you've reached the dumping phase and I'm not about to give you a sex education lesson."

"Dumping phase? How did—what do—how did you know I was going to break up with him?" I stumbled through my response, my voice nearly giving out several times in my attempt to speak. "I don't need a sex lesson from you."

"Really? We've been friends for ten years. I think I know how this is going to go."

I rolled my eyes. "You have no idea how it's going to go." I paused, biting my lip. "Do you?"

Liam waved at his manager when he began to shoot him impatient looks. That was Liam, totally unconcerned about the fact that he was supposed to be actually *working*. It drove me almost as insane as his ability to see right through me did. "This isn't the first time you've brought a guy here when you want to break up with him and I doubt it'll be the last. What's the reason this time? You two have been kicking it for longer than usual. He do something stupid like propose?"

At my silence, he straightened and tried to keep a straight face. "Holy shit, did he propose?"

My hands knotted, and I looked away.

He snorted. "You're kidding." When I didn't answer, his expression grew serious. "Whoa. You're not kidding. Congratulations? I guess a lifetime of nice sex may be someone's idea of a happily ever after, though I'm not sure *who*."

For the first time in my life I understood the phrase about gazes shooting daggers and I wished mine would. He'd be dead ten times over. "Don't be ridiculous."

"Ouch. Poor guy. Now I actually feel bad for him."

I followed Liam to the bar and accepted the beer he offered. I figured I'd need more than one before the night was over and drank deeply, hoping the cool brew would soothe the dryness in my throat. "I didn't mean for it to go this far. We got along so well and he seemed to understand I wasn't looking for anything serious."

"This is what I mean about you and these guys. That's how I know you're about to break up with someone. You always bring them here. I almost feel bad for him," he said as he studied Andrew. "He has no idea you're about to break his heart."

"I don't break their hearts!" I sipped from my beer, contemplating his words. *At least, I don't think I do.*

Liam took an order from a couple who could barely keep their hands, and mouths, off each other while I worked up the nerve to walk over to Andrew and get it over with. It didn't escape my notice that I'd never been so into a man, Andrew or otherwise, who got me so hot I forgot we were in public. Maybe Liam was onto something about *nice* meaning something bad.

"Don't worry," Liam said when he was finished with the couple. "I'll keep an eye on him in case he freaks out."

"You're making this out to be a bigger deal than it is." Maybe if I repeated it enough, I'd start to believe it.

He leaned on the counter after handing me another beer. I hadn't even realized I'd downed my first. "C'mon, Charlie. You and I both know you've left a trail of men in your wake. It was only a matter of time before one of them got serious before you managed to shake them loose."

"You make me sound terrible." *Was I really that bad?*

"No, you're not that bad." He was smiling again at my habit of speaking my thoughts out loud, but this time at least I didn't want to punch him. This time I was thankful he was my best friend, so he could lie and tell me all the things I wanted to hear instead of the truth. "But you better let him down gentle."

I polished off my beer and accepted a third. I had a feeling I was going to need it. "Thanks for being here, Liam."

"Anytime, shortstack. Don't be too hard on yourself." He winked at me as he straightened. "Besides, you need someone who'll rock your world. Not someone who's *nice*."

"You're really asking for it," I told him.

I could only sigh as I made my way through the crowded bar to Andrew's side with guilt hanging like a heavy weight on my shoulders and settling uncomfortably in my stomach. It didn't help that when he heard me approach, Andrew turned to me with a wide, slightly wobbly smile on his face.

"There you are! I was about to come looking for you."

"I'm sorry I took so long. You know girls' bathrooms." I waved a hand, but he still mostly looks confused.

"I ordered you a cosmopolitan, but I see you've already gotten a drink." We'd been together long enough he'd memorized my drink order. It should have caused a pang of affection to chime in my chest, but there was…nothing. I frowned as he pushed the glass across the table. Noticing my expression, he asked, "Is something wrong?"

My smile wobbled and I downed half of the cosmo for liquid courage. It joined the beer already sloshing around in my stomach and the combination ignited. *Not a good idea, Charlie.* I set the drink down and moved it out of reach. *Get it over with.*

"Actually, Andrew, there's something I think we should talk about."

He rolled his shoulders and shifted in his seat. "Good, I'm glad you mentioned it. There's something I wanted to talk to you about, too."

Caught off guard my throat closed on the words and I gestured for him to continue. A sense of foreboding settled over me like a dark cloud and I glanced around surreptitiously for Liam's comforting presence, but he was still busy at the bar. Besides, I didn't need him to come to my rescue. I could handle Andrew. *I hope.*

Andrew took my hand in his and all I could think about was how clammy it was. I had to resist pulling mine away. "You know how much I care about you," he said and tried to look deeply into my eyes. I hated when people did that. It always made me feel so incredibly uncomfortable. "We've been dating for a while now and…"

I couldn't take it anymore. I wasn't sure how I'd react if he actually proposed, but I knew it wouldn't be pretty. "Stop,

Andrew. I think I know what you're going to say." My heart is beating triple time and I wouldn't be surprised if it leapt out of my chest and onto the table in between us—but not in a good way.

His shoulders relax and he sends me a grateful smile. "You do? Good. I was afraid we were on the wrong page."

Oh, you have no idea.

"I found the ring," I blurted.

His head jerked back so suddenly his whole chair moved with him, making an awful sound against the wood floors. People in our immediate vicinity turned in our direction. I wanted to melt into a puddle at the floor. I should have waited until we were in a private place. It hadn't even occurred to me he could make this into a scene.

"*What?*" I'd never heard his voice quite that high before.

I lowered mine in response, hoping to smooth his ruffled feathers before he got upset. "The ring. The engagement ring? I found it when I was at your apartment last week."

Silence filled the space between us and my ears began to ring, blotting out the sound of the bad karaoke from a couple of sorority girls in the corner. But over the ringing, I heard Liam's voice berating me for my love 'em and leave 'em attitude.

"You thought I was going to propose to you?"

Then it was my turn to gape at him like a fish. "Weren't you?"

His eyes flicked back and forth as he studied me. He leaned back and crossed his arms in front of his chest. "You were going to break up with me, weren't you?" He actually laughed and then leaned in across the table. "You were going to break up with me even though you thought I was going to propose."

The warmth from the alcohol curdled in my stomach. I swallowed hard and pressed my hands into the table for balance. I wasn't going to throw up in public. I didn't even do that when I was fresh out of high school and acclimating to the constant flow of booze as a frosh. "You could do so much better than me, Andrew. I'm leaving this summer for a volunteer opportunity overseas. We wouldn't even get to spend a lot of time together." All my carefully rehearsed reasons now sounded pathetic and flimsy in light of Liam's accusations and the pure disbelief on Andrew's face.

He shook his head and got to his feet. "You're a real piece of work, Charlie. But for the record, I was never gonna propose to you. That ring is a family heirloom. My mom gave it to me last week for my twenty-fifth birthday."

I opened my mouth to respond, but he was already walking away. I downed the rest of the cosmo to wash out the bad taste in my mouth, but not even it could drown out the sound of Liam's words and Andrew's accusations.

CHAPTER 2

LIAM

kept an eye on their table as best I could, but the bar was packed on a Saturday night. By the time I looked up, I'd lost sight of them and their table was empty. As I filled drink requests for person after person my gaze flitted around the room trying find either of them. I cursed under my breath. Never should have let her do this on a night when I was working so I couldn't keep a close eye on her.

A half-hour later, it seemed half of the university had decided to show up so I hadn't been able to tear myself away. My eyes are gritty from the flashing lights and lack of sleep. I wish I could say it's because I've spent it with a woman, but I picked up extra shifts here and the pet rescue where I work as a vet tech for extra cash. If I was being honest it's been a hot minute since I've even had *time* for another woman.

The next girl in line, a pretty brunette with skin-tight jeans and a killer smile, didn't even do anything for me. "Sex on the beach," she requested.

But it did nothing for me. Not even when she perched on the bar stool and arched her back to thrust her pretty breasts in the line of my gaze. "Coming right up," I told her. I was still focused on scanning the crowd to try and spot Charlie and her latest guy, so I only gave her breasts a cursory glance. The brunette pouted until I placed her drink in front of her and she flounced off for another target.

Normally, it didn't bother me that Charlie chose my job as her dumping ground. It kept her close in case something went wrong that way I could be there to handle things for her. But something about this particular one was making me twitchy.

"The hell's wrong with you?" asked the other bartender on duty. He was a pretty chill dude who played ball for FSU named Tripp. I wasn't as into sports, but we got along well enough. He and Charlie lived in the same apartment complex with her friends and they always ended up hanging out together.

"What do you mean?" I leaned around the next customer to study a flash of blonde hair. *Not Charlie.*

"You're being twitchy."

I turned to him and grabbed the vodka for the drink I was making. "I'm not being twitchy."

"If you were any twitchier, I'd think you took one too many balls to the head."

The mental image produced by his words made me wince. "Charlie broke up with another one of her guys tonight. I've got a bad feeling about it, that's all."

Tripp snorted. "Are you sure that's the real reason?"

I started cleaning the counters between customers to keep my hands busy. *Twitchy, my ass.* "Of course it's the real reason. What else would it be?"

He elbowed me, knocking me off balance. He may be leaner than me, but it's all muscle, the little shit. "Can you think of another reason why you'd be so worried about who she's dating?"

"Aside from the fact that she's my best friend and I want to make sure she's okay?"

Tripp rolled his eyes as he prepped his next drink. "If that's what you want to tell yourself."

"That *is* the reason." I was pretty sure.

"I'm friends with Charlie and I've never been that concerned with her love life, let me tell you."

I wiped the counters again, even though they were still pristine. "I'm not concerned with her love life. Jesus, dude. I don't like the look of that Andrew guy and I've always kept an eye out for her."

"Sure, if that's what you wanna call it." He paused and gestured toward the counter. "Pretty sure it's clean enough."

"Fuck off," I told him as the next person stepped up to order a drink. My body relaxed when I saw it was the man I was looking for. "Andrew. Hey, man."

His lip curled. "I need the key to Charlie's place. She said you'd have one. We broke up and I have some stuff of mine to get and she won't be going home for a couple hours. I want to get it tonight."

Relieved at the fact that he hadn't flipped his shit and having spotted Charlie by the end of the bar nursing another beer, I pulled the key off my ring. She'd let him borrow it before, so I didn't even think twice. I was more worried about checking on her. "I'm sorry to hear that. If you'll lock up and leave the key on her counter for her, that'd be great."

He left without another word after pocketing the key and wound his way through the crowd to get to Charlie.

"Why does she even go for those losers?" Tripp asked.

I shook my head. "She's determined to find the perfect guy for the perfect version of her life she has mapped out in her head. As soon as one of them shows a side that doesn't fit in with the man she's conjured up, she checks out."

"That's messed up. No one's perfect."

"Pretty sure she'd have the perfect guy and come up with an excuse to bolt," I said absently as I glanced back over at the two of them. Charlie's face was tense, her lips pressed together like she was holding back her words. Never a good sign.

"Still, maybe he was a good guy."

I took a step closer as I saw Charlie's face blanches of all color. "If he were the right guy, he would have fought for her, you know?"

"Maybe he was scared."

"He had an engagement ring, she said. That normally means it's pretty serious."

I still didn't know how I felt about that. She dated and sometimes it got serious, but never permanent-serious. She'd never gotten close to getting engaged. I couldn't sort out why my stomach had dropped when she'd told me about the ring. Maybe it was the thought of things changing. Maybe it was the threat of losing my best friend. If Tripp had it his way, he'd say it's because I had feelings for her.

That couldn't be it.

Could it?

I shoved the thought away. There was no way in hell that had happened. We've been close for a long time, but it's always been platonic.

"You okay?" Tripp asked, no longer teasing.

I couldn't answer because I wasn't sure if I was. It was as though the Earth had shifted right under my feet. Everything around me was the same, but something intrinsic had changed. I just didn't understand what.

From the distance separating us, I could see a tear slip down Charlie's cheek and that broke me from my stupor. It didn't matter what was happening. She was clearly upset, and it was time to get her away from that guy, I didn't care if it pissed him off.

I didn't know what the hell he'd said, but it looked like she was about to full-out cry, which she never did…ever. Her face was red and her eyes bright with unshed emotion. The single tear she'd let go had left a shimmery trail down her cheek. He had her pinned in a corner against the bar and I could hear his outraged voice above the din, though I couldn't distinguish what he was saying from so far away. I found myself pushing through the crowd without another thought and was beside her in less than a minute.

"My mom was right about you," I heard him say as I got closer. "I never should have wasted my time on someone so worthless. I never would have proposed to you. I can't believe you'd even think so. Marrying you would have been the worst decision of my life."

"Ready to go home?" I asked Charlie. I paid no mind to the fuck-stain who turned to gape at me. As far as I was concerned, he no longer existed. I'd have Tripp cover the rest of my shift. If my manager gave me shit, I'd tell him to screw off.

Fuck-stain glared at me. "We're talking here."

Charlie's gaze skittered over to him, but I cupped her chin and brought it back to me. "Let's go home," I said, my tone gentle. "I'll pick you up some wine and we'll watch all the chick shit you want." A huge concession, considering I loathed all those girlie movies. My mom and sisters watched them non-stop growing up and sitting through one was enough to make me hurl.

Fuck-stain scoffed and glared some more, and I wondered how I'd ever thought he was good enough for her. Until further notice, *no one* was good enough for her. He was lucky I didn't put my fist in his face.

"I'd rather watch an action movie," she said. The corner of her mouth tilted up, and if it hadn't wavered, if there hadn't been the slightest glimmer of sadness in her eyes, I wouldn't have done what I did next. We would have gone out, grabbed some wine and food, and continued with our lives the way they were.

But it was that show of vulnerability that hit me right in the gut. She was hurting and all I wanted to do was take her up in my arms and make it go away. This guy had beat her down, torn up her self-esteem, and when she'd stood up to him, he hadn't been able to handle it.

"I'm ready to go," she said and squared her shoulders, but I was still staring at her mouth.

Fuck-stain made an angry noise in the back of his throat, but neither of us were paying any attention to him.

Ignoring him, my own objections, and common sense, I closed the distance between us and pressed my mouth to hers.

After a moment of surprise where her body froze against mine, her lips parted with a little moan, and it burrowed deep down inside me and took root. All I could think about as we were pressed together was how right it felt. She leaned against me, her breasts pressing against my chest, and I slid a hand down to the small of her back to keep her close. My senses both sharpened and dulled at the same time. Everything involving her was crystal clear, but everything else—the pulse of the music, the dull roar of conversation, even her fuckin' ex—all faded to the background.

There was only her. It had taken me most of my life to really see her. And now it was like I only had eyes for her.

CHAPTER 3
CHARLIE

Liam was kissing me.

Liam. My best friend.

What the fuck?

"What the fuck?" Andrew echoed.

I pushed Liam away after a long moment and turned my head, unable to process what had happened. His harsh breathing sounded like he'd run a marathon, whereas I seemed to forget how to breathe altogether. The alcohol made my head spin and the repeated sound of Andrew shouting was giving me a headache.

"Can you not?" Liam said. His body vibrated against mine. I chanced a look and would have pulled back if it weren't for the hand he had pressed against my back. I'd never seen him so furious.

As my body relaxed, he pulled me even closer. He was protecting me, like he had since the day my mother abandoned me with my dying father. My assumption was confirmed when he let go of me to push me behind his back. From the view over his shoulder, I could see Andrew fuming, his face red and his hands fisted at his side.

"Screw you." Andrew's voice shook and a vein pulsed at his temple.

"Just go, man," Liam snapped. "We're done here."

Andrew's eyes turned cold, determined. "Not even close."

Liam kept me tucked behind him until Andrew pushed his way through the crowd, then he turned and cupped my face with both hands. "God, I'm sorry. You okay?"

"Well, I guess you were right," I mumbled.

His thumbs traced my cheeks in one last lingering touch and then he pulled me away from the curious crowd to a pair of empty bar stools. He tugged me onto one and braced an arm on the bar. We were sitting so close I could hear him above the music and shouted conversations. It reminded me of how it felt when his body was pressed against mine and I shivered.

"About what?" he asked. His lips glistened in the glow of strobe lights. I'd never paid attention to them before, but now I knew what they felt like. I couldn't help but wonder, despite everything, what it'd be like to feel them on mine again.

I shook my head at the memory of his heat wrapped around me. The kiss was a way to get Andrew to back off. That's all. "That I break their hearts. I never would have done this here if I'd known he would cause such a scene."

He scowled. "Don't apologize for that dipshit. He's only upset because he knows what he's missing."

I sniffled and wiped at my eyes. *I was* not *going to cry.* "He wasn't going to propose. Didn't you hear? I'm not good enough for his perfect family. I don't know why I keep dating. It's a good thing I'm leaving after this semester."

Liam straightened. "You're what?"

All I wanted was to go home—not the little apartment I rented near school—but home, where Liam and I grew up. It's funny, my mom had run out on us when dad got sick when I was thirteen and I'd always promised myself I'd never turn out like her. I guess some things run in the family.

"I was going to tell you later, but I got offered an opportunity to volunteer overseas. They need nurses to give vaccines, run free clinics. That sort of thing."

He rocked back on his stool and rubbed a hand over his face. "Wow, Charlie, that's great."

"Thanks. I'm sorry I dragged you into all this. Next time, I'll make sure to find another place to break up."

His gaze met mine. "Next time?" Was it a trick of the dim lighting or was he upset?

The heat in his eyes prompted the memory of the kiss. I had to knock it out of my brain before all I could do when I was around him was think about kissing him. "Well, probably not since there's no point in dating if I'm leaving soon anyway." At his silence, I kept babbling. "Anyway, thank you for jumping in. Kissing me was probably a better choice than punching him and getting fired. He was so sure you and I had something going behind his back, so it must have pissed him off something bad. Joke's on him though, right?" I attempted a smile, but I could only muster up a grimace. This was why friends never kissed. It made everything awkward as hell. I could only hope our friendship would survive it.

He looked away and eased himself back. "A joke. Right."

Silence filled the space between us and I didn't like it. There had never been space in our friendship before and I hated to be the reason there was now.

"Liam, is everything going to be okay?" My voice trembled, but I carried on. "I don't care about Andrew, but I can't lose you. I know you were trying to protect me. You're a good friend. Can we just...go back to the way things were?" Somehow I'd gotten my hands on a cocktail napkin. I looked down in my lap to avoid his expression as he considered my words. The napkin was shredded in a pile on my thighs.

His hand covered mine as I began to shred the pieces into even smaller ones. I looked up and found him smiling at me, the traces of awkwardness gone. "It's alright. I was protecting you, like you said. Besides, I'd never let a douchebag like him mess with us. We're good."

I slumped and laughed, but it was shaky. For a second there, I thought maybe he'd been seriously hurt. For a second there, I'd even given half a thought to what it'd be like to kiss him on a regular basis. Then, I remembered what he said about me breaking hearts. I'd never want to hurt Liam. He was the most important person in my life. "Good. You had me worried."

"Naw, it was only a kiss."

"It wasn't even a good one," I said with a smile to soften the burn as I gathered the remains of the mutilated napkin and left it on the counter. Joking seemed easier than acknowledging that I hadn't wanted the kiss to end.

Liam grinned back at me and I knew everything between us would be okay. At least until I left, but I'd worry about that later. "Now I know you're talking out of your ass," he said. "Do you want to get out of here?"

I pressed a hand to my aching head and nodded. "What about your shift?"

"Screw it. I'll have Tripp cover for me. He owes me for when I switched with him for his tournaments."

"Are you sure?" Part of me needed space, but another more dominant part wanted me to cling to Liam for all I was worth. Tonight had shaken me down to my core and the thought of going home alone scared me more than it should. I knew it wasn't the same, but I couldn't help but remember the night I came home after a volleyball game and the house had been empty, my mother nowhere to be found.

He gave me a look that said don't be stupid and said, "I'll get my stuff if you want to meet by my truck."

I nodded and my stomach nearly dropped to my feet as he got to his and paused to kiss my forehead before disappearing into the mass of throbbing bodies. I almost thought he was going to kiss me again.

Cut it out, Charlie.

If I wasn't already sick from the four drinks I already had, I would have ordered another to steady my nerves. I'd never been so off-balance around Liam before. It had been a long day, that was all.

I slung my purse over my shoulders and navigated through the crowd to the door. The slap of fresh air against my face helped to clear my head. Clusters of giggling girls clung to each other as they navigated their way up the busy streets. A niggling worry at the back of my head had me pulling out my phone and unlocking it just in case. I didn't think Andrew would be waiting for me, but I'd rather be cautious. I never thought he'd explode the way he had, either. I let go of the breath I was holding when I got to Liam's truck in the well-lit parking lot by the back door.

There were a few tense moments where I was certain I'd see Andrew emerge from the shadowed streets beyond the parking lot, but I brushed them off. Liam pushed through the back door to the bar, followed by a short burst of music and laughter. The door slammed and his boots crunched in the gravel to the truck.

"Are you sure you won't get any trouble for leaving early?" I called out.

"Jesus, fuck, Charlie, who are you my mother? I said it's fine. Now do you want a ride or not?"

Remembering the creepy suspicion Andrew was watching, I nodded. "Yes, of course. Thanks."

"You know what?" he asked as he unlocked the truck and we jumped in.

I was already feeling better as the familiar surroundings of his old truck soothed my nerves. "What?"

"Maybe we should go home for a couple of days," he suggested, revving the engine. "That way you can take your mind off things for a bit. I'm sure my family would love to see you."

I rolled my eyes and frowned at my lap. I wanted to go more than anything, but I didn't want to seem needy either. "I have class next week. I'm not sure that's a good idea."

"Well, you don't have a say in the matter," he told her and pulled out onto the street. "You've got shit in our spare room. I'll call my mom and let her know we're on our way."

"You don't have to do this, you know," I said.

He palmed my head with one hand and shoved. "Don't be stupid."

"Yes, sir," I said, and relaxed. This was the Liam I was used to. Maybe I'd imagined everything else.

It gave me hope that it wouldn't be as hard to go back to normal as I thought it would be.

"Don't do it," I begged an hour later.

Liam grinned and quirked his eyebrows, his dimple making an appearance. I was back to wanting to slug him. "Are you sure?"

"I'm begging you, please, Liam. No."

"Just one more."

I righted myself in the seat and turned in his direction. My eyes narrowed in warning. "If you skip through another song without listening to it all the way through, I will personally rip the radio out and throw it in the nearest swamp as gator bait."

He gasped, and his hand dropped from the controls. He looked as offended as he had when I forced him to wear a pink tie to prom to match my dress. "You wouldn't dare."

"Try me," I said through gritted teeth.

His lips pulled into a smile and we both jumped when the car behind us laid on the horn. He snorted out a laugh and hit the gas. "You win for now."

"Seriously, I don't understand how you listen to music that way. You never finish a song. What's the point? And don't you dare quote *Supernatural*! You're the one who dragged me on this trip, so shotgun gets to pick the music."

"Fine, fine. This one time you can choose."

He patted my knee and I flushed at the feeling of his palm on me. It may have been through the fabric of my jeans, but now that my body knew how he felt in other places it was like I couldn't stop thinking about having his hands on me...everywhere. I swallowed, hoping my voice wouldn't betray my thoughts. "You're such a good friend," I said, more to remind myself than him.

"Don't make me regret this," he warned. The twangy plucking of guitar strings filled the truck, and he sighed heavily, removing his hand. "Charlie."

I frowned at the disappointment that flooded me. Maybe going with him so soon after hadn't been such a good idea. Even though I was afraid of losing him this summer, the last thing I needed was to be cooped up in a small space with him and wishing he would touch me. I tried to refocus on the banter that had always come so easy to us, but any conversation took monumental effort. "Don't judge, Walsh. You focus on the road and let the DJ handle the tunes."

"I'm already regretting it," he said. Thankfully, he didn't seem to notice my inner turmoil. I should be thankful, but in the back of my mind I wondered how he could be acting so normal after what had happened.

I flicked a glance in his direction and cast out a mental net for another safe topic of conversation. One that didn't involve tongues, or hands, or close spaces. "Was your mom okay with us coming over?" I asked. There. His mom was *definitely* a safe topic. She loved me, but I'm certain she wouldn't think too kindly if she knew the thoughts I was having about her son.

"Yes. She said she's looking forward to seeing the both of us. She wanted me to remind you that you promised to help her weed the garden and she's holding you to it while you're visiting."

I went quiet for a few minutes as I scrolled through his phone and tried to think of something else to say. His playlists numbered in the thousands and it always made me smile to tease him about how he hoarded music like I hoarded chocolate. I glanced up to study him as he drove. The glow from the dash illuminated the strong, clean lines of his face. His close-cropped hair was now covered in a baseball cap, Braves I bet. He was a die-hard fan. My heart squeezed inside my chest and I looked back down at his phone.

He flicked my ear and I scowled up at him. "You hear me?" he asked.

I rolled my eyes. "Yes. God, Liam. I heard you."

"You don't have to call me God," he said with a smirk.

Despite my worries, laughter bubbled up from my throat. "You're so full of yourself."

He tugged on one lock of hair framing my face. "That's why you love me."

My response stuck in my throat and I could only smile shakily.

I loved Liam, I did. But I didn't *love* him.

Right?

CHAPTER 4

CHARLIE

Something tickled my face and I groaned, trying to bat it away with one hand.

"Charlie."

"Ugh," I mumbled, and turned my face away from the annoyance.

"C'mon. Char. We're here."

I cracked open one eye and tried to invest as much of my burning hatred into my glare as possible. "Here, where?"

"My parents' house," Liam said in an over-exaggerated voice. "Just a quick warning. Grandma Dorothy isn't doing so well, so she moved in with them a couple months ago."

That cleared the cobwebs from my brain. I sat up straight, nearly knocking heads with Liam, who dodged back just in time to avoid the collision. The fear for his grandma, who was as much my own, erased most of the awkwardness from earlier. At least for now. "What do you mean, she's not doing so well? Why didn't you tell me?".

A shadow of emotion crossed his face, but it was gone too quickly for me to decipher. "Her dementia got worse. The doctors recommended she either go to a nursing home or we get her full-time care. Mom didn't want to put her in a nursing home yet, so they hired a service to help take care of her here."

I pushed a hand through the flyaway hair that had come loose sometime during my nap. Grandma Dorothy had been as much a part of my adolescence as Liam's, considering how much time we spent together after my mother left and my father got sick. My aunt's house wasn't exactly a refuge, even though she raised me after my dad died, so I treated Liam's place as a sanctuary. Thankfully, his family took pity on my gangly self and fed me regularly. They even came to graduation with one of those cheesy poster board signs with my name on it.

"Did your parents not want you to tell me?" I asked, my voice so low I wasn't sure if he could hear me or not.

He did a double take. "What? No. It wasn't like that at all." He paused before continuing. "She called before everything with fuck-stain and I didn't get the chance to tell you."

"Fuck-stain?" I didn't want to touch that one, so I said. "What did your dad say?"

Liam scowled. "The same thing he always says. That I should come back to work for the family. That going to school is only going to put me into debt. The family could use me at home to help with chores and take care of her. The usual."

"I wish you would have told me. I wouldn't have said yes to coming if I knew things were still bad between you two."

He gave me the same look he used to when I was being particularly boneheaded. "Don't you dare say that. I didn't just do it for you. If grandma is as bad as Mom said then I want to be here to spend time with her and I knew you would, too. So get your ass out of the car before I drag you out."

I wanted to protest. I even opened my mouth to start, but the more I thought about it, the more I realized Liam was right. Without looking up, I said, "I didn't mean to--"

Liam nudged my chin up with his hand. "You don't have to apologize, Char. Trust me. I wasn't kidding about dragging you out. I may even throw you over my shoulder if I have to, which may give grandma a heart attack," he added with his customary wicked grin.

I smacked him on the arm, grateful for the broken tension. If he was going to ignore the kiss, then I was, too. It's the only way things will go back to the way they used to be. "Let's get inside before I have to murder you on your front lawn and your mom has to clean up the mess."

"Remember that time we TP'd the street and she made us take it all down?"

We shared a laugh as we started walking up to the front door. "I thought we were never going to get that shit out of the branches. We were up there for hours."

"It was your idea to do my house," he argued. "I knew it was gonna come back and bite us in the ass."

"You liar! You're the one who said they'd never suspect us!"

By the time we reached the front steps we were both giggling, and I smiled for the first time since the night before. The heaviness was still present, waiting for the moment when I let my guard down and it could take over, but for now, I had Liam to distract me and if he was good at anything, it was distraction.

"Suspect you for what?" came a voice that sucked the laughter right from our lungs.

"How much I missed you," I said as I opened the creaky screen door to get a better look at her. I had to force the words passed the lump in my throat. "Hi, Mrs. Dorothy. It's so good to see you."

Grandma Dorothy stood behind the screen door. I wish I could say she looked the same, but the ravages of time were more evident than ever. I swore she was a good three inches shorter, her spine curved and requiring her to stoop over. The thin curls she religiously colored a soft brown every eight weeks had thinned and lost their bounce. My heart squeezed. How had I let so much time pass since the last time I visited? I knew the answer, I just didn't want to admit it to myself. I'd gotten so used to leaving people before they could leave me, I was doing the same thing with Grandma Dorothy that I'd done to Andrew. And neither of them deserved it.

After a quick look at Liam for reassurance, I wrapped my arms around her frail body for a hug. The familiar scent of peony body spray filled my nose and instantly caused the tension inside me to loosen. *Home*, it said. Finally.

I hadn't realized how much I'd missed it until Dorothy said, "Well, get inside. You're letting all the cool air out."

I giggled and released her to let Liam inside. He stooped down to give her a kiss on her papery cheek. He was so much taller than her that she had to lean her head way back to see him. The sight of them together pulled at me in a softer, sweeter way than kissing him had. My breath caught in my throat and Liam glanced at me, his eyebrows drawing together. I shook my head.

Grandma Dorothy interrupted the moment and I was thankful until I heard her words. "Willy, is that you? My, you've grown two feet if you've grown an inch."

The two of us froze and stared at each other with wide eyes. Liam was named after his father. William Walsh, Sr., who everyone called Willy. They'd shortened William to Liam to differentiate the two.

I watched as Liam's throat bobbed and his eyes softened as he stooped down to her level. "No, Grandma. It's me, Liam."

Dorothy shook her head and beckoned us to follow down the hall. "I know that, silly goose. Let's go find your mother so we can tell her my two favorite people are home."

I took Liam's hand despite the fact that I couldn't stop thinking about the kiss when I touched him. No matter what weirdness was going on between us, sometimes he needed me to protect him, too.

CHAPTER 5
LIAM

With her hand in mine, I could face seeing my father.

Grandma Dorothy went to the fridge and began pouring tea. When I noticed her hands shaking too much to hold the pitcher steady, I went to her side.

"I'll get that for you grandma." I took the pitcher from her hands and guided her to the breakfast nook where she sat across from Dad. He hadn't looked up from the paper he was reading. A steaming cup of coffee sat at his elbow.

She beamed up at me. "You're a good boy. Thank you, Willy."

"Anytime." I told her, deciding not to comment on her error about my name. Ignoring the issue wasn't healthy by any means, but it was better than focusing on how quickly she had changed. To Charlie, I said, "Do you want a cup?"

Charlie gave my hand an extra squeeze, then took an empty seat next to Grandma Dorothy. "Sure, thanks."

"Hey, Dad," I said when I couldn't put it off any longer.

"Liam," was all he answered. *Was it just me, or did he look…*

older? I didn't want to believe it. In some ways, I still wanted to think my father was invincible.

I poured iced tea for the three of us and served them. "How have you been, grandma?" I asked to break the silence. Sometimes silence was worse than my father's dictating to me. His blatant lack of interest in having a conversation screamed how little my life mattered to him these days. But, oh, how he'd come to life if only I did everything right—which meant his way or nothing at all.

"Just fine, dear. How's school?" Under the table, her foot began to tap against the floor and when her hands weren't busy with the glass they were constantly rubbing together. Once we'd learned she'd been diagnosed with dementia, the first thing Charlie had done was look up all she could about dementia. She quizzed her nursing instructors, scoured any available medical texts and gracefully agreed to help advise my parents when they chose home health care, even though she didn't think she was experienced enough to be of any assistance.

I always thought I was the one who took care of Charlie, protected her...but she did her fair share of taking care of me, too.

"Just waiting to hear back about applications for school in the fall."

My father snorted into his coffee and set down his newspaper. The full force of his gaze turned to me, pinning me to the sink where I was rinsing the empty pitcher. I'd been right earlier, he does look older. But that wasn't the only thing. He looked like an older me. Was this what I'd turn into if I spent the next thirty years fighting to pull life from an unforgiving patch of earth? His weathered skin had deep grooves that reminded me of cracked mud when the farm went too long without a good rain.

I ignored him because I didn't want another argument in front of Charlie and grandma. Raised voices agitated her.

"That's great," Grandma said, beaming. "What about you, Charlie?"

Charlie smiled at her, her cheeks pink with pleasure and she told grandma about her classes and the kids she saw on rotation at the hospital during her rounds. I'd forgotten how much she loved being here. She even said once being around my family, even when they fought, was like a relief for her. I relaxed a little, ignoring Dad's scrutiny. I could deal with his bullshit for one weekend if it gave Charlie a reprieve.

"Where are Janie and Marie, Mr. Frank?" Charlie asked my dad. She never had a problem talking with him and he treated her like a third daughter.

"They're sleeping over at a friend's house for the weekend."

"I was wondering why it was so quiet," she said, eyes twinkling.

He mustered up what passed for a smile in her direction and it hit me how Charlie always manages to pull people out of their shell, even miserly old bastards like my dad.

"Those two do more caterwauling than the barn cats."

Grandma was tapping her feet again and Charlie reached over to hand her the glass of tea without a second glance. My father looked at Charlie with such warmth in his eyes and Grandma Dorothy began chattering happily about the TV programs she'd been watching, I leaned against the kitchen counter, my heart stuck in my throat. Charlie fit. I couldn't imagine being here without her.

I wanted to kiss her again.

The urge slammed into me with the intensity of an avalanche. I wanted to cross the kitchen, pull her to her feet and plant a kiss on her she'd never forget. Not a hasty, spur-of-the-moment kiss. Right here in front of my family, alone. It didn't matter where. I wanted her. And it terrified me.

"Did you hear me son?"

I focused in on my father, who was standing in front of me,

his coffee cup in his hand. That was one way to get my thoughts off the carnal route they'd taken. "What's that?"

"I could use your help outside, if you have a minute."

It shamed me, as it always did, that my first response was to tell him no. I didn't want to spend the whole weekend doing chores and listening to him gripe about how I was abandoning the family to get a degree I didn't need. Then I took another look at those new lines on his face and relented. Besides, it'd get my mind off kissing Charlie, or at least, I hoped so. She has enough on her plate with what went down with Andrew and now she was leaving in a couple months. *Forget about it, Walsh.* I'd be content with the way things were. I had to be.

"Sure, dad. I'll be outside in just a sec."

He nodded, reached around me to put his cup in the sink, then pushed out the squeaky back door, the screen slapping behind him.

I crossed the scuffed checkerboard linoleum to the table and stopped to give Grandma Dorothy a kiss on her hair. I met Charlie's eyes over grandma's head and said, "Will you be okay here for a little while?"

She smiled, but there were questions in her eyes. "Sure. I bet Grandma Dorothy and I can find something to keep us plenty busy."

"You sure?"

Grandma twisted in her seat. "You heard the girl. Now get outside. Your daddy's been busting his back for months, but he's not as young as he used to be and could use your help."

Charlie sent me a sympathetic look and I sighed. Sometimes, despite her patchy memories and tics, Grandma could send an arrow straight through to the bullseye. "*Go,*" Charlie mouthed.

It wasn't that I didn't want to help my family. I wanted to, I tried. But living my father's life wasn't *all* I wanted for my own. I had my own dreams. My own goals. He was stubborn enough that he didn't want to bend, and I was stubborn enough that I'd never ask for help.

I found him in the old barn situated a healthy walk behind the house. Whatever color it had been painted when it was new had long since faded. My dad, and sometimes I, had kept it in good repair as best we could. Replacing the roof, rotted beams, weathered siding. It was a patchwork mess but the scent of fresh hay for the horse and motor oil was a familiar and welcome reminder of all the years I'd spent here. I thought of Charlie, who'd come to love my family in place of her own and felt guilty about even wanting to run from this place.

Dad called out from where he was sprawled underneath a tractor. "You're taking your sweet time, aren't you?"

Still thinking of Charlie, I swallowed my angry reply and hunkered down with one hand keeping balance on the side of the rusted old machine. "What do you need?"

We were more alike than I wanted to admit, because I saw him choke on his own response before he bit out, "Get me that wrench there."

Like they'd been a thousand times before, the tools he needed for the job were laid out on a towel, a dirty one, but as organized as you could get in a country barn. I found the wrench and passed it to his outstretched hand. Metallic clanks echoed throughout the bowels of the tractor.

It would have been so easy to be the son he wanted me to be. Easy in that I could see how much he wanted the kind of man who'd proudly carry on the traditions he'd started, who'd farm the land he slaved over his whole life. The irony was it was the very farm that had inspired me to become a vet. We had horses, donkeys, a cow or two, plus a slew of chickens, goats and barn cats. It wasn't out of the ordinary to have the large animal vet visit a couple times a year. Dad hadn't thought anything of my tagging along back then, but it had molded me in the way that I knew he still wished the farm would.

The conversation we should have been having hung over the rest of the afternoon like a dark cloud, but neither of us could make the first move. Instead, the only words spoken were requests for more tools or polite small talk. I wished as I handed him a screwdriver and followed his directions for guiding in a part that I could talk to him like I had when I was a kid. Then he'd ask for something else and the moment was lost.

It wasn't until he slid out from under the tractor that he looked me in the eye for the first time since I got home. He wiped his hands with a rag and sighed. My body tensed in preparation.

"We're selling the farm," he said.

CHAPTER 6
CHARLIE

"I'm so happy to see you again," Mrs. Walsh said as she smiled at me over a glass of milk after dinner that night. Liam had come in after a couple hours with his dad looking like a thunderstorm rolling in, so I kept my distance. He'd only surfaced when his mom started making dinner with a healthy side of homemade chocolate chip cookies. "I kept telling Liam he needed to bring you around."

A pang of guilt made my stomach clamp down on the contents of rich chocolate-y goodness. "I know. I'm sorry I haven't visited. I've had…a lot going on."

She tutted at me. "No need to apologize, honey. Liam told me all about the boy you've been seeing. Andrew, right? How's that going?"

Liam, who'd been happily stuffing his face with his mother's homemade chocolate chip cookies, paused, and his eyes came to me. I shook my head subtly, and he chugged a glass of milk to help the cookies down.

I shrugged in his mother's direction. "It's going alright." I hoped my response was nonchalant enough. Mrs. Walsh had a bullshit detector like you wouldn't believe.

Which was why when she said, "Now, I don't believe that for a second, but I'll let it slide until you're ready to talk about it, sugar bean," I couldn't look her in the eye. "Don't you worry," she added, "these things have a way of working themselves out."

"I sure hope so," I managed.

"You two clean up after yourselves. I'm gonna check in on Grandma Dorothy."

"Thank you, Mrs. Walsh," I said.

"No need, honey. You're family."

She stopped to kiss us both on the head like we were twelve instead of twenty-two, and I realized I needed this much more than I thought I would. I turned to Liam, who was licking the chocolate off his fingers. I ignored the pang of heat the sight ignited in my stomach and focused on my own cookie.

"Thank you for this," I said around a mouthful. "How did you know it was what I needed?"

He shrugged. "I didn't. I just tried to think of the one place that makes me feel better when something bad happens, and this was what came to mind. Besides, I had a wicked craving for homemade cookies, and I figured you wouldn't be open to baking for me."

We both knew he was joking, but I was grateful for the change of subject. "You're such an asshole."

He batted his eyes. "But you love me."

"Debatable," I said, but I was smiling. He had a knack for making me smile when I absolutely did not want to. We'd be in the middle of arguing about God only knew what and he'd start cracking joke after joke, because—as much as he wanted to win the argument—he wanted me to smile more. Or so he said. "What are we doing today?"

"Since chores are done and dad can't guilt me into helping out anymore on Mom's orders, I have a surprise," he said, then rounded the table to pull me from the chair and push me out the back door to the attached garage. "No time for thinking right now. If you start thinking you'll overthink it, and I can't handle the drama."

At first, I thought he was talking about the kiss and then I realized he must be talking about Andrew. I really needed to stop thinking about ways to go in for round two.

"Are you going to tell me what you and your dad talked about this afternoon?" I blurted out. *Great job, Char. Real subtle.* "You came back looking like he was drowning kittens or something."

"Long story. We can talk about it when we get where we're going."

I stumbled in the darkened garage, my hands outstretched to keep from running straight into something. "Where in the world are you taking me? Liammm. I do *not* want to go skinny dipping again."

He snorted and then placed his hands on my shoulders to guide me. I heard the rattled groan of an old truck door opening followed by a waft of leather, grease, and earth. "Scoot in," Liam said, and gave me a little heave into the cab of the truck.

"Umph," I grunted. It was his father's old truck. The one they used during the summer to tend to his part-time handyman business in addition to all the work they did on the farm. "Is this going to be a theme? You shoving me into vehicles and taking me off on a whim?"

"It would be if you'd shut your trap."

"I can't help it. I'm not the ride-or-die type. I have too many questions."

"Clearly," he replied as he hit the button for the garage door opener, then backed the truck into the driveway.

Before I could ask any more questions, he'd thrown the truck into Drive and we were bouncing along a rutted country backroad. The sound of night birds filled the truck over the smooth crooning from the latest country star. Being down one sense heightened all the rest and despite my constant reminding, my brain was especially attuned to how close Liam and I were on the bench seat.

"Should I be worried?" I asked to cover my nerves. This was *Liam*. I've known him forever. I shouldn't be nervous. It was like we'd crossed a line into a different territory and my eyes were open to things I'd noticed, but not at this level, not with this amount of intensity.

"You know I'd never let anything happen to you," he said.

"I know, but you've also never done anything like this before."

"I had a feeling we could both use a break."

The truck eased to a stop with a squeal of brakes. We unbuckled, and Liam tugged me into his arms and carried me to the back of the truck where he tossed me bodily into the bed. A godawful, scream-queen-worthy screech ripped from my throat as I sailed through the air and landed, not on the hard metal like I was expecting, but on soft, downy fabric.

"Listen, Walsh," I said when I finally caught my breath, "I appreciate you kidnapping me and throwing me around, but I have to say, your attempts to cheer me up leave a lot to be desired."

The truck creaked as he heaved himself over the side and plopped down next to me. "Shut up for a minute and just look."

"Look?" I prompted, but he slapped a hand over my mouth and tipped my head back, and the view made me swallow my protestations.

"You don't get stars like that in the city, do you?"

I swallowed past the lump in my throat and relaxed into the blankets. "No, you don't."

"I would have dragged your ass to the treehouse, but I figured the freshmen fifteen you put on might take the place down."

"You're such an ass, Liam," I said, but I leaned my head

against his arm as we settled into the pillows. Surrounded by the sounds and scents of days gone by, it made it easier for me to digest all the mistakes I'd made when they were so far away— which was exactly his intention, I realized.

"I thought my attempts to cheer you up left a lot to be desired?"

"You know what I mean."

"Mom had mentioned she and Dad used to come out here and do stuff like this. I figured it was shit you girls got off on."

"How romantic," I teased with my heart in my throat.

"Shut up."

"Your mom didn't think it was weird we're going to stay out here?"

He grinned. "She thought it was sweet. Said she was gonna bug Dad to take her out dancing or something because they never do anything fun anymore."

"So, c'mon. What happened with your dad?"

Instead of answering, he pulled out another blanket and draped it over us. I tried not to think about how close we were. How our heat mingled together underneath the fabric. It'd be so easy to lean over.

"They're selling the land. The farm," he said after a while, breaking me from my fantasies. It was as effective as an ice bath.

"What?!"

His fingers pulled at a string on the blanket. "Yeah, dad told me when we were out fixing the tractor. There's some fancy big shot who wants to develop the land into a country retreat or some shit."

"He didn't give you a hard time about it, did he?"

I knew how much tension there was between the two of them. They tried to hide it, but men weren't as subtle about their emotions. They liked to think they were all stoic and that women were the emotional ones, but it was the other way around. I wanted to reach for him, but I stuffed my hands between my thighs to keep from doing it.

"Actually, he didn't…and that was somehow worse."

"We're a pair, aren't we?" I wasn't as good at lightening the mood, but he smiled anyway.

"Yeah we are. But enough about me. We came here for you. I don't want you to beat yourself up about what happened. Andrew's a grown man. You deserve better. When you find the right guy, you won't be running away from him. The right guy will make you want to stay put. Your mom left you, your dad died. Everyone you've ever loved leaves you. You're scared of having someone else do it, too. You think I've been here all these years and not noticed?"

"I—" my voice cut out and I had to turn away to keep from letting tears spill over my cheeks. How could he see straight to the heart of me so easily?

"Aw, fuck, Charlie. You know I hate it when you cry. I take it all back." He tugged on my arm and pulled me close enough that he could wipe away my tears with the hem of his shirt. The familiar scent of his cologne wrapped around me on my next ragged inhale. I caught the barest glimpse of his abs which made all the emotion his words inspired clog inside my chest as a wave of heat swept over me.

Determined to ignore my response to him, I took several deep breaths to clear my head. "So you're saying I should have stayed with him?"

"Hell no." He sounded so offended I laughed. "If he was the right guy he wouldn't have let you go in the first place. If you did run, he would have chased after you."

"What about you?" If we had to talk about me any longer I'd go crazy. "I don't see you running down the aisle." It wasn't just a diversion, I was honestly curious. Even if I wasn't preoccupied with his mouth since the kiss, I knew he was attractive. There were enough girls always checking him out to clue me in if I'd been completely oblivious.

"I'm in no place to be in a relationship." I'd be lying if I said my heart didn't stop a little at his comment. But I was being silly. He was going to school, I was leaving. It'd never work. "Even if I could devote my time to her during vet school, I don't want to be in a serious relationship until I'm situated in my career and stable with a steady income."

"Is that why you rarely go on dates?" I asked.

"I date," he said and pinched my waist. I smacked his hands away, but snuggled closer to listen for the rest of his answer. I didn't even mean to do it, it was just habit. When he didn't push me away, I relaxed, listening to the way his words reverberated in his chest. "I just don't want to get serious yet."

I found his hand and took it in my own. His long, capable fingers were warm and callused as they cradled my smaller ones. "But things will never be just as you want them, Liam. My life is a testament to that. Just as you think things settle down and you have a good thing going, it throws you another curve ball. I survived my mom leaving, and then my dad got sick. I survived taking care of him, and then he died."

"You've seen how my parents can be sometimes," Liam said after a moment. "The stress, the arguments."

"They love each other," I insisted. "People argue."

"Sure they do, but it's not always enough. They've struggled my whole life putting food on the table. Providing for me and my sisters. I don't want a hard life like that for my family. I don't want to become my father, busting ass every day for a job that barely pays the bills and then having to sell it just to make ends meet. Besides, could you imagine me settling down? I can barely commit to listening to one song all the way through."

I laughed, then sobered. "Be serious."

He sighed and closed his eyes. "C'mon, Charlotte, you know I'm no good at this emotional shit."

"You always say that, but you know exactly how to make me feel better, so you must be good at *something*." Which wasn't a lie. After mom left and dad got sick, Liam was the only one who could deal when I finally broke from the strain. "And don't call me Charlotte," I added, though I knew it was pointless to remind him because in the years we'd been friends, he'd never listened.

"Well, you're pretty easy to cheer up. Cookies, a little time away. Piece of cake. Maybe I would kickass as the committed boyfriend."

I ignored the boyfriend comment. "You make everything seem so easy," I said as I lost myself in the deep blue-black endlessness of the night sky. "I wish I could be like you."

"Bullheaded?" he said with a laugh.

"To a point," I said honestly.

"You don't wanna be like me," he replied and tugged me closer to his warmth. My eyes began to flutter closed. I was warm, surrounded by Liam and felt safe. I always felt safe when I was around him and that was more important than any kiss. "You're perfect just the way you are."

CHAPTER 7

LIAM

We must have fallen asleep in the back of my dad's old truck because when I cracked open my eyes what felt like seconds later, it was morning and I was fucking freezing, despite the blanket. Charlie had curled into a ball beside me, and at some point during the night, I'd wrapped myself around her to keep warm. I wished I could blame my baser human instincts for what happened next, but I'd be lying to myself if I tried.

Her forehead was braced on my chest and my nose was buried in her hair. At first, I didn't realize where the scent was coming from. I got excited thinking my mom was baking apple pie first thing in the morning until I remembered it was a Sunday and she was probably more interested in sleeping in than cooking.

Then Charlie shifted a little in her sleep and the green apple scent met my nose, nearly causing me to groan out loud. Not that she would have noticed, as she was still snoring softly, her hands tucked in between our chests. But I certainly still wasn't asleep. Nope. Every single part of me had woken the hell up and was ready to go.

Head still cloudy with sleep, veins full of spiky adrenaline and the sweet, seductive call of lust, I didn't fully realize what I was doing at first. It's never been in my nature to curb my instincts and I've always been affectionate. So it didn't occur to me to resist the urge to pull her closer, pressing her soft curves to me. She shivered and made a little sound in her throat that I felt all the way down in my dick.

"Liam!" my grandma shouted from somewhere back in reality.

The sound of her voice was too close, and it jerked me so thoroughly back from the sex-fueled haze I'd been under that I threw myself backward, knocking my head on the toolbox and causing me to see stars.

"Fuck!"

I rolled to my side and away from making what could possibly be the biggest mistake of my life and was grateful for the pain spearing through my head. It kept me from thinking about how goddamn good she'd felt in my arms. It also quelled the raging morning wood.

But it didn't help the craving for her.

My whole body was still screaming that she fit so perfectly against me. I'd spent all weekend trying to forget the moment of insanity that had caused me to kiss her. Waking up wrapped in her brought back every second of how it felt to have her tight little body against mine. How, for just a split-second, she'd responded to me in a way that made me want to taste and take until we were both spent from it.

I forced myself to get up and slide down the tailgate. I waved to Grandma, who was on the back porch not too far from the barren field where I'd parked us for the night. She waved back and went inside the house, the screen door slapping shut behind her.

"Are you okay?"

The sound of Charlie's rusty morning voice had all of my

muscles clenching down to keep from reaching for her and pulling her back against me. The groping, fumbling jerk wasn't what she needed right now. She'd opened up to me and I'd be damned if I'd be another Andrew who used her for what she was willing to give and then dropped her as soon as they were done. She meant more to me than that. It was just my dick who couldn't seem to get with the program.

Remembering that she was waiting on my answer, I composed myself long enough to nod and say, "Yeah, I'm fine. Just forgot where I was for a second, I guess."

"Did you have a nightmare?" I could tell from her tone she was smiling. Even though my head was pounding and I was mired between confusion and annoyance, I smiled back.

"No, I didn't have a nightmare, Charlotte. Grandma Dorothy scared the shit out of me." I pushed my fingers into my eyes, then rolled my shoulders.

"I can't believe we fell asleep out here," she said as she sat up. The blanket fell to her lap and my mouth watered at her rumpled state. It made me want to push her back against the blankets and kiss her 'till the sun was high in the sky.

"Me either." Though falling asleep in my truck was the least of my worries.

She began picking through her dark hair with one hand as she yawned. She didn't look any different, which confused me more than anything because when I looked at her, all I could think about was how much I wanted to see if there was anything else I'd missed about her over the past twelve years. I couldn't even count how many times she'd been close enough for me to catch the scent of her hair, but it had never hit me like it did this morning, and it only made me want to find out what other secrets she'd been hiding.

It must have been the kiss. Knowing what she tasted like, how she felt under my hands. It was driving me crazy wanting to do it again.

"What?" she asked, jerking me from my thoughts. "Do I have something on my face?"

She started rubbing at her cheeks. I cleared my throat and started cleaning up the blankets, folding them as though I had a clue how to fold shit. If I didn't keep my hands and mind busy, I was afraid I might do something really fucking stupid, like bury my face in her hair for another whiff of her shampoo.

"Nah," I said once I was certain I could control myself. "Just need some coffee and a shower. Which do you want first?"

Charlie brightened at the mention of her addiction. "Coffee," she demanded. "Like you even have to ask."

She climbed over the side of the truck and reached out for me. I took her in my arms out of habit and helped her down. Minutes later we were pulling into the garage. A shower would help get my head on straight. Then we'd be driving back to campus and I'd have applications, deadlines, and papers to fill the spaces in my brain that were fixated on her.

"Don't even mention how short I am before I've had my first infusion."

I snorted, relieved to find that whatever the hell had happened this morning hadn't made shit even more awkward. As long as it never happened again, we'd be okay.

"Then I won't mention that you should come with your own footstool," I told her as I held the front door open for her.

"Not. Another. Word," she growled. Her nose twitched as she followed it to the happily bubbling coffee pot. She'd been to my parents' house so many times, she went right to the cabinet with the coffee cups, dove into the fridge for creamer, and sat herself at the kitchen table.

"I'll leave you to it and take the first shower then. Once you're sufficiently caffeinated you can have the next."

She waved me away as she snatched the fresh pot of coffee to fill her cup and I shook my head. She'd wouldn't be fully coherent until she had at least two cups in her, which would only serve in my favor.

I checked on Grandma Dorothy, who was happily clicking away at the TV as she crocheted a God-awful fluorescent orange blanket. "For your house," she announced cheerfully when she saw me standing in the doorway.

"I can't wait," I told her after pressing a kiss to the papery-thin skin of her cheek. "It looks awesome."

"I'll make one for Charlie, too. That girl is always cold. A woman shouldn't be living alone like that, I've said it before and I'll say it again. She needs a nice boy to look after her."

The reminder of her engagement to Andrew put a sour taste in my mouth. "Don't worry, Grandma. I take good care of her."

"Of course you do, dear," she said, then squealed. "*Wheel of Fortune*'s on. Spin that wheel!" I chuckled as I ascended the stairs to the bathroom, leaving Charlie to her caffeine fix and grandma to her TV shows and crocheting.

Twenty minutes under the warm spray hadn't been the best idea. The erection I'd tamed sprung back to life and I'd closed my eyes and wrapped my hand around my dick, trying and failing, not to think of her as I rubbed one out. The hot water cleared my head and jerking off at least kept me from fantasizing, but I doubted either would keep me sane for long.

It occurred to me as I got dressed that I was being a fucking chick about it. We got along. We had a good time. I was obviously attracted to her and based on the way she'd kissed me back, even if it was only for a second, she had to be at least a little attracted to me, too. Why couldn't we date? I'd spouted bullshit the night before, but Charlie wasn't just some one night stand. She was…Charlie.

The thought of asking her out made me nick myself as I was shaving. I cursed underneath my breath and tried to make myself see reason.

Just because I wanted to kiss the hell out of her didn't mean I should.

With that in mind, I finished shaving, but a call interrupted my thoughts. "Walsh," I answered.

"Liam, it's Matthew from the bar. Look I hate to do this, but you left me short Friday without notice."

My stomach sank, and my head filled with the memory of my bare kitchen cabinets and the stack of bills on my desk that I had due. "I know, I'm sorry. I had Tripp cover for me."

"I'm sorry, Liam, but I'm gonna have to let you go. There are a hundred other kids who'd kill to have your job. I need someone more reliable."

I sighed. I wanted to argue, but I could tell by the tone in his voice it would be no use. I'd simply have to find another job. Besides, it had been worth it to make sure Charlie was okay. I might have to survive on microwavable dinners for the next few weeks, but I'd make it work. "Alright, Matt, I understand. Thanks for letting me know."

After hanging up with my former boss, I found Charlie in the kitchen, watching my parents cook breakfast. I paused in the doorway as I observed her studying them. The naked longing on her face punched me in the gut and obliterated any lingering traces of disappointment from getting fired. I'd known her parents for most of my life, and when her mom left and her dad died, it was the first time someone I knew had passed away. It didn't compare to what she went through, but I knew I'd do anything I could to take away her pain.

Even if it'd put my future in jeopardy.

My mother turned and smiled. "Just in time for breakfast."

"As if that's something new," Dad said.

"Something smells good," I told her.

"Charlie said you two were outside all night watching the stars like we used to." She turned to my dad and narrowed her gaze. Then said, "I figured ya'll probably worked up an appetite."

Charlie eyed the plate of scrambled eggs, sausage, and toast my mother sat down in front of her. "You're a goddess, Mrs. Walsh."

My dad wrapped an arm around mom's waist and kissed her cheek. "That's what I try to tell her every day."

Mom bumped him with her hip, but she was blushing. "You both eat up now," she said to us, even though her eyes were on my dad the entire time.

They left together, my mom's giggles trailing behind. I shook my head as I sat down at the table across from Charlie.

"You'd think they were the ones in college instead of us," I said.

Charlie had thrown her hair up into a haphazard bun while I was in the shower. The sun shone in through the kitchen window and caught all the different colors, turning them into spun gold. It glinted in the light as she cocked her head to the side and sighed.

Without thinking, my mouth opened and I started to ask her if we could maybe take a chance. See where that kiss would take us.

Then she said, "I guess we better hit the road if we want to get back on time," and I lost my nerve. I had the drive back to campus to think about it.

Part of me already knew I was going to ask her. It was just a matter of getting up the balls to do it.

CHAPTER 8
CHARLIE

I couldn't put my finger on it, but something was off with Liam. I chalked it up to the patchy sleep he must have gotten from snoozing outside in the truck and resolved to make it up to him the first chance I got. I really couldn't ask for a better friend. It was starting to wear on me how much I had to remind myself that's all he was, all he could be. What excuses I did have didn't seem to carry much weight anymore. Not when I spent the night wrapped in his arms. At first, I thought I'd been dreaming, but there was no denying how turned on I'd been when I'd woken up.

"Is everything okay?" I peered over at him since we were nearing our exit and he'd barely said more than one-word answers in response to my questions. "Is it about your parents having to sell the farm? I didn't want to push, but I'm here if you need to talk."

He scowled at the mention and I instantly regretted bringing it up. "It's that and some…other things. It'll be alright, short-stack. I don't want you to worry about it."

"C'mon, don't go all strong and silent on me. Talk to me."

His scowl turned into a grin. "Since when did we become girlfriends? 'Cause I sure as hell don't talk like this with Tripp."

I rolled my eyes. "Don't deflect. I know something's bothering you." My left foot was already tucked under my right thigh, so it was merely a matter of twisting my upper body to direct all my attention to him.

"I don't know, Charlie. I didn't want the family business, you know that." I nodded, even though his eyes were on the long stretch of road in front of us. "But it's still where I grew up, it's all my sisters have ever known. I hate that I could have saved it if I hadn't been so determined to do my own shit."

"Don't say that. You can't sacrifice yourself for something your heart's not in. That's the difference between you and your dad. He gets up every day and works his ass off because he does love it. If you were to quit school and help him, you'd resent him and hate yourself within six months. That's no way to live." I lifted a shoulder. "Life is just too short."

He reached over and wrapped his hand around my knee, squeezed then released. I could feel the heat from his palm shoot straight to my belly. I swallowed hard.

"In my head, I get all that. I don't know, man."

"You hate to disappoint him."

"Yeah, I guess I still do," he said with a snort. "I guess some things you just never grow out of."

I nodded, but I didn't think that was all that was bothering him, but I didn't want to push too much. He'd tell me the rest when he wanted to. He always had. What I didn't want to do was smother him. He'd done enough this weekend, whisking me away when I needed space and time to regroup after the blowup with Andrew.

"I know you probably have work to catch up on or something. I texted the girls last night and they wanted to get together to bash men and have a drink. Would you mind dropping me off at The Georgetown on Tennessee?"

His head snapped over to me, his gaze intense. *Had I said something wrong?*

"You don't want to stop by your place?"

"If you don't mind leaving my stuff in the back of your truck, I'll get it after. Unless you want to leave it in my place on your way home?"

He was quiet for a few long seconds. Something else was definitely going on. Whatever it was, the mood inside the cab of the truck had gone electric. I shifted in the seat and pulled at the thin material of my jersey top.

Finally, he said, "If you're heading out, I can get some studying done at the library. I'll pick you up when you guys are done so you don't have to get an Uber."

"Are you sure?" I'd never wanted to back out of meeting my friends before, but they'd been begging for the low-down on what had happened with Andrew and I couldn't keep putting them off, despite how much I wanted this weekend with Liam to never end.

He gave me a look that said don't be crazy as we left the I-10 and began driving into the heart of town. In no time at all he was pulling into The Georgetown's parking lot.

For a moment it looked like he might ask me to stay, then he said, "Of course I'm sure. I can't keep you all the time, can I?" He said it lightly, but was there a hint of wistfulness in his tone or was that just wishful thinking on my part?

I spotted Layla and Ember by the entrance to the restaurant and sighed. I loved my friends, but all I wanted was my bed and maybe some ice cream. Wine would be a good substitute in the meantime, I decided. Lots and lots of wine.

"Call me when you're done and I'll come get you," he said as he came to a stop in front of the entrance.

"I will. Don't study too hard, Dr. Walsh." I hopped from the cab and turned to give him a smile.

"I like it when you call me that, Nurse St. James." He waved to Layla and Ember, who'd come up behind me. "Ladies," he said with a killer grin before driving off.

"Boy have you got some 'splaining to do," Ember said, and she tucked mine and Layla's arms into hers and marched us to the door. "But first, wine."

I couldn't argue with that.

Normally we'd all meet in Layla's apartment for a Tequila Tuesday game night, but this week we all had cramming to do for papers or tests and even though we'd been around the block a time or two none of us could risk failing. I followed the girls and the hostess through the dimly lit restaurant to a seat in the back. After taking our drink orders, a sangria for me, white wine for Layla, and a margarita for Ember, the waitress left us, and I almost called her back to save me based on the way both of their stares honed in on me.

"What?" I said and resisted—barely—the urge to cross my arms over my chest.

They shared a look.

"Don't 'what' us," Ember said as her dark green eyes sparkled with attitude. Her dark red hair came to life in the wash of the flickering candlelight despite the messy topknot she wore it in. She was a knockout, but she didn't have time to fuss with it much considering she cared for her two younger siblings and still managed to save lives as an EMT.

Layla's beauty was quieter, subtler. Her dark hair fell in soft waves around her pixie face. She wore thin-framed glasses that accentuated her big blue eyes and despite her aversion to makeup, she was a dab hand with eyeliner. "Yeah, what the hell happened?" she asked.

I snatched one of the napkins from the dispenser and began ripping it to shreds. It wasn't the memory of what happened with Andrew that had me nervous. Honestly, he was barely a blip on my memory. It was Liam.

I don't know when it had happened, but he'd shifted from a

support role in my life to the leading man and I wasn't sure what to think of it.

"I thought he was going to propose—"

"What?!" They screeched simultaneously.

"Whoa, wait a second," Ember said, holding up a hand. "Rewind and start at the very beginning."

By the time I finished relaying what happened, we were on our second round of drinks. "And then, um, Liam got him to leave me alone and brought me back to Nassau so we could visit his parents for the weekend."

Layla leaned back in her seat and drank deeply from her glass. She gestured in my direction. "There's something you're not telling us. Did you want to say yes to his proposal?"

My head shot straight up. "*No!* Of course not."

"Then why are you on your fifth napkin?" Ember asked.

Shocked, I glanced down at my lap and found a veritable mountain of shredded paper. I forced myself to knot my hands on the table. "Look, it's not a big deal."

"I call bullshit," Layla said primly.

Ember nodded emphatically. "So do I. Spill."

"Well, Liam came up when Andrew was saying all these awful things," I had to take another long draw from my glass of sangria to keep from choking up. "Anyway, Liam was working that night and he must have heard or seen Andrew come up to me. The next thing I know, he's kissing me and then Andrew left."

"Whoa, whoa, whoa," Ember said. "Liam. *Liam* kissed you?"

"Wow," Layla added, adjusting her glasses. "I definitely didn't see that coming."

"You and me both."

"Then Lay, you may need to get your glasses checked because you're blind. They're perfect for each other."

I carefully gathered up the mess of napkins and rolling them in another to keep from spilling everywhere. "It doesn't matter.

He just did it to get Andrew to go away. It didn't mean anything."

"Honey, a man doesn't kiss you and then take you on a weekend getaway if he doesn't want it to end up with more kissing," Ember said. She'd been in a relationship since high school, not a serial dater like I was or a dater-avoider like Layla, so we mostly deferred to her when it came to the opposite sex.

But she was wrong about this. "Not Liam. He didn't try anything else afterwards and we talked about it."

Layla jabbed her finger in my direction. "You're in complete denial, but we'll circle around to that." Her face fell and I reached for her hand on the table.

"What's wrong? Here I am blathering on and I haven't even asked how you guys have been."

"My *mother*. Well she called to tell me the other day if I insist on keeping my major in art that I can forget any financial assistance for senior year and not to even think about asking her for help with graduate school."

Layla's mom was a straight bitch. She was a living testament to why I never bothered looking for my own. Whereas mine abandoned me, hers never lets up. My phone rings, but I don't recognize the number, so I send it to voicemail and shift my attention back to Layla.

"Now you're the one who needs to listen. You don't need to live your life according to what she wants. She doesn't get a do-over. You deserve to be happy," I told her.

Layla took a deep drink from her wine and signaled for another. "I hear what you're saying, but that's a whole lot easier to say than to do."

"One step at a time, sweetheart. You have to cut those strings at some point," Ember said.

"And just when are you going to realize when you don't have to take care of your sisters and that it's your parent's job?" I asked Ember.

"Not up for discussion," Ember said. "Besides, my twin terrors are a hell of a lot less of a pain in the ass than Layla's mother and Liam put together."

I giggled and slurped down the rest of my third sangria. "Look who can dish it, but can't take it."

Layla was giggling, too, her cheeks flushed. "I think we've opened enough wounds for one Girl's Night."

"Yeah, but I always feel so much better after," Ember lifted her glass in a toast.

Layla and I touched ours to hers. "I'd say we should do it more often, but you two ladies drink too much," Layla said, then polished off her wine.

I did the same with my own. "Way too much," I said with faux graveness.

We were still laughing as we stepped out into the chilly night air. Their Uber was waiting by the entrance and I gave them a hug and helped them into the back seat.

"Text me when you get home, okay?" I said as I waited for them to buckle up.

"Yes, mom," they both said.

"You too," Ember added sternly, ever the mother hen.

"I will," I promised. I waved at their smiling faces in the back window as the Uber pulled away.

I may have had to concentrate extra hard on my way to the bench at the front of the restaurant. Remembering I promised to text Liam when I was done, I pulled out my phone and fumbled with the lock screen.

ME: I'm reaaaaddddyy.

It only took a few seconds for Liam to respond.

LIAM: Omw

I wanted to think it was the sangria, but the delicious anxiety I felt had nothing to do with having too much to drink. It was Liam. All Liam. The cool breeze laden with the scent of grease from a burger joint nearby did little to combat the flush in my cheeks. I had to get a grip on myself before I did something stupid.

Like kiss *him* this time.

Talking myself out of my nerves wasn't helping, so I decided I needed to walk it off. As soon as I stood up, the blood seemed to drain from my head and I swooned, reaching out a hand to grip the back of the bench before I stumbled and fall face-first into the concrete.

But I didn't.

A hand gripped my arm, and I looked up to find Liam standing in front of me. I blinked a couple times to clear the blurriness from my vision. "Careful there, Charlotte," he said with a mile-wide grin. "Wouldn't want you to hurt your pretty face."

My belly flipped and I barely resisted the urge to lean into his grip. I managed to roll my eyes instead, which was a bad idea as it caused me to wobble in my heels. Then I narrowed them, because even with the three-inch assist, Liam was still ridiculously tall. "Don't call me Charlotte," I told the two of him. "You got here fast. You better not have been speeding."

"And you've been spending too much time with Ember, clearly. I didn't speed. I'd just gotten your text as I was leaving the library."

Because I wanted to step into his arms, I took one back. I controlled my wobbling by sheer will. "Let's just get out of here," I said, but it sounded a little desperate to my ringing ears.

"Done," he replied, and wrapped an arm around me to help me to his truck. When I stumbled, he pressed me more securely to his side. "Have a little too much to drink there, shortstack?"

"Just a couple glasses of wine. Don't judge."

He opened the door for me and kept me steady with one

wide palm as I clambered up. "No judgement," he said, but I could clearly hear the smile in his voice. Instead of pissing me off, though, it made me want to laugh.

"You're such a good friend, Liam," I said as he buckled himself in. My eyelids were heavy and now that the rush of adrenaline was gone, I could feel myself starting to crash. Surrounded by the comforting scent of him, knowing I had nothing to worry about as long as he was there, I turned sideways in the seat and leaned over so I could lay my forehead against his shoulder.

He reached over and rested his palm on my thigh like I knew he would. "Any time."

I only meant to close my eyes for a second, but I must have dozed off, because when I opened them again, I found myself in Liam's arms. Blinking rapidly, I looked around and discovered we were in my apartment complex's elevator. Too emotionally and physically exhausted to move, I let my head drop back against his chest.

"Y'know, Charlie, after more than a decade of knowing you, I should have known that a couple glasses of wine knocks you out."

I smiled against the material of his shirt and marveled how that it was even possible after the past few days. "I just want to take a shower, change into a pair of yoga pants and a T-shirt and eat a gallon of ice cream." I yawned and then tapped him on the shoulder. "You can put me down now."

He set me gingerly on my feet, his hands on my arms to steady me.

"I'm fine, I promise."

"You sure?" he asked as the elevator dinged.

"I promise. I don't think it can get any worse," I said with a laugh.

And then we stepped out into the hall and found nearly a dozen men in uniforms going in and out of the yawning door to my apartment.

CHAPTER 9

LIAM

The easy, relaxed mood Charlie had been in since I'd picked her up from the restaurant disintegrated at the sight before us. Her shoulders tensed and her breathing grew shallow and sharp. My own gaze narrowed and I kept myself in check so I didn't go charging over demanding to know what the hell was going on. There'd been a ton of trucks in the parking lot and a whole mess of people congregated on the first floor, but I'd been too focused on Charlie to give any thought to why they were there.

Big mistake.

"Are you seeing what I'm seeing?" she asked and I kept my hand on her arm in case her knees gave out from under her again. Mostly it was for my own benefit. I needed to know she was okay.

"Yeah, what the fuck?" was all I could manage through gritted teeth.

Charlie inhaled and exhaled slowly, then she straightened her spine and marched across the hall to the disaster zone that was her apartment. She only wobbled a little on her heels until she came to a stop beside two middle-aged men in coveralls. After tapping one of them on the arm, she squared her shoulders.

"Excuse me. This is my apartment. What's going on?" she asked.

The two men turned to her and immediately their eyes went to the slight V of her neckline. I gritted my teeth and stepped up behind her. Catching my eye, they straightened their gazes, both turning red.

"Ma'am, your apartment flooded. We didn't find out until this evening because the space below yours is empty. The building manager had an emergency at another complex, so he'll be by in the morning to talk about your options. Until then, your apartment will be inaccessible."

She swayed in front of me, so I placed my hands on her shoulders. "F-flooded you said? But that's impossible. I haven't been here since Friday and there wasn't anything leaking at the time."

I thought back to Friday when Andrew had asked for her key to get his stuff from her place. Had he done this? Was he that spiteful? Then it hit me. If I hadn't given Andrew the key, she wouldn't be essentially homeless right now. This was entirely my fault.

"How long will it take to repair the damage?" I asked. I had to fix my mistake.

One of the guys, whose name tag read *Mac,* lifted a shoulder. "Four to six weeks depending on the severity. Once we clear it up a little bit, you can go in and assess your damages and gather any items you'd like." He pulled a business card from his breast pocket. "If you'll call the landlord's office tomorrow, they'll be available to go over your options."

"Options," she repeated.

"Hey, Mac!" came a shout from inside her apartment.

"Excuse me," Mac said, and disappeared inside.

Charlie turned, her eyes unfocused and her face devoid of expression. "Well, shit," she said after a minute of silence.

"Don't worry, we'll figure something out. But we should talk about this somewhere else."

"Somewhere else. I have nowhere to go." She barked out a laugh. "Have you looked inside there? It's a disaster zone, Liam."

"It's just stuff. It can be replaced." I guided her by the shoulders out of the melee while I figured out how to tell her what had happened. I'd tried to protect her and I'd wound up causing her even more damage.

For a few minutes we just watched the parade of repairmen go in and out. Each time they stomped over the sodden carpet, Charlie winced. As the minutes passed, her shoulders grew tighter and tighter until they were somewhere up around her ears.

"Why don't you stay at my place?" I said. I didn't know I was going to offer until the words spilled from my mouth. The more I thought about it, the more the idea made sense. It wasn't going to be forever. We were best friends, for fuck's sake. Of course she could bunk with me. It was my fault she was without a place. It was my responsibility to make it right.

"What?" She blinked owlishly up at me, like she was waking from a dream. "I'm sorry, what did you say?"

"Why don't you stay at my place until they've got yours sorted?"

She blinked again, her mouth hanging slightly open. Then she shook her head and said, "No, I couldn't do that to you. You love your house. We just talked about how you didn't want to settle down and all that."

I shrugged, feeling awkward as hell. "It's not that big of a deal, and it's not like I'm asking you to marry me. It would just be for a couple weeks."

"I can't move in with you!" I wasn't sure her eyes could get any bigger.

I shot a pointed glance at the ruins of her apartment. "Well you sure as hell can't live here."

A variety of emotions crossed her face, starting with irritation and ending with resignation. "Just for tonight," she said after a while. "Just until I can talk to the super and figure out what my options are."

Our building manager had never been what you'd call responsible, so I didn't have any high hopes about her "options", but she'd already had enough shit dumped on her in the past couple of days, so I agreed. I waited outside her front door while they let her run in and grab a few things that weren't completely soaked. I would have offered to help her, but she had the wrinkle between her brows that meant she was looking to fight with someone.

As soon as she came out with a couple garbage bags full of her stuff, I took them from her hands and said, "C'mon, I know you're hungry. Let's heat up a pizza and I'll get you some medicine for the headache you've got."

She squinted at me. "How did you know I have a headache?"

After reaching the elevator, I turned to her and pressed the crease between her brow. "This right here."

She only sighed, and I figured I wouldn't push her for the rest of the night. She had enough to deal with. We loaded her things into my truck and she was silent for the short drive over to my squat little duplex. The paint on the clapboard siding needed refinishing. The door was a little cock-eyed and the landscaping was practically non-existent, but it was dry and it was as clean as a bachelor pad could get, which was a hell of a lot better than her place. And it'd save her more money than if she got a hotel.

I set her bags down underneath the kitchen bar as she kicked out of her shoes. While she threw herself on the couch with a grown, I grabbed a frozen pizza from the freezer, unwrapped it and set it on a cookie sheet while the oven preheated. I shook a couple Tylenol into my hand and brought them over to her, along with a glass of water.

"Take these."

She did as I'd instructed and gulped down the whole glass of water. "Thank you," she said on a heavy exhale. "I guess I'll know better than to think things couldn't get worse in the future."

I chugged my own glass of water, hoping the knot in my throat would dissolve. "I'm sorry, sweetheart, but we'll get it taken care of."

"I know. I just I hate it when things are out of my control." She frowned, and I couldn't help but laugh. "What?" she asked indignantly.

"You're gonna go through your whole life frustrated if you think you can control everything. If my family had taught me anything, it's that you have to learn to roll with the punches. Cliché, but it hasn't done me wrong yet."

She shook her head, then winced and slumped down against the couch. "I'd rather know what's happening. Have a plan. That way if something does go wrong, I'll know what to do."

"So, you're saying you should have planned to lose your apartment?" Maybe I was wrong about understanding this woman in particular. I scratched my head.

Tears thickened her voice and it froze me to the spot. Those tears were because of me. I'd done this to her as surely as fuckstain. How I'd ever thought I had a right to ask her for more was beyond me. "I should have had renter's insurance at least so that would have covered any possessions that are damaged so I could replace them. I should have had someone come over to check on the apartment while I was gone. If I hadn't been so distracted by what happened with Andrew, maybe this wouldn't have happened."

Guilt drew my eyes to the countertops. I could barely look at her. "Clearly you're still intoxicated because that's the biggest load of crap I've ever heard, and sometimes you can really be full of it."

"I don't want to argue with you tonight, Liam," she said with a sigh.

"I'm not arguing." I glanced over as the oven chimed and got up to put the pizza inside. "All I'm saying is you shouldn't be so hard on yourself. You can't control everything."

"I can try."

With the pizza in the oven, there was nothing else I could do to distract myself from telling her the truth. I braced my hands on the island and forced my gaze to her. God, she was gorgeous. Even sprawled across my couch, her face splotchy with the remnants of tears and her makeup faded, she was gorgeous. "Look, this wasn't your fault. If it was anyone's, it was mine."

She threw a hand over her eyes. "No, it wasn't. If anything, you're the only thing holding me together."

I flinched. "He flooded your apartment because of me."

"What?" she asked as she straightened, her red-rimmed eyes coming to me. "What are you talking about?"

"Friday after you broke up with him he came over to the bar asking for your spare key so he could get his stuff. I didn't even think about it because I was so pissed off from the things he said." I didn't even want to touch how scrambled my brain had been after kissing her. "I should have asked you if it was okay. I should have known he'd try something after the shit he pulled. I'm sorry, Char. Just tell me how I can make it up to you."

She wiped her face and took a shaky breath. "You gave him a k-key?"

I wished she'd yell. It would be so much easier than the heartbreak on her face. "Yes. I'm so sorry. If I could take it back I would."

Her shoulders slumped and she blew out a long breath. I

braced my hands on the island, preparing for a thorough tongue-lashing. Bare feet appeared in my field of vision where they paused opposite the island. She was so close, but she'd never felt so far away.

"I don't know what to think about this right now," she began, then her voice cut off. I stared at her bare feet and realized she hadn't been able to get another pair of shoes. Because of me. "I don't want to be angry with you, I can't even remember the last time I truly didn't want to look at you. But that's how I feel. I'm tired. I'm overwhelmed. I'm homeless. It's too much. I'm going to go get a shower and get some sleep and maybe tomorrow I'll know how to handle everything, but right now, I think I need some space."

"I understand." My voice sounded like shit. I cleared my throat. "Do you need anything? Towels or—"

She shuffled her feet. "I can find them." Silence descended and I didn't dare break it. "Goodnight, Liam."

"'Night," I called to her retreating back. I wanted to say more, but I bit my tongue. She was right, she needed space. I'd done more than enough. I just hoped she could forgive me.

CHAPTER 10
CHARLIE

My confusion haunted my dreams. Not only was I in an unfamiliar place, but the sense of losing all my things, of being displaced again brought back all the insecurities I felt after my mom left. I dreamt of her for the first time in nearly a decade that night. Every time I woke up in a cold sweat and tried to talk myself down until I passed out again, only for the cycle to continue on relentlessly. By the time the sun rose, I didn't feel any more rested than I had when I'd first put my head to a Liam-scented pillow.

I'd set several alarms the night before in five-minute increments and it took every single one of them to get me fully awake and out of bed in time for my clinical rounds at the crack of dawn. Luckily, I kept a couple changes of scrubs in my car so they weren't damaged and had grabbed them before coming to Liam's. I tossed them in his dryer as I padded around his place, trying not to make any noise.

I spent quite a bit of time in it since we'd left Nassau for Tallahassee to go to FSU, but I saw it with new eyes now that I'd be staying for God only knew how long. Unlike me, he hadn't moved around each year trying out new complexes and trying to find one that fit. He'd found this dinky little duplex our freshman year and had stubbornly stuck to it.

It was in a prime location just off of Lake Ella where we'd often jog together when our schedules matched. I'd point out the cute puppies and he'd patiently let me pet them or coo at the geese and ducks. But there'd be no jogging this morning. I wasn't sure I could look at Liam. He didn't have class until ten-thirty or work until five. Part of me wanted to see him peek out his door, but another was grateful he was still asleep. I didn't want to look at him and still be mad.

I pushed thoughts of jogging out of my mind and focused on getting ready. I didn't have any food here—I'd have to go shopping after clinicals and classes, another expense I couldn't really afford. Then I spotted the note on the counter. It was written on a flashcard in Liam's precise handwriting and propped against the coffeemaker.

Help yourself to anything you need. -Liam P.S. I'm a jerk.

Tears prickled the back of my eyes and then I gasped as the coffeemaker gurgled to life and began to drip hot, fresh coffee into the pot. The scent perked my groggy brain right up and it was ready and willing to forgive Liam all his transgressions. I hadn't had time to process everything, but coffee was always the way to my heart and he knew it. I filled a thermos from his cabinets and relented by taking a slightly overripe apple and a granola bar. His pantry was pathetically bare—men, I scoffed inwardly—and I decided I'd grocery shop that afternoon. Who cared if I wouldn't have any money left? I'd need ice cream after I met with my building super this afternoon anyway.

The dryer beeped as I polished off my first cup of coffee and poured a second. I quickly dressed in my school-issued scrubs and packed a second plain pair to use for work afterward. I pulled back my hair into a serviceable ponytail and scrubbed my face with warm water and a hand towel. I made do with what little makeup I carried with me in my purse, a little concealer, some eyeliner and called it good.

I packed the snacks in my bag along with my change of scrubs and paused by the front door. I gave half a thought to waking Liam up, then I glanced at the clock. I wouldn't have time. Besides, I still wasn't sure what I wanted to say.

I dragged myself into work after a long round of clinicals and an endless morning of classes. It was only the thermos of coffee I'd filched from Liam that kept me going. It didn't taste good after about the third reheat, but it kept my eyes open long enough to keep the patients I saw to alive and take notes during my lectures. The only negative was it constantly reminded me of him, what he'd done, that I'd see him in just a couple hours. I hated being on the outs with him. It felt unnatural.

He'd texted me once during the day, but I still hadn't replied. I was putting it off. The therapist who I'd been required to see after my mother's disappearance and my father's death told me I had an avoidant personality. I thought she was a quack at the time, but maybe she'd been onto something. I'd happily put off this confrontation, oh, *forever*.

Which is why I was at least looking forward to work. A lot of people looked down on elder care, but it soothed me. It reminded me of my dad's last days in hospice, of Grandma Dorothy and the good men and women who cared for them. I liked being that person for someone else's family. Eventually I'd like to go into critical care, but for now this paid the bills and gave me purpose.

"Good morning, Mr. Williams," I said as I pushed through the door to my favorite patient's room, but it was empty. I knocked on the attached bathroom door. "Mr. Williams?"

My heart began to thud dully in my chest. Had he left? Had he…passed away?

I couldn't bear the thought of it. I began to speed out the door when it pushed open and Mr. Williams, a thinly-built man with a shock of white hair and watery green eyes, lit up when he saw me.

"Charlotte!" he exclaimed and I smiled. He was the only person, after my dad, who I let call me by my real name.

"Mr. Williams. You scared me. I thought you'd left." I stepped into his embrace and inhaled the scent of Old Spice and antiseptic. My insides unclenched.

"You couldn't run me away, sweetheart. Who else would play chess with me and let me win?"

"No one," I said fondly as I got out the board and began setting up the pieces. "Did you take your medicine?"

He scowled, but we both knew it was only for show. "You should know better than to torture an old man."

I tutted at him and retrieved his medicine from the pharmacy station. "Bottom's up!" I said and his scowl deepened at my cheerfulness, but he complied. "Now let's see if I can beat you again."

"Not a chance, missy."

"Did you have a good weekend?" I asked as I carefully considered my opening move. It wouldn't matter what I did. Despite his age and my teasing, Mr. Williams was a shark at chess and I'd only ever beat him once and that was only because he'd just had surgery to repair his hip and had been on some serious pain killers. I chose a pawn at random and immediately regretted my decision when his beard twitched.

He mimicked my move, but I had no clue what he was planning. A chess genius I was not. "It was boring here without you to keep me company," he said. "What did you do?"

"I went to visit Liam's family near Jacksonville for the weekend." I moved another pawn, but he struck and captured it with a masculine laugh.

I felt the tension leech from my shoulders the longer we played. I told him about Grandma Dorothy and her new fluorescent orange blanket. He had a similar one, this one an unearthly yellow, draped over the foot of his own bed. I even told him about the trouble with my apartment and how Liam had a hand in me losing it.

Mr. William's had three-quarters of my pieces by the end of my update. "Don't be too hard on him. He sounds like a good friend from what you've told me. He's probably madder at himself than you are at him."

I thought of the note he left me, the coffee he'd made. "I know that, but it just sucks all around."

"I know it does, but you can find another place to rent. You won't be able to replace a friend so easily." With that sage advice, Mr. Williams moved his bishop and crowed, "Checkmate!"

I frowned at the board. "You're diabolical," I said, then began cleaning up the set.

"You're getting better. One day you may even beat me."

"Thank you, Mr. Williams, it's nice of you to say, but we both know I'm hopeless." I smiled at him and lifted the chess box in greeting. "Rematch next week."

"You got it," he said as he settled into his hospital bed and turned on the TV to the news. "You'll have to update me about you and your young man."

"We'll see," I said over my shoulder.

I finished my rounds with Mr. William's words fresh on my mind. I knew it wasn't Liam's fault for what happened, not really. Andrew had used the spare key a couple times before to get a spare set of scrubs for me when I was tied up in class or get something of his he left. It wasn't completely unreasonable for Liam to give him the key. After Andrew blew up at us…after the kiss…suffice it to say we were both distracted.

The girls weren't much help when I texted to let them know what was going on. They both lived in the same complex and had noticed all of the commotion that morning. I didn't get a chance to reply until I finished my shift.

> EMBER: OMG!!! That rat bastard! Do you need me to come over and help you clean up? I'll see what I can sneak in and salvage since they won't let you in. If you don't have a place to stay, you can crash here.

> LAYLA: Tequila Tuesday at my apartment next week. Not optional! I'll even provide the tequila this time. Let us know what the super says or if we need to put a hit out on him.

I sent them both thank yous and promised to keep them updated. I didn't have a good feeling about my meeting with the super, but I headed there after work to get it over with. I'd feel better once I knew my options…I hoped.

I knew the meeting with the building manager wasn't going to go well when he had me wait for half an hour in the small lobby on the first floor of my apartment building. I never liked to linger there because it always smelled like spoiled milk despite the heavy rose-scented air freshener they had plugged in to every available outlet. By the time he called me back into his office, I was tired, nauseous, and ready to put my feet up after a long day of clinicals.

"Ms. St. James, thank you so much for your patience."

"Of course," I said as I took a seat opposite the ancient desk in the middle of the cramped office.

Despite the comfortable bed in Liam's spare room, I hadn't

been able to close my eyes and turn off my brain. It was like everything that could go wrong, had. And I didn't get a good feeling about this meeting. I didn't know if it was leftover nerves from the day before or what, but there was a knot of tension in my stomach that no amount of chugging water would make go away.

Mr. Jergan, the building manager, was in his late forties or so with a shiny pink head and the remnants of hair he trimmed fastidiously around its rim. His mustache matched the salt and pepper of what hair remained and was trimmed razor straight. It twitched as he sifted through paperwork.

"I have some unfortunate news about your unit. It appears the sink in the bathroom had been blocked with a washcloth and overflowed all over the unit."

I swallowed around the lump in my throat and fought the urge to cry in frustration. If he got away with this I was going to kill him with my bare hands. "I understand. An ex-boyfriend of mine used the spare key to get some belongings, or so he said. I never had any idea he'd do anything like this. I don't have renter's insurance, so he's cost me everything. Please, can you help me?"

His expression was unforgiving and my heart sank. "Seeing that the damage, though accidental, was at the hands of someone you're responsible for we're holding you liable for the damages. You're going to have to forfeit your deposit, you understand." His mustache twitched again and I focused on it as I considered my response.

"Sir, I can appreciate your position, but there has to be another apartment you can lease me in the meantime. If not here, then at some other building?"

"Currently, all of our units are full. Normally, we'd offer another for your use per the terms of your lease, but there are none available here or at another property. We will make our best effort to have the unit repaired in a timely fashion, but we won't be able to offer you accommodation in the meantime. I do apologize for the inconvenience. You're more than welcome to retrieve the rest of your belongings as soon as the maintenance crew has given me the all-clear."

Numb and disbelieving, all I could do was nod. "Do you know how long it'll take for my apartment to be repaired?"

He leaned back in the seat and tapped his thumbs on the armrests. "Hopefully within in the next two months, as long as the contractor stays on schedule."

It felt like the breath was knocked out of me. I couldn't afford a hotel for that length of time. Without the return on my deposit, I couldn't afford a first and last deposit either. Not without dipping into my overseas fund and I was reluctant to sacrifice my dream. But I'd have to if I couldn't figure out an alternative.

"If you'll sign and date these papers here, we'll get you all taken care of."

I glanced at the papers as he handed them over and decided I wasn't going to let him screw me. I took them and stood abruptly.

"Erm, Ms. St. James—"

"Thank you so much, Mr. Jergan. I'll give these a once over and return them to you once I've signed them. I hope you have a wonderful evening."

Without another word, I spun on my sensible white sneakers and marched out of his office and to the garage where I'd stored my car. I'd managed to use the bus to get it this morning before clinicals. Practically vibrating with frustration, I jabbed my key into the ignition and forced myself to drive carefully through the maddening evening traffic. College kids, liberal amounts of alcohol and unfettered free time did not mix well. Especially at a school like FSU with its notorious reputation for an epic social life.

I was still livid as I stalked through the grocery store closest to Liam's duplex. I practically sprinted down the aisles loading my cart with comfort food. Aside from the brief respite of chess with Mr. Williams, it had been a hell of a day. I paid for the groceries and bundled them into the car.

Despite my pleas otherwise, traffic had cleared by the time I left the grocery store and I made it across town to the duplex in record time. Liam's truck was parked in the driveway and a light shone in the living room. I didn't want to be mad at him anymore, I decided. I missed my friend and it had only been a day. There was no more avoiding him.

I weighed down my arms with the bags because I'd rather lose circulation in my arms than have to go back for two trips. It was a stupid decision because it meant I didn't have a free hand to open the door. I sighed and kicked it with my foot and wondered if sleeping in one of the empty rooms at the adult care facility was an option. The last thing I wanted was for things to be awkward between us.

He came to the door without a shirt on and my tongue stuck to the roof of my mouth. He froze at the sight of me for a second, then took half of the bags in one of his hands causing his muscles to bulge. Needing to keep my distance from him was practically impossible now that we were living together.

"Thanks," I croaked and purposefully shifted out of the way and closed the front door behind me, the remainder of grocery bags slapping against my leg along the way. I slumped against the wall with a frustrated growl, let the bags drop to the floor, and squeezed my eyes shut. Maybe if I clicked my heels together the world would go back to normal when I opened them again.

"Guess your meeting with good old Mr. Jergan didn't go very well." I heard the rustle of the bags as he carried them to the kitchen and then returned for the ones by my feet.

"You can say that again," I told him without opening my eyes. An epic headache started to beat a wicked tattoo in my temples. "Apparently because Andrew technically had access to my place because he had a key, his damage was my fault. So I'm out my apartment and a deposit. I don't exactly have a ton of money, so I'm pretty much screwed here because it'll take me forever to save up first and last month's rent for another place unless I dip into my overseas savings."

"That's fucked up," he said, and I was glad he didn't try to comfort me. One show of sympathy and I might have broken. "You know I can help you with the money, if you want."

But we both knew it was mostly a kind gesture. Liam was a broke student saving for vet school like I'd been saving for my volunteer gig. I sighed. "I'm sure I'll figure something out."

I kept my eyes squeezed shut. Just a few more minutes. Maybe it was the headache, maybe it's because I didn't want to see him feeling sorry for me, but mostly it was not wanting to stare at him like a psycho.

"I wasn't kidding when I said I was a jerk," he said. "You wouldn't be in this position if it weren't for me. I can't say I'm sorry enough, but I can help you. You can stay here with me."

At that, I cracked open an eye. He'd taken everything out and had begun putting things away. "You can't be serious."

He leveled me with a look that clearly said how stupid he thought that statement was. "Of course I'm serious. If it makes you feel more comfortable, we can put a time limit on it. However long you think it would take you to save up money for first and last for a new apartment. If you can forgive me that is. Even if you can't, you can stay here as long as you need to and I'll keep my distance, I swear."

It was the way he held himself apart that broke me. This is *Liam*. I knew he meant what he said. If I wanted to use his generosity to stay here and not talk to him again he'd let me. Because that's just who he was. I pushed off the wall and crossed to the kitchen where I wrapped my arms around him. "I forgive you. Please don't blame yourself anymore." I was aware of his bare skin beneath my cheek, the thump of his heart in my ear, but I tried to focus on him, on not fucking things up more than they already were. "I'm sorry for being pissed off. It was just too much."

His arms came around me and I felt his sigh of relief. "You don't ever have to apologize to me, Char. It was my fuck up. Just tell me we're okay."

"We're okay." I felt such relief in his arms that I knew I made the right decision. I could never stay mad at Liam for long anyway and I knew he'd never do anything like that intentionally. "I really don't want to put you out any more than I already have, but I have nowhere else to go right now."

"You aren't putting me out. I'm offering. Understand?" When I didn't answer right away he tipped my chin up with a finger and prompted, "The correct answer is 'yes, Liam'."

I tucked myself back against his skin. *Just one more minute.* "Are you so demanding and obnoxious with everyone or am I just lucky?"

I felt him smile against my hair as he leaned down and pulled me closer. "I save it all up just for you. Besides, you're not the only one in dire straits. My manager at the bar wasn't too thrilled with me this weekend. I got fired."

"What?!" I screeched. "Liam, no. You can't be serious."

"Don't worry, shortstack. Jobs like those are a dime a dozen, but it'll help me out to have you here for a bit while I look for another."

I pulled back to frown at him. "Well now I feel like a little shit for being upset yesterday. You have every right to be mad at me, too."

He shrugged and moved away to open the fridge for a beer. "Why don't we just call it even? You can have the spare room, we can split everything else and maybe we'll both get what we need. You get your overseas thing and I don't have to spend any of my college fund for vet school."

"Are you sure?" I asked.

"Don't worry, I plan on putting you to work." He threw

himself on the couch and turned on the TV. "Cooking, cleaning. The usual."

Laughter bubbled out of me until he didn't join in. "What? Wait, are you serious?"

"Of course not. We'll split the rent and bills. Don't be a slob and we'll be fine. It's not like it's forever, Charlie."

Too exhausted to think of an alternative, I plopped down on the couch beside him and propped my head on a pillow against his thigh as he flipped through shows on Netflix and sipped his beer. After selecting one, he began sifting his fingers through my hair until I purred in the back of my throat.

"That feels good," I said sleepily.

"Just relax for a while. Everything will work out."

Maybe everything had worked out for the best. It wouldn't be a good idea to act on my attraction to Liam now, not when we would have to spend the next few months together. If one of us caught hard feelings and things ended badly, I'd be forced to move again and I'd have to sacrifice the volunteer opportunity.

Not only that, but I'd risk my friendship with Liam. It might survive a failed relationship, but it'd certainly never be the same. I already worried it was fundamentally different because of one kiss. After almost losing him because of this crap with Andrew, I knew just how much it could hurt me and I knew first hand relationships weren't worth the risk. My own mother taught me that well enough. What I had with Liam was so much stronger...so much more important.

As he played with my hair and I drifted in and out to the sounds of *Criminal Minds*, it was almost impossible to ignore how much I enjoyed him touching me, but I'd have to get used to being this close to him...and doing nothing about it.

If we were going to live together, anything more than just friends would have to be off limits.

CHAPTER 11

LIAM

There was something that looked suspiciously like breakfast waiting in a covered dish on the island.

This was impossible for three reasons:

1. I didn't have anything resembling cookware in my house (and probably hadn't since I'd moved in two years ago).

2. I wasn't sure anyone my age actually knew how to make food that didn't require a microwave.

3. The last time Charlie cooked something, we both wound up with food poisoning.

It wasn't until I spotted the takeout containers in the trash that I deemed the biscuits and gravy safe to eat and tossed them in the microwave to heat up as I got dressed. I didn't have class until eleven, but I liked to get up a couple hours early to hit the gym for a quick workout beforehand. I wolfed down the biscuits and gravy and shot off a quick text to thank Charlie for the food. I felt a twinge of guilt that she not only stocked the cabinets and fridge the day before, but that she'd sprung for breakfast as well.

I hadn't been kidding when I asked her to move in. I'd been prepared to beg. Not only had I gotten fired from the bar, but bills were coming due and I'd been surviving on canned soup for longer than I'd cared to admit. This weekend at my parents was the first time I'd had anything home cooked since Christmas.

I could have asked my parents for help, but there was no way in hell I wanted to hear my dad bitch about how much money I was wasting living in a different city going after a useless education when I should have been helping him. The guilt and shame of having the gall to go to school when they were struggling was already overwhelming.

My phone rang as I jogged to my truck. I answered it, breathing heavily. "Hello?"

"Willy, you forgot your good jacket at the house. You're gonna have to turn around and come pick it up so you don't catch a chill," came Grandma Dorothy's voice through the crackling line. She must be on the house phone. It had a lot of static on the connection. My parents didn't want to get rid of it because Grandma Dorothy liked to call her friends when she was of a mind to.

"Hey Grandma, it's Liam."

"Liam?" she asked, her voice breaking in the middle of my name in a way that made me stop before I unlocked my truck and lean my head against the window. She'd always been the strongest person I'd ever known and to watch her deteriorate before my eyes was worse than if she'd been taken without warning like my grandfather had.

I swallowed back the choked feeling in my throat and told myself to stop being such a fucking pussy. "Yeah, Grandma, it's me. How are you doing?"

There was a lengthy pause as she sorted through the labyrinth her mind had become, but I was patient. Even though I'd been in a hurry to get to the gym, everything had ground to a halt when she called. If I'd learned nothing else from being friends with Charlie, it was that each moment with your loved ones was precious, and there wasn't a chance in hell I was gonna miss out on any of them.

"I'm doing fine, sugar. You should come by and see your grandma sometime. I sure do miss you."

I didn't remind her that she'd seen me just a couple days ago, but it still stung like a son-of-a-bitch that she didn't remember because I knew there'd come a day when she wouldn't remember me at all.

"I'll try to come up this weekend when school lets out. I promise."

She made a humming sound that was as much a part of my childhood as the taste of her sugar cookies. I urged myself to hold it together as she said, "How's school, honey? Are the other kids playing nice?"

Laughter burst free, but I choked it. I rubbed at my eyes. "It's going pretty well. Passing all my classes and the other kids are treating me just fine."

"Good. That's good to hear. You'd tell me if someone was bullying you, right? I won't have none of that nonsense with my grandson. You hear me?"

"Yes, ma'am," I said obediently. I was reminded of all the times she'd been forced to discipline me for one harebrained scheme or another I'd concocted while under her care. For such a small woman, she could sure as hell be intimidating, even though I towered over her, both then and now.

"I'm glad you brought that Charlie over. I've been thinking about her. She seemed upset, though. Is everything okay?"

I thought of Andrew and considered, not for the first time, what I'd like to do to his ass if I saw him again. "She and her boyfriend broke up, so she's having a bit of a rough time."

Grandma hummed again. "That poor girl. I'm glad you brought her by, then. People need to be around family when they're hurting, and I've always considered Charlie to be part of our family."

"She feels the same way," I said.

"Alright now, I think it's about time I put on my stories. You call me tomorrow, okay, honey?" For as long as I can remember, Grandma Dorothy could be found watching her soap operas from morning to afternoon. It was good that some things hadn't changed. Yet. "Here's your mom, she'd like to talk to you."

"Okay, Grandma. I love you." I used to feel awkward saying it. My whole family loved to say "I love you". It didn't matter the reason or occasion. There was always a chorus of them when we got together. I didn't get it until the day I visited Grandma in the hospital for the first time and realized she might never hear me say it again. Ever since then, I've made it a point to say it every chance I got.

"Love you, baby doll. I'll talk at you later."

"Later," I said with a laugh.

"Liam?" Mom said as she fumbled with the phone.

"Hey, Mom, what's up?" It had to be important if she was calling the day after I saw her.

"Sorry about that, honey. Your grandma hasn't been feeling well lately and she's been antsy all night wanting to talk to you."

"That's alright, mom. You don't have to apologize. I wish I could help out more, but I couldn't miss anymore classes this semester."

"Don't you think on that for a minute. We were glad to see you. I was going to talk to you about everything this weekend, but Charlie seemed upset and I didn't want to intrude."

My stomach dropped. "What is it?"

"Your father mentioned he told you about the plan to sell the land?"

"Yeah, he did. I hated to hear that, mom. I wish there was something we could do."

"Well, there was a reason why."

"What is it?"

"It's Grandma Dorothy, honey. Her doctors tell us she's in a rapid decline. She needs to be hospitalized soon, for her health and safety. We do our best, but she needs more care than we can provide at home. It's one of the reasons we're selling. It's the only way we'd be able to afford for her care."

Guilt twisted at my heart. "Are they sure?"

Mom sighed over the line. "They're sure. I just wanted to let you know. Your dad was going to tell you, too, but it's been really hard on him. He may seem hard, but he has a big heart."

"Thank you for letting me know. Keep me updated, okay?"

"Of course. You call me if you need anything, won't you?"

I managed to say goodbye before I lost it.

"You look worse than I did yesterday," Charlie said as soon as I stepped in the door.

I grunted in answer and dropped my bag of school shit by the front door and toed off my shoes, leaving them by my bag. After a brutal morning at the gym where I tried to erase the conversation with Mom from my brain and an even longer afternoon of classes I was beat. None of the applications I'd submitted the night before had returned any results and I had another stack of overdue notices crammed in along with my textbooks and dirty gym socks.

"Well, hello to you, too," I said.

"Everything okay?"

I snorted. "Yeah, sure."

"I ordered pizza," she said with false cheerfulness.

At her hollow tone, I grimaced. I was being a dick. "Charlie..."

"I got you the cheese and mushroom you like," she interrupted.

"You don't have to take care of me, Charlie. Breakfast and now pizza. You don't have to be weird about living here."

"I'm not being weird. I'm trying to be nice," she said as she pulled out paper plates. The scent of cheese and tomato sauce filled the air, reminding me I'd stupidly skipping lunch after the gym. Well, skipped is a strong word. *Didn't have the money for* would be more accurate.

"Didn't we already have a conversation about being nice?"

She rolled her eyes. "Let's not go there."

"Sorry. It's just…it hasn't been a very good day." I scrubbed a hand over my face. *That was the understatement of the year.*

Charlie loaded up the plate with a gargantuan sized pizza from Momo's, a local legend for pizza slices bigger than your head. "Well, I'm here and I have ears if you want to tell me what's got you looking like you're going to incinerate innocent civilians with your eyesight."

I tore into the pizza still standing and said, "I'm never letting you watch *X-men* again."

She took a bite of her own, licked the sauce off her lip. I cursed myself for the thin athletic shorts I was wearing and casually slid onto a stool at the island so she couldn't see the outline of my dick through them.

"Seriously, though. What's wrong?"

"Mom called me today."

Charlie set the pizza on a paper plate. "What is it?"

She'd gone completely white. "Shit, Char. This is why I didn't want to tell you."

"Is it your parents? Grandma Dorothy?"

The knot in my stomach hadn't dulled with an hour in the gym. It intensified under Charlie's agonized expression. I swallowed a bite of pizza, but it was a struggle. "Grandma isn't doing so hot. They have to put her in a home. It's why they're selling."

"God, Liam, I'm so sorry.

I stood, suddenly unable to sit here with her soft brown eyes looking up at me. It made me want to hold her, comfort her. Those things were alright before, but hell if I understood why they made me so damn irritable now. I couldn't deal with any of it. I didn't want to. "I'm gonna grab us a six pack to go with this pizza."

She took a step back, dropped her hands When she spoke, her voice was tentative and I immediately felt like a dick. "That sounds great. We can have another movie night and veg out, okay?"

"I'll be right back," I told her.

The short run to the convenience store down the road allowed me to put a lid on my bullshit. She had enough on her plate without dealing with me. I'd find another job and she'd go off to wherever and things would get back to normal. They had to. By the time I got back to the duplex, I had that lid screwed on so tight I practically vibrated with it. Sitting next to her on the couch was like torture.

"Thanks for the pizza," I told her after the movie, getting to my feet almost before the credits rolled. "Even if you're still fucking weird for not liking mushrooms."

She pulled a face as she picked up our empty bottles and rinsed them. "They're so gross. I still don't see how you eat them."

I licked my lips. "Mmm-mmm, good," I said.

She laughed and slapped at my shoulder. "Do you mind if I take the first shower? It's been kind of a long day."

"No, go right ahead. I've got some studying to do anyway."

With a nod and a small smile, she turned around, then paused and turned back. "I'm here if you need me, Liam."

I lifted a shoulder. "Thanks."

"I'm serious. You were there for me. I want to be there for you, too," she said.

"You don't owe me anything, Charlie."

"Of course I do," she said, then disappeared into the bathroom.

I heard the shower turn on a minute later, and I took my books into my room, turning on the light beside my bed before throwing myself onto the mattress. Five minutes turned into ten, and I realized I couldn't remember a word of what I'd read. I shrugged my shoulders, figuring it was because I wasn't used to having someone else in the house. After nearly four years of living by myself, I'd kind of gotten used to it, even though I'd spent most of my life crammed in a house with my sisters.

The truth was, I'd never had a woman stay the night at my place before.

Charlie would hang out, but sleepovers had never been our thing.

Now I realized why.

I slammed the book closed, tossed it on the floor, and relaxed back onto my pillows. I couldn't seem to focus, couldn't get rid of the tension in my shoulders. It was probably because of my parents and bills.

As my thoughts drifted, I found them going to the shower, to Charlie. For a second, it occurred to me that she was naked in the house with me. I stumbled to my feet and stubbed my toe on the book. I muttered curses and kicked the book across the room. Limping, I turned in a circle and considered going back to the gym for another workout, then rejected the idea.

Instead, I hobbled to the door, pulled on my shoes with a muttered curse and went out for a jog. Everything was going to shit and all I could think about was what my best friend looked like naked.

CHAPTER 12
CHARLIE

The blare of my alarm woke me from a dream, a moan still clinging to my lips. My cheeks were flushed, my thighs clenched, and my hands twisted in the mangled remains of my sheets. My ears rang, but it wasn't from the drone of the alarm. I'd been holding my breath and it came out in one long exhalation, lungs burning with the effort to draw new air in. Spots studded my vision.

"Jesus Christ," I managed as I sat up, carefully releasing my strangle-hold on the sheets.

With numb hands, I fumbled with my touch screen until I silenced the alarm. But it wasn't the sound replaying in my brain. It was the sound of Liam's groans echoing in my ear from the sordid dream I'd been torn from.

This was bad.

I covered my face with a pillow hoping to drown out the memory of his hands on my skin, his filthy words in my ear, but I couldn't. The door had been opened weeks ago when he'd kissed me and there was no amount of locks that would keep it closed. No amount of forgetting could wipe away the memory when he was on the other side of a thin wall, refreshing it day in and day out. Especially not if I was going to start having wet dreams with him in them.

We'd been living together nearly a month now and I'd thought everything was going to be fine…apparently my body and brain had other ideas.

I rubbed my thighs against each other in an effort to sate the aching emptiness between them, but there was no quenching it. Sex with Andrew and I had been sporadic at best and before we broke it off, we'd been in a bit of a dry spell. I dipped my fingers between my legs and stifled a moan. There was no doubt that the dry spell was over.

It should have embarrassed me to realize Liam was the reason, but I was too turned on to think of anything but finishing what the dream had started.

As I was rubbing furiously, my lip clamped between my teeth, I heard the tell-tale sound of Liam's door opening and his feet padding against the creaky wooden floor outside my door. Oh, God, I knew I should have stopped, I knew I should have pushed all thoughts of him, and that kiss, out of my mind, but the forbidden aspect, the thrill of knowing he was on the other side of the door made the walls of my pussy clamp around my fingers in vicious delight.

I tensed my stomach and held my breath hoping to force the orgasm before I truly fucked up and let him know what I was doing. The mere thought of having him burst through the door and catching me in the act had my fingers quickening their pace. Sounds were coming from the bathroom now, right across from my room. The light shone in the thin space underneath my door. His shadow danced across the floor inches from where I lay in bed touching myself to the thought of him.

My chest burned for air and I gasped, sucking it in as quietly as possible when I could hold it no longer. His shadow paused and I nearly squeaked in surprise. Even though shame burned in my stomach it was no match for the rising undulation of pleasure. My free hand dove under my shirt and cupped the swollen weights of my breasts, my nipples already hard and aching against the flat of my palm.

Water splashed in the sink and I recall the many showers I'd taken in the three weeks since I'd been living in Liam's duplex. I'd done my level best to think of anything but the fact that he was on the other side of the door while I was naked. As my fingers dipped into my wetness I couldn't think of anything else. He'd been the one to kiss me. Had he been thinking of me like this too?

Heat covered my whole body.

Had Liam been touching himself like this to thoughts of me?

Maybe another person would have been turned off by the thought, but it only made me bite my lip hard enough to taste the copper tinge of blood. I sucked away the sting and arched my neck as my hips began to roll.

He had no idea I was awake, let alone what I was doing, but that didn't make it right.

In fact, it probably made it worse.

Sharing his place with me was a show of trust. That he could trust me not to snoop, not to be a dirty Peeping Tom as his new roommate. I was his friend, and by taking advantage of the little sliver of invitation, I was betraying our friendship. But dammit, a nuclear bomb couldn't have stopped me from shifting to thrust my fingers inside and imagining they were his. Oh God. I'd never be able to think of his hands without wanting them inside me again.

This was such a bad idea, but I couldn't stop.

The faucet turned off in the bathroom and I swore he could hear my heart beating right through the door it was so loud. I tried to swallow, but my mouth was so dry, it was impossible. Did he do something to the heat? He must have, because my clothes were sticking to my skin and I was about two seconds away from having a heat stroke. Could that happen in the middle of March?

His footsteps drew closer to my room and I felt everything inside of me reaching a fever pitch. A knock came at the door and a desperate cry hovered on the edge of my lips. He knocked again and knowing he was there pushed me right over the edge. I turned my face to the side and allowed a soundless cry to escape into one of the pillows he'd given me that still smelled of him.

"Charlie?"

The crest overtook me a second time at the sound of his voice and I shuddered in silence, my thoughts fractured and conflicted. My alarm blared again, a sharp splinter of light in the fog of pleasure. I slapped a hand on it with a muffled shriek.

"You awake in there?" Liam called as the alarm cut off.

A shaky breath rattled free from my lips and I sat up in bed, pulling the sheets up as far as they would go. "Yeah, I'm up." I hoped my voice didn't sound as warbled and breathless as I thought.

A thud came from the other side of the door. I pressed my back into the headboard and gulped in deep breaths.

"You mind if I come in real quick?" he said through the door.

Mind? I wondered desperately if he'd be able to scent my orgasm the second he opened the door. Would he see it on my face? I had to hope not.

I frantically straightened the comforter and hoped it said restless sleeper rather than recently masturbated about its occupant. "Come in!"

The way the room was situated, the door opened right to the dresser and I spotted Liam's reflection in the mirror above before he pushed all the way through. In it was a half-naked body. Liam's half-naked body.

This is wrong, I told myself as the aftershocks danced along my nerve endings. So, so, so wrong.

The reflection in the mirror turned, offering me a delectable profile view. It really wasn't fair how good-looking he was. It was unnatural, I decided. Even so, I couldn't tear my eyes away.

The verdict was in. I was a terrible person. Because no one should look at a friend the way I was looking at him.

He leaned around the open door and I forced my gaze up to his eyes. "What's up?" I asked.

"I just wanted to let you know I got a call back for a job at a different restaurant, so I won't be back for a couple hours. If they hire me, I may start work tonight."

My lips twisted into what I hoped resembled a smile. "That's wonderful! I'm so happy for you."

I knew how hard he'd been looking for a job to replace his bartending gig. I felt wholly responsible for him getting fired. The past couple weeks I made it a point to help him scour the local listings and helped him beef up his resume to atone.

"Thanks, I..."

His eyes left mine and traveled down the length of my body encased by the comforter. "How are you not burning up? It's like a furnace in here."

I chuckled nervously. "Oh, it's nothing. I must have gotten cold."

Was it my imagination or were his eyes boring holes into the fabric?

"Was there something else?" I asked. The sooner I could get him out of my room, the sooner I could take my own shower and wash this whole morning away. With his eyes on me and the memory of the orgasm still dancing along my skin it was almost too much.

I was too close to asking him to stay.

Too close to taking another kiss.

Too close to wondering what it'd feel like to have his hands bring me to the edge instead of my own.

"I'm done in the bathroom if you need to use it."

My cheeks reddened as the image of having him in there with me surfaced. Get it under control, Charlie. "Thanks, I'll be out in a minute."

He shifted, pausing in the doorway for another tantalizing second, then turned and left me with the image of his ass framed in a thin cotton towel seared into my brain.

I didn't get out from under the covers until I heard his bedroom door shut behind him, then I sprang into action, grabbing whichever clothes were closest and my phone, then zipping to the bathroom. My muscles didn't relax until the bathroom door was also shut between us. I stripped down, my whole body tingled with awareness. I needed a cold shower immediately.

My phone rang as I was stepping into the shower, but I didn't recognize the number, *again*, so I ignored it and forced myself under the frigid spray instead. As I soaped up, I slowly turned on the hot water until I was no longer shivering. By the time I finished washing and conditioning my hair, I could breathe normally again. After I exfoliated and shaved, my thoughts settled. When I stepped out to towel off and lotion up, I was convinced I could handle seeing Liam again and not think about the dream, my fantasy, or what he looked like in that towel.

That is, until I got dressed and nearly bumped into him in the hallway and then backed up so quickly I collided with the wall.

Dressed in crisp black slacks and a long sleeved button-down shirt, he was as mouth-watering as he had been in the towel. I couldn't decide which version of him I liked better. It wasn't fair he looked as good fully dressed as he did half-naked.

"Jesus, Char. You okay?"

I rubbed the back of my head. "I'm fine," I said to the notch at his throat. His heartbeat fluttered there and my first thought was that I wanted to kiss him there, right where his scent was strongest. "I'm fine."

"You sure?"

"Yeap." I spun around and marched to the kitchen where I pulled out the makings for cereal. "You want some?"

He sat down at a stool by the island. "Sure. Thanks. Are you sure you're okay? You've been acting...weird this morning."

I busied myself with the bowls. "Yeah, I'm fine. Just an early morning."

He chuckled. "It's nearly eleven."

My glare didn't incinerate him like I'd hoped as I handed him his cereal. "Eat your food," I ordered, then began smashing buttons on the Keurig hoping at least one thing would go right.

"Stop, stop," Liam said, as he got to his feet and put his hand over mine on the machine. "You're going to break it like that."

All I could do was growl.

"Go sit down," he said with a laugh.

I took my seat next to his and stuffed my face with cereal so I wouldn't do something stupid like ask him to kiss me again.

CHAPTER 13

LIAM

For the first time in all the years that Charlie and I had been friends, things were fucking awkward and I didn't know what to do to fix them. In any other situation, I'd know what to do to dispel the tension. If she were any other girl, I'd be able to bullshit my way out of any circumstance. But this was Charlie and none of my moves seem remotely appropriate.

Each day since she'd moved in had been pure torture.

Not that she wasn't a great roommate. She was reasonably clean, quiet, and at some point, had learned to cook like she'd been doing it for years. Hell, under any other circumstances, I'd be asking her to room with me for the foreseeable future, but that wasn't what was driving me crazy.

It was all the things I'd never noticed before because I'd framed her as a friend and nothing more. It was all the things I'd conveniently forgotten because she was "one of the guys" instead of one hundred percent woman.

But now I couldn't escape them.

We're both sitting at the island pretending to eat cold cereal and looking at our phones, except I can't focus on anything but the way her shirt is hugging her breasts and how I'm dying to know what she's hiding underneath it. If anything. I shifted in my seat and gulped down my soggy cereal, but no amount of distasteful visualizations can undo the reality of her oh-so-delectable body sitting across from me.

When I managed to pull my eyes away from her tits, I realized she'd been watching me, and I clear my throat. "I'm sorry, what?" I'm such a tool.

"I said, what time is your interview?"

How had I never noticed her lips before? They were slightly top-heavy and the most delicious shade of pink. Last night she'd made pasta for me and she'd licked away some sauce from her bottom lip. I'd nearly lost my ever-loving mind. With any other woman, I would have pushed her back against the refrigerator and taken that mouth. I would have had my hands everywhere on her body, anywhere they could reach. With any other woman, I would have slipped her little pajama shorts down over her hips and thrown one of her legs over my shoulders to feast on what I was really craving.

It didn't help that I was 99.9% certain I'd nearly caught her playing with herself this morning.

In that one moment I'd nearly taken back all the promises I'd made myself about keeping my distance. I'd weathered the nights with her a few feet away in those frequent showers. It nearly killed me going for a run every time she took one, but I made it work. The mantra that we'd only need to live together for three more months is what kept me going.

Then, I'd stepped into her room and seen her red-faced and hiding underneath the comforter. At first, I thought she hadn't been feeling good. I'd almost offered to get her, I don't know, some soup or some shit. Then, I realized she couldn't meet my eyes. I'd barely been able to speak, let alone keep my dick from tenting the towel I'd stupidly worn to talk to her. I don't even remember what I'd said, but I do remember catching the scent of her arousal. It was burned into my brain.

Despite all the voices in my head telling me it would be a mistake, it was hard to listen to reason when my whole body was screaming yes.

She snapped her fingers in front of my face. "Liam? Hellooo? Did you study too hard last night, or what?"

"Yeah," I managed to say, then dumped the rest of my breakfast. There was no way I was going to be able to focus on anything other than what was going on beneath her sexy-as-hell scrubs. Christ, she was driving me insane. Since when were scrubs sexy? "I mean, I must have."

I'd braced my hands on the sink as I tried to control my reaction without looking like an idiot or coming off as a jerk for staring at her body. God knows I didn't need to be just as much of a dick as her ex. I was supposed to be the person she could trust not to be an asshole. Not the guy who took advantage of her when she was vulnerable. This was Charlie. I shouldn't have to remind myself, but I did. I repeated her name over and over in my mind. Tried to remember all the times I considered her to be one of the guys.

Her chair scraped against the linoleum floor and her feet padded toward me. The warmth of her hit my back, followed by a soft cloud of that fucking green apple shampoo. I was going to have to find every bottle of it and hoard them when she left.

Then it hit me. She was leaving. It wouldn't be now, but in a few months she'd be hundreds of miles away doing God-only-knew what and I wouldn't get these early mornings with her.

"Is everything okay?" she asked from behind me.

Her voice was smoky with sleep and sexy as hell. I wanted to hear her screaming for me in that voice. Pleading in it. Then I wanted to make her breathless until she couldn't speak at all.

My hands fisted on the counter and I straightened without turning to run cool water from the sink and splash it on my face. "Yeah. Yeah, everything's fine."

Everything was not *fine.* I was about ten seconds away from doing something I'd regret. Like taking her back to her bed, *my* bed, and giving her a round two that'd have her seeing stars.

"You sure? You don't sound so good. Are you getting sick? I could run you to the clinic. Of course, I'm almost an official nurse. I could probably give you an exam right now." She wiggled her eyebrows at me. Normally I'd give as good as I got, but if I wasn't on fire before, the thought of her stripping me down and playing doctor sure pushed me over the edge.

I shoved away from the sink, keeping my back to her. "I'm fine, Charlotte." My tone was too harsh to be teasing.

"Don't call me Charlotte just because you're in a pissy mood," she said to my back. I knew if I turned around I'd find her with a hand on her hip and her eyes shooting fire. It was almost worse than seeing her all soft and sleepy.

Keep walking Walsh.

"I'm not in a pissy mood."

"Could've fooled me! If you have a problem with me living here, just man up and say so. You don't have to be a dick about it."

I sighed heavily as I enter my bedroom. "Look, I'm just in a shit mood, that's all. It has nothing to do with you."

"Are you sure?" she asked, following behind me and plopping down on my bed, which I was determined to ignore. I'd already spent too much time imagining her there. I didn't need the reality right in my face. "Because ever since I moved in you've been acting really weird. If I did something, just tell me. This is exactly why I didn't want to move in with you in the first place."

I could only hope I got the job and started tonight. The less time I had to spend at home with her, the better. At the very least I hoped working long hours would make me too exhausted to get horny, but who was I kidding. It didn't take much for me to get turned on around Charlie these days. "I'm sorry. I promise you haven't done anything wrong. I like having you here. To be honest, I probably get more from it than you do. You've been a great roommate. And friend." I had to keep reminding myself of that.

"Then what the hell is going on? You can't even look me in the eye anymore." She put an arm on my bicep and turned me to face her. Staring into her gaze "Please, Liam. Whatever it is, I can help. I don't want to make you feel like a guest in your own home, and besides, we're supposed to be able to talk to each other. So talk to me."

But that was the problem.

The last thing I wanted to do was *talk*.

"There's nothing to talk about. I've got that interview and I need to head out soon. Do you need anything before I go?"

Her mouth twisted and she took a step closer, pressing me against my dresser so I couldn't escape. The closer she got the less oxygen there seemed to be. My heart began to race like I'd run a couple miles.

"You're really not going to talk to me?" She sounded hurt, which didn't help my self-control. "Since when do we do the silent treatment?"

I shoved out from under her touch, unable to stand the feeling of her hands on me and turned to walk away. The destination didn't matter, the only thing that did was getting away from her until I could remember all the reasons I'd been repeating to myself for the past few weeks.

We both needed to save money by sharing the house.

Sex would only complicate both of our lives.

We were friends.

Then she reached out a hand and took mine. Heat shot up from the contact and I'd never known there was a temperature hot enough to freeze, but that's what it did. Her touch froze me down to the core, stopping me in place. No amount of reason could have spurred made me leave when her hands were on me.

I turned, my whole body tense with indecision.

Her brows furrowed and her hair was a wild mess around her face. She bit her lip, sucked it into her mouth.

Fuck just friends. Then took a step toward her, come what may. *We could be so much more than that.*

My hand tightened on hers, then tugged, reeling her in. She glanced down at where I held her and her mouth opened into a little *O* of surprise. I licked my own lips in anticipation. That mouth. God, I wanted that mouth.

"Liam?" she asked, her voice quavering. "What are you doing?"

I crowded her into the dresser where she'd had me pinned just moments before. Her expression wasn't confused anymore. And she wasn't nervous like she'd been the first time we'd kissed. Some part of me recognized the flare of arousal in her eyes, the same part that had made the split decision to kiss her in the first place.

"I changed my mind."

She squeaked out a sound of surprise when her back came in contact with the dresser and her hands grappled for a hold, but slipped once before she could steady herself. "A-about what?"

I bracketed arms around her and smiled a little at the way her breath caught at my closeness. I liked her nerves. I liked having her off balance. "This kiss. What if it wasn't a one-time deal?"

Before she could respond, I dipped my head and nuzzled into the curve of neck and shoulder. I didn't kiss her there, not yet. The last time had been rushed. If I was going to hell for this, I was going to take my time about it.

"But I thought you said—"

"Forget what I said." My lips were close enough they brushed against her skin as I spoke and she shivered.

"But we can't," she said and her voice was as breathless as I felt.

I continued my exploration until my lips met the shell of her ear. "Wanna bet?"

CHAPTER 14
CHARLIE

couldn't seem to think straight.

Just like the last time he'd been this close to me, nothing was making sense. I released the death grip I had on his dresser and brought my hands up to his chest, not only to hold him at a distance, but to keep myself upright.

When I didn't answer, he shifted closer. "What were you doing this morning?" he asked, his voice deep and thick with something I'd never heard directed toward me before.

I was lost in it for about two seconds, then I pushed at his shoulders to give me room to breathe—to think. "I don't know what you're talking about," I said, but I couldn't meet his eyes.

His lips came back to my ear with that same voice that made me weak at the knees. "I think I know what you were doing."

"No you don't!" He couldn't. *Oh, God, could he?*

"It's probably the same thing I've been doing in the shower every day since you moved in."

Well, that distracted me from my own mortification. "What?" I shouldn't want to know, but at the same time, now it was all I could think about. This was so bad, but I couldn't seem to pull myself away.

He brought one hand to my mouth where he thumbed my lower lip. I gave up trying to convince myself it was a bad idea and instead focused on drawing in enough air to keep from passing out. His forehead pressed against mine and he exhaled roughly at the same time I drew in a breath. It felt more intimate than any lover I'd had in my short life span, sharing breath with him.

My own eyes shuttered closed and it amplified the sensations of having him so close to me a thousand-fold. The hand at my mouth coasted down my neck, over my collar-bone then down to my trembling hand. He took it in his and that same thumb pressed into the wildly fluttering pulse point at my wrist. Then he palmed my hand and brought it to my waist and turned me around to face the mirror above his dresser.

His lips found my ear again and I met his gaze in the mirror with half-lidded eyes. "I think you were doing this," he said and guided my hand down from my stomach to rest above the waist-band of my scrubs.

The drowsy-laziness of arousal snapped clear with recognition, but he wouldn't release my hand when I began to struggle. "I don't know what you're talking about," I said shortly, cheeks burning.

He merely smirked. "I think you know exactly what I'm talking about."

Stubble scraped along my shoulder and I melted a little. "Liam," I warned but I wasn't sure if it was because I wanted him to stop or because I wanted him to keep going.

"Let me show you," he said in that rumbly voice. I had no way to defend myself against it and it was like he knew. Maybe because he knew me better than anyone else in the world. Maybe because I hadn't been able to stop thinking about him like this. Or the Liam-inspired orgasm I'd had not even an hour before had turned my brain into mush.

That had to be why the words "Show me what?" tumbled from my mouth instead of a refusal.

His hand began to move over mine, this time to guide it further south…and underneath the waistband of my scrubs. "We can't," I said again, but if he stopped I was pretty sure it would kill me. "You have to leave."

"Shh. I'm busy here," he said.

Our hands were over the material of my panties and he was right. There was no point in talking. My throat was so dry I couldn't form any more protestations even if I wanted to.

He nuzzled my ear. "That's my girl."

Seeing us in the mirror and feeling the slow, torturous exploration of our hands together was an assault on my senses, short-circuiting what was left of my self-control. As I gave into him, he guided my hand over my thighs in a gentle, loving caress and for once I was grateful for my scrubs and how easily accessible they were.

With languid strokes, he directed my hand over the tops of my thighs and down between my trembling legs, but never where I wanted him to go. My head dropped back against his shoulder when the sight of us in the mirror became too much for me to handle. He used his free hand to angle my head to the side so he could kiss my neck as he continued the torture.

"I think I've been wanting to do this for a long time. Too long. When I saw you with that jerk and the things he was saying about you. I snapped. It wasn't just because we're friends. It took realizing one day some man is going to propose to you for real for me to wake the fuck up."

My breath caught in my throat as he nudged my hand further between my legs. If I weren't already embarrassed by being caught, the evidence of my arousal dampening my panties would have been enough.

It didn't bother Liam though. As his fingers pushed between

mine, he felt the proof for himself. His resulting groan sounded just like the one from my dreams and I fairly collapsed against him in response.

"We should stop," I croaked out even though it was the last thing I wanted.

"No way in hell," he growled.

"But what about—"

He brought my gaze back to his in the mirror. "We don't have to make any decisions now, Charlie. The only thing that matters is that I want you and I think you want me, too. If not, tell me now and I'll stop and I promise you I'll do everything in my power to make sure things go back to normal."

I hesitated, but it was only for a second. If it were anyone else, I would have walked away and not looked back, but it was Liam and it felt righter than anything else in my life. I've spent almost every day feeling uncertain about something. My past, my parents, my future. But I'd never questioned Liam, who'd always been there. I didn't know how this would change everything between us, but I trusted him. Even with my heart.

Even if it scared the life out of me.

"Do you want me to stop?" he asked as he brushed my hand away. He tugged the crotch of my panties to the side and then, with the gentlest touch, pressed the pads of his fingers against me and stole what remained of my resistance.

"Don't stop," I whispered as I wrapped my hand around his neck and pulled his mouth to mine. "Don't ever stop."

"I've got you," he said and despite myself and my fears, I relaxed against him because I believed him.

His fingers parted my folds and I sighed in pleasure. As he rubbed all the sensitive parts of me, it was almost as though he could read exactly what I wanted. Maybe he could. Maybe our years of friendship had prepared him to understand me in ways I'd never anticipated.

"The sounds you're making, Char. God, you're killing me."

His lips fluttered against my ear and bucked against him in response.

My fingers latched onto his wrist as my body worked itself to a frenzy. There'd be bruises from the grip I had on him, but I couldn't work up the energy to care. I was so close. Already primed from the orgasm in my bed, it didn't take much from him to bring me back to the brink again.

"Please." My vocabulary had been reduced to one word and I repeated it endlessly. I whispered it. Screamed it. Crooned it. No matter how I said it, he'd murmur sweet words to me in response. He was so patient it made me want to crawl out of my own skin, but he wouldn't let me do that either. Liam merely held me against him as his fingers drove me to insanity.

When I thought he'd never bring me over the edge, he turned my face to his and kissed me. I thought I'd need penetration, at least from his fingers, to finish the job, but no. Everything, it seemed, was different with Liam. All I needed was the sweet, seductive rhythm of his fingers and the gentle pressure of his lips.

The orgasm rolled over me both tender and relentless in equal measure. I whimpered against his lips as it wrecked me from the inside out, leaving me somehow altered in its aftermath. He didn't withdraw his hand at first, merely cupped the delicate flesh until the aftershocks faded.

When the last of the tremors were gone, he turned me in his arms and tucked me under his chin as his hands stroked over my back and soothed away any doubts I may have had, at least for the moment.

"You okay?" he whispered against my hair.

"That was…" I couldn't find the words because I didn't have any. If I thought there was no going back after the kiss…there was definitely no going back now. What scared me even more than that was that I didn't want to. "That was incredible."

He tipped my chin up and studied my expression. "Are you sure?"

"A little too late to be asking that now."

"Come on, sweetheart. Don't be like that."

I didn't know when shortstack had turned into sweetheart… but I liked it more than I should. It filled my chest with a warm glow—something I'd never had with anyone else. I wasn't sure if it was the orgasm or Liam, or maybe a combination of both, but I *liked* it. It may be a mistake, but I wanted more.

"I'm fine, Liam." I searched his gaze, but found nothing other than concern in his expression. "Are *we* okay?"

The corners of his eyes crinkled and his dimple winked when he smiled. "We're better than okay."

He dove down for another kiss and I promptly decided I could be a few minutes late for work. As we kissed, we stumbled backward until I was bent nearly over the dresser. The edge bit into my back, but I didn't care. I'd had a taste and this time I wasn't going to let anything stop me from getting another.

My phone began to ring in the background, but I'd gotten so many hang ups and calls from random numbers I ignored it. Whoever it was could leave a message.

"You should get that," he said against my lips as his hand molded my breast over my scrub top.

"Later," I replied and fisted his shirt in my hands. "Bed."

He twirled me around immediately and I giggled against his lips. We tumbled onto his bed and he landed on top of me, bracing his arms on either side to catch his fall. My legs parted to make room for him and we both groaned as I pulled him closer.

For the first time in my life, I was considering calling into work to spend the day in bed. I'd never canceled plans for a guy, not even if it was Liam, but as we began to grind together, I was seriously giving thought to changing my mind.

It had never occurred to me before that there would be a guy who could convince me to make an exception.

Or that that guy could be Liam.

Our mouths collided, parted, then collided again. Lips parted, tongues tangled, and teeth clashed until I gave up worrying about work altogether.

My phone began to ring again, but this time it brought back a shock of reality.

We had to stop.

CHAPTER 15

CHARLIE

Liam paused, breathing heavily. "You're right. I have to get to the interview and you have to work."

I nodded even though everything inside me was screaming to keep going. I wanted those clothes off him, wanted to know what it felt like to have his bare skin against mine. More than anything, I wanted to continue what we started, but the annoying blaring from my phone had broken the mood.

"Let me get that," I said, then awkwardly maneuvered to my feet.

"Tell whoever it is to go to hell," Liam shouted at my back as I padded to the kitchen on wobbly legs.

Oh my God, I mouthed to myself when I was out of view. I nearly tripped twice as I made my way to the island to answer my phone.

As I hopped on one foot, I swiped at the screen and pressed it to my ear. Whoever it was had better be on their deathbed. "Hello?"

"Charlie, thank God. We have an emergency."

Liam walked out and now that I could ogle him without repercussion, my eyes feasted on the way his shirt accentuated the lean muscles of his chest. I'd been this close to having my mouth all over him. *This close.*

"It better be," I said under my breath and Liam smirked.

"What?" Layla asked.

I turned away from him so I wouldn't be tempted to drag him back for another kiss. "Nothing. What's up?"

"My mother is forcing me to attend a mixer tomorrow night with some of her partners from the firm. I need a buffer. Can you come? I promise all the wine you can possibly drink."

I thought of Liam and what we'd come so close to doing… how much I wanted to do it again. "I'm not sure. Where is it?"

She rattled off the name of an exclusive restaurant. "You have to come," she said, sounding desperate, which was out of character for Layla, who valued control above all else. "You can't leave me alone with Dash. His whole family is going to be there apparently and you know how he loves to torment me."

Dash Hampton was Layla's mortal enemy and competitor in all things from parking spaces and lab partners to grades and prestigious honor society positions. They'd been going at it, and not in a good way, ever since he beat her out as Valedictorian their senior year of high school. It would nearly be worth going to the mixer just to see the two of them argue. Ember and I used to joke that whenever the two of them were in a room together, it was like getting free entertainment for the evening.

"Why is he even going to be there?" I asked as Liam came up behind me and pressed a kiss to my neck. I nearly dropped my phone as pleasure zinged across my nerve endings. My eyes shuttered closed. He had to stop doing that or we were both going to be late.

"That's what I said," she fairly yelled in my ear, managing to distract me from my Liam-induced stupor. I carefully edged away from him and glared, but he only smiled in return.

"You have to come," she begged. "Otherwise I may commit murder. Save me." I wasn't sure if she realized how often our conversation turned to Dash, but I wasn't about to bring it up. There was no way she was open to a discussion about why she responded to his goading. Hearing his name was enough to make her rant.

"One second," I told her, then muted the call. "If you don't have to work tomorrow with the new job, Layla's forcing me to go to this thing for her mom's firm." I paused, then forced myself to continue. "Do you want to go with me?"

Despite what had just happened between us, my heart pounded in my chest. I'd never risked so much for anyone before. If it had been any other man, I simply wouldn't have done it. I chose my potential love interests carefully to make sure I wouldn't get overly involved. Apparently, I couldn't seem to follow my own rules when it came to Liam.

He adjusted the cuffs of his shirt and glanced in the mirror above the sofa. "Depending on my shifts if I do, I'd be happy to go with you." When he was satisfied with his appearance, he turned and prowled toward me. "You realize this sounds like a date. You asking me out, Charlie?"

My heart was in my throat. If I had a napkin in my hands it would have been in shreds in seconds. "I know we haven't discussed it, but we hang out all the time. It wouldn't be weird if we went together. We don't have to tell anyone anything. It'd just be hanging out. If you don't want to it's okay, I'd understand."

He smiled and cupped my cheek. "You're rambling. Of course I'll go with you. We don't have to define anything now and we don't have to tell anyone if you don't want to."

I bit my lip. "Are you sure?"

"I'm sure." He kissed my nose, then crossed the room to bend down and pick up his shoes. I guess one of the upsides about living with him now was I could ogle him at every opportunity without being weird.

I had a feeling it was going to become a habit.

After unmuting the call, I said to Layla, "Count Liam and I in."

"You sure you don't mind going with me?" I asked the next day. "I didn't get to talk to you much after you got back from the interview."

I couldn't read his reaction because his arm was thrown over his face. I tried not to notice that his skin was still slightly damp from his workout. The waistband of his sweats rode dangerously low on his hips, leaving my mouth bone-dry.

To say I was *frustrated* was an understatement.

That had to be why I couldn't tear my eyes away from the golden trail of hair dusting his chest and abdomen. It was the only logical explanation for the way my fingers itched to tug down his sweats to see how far down it went. The slight bulge between his legs hadn't escaped my notice, either, but I was trying to be good. We'd kissed twice now. He'd made me come. I wanted to do both again more than I should and I was only one flex of his abs away from begging.

"I already told you I'd go with you, sweetheart. Besides, we have to do something to celebrate my new job," Liam said and I managed, barely, to tear my eyes away from the visual feast that was his body. He caught me staring and grinned. "Unless you'd rather stay home instead."

Heat filled my cheeks and I shifted from foot to foot. "Don't distract me. Layla would kill me if I didn't show up."

He did an ab crunch and his hand shot out to grab my wrist before I could move out of his reach. I squealed as he tugged me down to the bed. "Distract you like this, you mean?"

I should just forget about breathing when he's this close to me, I decided. His teeth nipped at my lips and my mind went blank. "What?"

Liam chuckled and slapped my butt. "You might wanna go get dressed. We don't want to be late for our first official date."

A date. With Liam.

I couldn't seem to wrap my head around it. The little voice that had kept me from getting too into any guy was drowned out by how right it felt being in his arms. Maybe this level of comfort is what I'd be waiting for this whole time. I didn't know how things would change once summer came, but for now…for now I wanted to enjoy him.

"What are you thinking so hard about?" Liam asked as he rubbed the furrow between my eyes.

"Just how crazy this is." I was afraid to even say the words. Maybe that's what had kept me from taking risks in my previous relationships. Why I kept running. I was afraid.

I leapt to my feet and skirted around his bed away from his reach. This could go so wrong. We could come to care for each other and then something could happen and we could break up. These are things I'd hadn't considered until the second he said date. Somehow being around people now made everything real in a way that it hadn't been while we were cocooned in our house.

He got to his feet and gripped my biceps. "I've got you, Charlie. I'm not going anywhere."

The knots inside my chest loosened. "I'm being silly."

"You are if you don't get your ass in gear and get dressed. I know you don't want to be late." Using his grip on me, he drew me closer for another kiss.

I practically floated back to my room, heart going a mile a minute as waves of cool air washed over my heated body. Note to self: drink lots of water and wear something breathable. I tore through my closet hoping to find something that straddled the line between indecent and classy because Layla would absolutely flip if I went out dressed in yoga pants again. Focusing on my appearance distracted me from how my lips still tingled from his kiss.

Well, at least a little bit.

I chose a casual but classy dress in siren red that I'd been too shy to wear with anyone else. It would drive Liam crazy and I liked the thought of making him as wild as he made me. I tugged on the dress and imagined how it would feel when he took it off again. A secret smile painted my lips as I ran my hands over the fabric covering my curves.

It's funny, because I used to make fun of the girls who pranced around dressed to the nines or pretended to be obsessed with his interest. They'd flounce around in baseball jerseys because he was a huge Atlanta Braves fan like Tripp or they'd agree to go four-wheeler riding after a hard rain because he enjoyed getting as dirty as possible while going as fast as possible. I never wanted to do those things. In fact, I vehemently protested whenever he'd drag me along to games or kept me out past dark driving through the thick of the woods. I thought I was better than the girls who vied for his attention because I never tried to be the center of it. I got it now. I wanted his eyes on me, no matter what I had to do to get them there. Even if it meant going a little out of my comfort zone.

I zipped up the dress and buttoned the closure at the back of my neck. The keyhole opening at the front showed off just the barest hint of cleavage and the hem of the dress skimmed my thighs. I couldn't keep a tan to save my life, but my legs were toned from hours of being on my feet at work and it had been a long time since I wanted to show them off. I left my hair down and misted it with product to enhance and define the curls. After a quick touch up on my makeup— nothing too dramatic, just a little eyeliner and mascara to define my eyes—I wandered out of my room in search of Liam.

The memories of the girls who used to drool over him had

left me feeling vulnerable. We'd explore whatever this was, but I had to remember to be smart while we did. If push came to love, I'd put our friendship first. Always. Relationships came and went, but what we had was timeless.

"Ready to go?" I asked my feet as I pretended to look for something in the small clutch I'd transferred my wallet and keys to.

He didn't answer, but I was hardly paying attention. The first thing I was going to do when I got to the bar was drink my weight in screwdrivers. Then I was going to find Layla, console her like I always did when her mother decided to focus attention on her. That should give me enough time to figure out how to deal with this Liam thing.

It took me a few minutes of mental preparation to realize he hadn't answered me, so I looked up, my brows drawn and found him staring at me, his eyes stormy and intense. "You okay?" I asked, clutch and personal miseries forgotten. I'd never seen him look at me quite like that before. It made my stomach twist—though not unpleasantly. If I weren't mistaken, he was looking at me the way a man looks at a woman he wanted, badly.

When I managed to tear my eyes away from his expression, I couldn't help but take in the rest of him and, oh, it got better with every. Single. Inch. He wore an old hat he'd had forever pulled down low over his eyes. It cast a shadow over his face, darkening the blonde five-o'clock shadow on his square jaw. He wore a plaid shirt with pearl snap buttons tucked into a new pair of jeans that fit him like a glove. I'd never had an opinion about pearl snap shirts, but they had instantly become my new favorite thing. I couldn't help but think how good he looked, but that he'd look even better if every stitch of it were on the floor.

I swallowed once, hard, and tried to control my breathing. I tried to speak, but my mouth was too dry to form words so I could only stand with my mouth opening and closing like a befuddled fish.

"You look nice," he said and his voice sounded like I felt. My body didn't care about my fears. All it wanted was another tumble on his bed.

"We'd better get going," I said before we did just that.

The dimple in his cheek winked and I knew *he* knew just what I'd been thinking.

CHAPTER 16

LIAM

As a college town, Tallahassee, boasted a healthy variety of bars, clubs, and restaurants. A couple years ago, I could be found in any number of them looking for a woman, a good time, or both. But I wasn't as interested in the casual thing as I used to be. Swiping through dating apps or trolling the night life for an easy tumble between the sheets wasn't appealing. Probably because it was just that—easy. Not to say I didn't appreciate a woman who knows what she wants, it had just become hollow. The last time I'd taken a woman home, I felt nothing.

I signaled to the bartender for a beer, hoping to feel a little more nothing. I wasn't sure what was worse. The endless line of women, so many at times their faces blurred together, or the thought of risking it all for a woman like Charlie. Just thinking about it made my hands tremble with nerves. The bartender placed a bottle in front of me. I took it with one hand and paid with the other, tipping generously for the quick service.

I spotted Charlie across the room and downed half my glass to sooth the rawness in my throat. She'd found her friends Layla--a stunning, if aloof, brunette, and Ember a fiery redhead with a mile-wide smile. They were in the middle of an intense discussion by the looks of it and even though I knew I should look away I couldn't.

She'd pulled her dirty blonde hair over one shoulder and I realized there was a matching cutout on the back of her dress that showed the dip of her spine. I'd never been so irritated and turned on at the same time in my life. I downed the rest of my beer and signaled for another. This one would have to last me the rest of the night because there was no way in hell I was going to let her out of my sight looking as good as she does.

I couldn't take my eyes off her if I tried.

It wasn't the dress, though she looked smoking hot in it, all long legs and shining hair streaming down her back. It was the heated looks she kept sending me and the way her eyes would light up when she caught me looking at her from across the room.

Tripp had come along with Ember and sidled up to me with a fresh beer. I accepted without turning away from the view of Charlie laughing with her friends a little ways down the bar. God, she was stunning when she smiled.

"Hey, man. I didn't know you were gonna be here tonight."

I managed to pull my eyes away from Charlie for a second to find Tripp standing next to me. A starter on the university baseball team, Tripp had been friends with Charlie's friend Ember for as long as I've known them.

"How's it goin'? You here with Ember?"

He signaled to the bartender. "I'll have whatever he's having. Yeah, she didn't want to come alone and begged me to tag along. "Something going on between you two?" he nodded to the three girls across the room.

"What's that?"

Tripp accepted a beer from the bartender. "You and Charlie. Something's different there."

"What the hell is this, social hour? We gossiping now?"

"Spring training. I'm going stir crazy so don't blame me. But you're evading the question, which basically tells me all I need to know."

"What the fuck ever," I said, but we both knew it was just bullshit. I still hadn't taken my eyes off Charlie.

He slapped me on the shoulder, his focus already on a pretty blonde a couple stools down at the bar. I felt for him almost as much as I did for myself. Everyone, and I mean *everyone*, knew he had a huge thing for Ember, but she was dating some grad student who kept stringing her along. Tripp spent most of his time drowning in women to pretend he didn't care about her, even though it was obvious to everyone but Ember.

As he moved in on the blonde, I made my way across the room to the girls. I pulled Layla close to press a kiss to her cheek. "Sorry to interrupt," I told them. "I just wanted to make sure this little lady didn't need a knight in shining armor."

"Thank you, Liam," Layla's eyes were as bright as her smile. "We were just talking about you since you're applying to vet school next semester. Did you get in? I asked Charlie, but she said she wasn't sure."

"Probably the *only* thing she doesn't know about you," Ember said, eyes twinkling. I had a feeling she'd cottoned on to the fact that I hovered close to Charlie's side and had a protective armed around her and propped on the bar.

I could practically feel Charlie vibrating in front of me and it made me want to smile darkly. I'd teased her plenty as friends, but there was a delicious new aspect to teasing her this way. Leaning forward so my lips were just near her ear, I said, "I have a few things to submit for scholarships and I've applied to schools here and a couple other places.

"You have?" Charlie asked twisting around to look at me, her eyes wide.

"Congratulations," Layla exclaimed. "That's amazing. I'm

sure you're going to do well wherever you go. I can't believe you haven't said anything!" she added in Charlie's direction.

Charlie just took a sip of her fruity drink, but she'd stiffened against me.

Unable to have her be uncomfortable, I placed a soothing hand around her waist, then said, "I haven't said much about it because I'm still weighing my options. There's been a lot going on, family wise."

"I hear you. The twins are driving me crazy. One of them wants to start ballet, the other one wants to start t-ball. With that, school, and my shifts I can barely see straight let alone apply for scholarships," Ember said, but she smiled. "I don't know how you do it."

Layla and Charlie frowned. "What about your parents?" Layla asked.

Ember gestured to the bartender for another drink and made a noncommittal noise in her throat. "They're both working double shifts. But it's alright. My neighbors watch the kids when I get a call or have to go to class."

"Are your parents still giving you a hard time about going back to school to become a paramedic?" I asked Ember.

She glared at Charlie, who shrugged, which caused her shoulders to brush against my chest. I brushed her hair off her shoulder absently and pressed a kiss to the bare skin there.

Layla and Ember shared wide-eyed looks, but Charlie was too dazed by the casual show of affection to notice. I was glad she wasn't concerned about me kissing her in public. That was progress.

Ember managed to answer despite her surprise. "They don't understand why I want to go back to school when I'm already making decent money."

"You mean they're disappointed you don't devote all of your time to raising their kids?" Layla corrected.

"We're family," Ember replied with a shrug. Her voice cut out and I glanced over my shoulder to see what caught her eye. Tripp and the blonde were in a very passionate lip-lock in a darkened corner. When I glanced back at Ember, a shadow crossed her expression but- it was gone as soon as it appeared. "Besides," she said with faux cheerfulness, "I like Tillie and Mollie. They keep me entertained when Chris is busy and I'm not working."

"You know I'm happy to babysit anytime you need help," Charlie offered.

Charlie's friends weren't my besties or anything, but they were sweet girls who mean a lot to Charlie. So when her offer to Ember made the sweet redhead's sharp green eyes go watery a burst of pride filled my chest. Charlie wasn't just a good friend to me, she was a good person in general.

"Now she's making me look bad," Layla said. "Fine, I'll help you, too. But I do not change any diapers."

We all shared a laugh.

"I think you're safe there," Ember told her. "The twins were potty trained by two."

The two of them had broken the somber mood and managed to distract Ember from Tripp escorting his newest lady out of the restaurant. I doubt Charlie had forgotten about my applying to schools, but she had to know that. Right? My goal was to attend a school here in Florida, if possible, but I'd go wherever afforded me the best opportunity. It was something we'd need to talk about…later. For now, we had a couple hours, an open bar, and some bad food to distract us.

"Layla," came a sharp voice that reminded me all too much of a snake. "Layla Lucille Tate!"

I turned to Layla, who unceremoniously downed the rest of her drink. "Your middle name's Lucille?" I asked with a grin.

She grimaced. "I hate you."

"Don't worry," Charlie rubbed her arm. "We'll be right here."

Layla squared her shoulders and sighed as she crossed the

bar area to a woman who must be her infamous mother. She was the spitting image of Layla, only a more severe version. Her dark hair was twisted into a tight bun at the nape of her neck. On Layla the sharp jut of her chin emphasized her fairy-like appearance. On her mother, the sharper edges of her jaw and cheekbones seemed as hard as steel and just as unforgiving.

"What's the story there?" I asked Charlie, who'd turned to lean her back against my arm on the bar.

Ember rolled her eyes and Charlie said, "Layla's mom wants her to go into finance, but Layla refuses. She's wanted to be a teacher her whole life and her mom likes to give her a hard time about it."

I watched as Layla's mom pushed her forward with a claw at the small of Layla's back. A group of fancy suit-types accepted her with fake smiles and her mom beamed proudly. My dad may be overly obsessed with me following in his footsteps, but he'd never treated me like an object or a prize. We didn't get along about everything, but he loved me in his own way. For the first time in a long time, I felt a shred of tenderness for the old bastard.

Maybe I'd give him a call soon.

"I'm gonna go keep an eye on our girl," Ember said as she polished off her own drink, leaving Charlie and I alone.

I twisted around until I had her pinned between me and the bar. "Having a good time?" I asked as I took in the rosiness of her lips and wondered if she'd let me kiss her again. If not here, then when we were back at home, alone.

Suddenly I was very appreciative of my moment of genius. Maybe having her move in with me was the best idea I'd had in forever.

She licked her lips and nodded. "I am. Thank you for coming with me."

"Should we help Lay and Ember?" The bar wasn't that loud, but I leaned closer like I was having a hard time hearing her. It made me smile when her breath caught in her throat. I enjoyed how much I affected her way too much and wondered if her heart was racing, too.

"What?"

I smiled. "Should we go save Layla from her mom?"

Charlie lifted a hand to my chest and rested it over my heart. Could she tell it was pounding, that she'd brought it back to life? Raised voices from behind me tore me away as I was about to lean down for another taste of her mouth.

A tall good-looking man who looked like he'd been born to wear a suit smirked down at a red-faced Layla. Her mother had disappeared, but Layla didn't look pleased with the fact. In fact, if I'd learned anything being raised with sisters, it was how to detect a full-on female rage fest.

"Let me guess," I said as I turned back to her. "That's the infamous Dash?"

Charlie sighed and one side of her mouth curled up. I couldn't tell if she was more amused or resigned. "I should probably go save her. Ember must have distracted her mom."

Before she could slip out of my grasp, I snagged her elbow with my hand. "After you save Layla, do you think we can get out of here?"

Her eyes widened slightly, then heated. She had to clear her throat twice before she could talk. "Yeah, um, just let me take care of this and then we can go."

With my hand on her arm, I pulled her closer. "I think we need to finish what we started yesterday."

CHAPTER 17
CHARLIE

t didn't take me long to reach Layla's side and tug her away from Dash with a murmured excuse. I don't remember what I said or even if it made sense. All I could think about was Liam's words and getting back to his place. I dropped Layla off with Ember and ignored both of their knowing looks as I sped back to Liam's side. Butterflies were having a rave in my stomach.

"Ready?" he asked as he took my hand and tugged me through the crowd.

I couldn't answer. I let him pull me along until we were back in his truck and heading away from the restaurant. The ride home was a blur. My hands were trapped beneath my thighs because otherwise I'd have them all over Liam's body. Causing a crash would severely wreck my plans for the evening so I kept them to myself.

When he slammed the truck in park with more force than necessary, I couldn't wait anymore and unbuckled to slither across the seat to his lap.

He hissed out a breath a second before my mouth closed over his. All I could hear was how he was applying to schools everywhere. I knew it in the back of my mind that he'd be leaving, that we both would eventually be busy, but it didn't hit me until tonight. It made me wonder why I had fought so hard to keep from having this with him?

After all, I should know better than anyone that life was short.

His mouth opened under mine and any doubts I may have had washed away as he gripped my hips to keep me close. "I want you," I said against his lips when I could catch a breath. Desperation had me pulling at the collar of his shirt. "Please."

"Jesus, Charlie. Let's get inside before I take you right here."

Somehow we made it out of the truck and to the front door. We slammed against it as I wrapped myself around him. He cursed under his breath as my lips attacked his throat. I moaned as the flavor of him bathed my tongue. It took longer than usual for him to unlock the door because he dropped the keys twice and pushed me against the wall for a kiss that was borderline violent.

We stumbled into the darkened house blind. It was only by pure luck we didn't fall into a heap on the floor. His hands found my hips like they were meant to be there. They slipped around my waist and guided me back down the hall, almost like a dance. My body followed his instinctively, unquestioningly. Somehow, I knew he wouldn't let me fall.

"Are you sure about this?" he asked as we reached the door to his room. "You can walk away right now. Go to your room and get some sleep. You've had a very hard week and aren't thinking clearly. You'll regret this in the morning."

I didn't know if he was warning me, or himself.

It didn't matter, because neither of us listened.

"I can tell you one thing for sure," he said as his lips grew even closer to mine. "The last thing I'd ever regret is being with you."

If I'd had any doubts, his words erased them. I wanted this, I wanted him. "I regret a lot of things, but this would never be one of them."

I didn't want to be alone anymore. I didn't want to keep pushing away the one good thing in my life when life itself was so short. My hands clung to the lapels of his shirt like he would somehow slip through my fingers. With exquisite care, he peeled my fingers away and pressed them against his chest as he led us back into the shadowed recess of his room. Beneath my hands, his heart thudded in a slow and steady rhythm. I leaned forward and pressed my lips to the triangle of skin bared by the opening of his button-up shirt.

Liam's hands went to grip my biceps, not to push me away or pull me closer, but as a reminder he wasn't quite ready to let me go. Reassured, if only for now, I lifted my fingers to his buttons and slowly unsnapped them, even though I wanted to rip them open. I bit back a moan of impatience as inch by inch of his tanned throat was revealed.

My fingers dipped beneath the folds of material and I pushed the shirt off his shoulders and down his arms until it fell at his feet. I glanced up at his face to make sure he was still okay and the heat from his gaze made my breath catch in my throat. Determined to keep going, I slid my hands from where they'd stopped at his wrists to the glint of dark blonde hair that lined his abdomen. The moment I touched him, his muscles contracted beneath my hands and he sucked in a breath.

"Don't stop," Liam said through gritted teeth. "Take them off."

As if that was a choice.

Instead of delving into the waistband of his pants like I knew we both wanted me to, I teased us both and slid my hands up his chest and paused at the darker skin of his nipples. My head tilted to the side, and I watched as my thumbs flicked over the sensitive flesh. I glanced up as his face darkened with a flash of need so intense, it was mirrored in my body. My thighs clenched from the emptiness of needing him, but something told me to draw the sweet ache out, make it last.

So I took my time instead. I studied all the parts of his body I'd never given thought to exploring. The dips above his collarbones. The sensitive skin just behind his ears. I covered each discovered spot with kisses and little nips.

He transferred his grip to my hips where his fingers bit into the material of my dress until it stretched skin-tight across my ass. He pulled up my dress until the material gathered at my waist. At the touch of his hands to the tops of my thighs, he groaned in my ear, causing me to shiver. I couldn't seem to get enough of him.

Momentarily distracted, I pressed my face into his throat with my eyes closed to drink in the sensation of having his hands on me. He'd leaned forward to grip just underneath my ass to lift me up. I didn't have time to let out a surprised squeak before we were moving.

He took two quick strides before falling back on the bed with my knees on either side of his hips. Unable to continue my leisurely exploration, my mouth found his with a desperate sound that he didn't hesitate to swallow up. He met my tongue with a thrust of his own and then any attempts at seduction or finesse were lost as I melted against him.

His hands clenched on my ass, causing me to grind into his erection. The old Charlie would have been embarrassed at the brazenness of my actions, but this was Liam, and I couldn't find an ounce of shame inside me for what was happening. There was only the need to get closer, so I didn't hesitate to spread my knees wider and press against him. I couldn't seem to get close enough.

"I can't wait," he said against my lips. "Take off your panties."

Apparently, neither could I.

With jerky, uncoordinated movements, I climbed off him long

enough to strip as he grabbed a condom. As I unbuckled his belt and unzipped his pants, Liam tore through my zipper and tugged my dress the rest of the way off and tossed it over my shoulder. My bra and his pants soon followed.

Seconds later, the condom was on and we were reaching for each other. He practically dragged me up his body until I hovered over the hard length of him. Our lips found each other's and then I lowered myself onto him with a ragged sound. His hand speared into my hair as I began to move over him.

"I can't," I said, but what I meant was, I couldn't wait, but the words wouldn't come out quite right.

"Then don't," he answered.

It was like I couldn't control myself, like my body was saying what I couldn't express in words. I rode him to the brink and came in an explosion that defied logic. I'd wear the bruises from his hands at my hips for days, but reason paled in comparison to wanting Liam as he flipped me onto my back.

I expected him to continue the frantic pace, but nothing could have surprised me more than when he began moving slowly. I tipped my hips up, trying to force him to go faster because my body craved him like nothing I'd ever imagined. My mind was fevered with need and all I could think about was coming around him again.

"Please," I begged.

Ignoring me, he maneuvered one arm underneath my shoulders so we were pressed against each other from chest to hips. My legs wrapped around his waist and my eyes rolled into the back of my head as he went even deeper. His free hand clutched my thigh as he slid in, then back out with aching slowness.

If my frenzied climb to orgasm had driven all thought from my mind, sending me into outer space, his own chase to the end brought all my thoughts to the forefront, and they all centered around him, around us.

Nothing had ever felt as perfect as being surrounded by him.

I wanted to cry at the rightness of it all, but I squeezed my eyes shut and turned into the pillow as he thrust back in, stealing my breath. I'd never known I could be so close to a person. Never known the act of making love wasn't just a physical action.

Whatever was between us wasn't just chemical, it was destiny. Like I'd been searching for the piece to complete me and I'd found it in the last place I'd ever expected.

With my best friend.

"Open your eyes," he said as he canted his hips and made me groan.

I forced myself to look at him, even knowing that when I did it would obliterate me. But denying him was unthinkable. As soon as I opened my eyes, his hand was in my hair and turning my head up to receive his kiss. My arms wrapped around him, needing to have him as close as physically possible, to anchor him to me when I felt like I was going to simply fly apart.

"Don't leave me," I said in a moment of uncharacteristic transparency. I was so desperate, my nails dug into his back.

"Not goin' anywhere," he said as he shifted to nuzzle into my neck. "I'd never leave you."

Another orgasm threatened causing my breath to quicken. My nails bit a ragged path from his shoulders to the swell of his ass. Even though I was making animal sounds in the back of my throat, he refused to move, which only made me even more frantic. The slickness on his back and the bite rust colored stains on my fingers told me I'd drawn blood in my need to make him move, but he was resolute.

I gave up trying to thrust up to him and instead attacked his mouth with renewed determination. The second our tongues touched, he gripped my hip and shifted his so he wasn't pulling out, but pressing deeper. The sensation of being filled, surrounded, surrendered, overwhelmed me to the point of deliriousness.

I froze underneath him, every muscle inside me going taut as the sweet-hot rush of pleasure overtook me. I'd never felt anything like it, not even close. It was more than just the body-destroying pleasure, more than the physicality of sex. It was the closeness I felt to him that came from our connection.

I clenched around him with a soundless scream that he swallowed. Even though I bucked and rocked underneath him, he was like a mountain being battered by the ocean, and I was the waves crashing against him, reshaping myself to fit around him.

"Open your eyes," I heard through the roaring in my ears.

When I did, he began to move, finally, and I couldn't tell what was better, the way I'd clasped around his stillness or the way each thrust now kicked my orgasm off into new heights.

When he went over, I held him close to me, taking him in as deep as I could and knowing whatever lines we'd unknowingly drawn in the sand between us had just been destroyed completely.

CHAPTER 18

LIAM

Charlie was the last thing I saw before I slipped into unconsciousness and the first thing I saw when I woke up, and for the barest second I realized that I could get used to waking up to her. I could get used to having her in my bed, her arms wrapped around me and her head resting on my chest. I'd had my fair share of relationships, but no other woman in my bed had ever felt as right as Charlie.

It should have scared the fuck out of me.

I knew when I had time to think with my head instead of my dick that reality would come crashing down eventually. But with her in my arms, all I could think about was having her just one more time. Just one more taste of perfection.

I shifted until she lay on her back and smiled when she made a sound of annoyance. Slowly, as if unwrapping a present, I tugged the sheet down to bare her body and marveled that I'd spent over a decade next to her without taking a bite. She shivered a little from the exposure and her pretty, dark nipples beaded up. Unable to resist, I leaned forward and took one into my mouth to tease it with my tongue. Her hips lifted and her hands slid against the sheets, but she didn't wake.

As I nipped and swirled, I caressed her skin with the back of my hand. Inch by inch, her body woke to my touch. When she was moaning and arching beside me, I moved down the bed to tug off her panties and spread her legs. My mouth watered at the sight of her and I ducked my head to feast.

I started slowly, tracing her wetness with my tongue, searching out the spots that made her come alive beneath my hands. Soon, her fists were gripping my hair and moans erupted from her throat.

"Oh, yes," she said, but her eyes were still closed and her voice soft still with sleep. "Yes."

Her hips bucked against my face, and it was unabashed, unashamed. I couldn't get enough of her response. I wanted her crazy and mindless for me. To wake to the edge of orgasm. To know her first thought was of me, that I'd be as branded on her as she was on me.

Her grip in my hair tightened and her legs by my sides lifted and spread even more. I grabbed the backs of her knees with my hands and pressed them wide and far, pinning them so she was completely vulnerable to me. My tongue engaged in a wicked assault that brought Charlie arching up from the bed, propped up by her hands, her eyes wide and her body on the edge of release.

I paused long enough for a quick, "Good morning," before I was back to driving her crazy.

"Oh, God, Liam. What are you doing?" she said between gasps for breath. "Oh, you have to stop. I can't…"

I gripped her hips more tightly and tilted them up to my waiting mouth. "Yes, you can."

As I watched her resist and then give in, I realized I wanted to do it again and we'd barely even finished. There was something beautiful about seeing her completely exposed and open to me. She'd always been able to tell me anything, but this was different. This was a side of her I never knew existed, and all I wanted to do was figure out what other parts of her I'd been missing.

I couldn't get enough of her taste. I wanted it to coat my tongue. I wanted to drown in her until there was nothing, no one else but her. The thought should have scared me, the intensity should have been overwhelming, but instead it was comforting. Everything inside of me was screaming to take her, to make her mine, but I wanted to give her this first. I wanted to know what she looked like when she went over the edge.

My arms went under her legs and the insides of her calves clutched and gripped at my shoulders, trying and failing to find purchase. Just when I heard her breathing catch, I pulled back and kissed her trembling thighs until her hips bucked up to me, silently urging me to come back to her.

I repeated the languorous teasing until her control broke. Her hands seized on the blankets, ripping them from the bed, searching for an anchor to hold on to. I moved impossibly closer until her hands found my forearms. Even if I had no sensation, I would have recognized the meeting by the deep inhale, by the way the tension melted from her body as our fingers intertwined.

I liked that connection, the way my touch grounded her just as much as my mouth enticed her to fly. My intention was to draw it out, make it last, drive all the doubts out of her mind by pure will alone, but there was something about the taste of her on my tongue that short-circuited my brain.

It started easy. Light teasing nips. The slow pass of my mouth and breath over her sensitive skin. Then languid licks and open-mouthed kisses. She lifted her hips up to meet me and I backed away until she groaned and pleaded. Then the process started all over again. I had myself under control until I followed the taste of her to the source and thrust my tongue inside.

"Liam, oh my God. Omigod." Her desperate words turned into mindlessly whispered pleas, which only served to spur me on.

I used the grip on her hands to pull her whole body closer to me. Without even thinking, she started to lift her hips to meet the thrusts of my tongue. Her hips became unglued and ground against me. I was hard as a rock, but nothing on God's green earth, not even my own discomfort, would have torn me away from the greedy draws of her pussy as she grew closer and closer to the edge of reason.

"Don't stop," I heard Charlie sigh. "Please, don't stop."

Her nails bit into my wrist as I shifted to lift her hips to my mouth. The muscles in her thighs and stomach clenched and her heels dug into my ribs. She was so close, and I'd never wanted anything more than to bring her there.

The strain caused her thighs to shake and I could tell she was holding back. Little growls ripped out of her throat as she chased the edge of release repeatedly. It was only the realization that she was probably thinking too much that tore me away.

She wouldn't look at me as I crawled up her body, but that was okay. I stretched out next to her and pulled her in to my warmth, making sure to tuck the sheets around us. The tension didn't completely go out of her body, but she turned to the circle of my arms, which I took as a good sign. She took in a deep breath and when she let it out, it was a little shaky.

"I'm sorry," she said, and I'd never heard her voice so meek. It made me want to gather her close to me and never let go. Christ.

"Don't be sorry, baby girl. You have nothing to apologize for." I pulled her close to me so she could lay her head on my chest like we'd done a thousand times before. Nothing had ever felt so right.

Only when I thought she was ready, did I place an arm on her thigh. Her heartbeat thundered against my chest, but I merely traced patterns along her skin until it calmed again. Then I increased the pressure of my hands and rubbed all over her stomach and thighs. It was as much to soothe her as it was to keep my hands on her. I couldn't seem to get enough.

With each pass, my hands dipped lower and lower. To the tops of her thighs. The globes of her ass, the small of her back. When I heard her breath catch again, I traced the inside of her thigh with one finger until her legs shifted, allowing me access.

My new favorite thing was listening to her breathing change as my hands mapped her body. I'd never known she could make such erotic sounds and I wanted to catalogue each one. Like how touching the skin just underneath her belly button could make her sigh or how scratching lightly over the backs of her thighs would make her shift and grind closer to me.

I was perfectly content to spend the rest of the morning letting my hands wander over her until there wasn't a part I wasn't familiar with, but she had other ideas. Without warning, she surged up and pulled my mouth down to hers.

"Please," she said against my lips as our tongues battled fiercely. "Please, Liam. Please. Please. Please." She said it over and over until I swore I'd hear her begging in my sleep.

My hands became more insistent, forcing their way between her legs until I found her wet and waiting. I plunged two fingers inside her and swallowed down her moan like it was water and I was two steps away from death.

"Yes," she whispered. "Oh my God, you feel so good. Oh God, please."

She was soaking wet and couldn't keep her hips still, couldn't stop kissing me. Her hands dug into my shoulders and pulled me even closer. I braced myself on one forearm, my muscles burning from the awkward angle, but I didn't dare move. She was clamping down on my fingers and I was so focused on the slow, gliding thrusts that made her plead with me each time I did it that I didn't care if I had to hold this position for the rest of my life.

When she went over, God, I didn't think I'd ever forget how she felt in my arms. She tugged me closer to kiss me wildly, open-mouthed and animalistic. She rode my fingers until her hips couldn't move any longer and I pulled back just enough to commit her pleasure-ravaged face to memory.

CHAPTER 19

CHARLIE

should have been embarrassed, but somehow, there wasn't room for it. I'd never been so comfortable with another man before. It didn't make any sense to me because it should have been awkward. I'd known Liam so long in every other way, him seeing me naked, him making me come should have made me want to run in the other direction. But it didn't.

It made me want to climb on top of him and do it again.

All I wanted to do was sink against him and stay in the protective circle of his arms. I'd always been relaxed around him, but this was different. It was as though I'd discovered another side of him, one that fit all my jagged edges like the perfect matching puzzle piece.

I blinked up at him, my tongue thick and heavy in my mouth. I didn't know what to say, but he seemed to know what I wanted without words and simply put a hand on my waist and wrapped me up in his arms, just like I needed.

I'm not normally a crier, but my chest swelled with emotions I didn't know how to handle. Instead of letting them out, I balled my free fist up in the sheets to cover his stomach and pressed my forehead against his chest. The hand on my back rubbed over me in a soothing gesture until my breathing went back to normal and all the blood returned to my brain.

"Wow," I said, when I could think again. "Just…wow."

He chuckled and pressed an absent-minded kiss to the top of my head that made it hard for me to swallow. "Good morning?"

"Very," I answered. I exhaled shakily. "Very good morning."

"You okay?" he asked, his mouth still resting against my hair.

"I think so."

He started to speak, but my phone cut him off. "Hold that thought. Some rando's been calling me for weeks. Let me tell them to stop calling," I said as I reached for it. "Hello?" But it came out split into two words because the second I answered, Liam's hand streaked up my thigh. I held it with one of my own.

"Hello?" came the tentative answer. "Is this Charlie St. James?"

The hand climbed higher, despite my grip on it. "S-speaking." I glared at Liam, but there wasn't a shred of regret to be found. As soon as the call was over, I was going to tease him until he begged for it.

"You sound just like me. I can't believe it's really you."

My hand went limp on Liam's and my heart began to race. "Who is this?" I scrambled for an explanation, but my mind was blank.

"Do you have a minute to talk?" came the woman's answer. I didn't recognize her voice. She said I sounded just like her, but I didn't note the resemblance. Besides, why would I sound like her? That didn't make any sense…

Then it hit me. I sat up straight, racing heart now in my throat. "Who is this?" I repeated. My voice was harsh, almost a bark, but I didn't care. "Tell me or I'm hanging up."

"Don't hang up. Please. I just want a chance to explain."

"Start talking, then."

Liam sat up against the headboard and his arm came around

me until his hand rested reassuringly on my thigh. "What's the matter?" he murmured.

I could barely hear him or the woman on the phone over the ringing in my ears.

"This is April. April Parrish." She laughed nervously. "I'm, God, I'm your mom, Charlie."

"P-Parrish. April Parrish," I repeated to make sure I was hearing things correctly. The word "Mom" ricocheted in my skull. I'd played this scenario over and over again in my head, but I never truly believed I'd ever hear from her again. Now that I had her on the phone, I didn't know what I wanted to say first, if anything.

"Yes, baby, it's me. God, it's been such a long time."

"Mom?" Someone answered. It took me a minute to realize the small sounding voice was my own.

"Mom?" Liam repeated. His hand tightened on my hip. I covered it with my own and squeezed, needing the reassurance his strength provided.

"I know. I can't believe it either," she said. I had to close my eyes to focus on the sound of her voice. She was right. I could recognize my own in hers. "I was at work and I came across your application for the volunteer trip. I almost couldn't believe what I was reading. It took me weeks to work up the courage to call you."

"You work for the volunteer organization?"

"Sort of. It's hard to explain, but I'd love to meet you in person. If you're up to that, I mean. I want to help you."

"Help me?"

"With the application. I know some people and thought I might push it along so they see it? If you were interested, I mean."

The happiness I'd felt waking up to Liam had leached away the moment I answered the phone and realized who was on the other line. "Why would you want to help me now?" I asked.

Liam's hand tightened on mine. I squeezed back for dear life, a little more at ease knowing that no matter what happened, he was there for me.

"I know nothing I say can ever explain away what I've done, but I thought, maybe it was a sign. Maybe enough time has passed that we can talk again. Nothing I say will ever explain away what I did, but I'd like the chance to give you my side of the story."

"Why should I?" I asked bluntly.

There was a pause before she said. "I thought you might like the chance to get to know your family."

"My family?" My throat closed around the words.

"Please, Charlie. Just give me a chance."

I hung up a few minutes later and slumped against the headboard, unsure of what to think. My mom. I'd just talked to my *mom*. I wanted to cry. I wanted to scream. I wanted a million different things and didn't know which one of them I should do first.

"Are you okay?" Liam asked quietly.

I shoved my face in my hands and sucked in a deep breath, but it didn't help. "I honestly don't know."

He kissed my shoulder and his breath fanned over my still-bare skin. I'd forgotten I was naked, but as soon as I realized it and how close he was, my body heated. Despite the shock, it still wanted him. I wanted him.

"Is there anything I can do to help?"

I turned to lean my head against his chest and my muscles relaxed as his warmth seeped into my clammy skin. "Just stay with me for a while, please."

"Of course." His hands traced my body, causing me to shiver. "Do you want to talk about it?"

I shrugged. What was there to say? I still couldn't believe what had happened. "She wants to meet me. To talk."

"Are you gonna do it?"

I closed my eyes and fitted my face into his neck. As though we'd done it a thousand times, he shifted to make room for my body. "I'm not sure."

"Whatever you decide, I'm sure it'll be the right thing." How he could be so certain, I'd never know. What I did know was he was my rock. The solidness of him beside me quelled the panic that threatened to rise.

Silence surrounded us, but it wasn't uncomfortable. Then I tilted my head back to look at him. "Will you do me a favor?"

He brushed the hair away from my face. "Anything," he said.

"Will you help me forget, just for a little while?"

His hand trailed down my arm, pushed beneath the sheet covering my bare hip and cupped my ass. "You mean like this?"

"Yes," I said on an exhale. "Please."

His voice dropped an octave. "I love it when you say that."

I strained upward until my lips reached his ear. "Please, Liam."

He groaned and settled between my legs. "Whatever you want, sweetheart. I'll give you whatever you want."

He slid inside, and I gripped his arms. "All I want is you."

An hour later, we were running very late to meet up with the girls, Dash, and Tripp for dinner and drinks. Since we all lived in the same building, we normally met at Ember's place on the first floor since it was the most convenient. She'd offered to let me stay with her, but her twin sisters and parents also lived with her. Ember had enough on her plate and I didn't want to be a burden.

"Sorry we're late," I said as I stumbled into her living room, tugging on my cardigan sleeve and trying not to blush. Liam had done exactly as I asked and made me forget everything but him. "I was doing…stuff."

Liam emerged from the door behind me with a self-satisfied smile on his lips. "I was stuff."

I slapped him on the shoulder, then shoved him into the wall. I turned, sniffed, then said, "Did someone save me a slice of ham and pineapple?"

Ember and Layla shouted, "I knew it!" at the same time and Dash and Tripp shared manly grins with Liam.

It wouldn't make our problems go away and we'd have a lot to talk about eventually, but for now, I had my friends and I had Liam and that was all I needed to forget everything else and lose myself in the moment for once instead of worrying.

CHAPTER 20

LIAM

left Charlie in my bed the next day without waking her.

Not only because she looked so peaceful as she slept, but because I knew if I looked into her eyes I wouldn't be able to do what I needed to do without feeling overwhelming guilt. But it didn't matter. I still felt regret gnawing away at my insides like a cancerous tumor. I rationalized it by telling myself there was no use in bringing up the scholarship as my options were still wide open. The last thing she needed right now was for me to bring up that I was applying to veterinary schools out of state.

The ride to the library on campus took for-fucking-ever and gave me too much time to think. Too much time to remember how Charlie looked the moment she took me inside her. How she made me feel like I was the only man in the world, in her eyes. It was heart-stopping, the way she looked at me.

I used to think I knew everything about her. I could tell by the sound of her voice if she was happy or sad. I could read her like a fuckin' book.

But the past couple days.

They'd been different.

They'd been more.

And it scared the fucking shit out of me.

It made me want things I shouldn't want.

Things I don't deserve.

She makes me want it all—with her.

I had to force all of it—including her—from my mind as I reached the parking garage for the library. The scholarship was for the University of California, Davis. It had been my first choice after the University of Florida. Or at least it had been before I realized how far away I'd be if I got it. How far away I'd be from Charlie.

I used to think being with Charlie was a simple as breathing. Now I realized it was so much more than that. Being around her was as essential, as life-giving, as necessary. The thought of losing her sent my body into an all-out panic. My chest ached and my brain screamed for just one more inhale.

I knew reality would return when deadlines for admission came, along with all my doubts, but for that moment, I wanted to breathe her in over and over, until she's was as much a part of me as the oxygen flowing through my veins. I wanted to enjoy having her by my side for as long as I fucking could.

Each step I took through the cavernous lobby put more and more distance between me and the one person I never thought I could abandon. I could feel myself moving farther and farther away from her, but I knew we'd both regret it if I put my plans on hold. Despite everything that had happened, we both had a future.

As I sat at the desk to review my paperwork, I realized I'd never considered the fact that our futures might not be with one another. And that thought scared me more than it should.

I was so troubled by the thought I pushed it from my mind and called my dad to stop from thinkin about it.

"Hello," he answered after a couple rings. I had to press my ear close to the speaker because my dad had a habit of getting distracted and not speaking directly into the microphone.

"Hey, Dad, it's Liam."

"Liam. Good to hear from you."

I cleared my throat. "You too. Uh, listen, I'm being considered for a couple scholarships for veterinary school and I need your help with the financial information. They're requesting copies of tax returns for the past couple years for verification."

Dad grunted.

"Would you mind emailing me copies, please? I don't have them and they need them in the next couple weeks before they announce finalists."

I didn't try to explain to him what the scholarships could mean for me. They were the difference between attending a top school in the country or settling for my second choice. The truth was, I wasn't sure he'd care about the difference. As far as he was concerned, I was chasing a pipe dream.

"Yeah, I'll see what I can do."

"Is that William?" came Grandma Dorothy's voice.

"It's Liam, Mom," Dad corrected solemnly.

I felt like a dick. Dad was just trying to do what was best for his family. He probably couldn't understand why I wanted to become a vet despite that I'd tried to explain it to him several times. He had to put his mother in a home rather than take care of her. Much as we butted heads, I needed to remind myself to cut him a break.

"Liam!" came Grandma's familiar voice as she took the phone. "I miss you baby boy. When are you going to come see me again?"

I thought of upcoming exams, work, and the acceptances I needed to sort through and make a decision about. "I'm going to try to head over there as soon as I can, okay?" I hated telling her no, but there was so much I needed to do.

"Oh, alright. Well, I miss you and I love you!"

"I love you, too. Give mom a hug for me."

"I will, baby. You take care of yourself."

"You, too," I answered, but she was already gone.

After a long day of classes and worrying about grandma, I was looking forward to going home, and if I was honest, seeing Charlie. We'd texted throughout the day, but I wanted to bury myself in her and forget everything else. I'd spent an hour at the gym after my last class, but it still didn't erase the unease pulling at my stomach. The only thing in my life that seemed to be going right was her…and I didn't want to lose her.

The scent of spices and grilling meat greeted me the second I opened the door and nearly brought me to my knees. I immediately made a mental note to give her the hardest orgasm of her life. It was like she knew I needed to come home to something like this today. I don't know how she knew, but I was grateful.

"Something smells good," I said as I dropped my stuff by the door and crossed the open living room to where she stood by the oven smiling at me.

"I hope you don't mind. After work I was craving some red meat."

I wrapped my arms around her waist as she stirred what looked like mashed potatoes in a pot. My mouth watered, but it wasn't only for the food. "Mind? I think you're an angel."

"You better quit it," she said when I started nibbling on her ear. "If you don't I might burn the food."

I backed away to sit at the island, but my eyes were on her. "Fine, but only because I'm starving. First I'll eat dinner, then I'll have you for dessert."

Her cheeks grew rosy and I smiled, feeling the tension leaving my body. "Is it always like this?" she asked as she turned back to add butter, salt, and pepper to the mashed potatoes.

I take a sip from the beer she'd already had waiting on the counter while I considered my answer. "What do you mean?"

She didn't turn to face me as she spoke. "I've never felt like this about anyone before. I never let myself. But I already care so much about you, it's like there's no stopping it now."

The beer washed away the knot in my throat. "Come here," I told her and she did as I asked. I pulled her between my legs so I could look into her eyes. I could have told her it was normal, that every relationship feels as intense as the connection between us, but I couldn't. "No, it isn't always like this."

"Is it because we're friends?"

Sitting down she was the perfect height for me to pull her lips to mine. "I don't have an answer for that," I said against her mouth. "But what I do know is I care about you. A lot. More than I have for any other woman. I didn't plan for this to happen, but I'm glad it did."

She let me take the kiss deeper until the kitchen timer trilled. "I better get that," she said and I was pleased to find she was little out of breath. "I have something to ask and if it's too much you can say no."

"What is it?"

"Will you go with me to meet my mom tomorrow?"

CHAPTER 21

CHARLIE

"You'll stay with me?" I hated that my voice wavered. I didn't want to care that I was about to see my mother for the first time in over half my life.

Liam squeezed my hand, reminding me that I wasn't alone. "Of course I will. I'm not going anywhere."

From my vantage point in a booth at the Chinese restaurant I'd chosen, I noted the parking lot was as empty as it had been for the past ten minutes. Part of me was afraid she wouldn't show. I almost hoped she didn't. It would be so easy to spend the rest of my life blaming her for everything that had gone wrong. Or maybe she would show and be worse than the villain I'd conjured in my mind. Someone I could pity and forget.

Normally, I loved the scents that wafted from the kitchen. Warm sesame oil, searing meat and garlic. Now they only exacerbated the nausea. A warm hand caressed my hip and settled on my waistline. Liam tugged me to his side and I closed my eyes against the vision of the parking lot and the images of my mother, pressing my face into the curve of his neck. He tucked his hand between my thighs and kissed my hair. As I snuggled closer in the booth facing the plate glass of the front window, I wondered how we'd spent so much time together without ever knowing how good it would feel to be this close.

"Thank you," I said.

"For what?" he asked.

"You know what."

I peered through my lashes, unable to keep them closed for long, but didn't see anyone I recognized outside the restaurant. Would I even recognize her? Would she look like me? I had pictures from when I was little. There weren't many because I think Dad got rid of a lot of them, but I couldn't tell from the ones I had.

Liam squeezed my hand. "You don't ever have to thank me for being here for you."

"Still," I said, squeezing back.

The parking lot was empty except for Liam's truck, so I knew the moment a small red Corolla pulled in that it had to be her. My whole body stiffened and Liam sat up to rub his hand over my arms to soothe me. Normally it would work and I'd melt into him, but no amount of touching could get me to settle right now.

Oh, God, this had been a bad idea.

I never should have agreed to meet her. What answers was she going to give me that I didn't already have? She wouldn't bring my dad back. She couldn't give me the family I'd been without. Liam's family had taken that place. His parents, sisters. Grandma Dorothy. Him.

But I had to at least give her a chance. That's why, as she pushed into the restaurant and peered around, I didn't duck into the bathroom to hide from her like the coward I was. When her eyes locked on me, I felt her gaze like a shock. She even had my eyes. The same warm brown eyes stared back at me for a long moment before her mouth curved in a tentative smile.

Liam's phone rang and he sent me an apologetic look and went to silence it. "No," I told him as I laid a hand on his arm.

"It's okay. I'm okay. Why don't you take the call while I talk to her?"

He hesitated, the phone still ringing in his hand. "Are you sure?"

I nodded as she reached the table. "I'm sure. Just stay close in case I need you."

"I'll be just outside." He inclined his head toward my mother in greeting before answering the call and stepping outside.

"Charlotte?" she asked, and I only barely kept from wincing.

"Charlie," I corrected.

Chagrined, she set her purse down on the table in front of her and knotted her hands. "Right, sorry. Charlie. Wow, you look just like your father," she blurted.

I touched my hair self-consciously. It was the same golden-blond his had been. "Really?" The off-handed comment meant more to me than she could possibly know.

"It's uncanny." I didn't know her well enough to guess, her voice thickened at the mention of him. "I was sorry to hear when he passed. Even more sorry when I never called to explain and when I didn't come back."

My mouth was so dry my tongue was glued to the roof of it. "Why didn't you?" I asked when I managed to unstick it. Apparently, it had freed the very question I had buried deep down inside of me. I hadn't wanted to ask that the first time I saw her, hadn't wanted to let myself be vulnerable, but it was out there and I was completely bare to this person who had abandoned me when I needed her the most.

She looked to her knotted hands as she spoke. "I wish I had a better answer for you, Charlie, but the truth of the matter is I was very young when your father and I got married. Very young, and very unprepared. When you came along, I thought it could fix the broken relationship between us, but it didn't."

"So you think that's a good reason to abandon him?" My voice was sharper than I intended. Anger burned low in my belly. I'd coached myself not to get too emotional when I finally saw her again, but no amount of preparation could stop the words from spewing forward.

She shook her head and looked down at her hands. She'd taken a napkin from the dispenser and had begun tearing it to shreds in front of her. That more than seeing her again, more than speaking to her speared me right in the gut. How else were we alike? Would I leave my family, too?

"I didn't want to leave, but nothing we did seemed to work. The more I tried, the more he turned to caring for you. Not that it was your fault. You were the best thing that ever happened to us, but when he got sick I couldn't face losing him. It was too much."

"Too much for you?" I scoffed and resisted the urge to get my own napkin to rip to shreds. God knew I wanted to rip something. "What about me? I was just a teenager. You left, and then he died, and I was all alone."

"There are no explanations for the things I've done. No apologies. I know I don't deserve a chance at getting to know you, I certainly don't deserve to be forgiven."

"Then what do you want?" I demanded.

"To give you something back for what I've taken away. Let me help you with this volunteer thing. Please, you don't have to do anything for me. I don't know any other way to say I'm sorry."

"I'm not saying I will, but first you have to answer a question for me. Why didn't you come back when he died? When he left me all alone with no one?" My voice was higher than I'd intended, and I lowered it a few octaves. "Why didn't you come back for me then?"

She couldn't look me in the eye. "I was ashamed and I felt like your life would be better, less complicated and happier if I weren't in it."

I was silent for a few moments while I digested the news. "Then why did you reach out to me now? What's different?"

Her eyes brightened and one of her hands went to her stomach. "I met someone. Someone who truly cares for me. I've changed a lot in the past few years and I wanted to give you—us—the opportunity to have a relationship, if you wanted. The man I married is a good man. He wanted our daughter to know you, too."

"I have a sister?"

She smiled the first real smile since she walked in the door. "You do. You have a whole family now, Charlie. And I'd like you to meet them."

We were silent on the drive back to the duplex. I'd spoken with my mother for another hour with Liam by my side after our initial conversation. She told me she had steady work as a volunteer with the organization planning my trip abroad and about her husband—my stepfather—John. She invited me to their anniversary barbecue the following weekend. I wasn't sure if I was going to accept, or if I'd even see her again, but I felt better knowing instead of guessing about who she was and where she'd gone.

Liam took my hand as we made our way to the front door. So much had changed in such a short time since I'd moved in with him. His parents selling the farm. We were both having to make decisions about our careers soon. My mother. God, I had a whole family out there I'd never known about and I didn't know how to feel about it.

"Do you want to talk about it?" he asked when we got inside.

I shook my head. "I will, eventually, but right now, I just want to be with you for a while. Everything else may not make sense, but when I'm with you, when you touch me, it's like I'm right where I'm supposed to be. Is that okay?"

"That's more than okay," he told me as he wrapped his arms around me. "I'm here for whatever you need."

I tugged him down with me to the couch, needing the security of the weight of him pressing me into the fabric. Nothing felt as good as having him surrounding me. I'd never felt more at home than I did in his arms.

Only a few days ago this space had seemed so small with the two of us in it. I'd wanted to run, needed room to breathe. Now, with Liam, it had become my refuge, my sanctuary. Hell, it could have been as tiny as his room and I would be perfectly content to spend the rest of my life in less than 1000 square feet.

When I kissed him, it was full of desperation. I ripped off his shirt, needing to feel his skin to ground me, to steady me. Even if everything else in my life was uncertain, the one thing I could be sure of was this, him. And for now that was enough.

If our first time having sex had been an adventure and our second a free-fall, the feeling that overtook me as I clung to Liam was desperation. There was an edge to my need that even I couldn't understand. An edge that made me cling to his arms a little tighter, lean in to him a little closer, savor his kiss a little more.

An edge that made me realize once more that some good things just don't last forever. And I should cherish them—him—while I was able.

CHAPTER 22

LIAM

"Are you sure you don't want me to stay home with you today?" Charlie leaned a shoulder against the door jamb and studied me as I got dressed.

"Not gonna say it again, Charlie. I'm fine. I don't need you to hover." If my tone was a little short, I hoped she'd forgive me. I'd make it up to her later.

"I'm not hovering. I can tell you're upset about Grandma Dorothy. I am, too, but she needs to be somewhere with constant care."

I hated that I wasn't going to be at home to be there when Grandma was transferred to elder care. I hated that my father had rubbed it in my face the last time I called to check in on the forms I needed. "I know that."

She crossed the room and stopped me from putting on my hoodie as I prepared for a run. "You should go see her this weekend."

"I can't I have to work. You know that." My new job didn't have substitutes and I was under a probationary period. Calling into work wouldn't endear me to my new boss who had been hesitant to hire me considering I'd been let go from the last place.

She frowned. "I was so excited for that new job, but it's keeping you busy."

"Gotta pay rent somehow." I didn't say it, but I also needed the money to save up to move…if and when I chose a school for next year. I was already cutting it way too close for comfort, but I needed those papers from my father, who hadn't returned my messages about the forms I needed.

"Do you want me to go with you?" she asked.

"Please. You hate running."

She laughed and it lightened my worries, if only a little. "That's true."

I kissed her lightly on the lips. "Don't worry about me, sweetheart. I'll be fine. Besides, don't you have a final to be studying for?"

She pouted. "It's not fair you already finished yours."

Deepening the kiss helped to distract us both. "Why don't you finish up studying while I'm gone and then we'll have something to eat. I'll cook this time," I added before she could offer. "You've catered to me more than enough."

Tossing her hair over her shoulder, she smirked at me. "Is that what you think?" she asked.

I noted the look in her eyes and carefully put distance between us. "Oh, no you don't. You're not going to distract me when you have to study. You know we won't get anything done if we get back in bed."

It was the truth. Now that we'd crossed that line, we couldn't seem to get enough of each other. I'd thought the need for her would have cooled eventually, but if anything it seemed to burn hotter each time I had her.

She gave me that look that meant she wanted me, now. It was a look she knew I couldn't resist. "Charlie," I groaned. "We can't do this now."

"Hush," she said and covered my lips with her fingers. "Let me do this for you."

"You don't have to *do* anything for me."

"I want to."

She dropped her hand and then fell to her knees in front of me. There wasn't time for me to prepare because a second later, she pulled down my cotton running shorts and had me in her mouth.

"Jesus fucking Christ," I said as the wet heat of her mouth enveloped me. She took me deep, stroking my dick with her tongue as she sucked me.

I scooped up her hair with both hands and tried to slow her down, but she wasn't having any of it. She gripped the base of my dick and stroked with each slide of her mouth. My legs shook and I gave serious consideration to collapsing back on the bed. She devastated me.

I wish I could say I lasted a long time. I wish I could say it didn't completely wreck me when she glanced up at me, but I couldn't. It only took a few minutes for me to reach the point where I tried to pull her away. We'd never really talked about things like *swallowing* for fuck's sake, but she wouldn't have any of it. She sucked me back even farther and stroked harder with the tight fist of her hand.

"Charlie," I groaned. "You gotta stop."

But she didn't.

I hunched over as the orgasm hit and I came into the sweet recesses of her mouth. She didn't stop for a second. Watching her throat work as she swallowed it down had to be one of, if not *the,* hottest moment of my life.

She rocked back on her heels after licking me clean and I pulled my shorts back up. It had only been a few minutes, but I felt like I'd run a marathon.

"Now you can go," she said with a laugh as she got to her feet with a wicked smile.

I stood there for a minute hoping my legs would hold me up. "I'm not sure I can."

Charlie began to back away. "You go for that run. I'm going to study. You definitely owe me dinner when you get back."

Somehow I made it to the front door without falling straight on my face. I shook my head as I stretched on the front porch. That girl was something else. Despite the growing realization Grandma Dorothy was never going to get better and everything else going on in my life, Charlie was the bright post. She always had been. I couldn't imagine my life without her.

God, I loved her.

The thought stopped me short as I reached the trail around Lake Ella opposite my house.

I loved her.

What the hell was I going to do about that?

CHAPTER 23
CHARLIE

woke up to a snoring Liam and I immediately smiled.

I was doing a lot of smiling around him lately. It was like I couldn't contain it. I was stressed about my mom, stressed about finals, and the final approval for volunteering, but as soon as I walked in the door it was like his mere presence could wash it away.

As I shifted, he cracked open an eye and smiled. His arms wrapped around me and he pulled me closer to kiss my hair. "Good morning, beautiful," he said, like he had every morning after I slept in his bed.

"What?" he asked when I didn't respond right away.

I pressed my forehead against his chest which, was warm from our combined heat under the sheets. Our skin stuck together where arms and legs were intertwined. I was completely wrapped up in him, under his spell. I nuzzled into the thin dusting of hair on his chest and suck in heady breaths heavy with the scent of him. The last wispy remains of yesterday's cologne and the cotton fresh laundry detergent he prefers.

"I like waking up to you," I told him with uncharacteristic honesty. It was akin to me offering him my heart on a silver platter. I wanted him to see me bare and defenseless, with walls down. For the first time, I wanted to let a man in, rather than barricade him out.

His hand brushed over my hair and I stretched like a cat against him. "Oh, do you?"

"I like the way you hold me."

His arms tightened around me. "Good luck trying to get me to let you go."

If I'd thought he couldn't get any more amazing, I was wrong. And that was after an amazing night with him once he got back from his run.

It hadn't been anything special, but to me, it was everything. We ate dinner and watched a movie cuddled together on the couch. I studied to the point where I couldn't see straight and he forced me to take a break, which of course meant we ended up making out on the couch until three o'clock in the morning.

I swear, I wish we'd made the plunge into dating sooner. I've never felt about anyone the way I feel about him.

It was as simple as feeling his heart beat sync with my own. He twined his fingers with mine and pressed them against his chest.

The words spilled out before I even made the conscious thought to say them. "I love you, Liam."

His body stilled under my hands and with anyone else, I would have rushed to apologize. To backtrack and apologize. At the first sign of commitment or weakness, my first instinct was normally to run, but the only running I wanted to do when it came to Liam was right back into his arms. I guess my mom and I weren't alike in that aspect after all.

When he didn't say anything, the first tingling of anxiety had me tilting my head back to gauge his reaction. I found him smiling down at me and taking my lips for a kiss I'd never forget.

"I love you, too, Charlie," he said when we stopped to catch our breath.

I dragged him back to me as warmth spread through my chest. My whole body felt as though it were weightless. I couldn't stop smiling even though we were kissing. By the time we were done, happy tears had blurred my vision.

"I hate to tell you this," Liam said as he looked over my head. "But I think you might be late for that final."

Still floating from the kiss, it took me a minute for the meaning of his words to sink in. "What?" I shrieked and flew from the bed. "Oh my god, I'm so screwed."

I stumbled across the hall to my room and grabbed at clothes blindly. I'm not sure any of it matched, but I didn't care. Failing this final would ruin me for the whole semester. Liam was waiting for me in the kitchen with a steam carafe of coffee. If I hadn't already fallen in love with him, seeing him standing in his boxers with just a mug of coffee would have done it.

"You're a god," I told him as I accepted the carafe and gave him a quick kiss. "See you later?" I threw over my shoulder as I hurried to the door.

"I'll be here," he replied. And I knew he would.

On my way to campus I sped through more yellow lights than I cared to admit. Speed bumps? More like suggestions. I only had two minutes to get to the final before the professor, who was notorious for locking doors on the hour, barred me from entering. I was just pulling into a spot when my phone rang.

Thinking it could be Liam, maybe hoping it would be, I answered. I was turning into a fourteen-year-old with a crush. I was smiling when I said, "Hello?"

"Charlie, I'm glad I caught you." I recognized April's voice. I wasn't quite ready to settle on calling her mom again. I might not ever be.

"April? I'm running kind of late for an exam can I call you

back?" My lungs burned with effort as I raced from student parking to the building where the final was taking place.

"This will only take a second," she said.

"Good, because that's all I've got."

"I received word that your application has been accepted. The volunteer spot is yours if you want it."

The news should have made me happy, but if it did, it was hollow. I frowned as I shoved through the double doors and hurried down the hall. "That's great," I told her. This was all I'd wanted for a long time. The chance to serve where I was needed, to give back to others the way I wanted to when my father was sick, but couldn't. It's the entire reason why I decided to get my bachelor's in nursing in the first place.

There was a pause. "You don't sound as enthusiastic as I thought you would."

I tried to muster some enthusiasm up. "No, I am, this is great."

She cleared her throat. "Look, I don't mean to be rude, but I pushed your application through. I had to pull some strings to get you accepted. I thought you'd be pleased."

My back stiffened. I wanted to close the gap between us, but I certainly didn't need her playing mother. "You shouldn't have done that. I didn't need your help. I would have gotten it on my own."

"I just wanted to help you."

I took the stairs two at a time and cursed under my breath. One minute. "Look, I'm grateful for your help, but my plans may have changed."

"Changed?" There was a pause. "This is about that boy isn't it. The one who was at the restaurant with you? Please don't tell me you're throwing this opportunity away for some guy."

I thought I'd gotten over her leaving. In fact, I was looking forward to meeting her family and mending fences. The second she attacked Liam however, I snapped. "Funny coming from a woman who threw away her daughter." I reached the classroom door just as the professor was walking up the aisle to lock it. "I've got a final, I have to go."

Click.

Pushing her from my mind, I gave my professor a nervous smile and took a seat in the back of the room. She had no right to judge any choices I made. Just because I was no longer obsessed with school and my career, didn't mean they still weren't important.

I was allowed to have a life in addition to work. In fact, I'd given it up in exchange for extra classes, volunteer work and my job for so long I'd forgotten what fun was like until recently. She had no place to tell me what to do, especially after she'd been absent for so long.

If I wanted to give up the volunteer opportunity to spend more time with Liam, there'd be other chances.

I couldn't say the same for me and Liam. We only had a couple short weeks before his lease ended and we had to make a real decision about what was happening between us.

For the first time in my life, I was open to the possibility of taking a chance.

As long as it was with him.

CHAPTER 24

LIAM

My email dinged as I was driving home from work later that day and I paused at a stoplight to check it. *Dear Mr. Walsh, unfortunately you are ineligible to receive the scholarship based on…*

A loud blare from the car behind me shook me out of my stupor. I ground my teeth together as I accelerated. I'd been so distracted the night before I'd forgotten to call and remind dad to submit the forms so I could finish the application by the deadline. The email had been a standard form rejection. With only a few words, my hopes at attending the best school in the country had been squashed.

Part of me had to wonder if it hadn't been a deliberate move on Dad's part. Now he had me right where he wanted me. I'd attend the University of Florida, which was a couple hours away but still close enough to stay under their thumb. I should be grateful I was accepted anywhere, that a partial scholarship I'd already received would cover some of the costs, but all I could think about was the opportunity I'd lost.

Because of him.

Charlie's car was already parked next to my space. I needed

to talk to her about what was going to happen this summer, but I didn't know what to say. How do I tell her I have to leave her when just this morning I'd told her I loved her?

Dread pooling in my stomach, but I strode to the front door in spite of it. I'd just tell her. She'd understand. Charlie always understood. We'd just have to make it work somehow. People did that sort of thing all the time. Besides, if anyone knew what I was feeling it would be her. She had her own future to think about. There's no way she wouldn't understand when I had to leave.

The moment I laid eyes on her all logic seemed irrelevant. She'd changed out of her scrubs after work and was wearing a pair of shorts and one of those drape-y shirts that girls liked now. It clung to her breasts and flared at her hips, skimming her thighs and making me consider how soft it would be under my hands.

"Hey," she said warmly. Her bare feet were propped on a rung at the island stool. There was something so sweet about how naked they were that had me stopping in the entryway. The words I'd so carefully considered evaporated.

"Hey," was all I could manage.

Before I could say anything else, she got to her feet and said, "I have some news."

I let out a breath. Here was my chance. "So do I, but you first."

She took a sip from the glass of wine in her hand. "I was accepted for the volunteer position."

"That's amazing! I had no doubt you would be."

I closed the distance between us, unable to hear her say anymore. I should be happy for her, but all I could think about was how empty my place would be when she was gone.

There was a long silence. I could tell she expected me to fill it, but I still didn't know what to say. "What about you? What's your news?" she asked.

I glanced at my watch, unable to look her in the eye. "Don't worry about it. We'd better get going or we're going to be late for Taco and Tequila Tuesday with your friends. I think we should celebrate your good news first. We can talk about this after."

"Are you sure?" she asked. "You're acting weird."

"I'm sorry. It's just been a long day. I could use some of that tequila."

A couple hours and several shots of tequila later, I'd pushed the email, the future and everything but Charlie out of my mind.

I couldn't get enough of her. Enough of looking at her, talking to her, kissing her. I spent most of the night imagining just what I'd do to her once I got her alone.

Tripp shoved my shoulder. "Someone's whipped," he joked. "Were you even listening to me?"

"Fuck you. You and I both know I'm not the only whipped individual here." I glanced pointedly at Ember, and Tripp sighed and sipped his beer. Taking pity on him, I changed the subject. "What were we talking about?"

"Graduation. How does it feel to finally have freedom on the horizon?"

The immediate answer should have been resoundingly enthusiastic, and would have been a couple months ago, but now, all I could think about was Charlie and leaving her behind. "It's good, man."

Tripp quirked a brow. "Well now I'm just overcome. C'mon man, seriously, what the fuck? I thought you had vet school all lined up."

I sipped my beer and wished it were another shot of tequila. "I did, I mean I do."

"Well, spill, dude. Where did you accept?"

I sighed. "I had a couple of places I was considering."

"You don't sound too excited."

"No, I am. They're a great opportunity. All really good schools."

"I'm happy for you, dude."

"Thank you." He lifted his beer to knock it against mine, but for some reason, I no longer felt like celebrating.

I downed the beer anyway, and went in search of Charlie. I needed to see her, hold her. I had to tell her about school at some point, but I wanted to make this moment last a little longer.

I found her playing Cards Against Humanity with Layla, Ember, and Layla's neighbor and rival Dash. They were falling over each other with laughter, faces bright from the tequila shots they'd been doing and stacks of messy cards in front of them. Charlie caught my eye and motioned for me to come sit next to her on the couch. Just being near her soothed me.

As I watched them play, I tried to remember if it had been the same way when we were just friends. It must have at least been similar, otherwise we wouldn't have been so drawn together for so long. Which made me wonder if we were together because we were such good friends or were we friends because this thing between us was so strong.

An hour later, I propped her up with one arm as we stumbled our way outside to an Uber. We'd both had one too many tequila shooters and after a couple rounds of cards had started giggling at every damn thing.

"Did you know your hair is just the cutest thing?" she squealed as I carried her out of the Uber to my front door. Tripp and Dash were following behind with my car. Tripp because it was spring training and he couldn't drink much, Dash because he didn't drink—at all. Ever. When I'd asked, Charlie wouldn't say.

"My hair, huh?" I said and had to fight to keep her hands

from wandering all over my body—at least until we got behind closed doors.

"I like having you around," she said when we stumbled inside. "You're like a sexy, snuggly bear."

"Oh, am I?"

Her giggle was muffled as she started kissing her way down my chest. Finally, I gave up trying to let her walk to the door while she was so distracted and simply picked her up again. This both helped and hindered because she was able to focus completely on kissing, licking, and nipping at my skin instead of walking, but I grew more and more distracted the longer she went at it.

"Jesus Christ, Charlie. You're killing me."

"I want you naked, Liam. You're wearing too many clothes." She said the last bit in my ear on a moan.

I was about ready to break the damn door down when it finally opened. I wanted it to last forever. I wanted to spread her out underneath me and take her slowly, torturously, but that's not what happened. We slammed into the house, the front door flying back and crashing against the wall.

"There goes your security deposit," Charlie said against my mouth.

"You mean there goes your security deposit."

"I didn't pay a security deposit for this place," she reminded me as I sampled her throat.

"Clearly an oversight on my part. Fine, we'll split any damages."

I felt her laugh vibrate against my tongue. "So chivalrous, Mr. Walsh."

Careful to catch her head with one hand, I guided her back against the wall and kicked the door close with my foot. "That's me, baby."

She snorted. "I'll believe that when I see it."

I carried her to the bedroom, then followed her down onto

the bed and for a while, nothing mattered but the sighs and moans I stole from her.

"What's this?"

I cracked open an eye to find Charlie standing by the bed. She was holding my phone.

Shit.

I sat up and pressed my fingers to my eyes, hoping the pause before I had to respond would give me time enough to come up with an explanation. "What are you doing?"

"Your phone kept ringing. I got up to get a glass of water and turn it off." Her voice was still hoarse from the shouting at Ember's place and then all the shouting I'd made her do after. "You got accepted to UF?"

I didn't want to lie to her. Couldn't. So I said simply, "Yes."

"I also saw you applied to California. You never told me."

I sat up and pulled the sheet over my lap along the way as I leaned against the headboard. "I applied to schools all over the country. California was just one of them. I can't afford to go there, but I'm going to take out loans. It's the best program for me."

She'd pulled on one of my shirts. It bagged around her and flirted with her legs. It made her look young and vulnerable. And hurt. Fuck, I didn't want to hurt her. That was the last thing I wanted to do. But I had and it was already killing me.

"Why didn't you tell me?"

"It just happened. I was going to tell you." I lifted a shoulder. "I just couldn't figure out what to say. Besides, you're leaving this summer, too."

"Were you?" Gone was the laughter, the bright eyes. Her lips were pressed into a hard line and the angry furrow between her brows was one I'd never really had directed at me.

"Why wouldn't ?"

"Actually, I turned down the position. You didn't give me a chance to say it earlier, but I was planning to stay." The only other time I'd ever heard her voice sounding so dead was the day she told me her father had died. "For you."

"You shouldn't have done that," I answered honestly. I never wanted her to give up her plans for me. That wasn't the Charlie I knew.

"Well, I did. Because you made me realize it wasn't the only important thing in my life." She was doing that thing where she tried to be strong, but I heard the reed-thin sound to her voice. "It's ironic, isn't it? The one guy I fall for and actually think won't leave me is the one who does."

"Don't say that." All my life, I'd been working to prove myself to my father. I'd dealt with the guilt from leaving my family, abandoning Grandma Dorothy. Charlie knew this. And yet the moment I saw her take a step away from me as I sat up to go to her, I would have given up everything I'd earned to have her happy again.

"Why not? It's the truth."

I shifted under the sheet. "Believe me or not, but I was gonna tell you. Last night just wasn't the right time."

Her voice hardened. She was turning to stone right in front of my eyes. Because of me. "How long have you known?"

"Does it matter?" There was no way she'd forgive me now.

"It matters to me."

"Look Charlie, things between us are still new. We're still getting used to…whatever this is. I didn't want to ruin anything."

"Don't you think moving halfway across the country is going to have an impact on whatever this is?" Normally the snarky tone she'd take when she argued would bring a smile to my face, but this time it made my stomach sink.

"Can we not talk about this now? It's early and we're both tired." And the last thing I wanted to do was have a conversation that could possibly bring about the end of us when we'd barely even begun.

She was silent for a long moment. Long enough that I thought maybe she'd agree to drop it. Then she moved quickly to tug on her jeans and slip into her flats. She was still wearing my shirt. For some reason that stood out in my mind. Like as long as she still had something of mine we'd always be connected.

"What are you doing?" I asked, sitting straight up.

"I think it's best if I leave. I'm gonna go stay at a hotel for the night. While you're at work tomorrow, I'll pack up so I won't be here when you get back."

"Wait a damn minute." I wanted to get up, to stop her, but she was already slinging her purse over her shoulder. By the time I hopped up and drug on a pair of sweats, she was already striding to the front door.

"Don't worry about it, Liam. We'll figure everything out when you get back."

"Dammit, Charlie. What are you doing?" Thunder rolled and I had to raise my voice over it.

"I'm leaving you before you have to make the hard decision to leave me first. I knew this was a stupid thing for me to do and I did it anyway. For you."

Then she spun around and slammed out the door before I could tug on my shoes and follow her. By the time I reached my truck, she was already peeling out into the heavy downpour of the sudden Florida storm. My hands fused to my steering wheel as I followed her out into the rain and onto the highway. All I could picture was her face and how I didn't want it to be the way we ended things.

CHAPTER 25

CHARLIE

The rain suited my mood. I wanted to drown in it, hide in it. But most of all, I wanted to run…and I hated myself for it. The second I saw Liam's acceptance letter it was like the floor had been torn right out from under me. I wanted to scream and cry and rage, so I did. In between stop lights and on long stretches of road. I screamed and tears poured from my eyes. It was so early, there was barely any traffic.

There was no one to see me break down. No one to save me now that I'd left the one person who'd always been there.

I was truly alone now.

I took a curve going a little too fast and slightly tapped the brakes. At first I thought it was my car. Maybe the damn thing had finally given up the ghost, but no. My car skidded across the rain-slick streets and began to hydroplane across three lanes of traffic, right in front of the semi in the inside lane next to me.

Even though my head screamed at me not to slam my foot on the brakes, my body reacted without thought. All I could think was I needed to stop before I slammed through the guard rail and into oncoming traffic. Everything happened so fast, but slow at the same time. The time in which I spent spinning across two lanes of traffic on the interstate and then into the grassy median seemed to take an eternity.

I braced for impact, but the muddy grass slowed me down—or maybe it was the death-stomp I had on the brake. Either way, my car came to a sickening halt facing north on the southbound side of the interstate.

Rain pelted against the hood of my car and sweat dampened my brow, my upper lip, and the backs of my knees in hot, uncomfortable pinpricks. At the same time, I trembled, skin coated in goosebumps from the chill. I was alive.

Then shock settled in and my hands began to quake.

I'd spent my whole life being strong. First for my dad after my mom split, then for myself when I was all alone in the world. I didn't want to be strong anymore. I didn't want to do it all on my own. I wanted someone I could trust to lean on, and maybe that's why I took the news about Liam's leaving so hard. I thought he was the one I could trust to always be there.

But now, none of that seemed important.

I was scared and alone and all I wanted was his arms around me to tell me it would be okay.

I fumbled in my purse for my phone to call emergency services to help with my car and report the accident, and to call Liam and apologize for overreacting. God, I wanted to apologize. But my phone was dead and I'd left my charger at his house when I'd raced out. The tears spilled over then and I banged my head against the steering wheel.

I forced myself to breathe normally—in through my nose and out through my mouth—until I calmed down enough to think rationally. Someone would have reported the accident. Someone would see my car stuck on the side of the road and they'd call the state troopers. I'd just need to wait until someone came out to check on me. Then I'd figure out what to do from there.

It didn't take long for the flash of someone's headlights to shine into my front window. Certainly faster than I thought their response time would be, considering the torrential downpour. Their lights were shining into my eyes, so I couldn't see who it was, but it didn't matter. I was grateful.

Unable to keep my head up any longer—crashing from the adrenaline, I guessed—I slumped against the wheel again as I waited for whoever it was to come to me. Normally, I would have gotten out to meet them, but I wasn't sure I could walk, let alone do so in the early morning in the rain.

My door flew open. "Charlie?"

The sound of Ember's voice sent a shock throughout my whole body, giving me enough energy to sit up. "Ember?"

For a second I was legitimately afraid I'd died. My thoughts were like sludge and it didn't occur to me that there'd be any other explanation.

"Jesus. Are you okay?" I started to move to get out, but she stopped me. "Wait until I can check you over really quick. Do you feel any pain anywhere?" Her fingers came away bloody as she inspected the wound on my head I only just realized was there.

I reached my own hand up and found a sizable bump on my temple that was freely bleeding. "It's just a bump. I'm okay." When there were no significant injuries, she helped me to her SUV to finish the exam rather than wait in the freezing rain. She must have gotten the emergency call when I'd gone off the road. I spotted the semi driver talking to a cop in the distance. I'd have to remember to thank him.

She frowned. "You're okay when I say you're okay. Stay still while I examine you." As her fingers poked and prodded, I stayed as still as possible.

"I'm fine. I promise." The sight of blood cleared my thoughts a little.

"What are you doing out here, Charlie?" Ember asked quietly as she bandaged the wound.

There was no point in trying to hide anything from her. She'd had too much experience dragging out the truth from her mischievous siblings for lies to work on her. "Liam and I had a fight."

She sighed and pulled me in for a hug, then shoved me back firmly to glare. "And you thought the smart thing to do would be go for a drive in the middle of a damn hurricane!"

I nearly rolled my eyes, but I didn't think she'd appreciate it. "This is Florida, there's always a hurricane."

"Be serious. You could have been killed. I've had to see a lot as an EMT, but what I never want to see is someone I love at a call." It was her serious tone that sobered me up.

"I'm sorry, Ember. I would never want to put you through that. To be honest, I was just driving. I didn't know where else to go." I hated to admit that, to be so vulnerable with anyone, but Liam seemed to have opened a damn of emotion I'd never realized had even been there.

Ember took my hand with hers. "You always have somewhere to go. With me, or with Layla. We love you, Charlie, so much. That's why we're friends. We don't have Liam's abs or his dimple, but we love you and you're always welcome with us."

I laughed, but it caused my head to ache and I winced. "Don't make me laugh, it hurts."

"We're gonna take a ride to the hospital to get that checked out, then you're coming home with me."

I opened my mouth to whine about going to the hospital, but one stern look from Ember had me shutting it. No wonder the twins shut up whenever she barked an order. She had the mom glare down pat.

Layla was waiting for me at Ember's apartment by the time we finished up at the hospital. I felt bad for making them cater to me at the crack of dawn, but at the same time, I don't know what I would have done without them. Which only made me dissolve into tears on Ember's loveseat. Quiet tears, that is, because the twins were asleep in the next room.

"Do you need more ibuprofen?" Ember asked as she leaned over to check the ugly ass bandage on my head.

"No, Mom, I'm fine." Then I sighed. "Speaking of, I have something to tell you guys."

I caught them up on the call from my mother and her offer to push through my application as well as the fallout.

"You're kidding!" Layla gasped.

"Unfortunately, no." The medicine helped, but the combination of a hangover, the knock on the head and the on-and-off crying left me wrung out and my head aching.

"You've been busy," Ember said after checking on her siblings, who thankfully hadn't been disturbed by my arrival after their sitter left.

"You could say that."

"Do you want to talk about Liam?" Layla asked gently.

At the mention of him, my heart twisted in my chest. "I'm not sure what there is to talk about."

Ember handed me a cup of hot coffee. She knew me so well. "We assumed after Layla's mom's mixer that something was going on between you two."

"It's okay if you don't want to talk about it," Layla added hastily after taking her own mug.

"It sounds like it happened so fast, because the physical aspect did, but we've been friends for so long it felt natural to move on to something more."

"I always thought there was something between you two," Ember said as she sat next to me on the loveseat.

"You did?" I asked.

"Duh," Layla answered with a laugh. "You both fit together so well. The only reason we never said anything was because you didn't seem ready to settle down. It would have been a disaster if you dated before you were ready."

"You mean like now?" I stared down into my steaming cup.

"No," Ember rushed to say. "Not at all. You never would have rushed into anything with Liam if you weren't serious about it."

Layla nodded. "No way you'd risk it unless you really care about him. You do care about him, don't you?"

"I do. Much more than I ever thought possible."

"So what happened? You both seemed fine last night." Ember asked.

My whole body hurt remembering our argument, and not just the residual aches and pains from the accident. "I don't know. I didn't mean to blow up about it, really. I just woke up and saw the notification on his phone that he'd been accepted to all these schools. Schools as far away as California, apparently and he'd never said a word about it to me."

Layla frowned. "He didn't tell you where he was going?"

I shook my head and took a sip of coffee and nearly groaned. Ember understood my love for all things caffeine. Since she often took calls at all hours of the night, she knew the horror of settling for gas station slop and made it a point to make the good stuff whenever she could. "I hadn't even thought of it because I was so focused on how good things were going. Maybe that's why he waited. I don't know. Maybe it's a good thing this happened."

"What are you going to do about volunteering?" Layla asked.

My eyes felt like they'd been filled with sand and then set on fire. I needed about a month of sleep. Maybe that would help the ache that had taken up residence in my heart. "I'm not sure. I've never been in this position before. Part of me gave up going for him, which was something I said I'd never do." Before they could pipe up, I added, "And don't you dare tell me never say never."

"I think this is a good thing," Ember declared.

"You do?" Layla and I said at the same time.

"Yes, I do. You've been so closed off for so long, there was bound to be someone who broke you out of your shell. Even better that it was Liam, who we already know is a good guy."

"But he lied to her," Layla said with a scowl.

"He's probably just as confused as she is. Relationships are hard enough without being friends first."

Layla and I both held our tongues. Ember and her boyfriend had been together for years, but things had been rocky since he started university in Miami. Long distance had been rough on them both.

I sighed. "I don't know what to do."

"You don't have to make any decisions now," Layla said, ever the reasonable one. "Take a couple days and figure out your next step. You both owe it to each other to work through the first hiccup. If you decide you don't want to keep being with him, you don't."

"What if I do...and he doesn't?" I almost couldn't get the words out. The coffee had cooled, but I no longer wanted it. The taste was acrid on my tongue.

What if I'd finally fallen for someone and got my heart broken? I'd spent so long running away from being hurt again that I was terrified to stop. Then Liam had kissed me and I'd forgotten to be afraid, if only momentarily.

Ember rubbed my back. "Then we'll be here for you. No matter what happens, you aren't alone, Charlie. Why don't you get some rest? We'll figure everything out in a couple hours."

"I don't know how to thank you guys."

"You don't have to thank us," Layla said as she crossed to me and kissed my brow. "We're your friends. No matter what."

"You can take my room that way the monsters don't bother you," Ember added.

I looked at my two friends and ordered myself not to cry again. "I don't know how to thank you."

"You don't have to thank us," Layla said cheerfully. "We fully expect payback whenever if and when our shit hits the fan."

"I'll remember that," I said as I stumbled my way down the hall to Ember's room.

I collapsed on her bed and wrapped myself in her sheets. As my eyes shuttered closed all I could think about was Liam. Too tired to cry anymore, I hugged a pillow close to my chest and fell asleep imagining it was him I was holding instead.

CHAPTER 26

LIAM

drove around in the rain for hours looking for her. I checked all of her favorite hangouts, her job. I even arrived for her first early-morning class, but she wasn't there and none of her other classmates had seen her.

Walking back to my truck, having no idea where she could be, I was damn sure I couldn't get any lower. My phone beeped with a message.

TRIPP: Yeah, I've seen her. Ember mentioned Charlie's staying at her place for a couple days. Why, what's up?

ME: Thx, man. I'll explain later.

The screen went black in my hands as I sat in the cab of my truck with the rain pouring down. I slammed the phone against the steering wheel until I heard something crack and then threw it in the floor well on the passenger side.

"Fuck!" I shouted.

I never wanted to hurt her. I promised myself before this ever started that I wouldn't. The look on her face…I'd rather she'd scream at me…hit me…anything other than the look she gave me before she left. Like I'd betrayed her.

I drove home in a fog, barely noticing the downpour, and only making it there out of pure luck. Her parking space was empty. The house was quiet without her in it and I'd never noticed how much she seemed to fill the space until she was gone.

Two weeks.

Two weeks and I hadn't heard from Charlie.

Well, other than to come home one afternoon after classes and realize some of her stuff was gone. I'd texted Tripp and he confirmed Ember and Layla had come by to pick up some of her things. I could barely spend any time in the house without being bombarded with memories of her.

I took a page from her book and fled for the first weekend I had free from my new job. I couldn't stand coming home and her not being there with food on the stove and a smile the second I opened the door. My bed was cold without her splayed across it. For a guy who'd spent several years chomping at the bit to leave a house full of women, I found myself aching to have her back.

And it pissed me off.

I tempted highway patrol by speeding the whole way home, but I didn't pass the first trooper. It left me itching for a fight.

And I knew just where I could get one.

Orange dust streamed behind me as I drove a little too fast on the dirt road that led to what was soon to be someone else's land. The thought didn't help me calm down. I ground my teeth together and knotted my hands on the wheel, the leather scrunching in protest under my fists.

I pulled into the front yard and parked next to my dad's truck. He was home. Good.

Metal shrieked as I slammed my door, but instead of my dad greeting me at the door, I found Grandma Dorothy, her round face upturned as she grinned in pleasure.

"Liam!" she said. She hadn't recognized me without prompting in longer than I could recall and it stopped me in my tracks on the top step. "It's so good to see you."

The hinges of the screen door groaned as I pulled it open to wrap my arms around her waist. She only came up to my chest, but when she encircled my waist with her arms, I felt seven-years-old again. Except she couldn't heal all my hurts with Kool-Aid and cartoons anymore.

"Missed you, Gram," I said as I bent down and pressed my lips to her hair.

"Missed you, too," she replied.

"Shouldn't you be at school?" A derisive snort followed the question.

"Don't start," Mom said with a stern look in my father's direction as she pushed past him and tugged me through down the hall. Gram followed close behind, humming. Mom pushed me into a chair at the table. "Something's wrong. Want tea?"

She was already making a glass before I could answer. "Nothing's wrong. I'm fine."

"Son, I've had twenty-two years of deciphering your moods. I can tell when you're upset." She set the glass of iced tea down on the table in front of me. "Now you tell me what it is, or I'll beat it out of you."

Grandma Dorothy sat opposite me and Dad skulked in behind, but veered off for his recliner in the attached den. I ignored him, but I could feel his presence like the threat of a malignant tumor or a lurking aneurysm. It was only a matter of time before one of us blew up at the other.

"Charlie and I had an argument." I had to take a couple deep swallows of tea to get around the knot in my throat. "She moved out."

Mom laid a hand on my shoulder. "I'm so sorry. What happened?"

The words burned in my chest. I took another sip of tea. "I didn't tell her something important and it hurt her."

Grandma Dorothy began waving one hand and the other tapped monotonously against the table. I could almost feel Dad straining to hear from the other room.

"What was it?" Mom asked.

I sighed and the bunched muscles in my shoulder wound a little tighter. "About my plans for school next year. I applied to some schools out of state. We—" my throat closed around the words. I cleared it with another swallow of tea. "We'd gotten… closer since she moved in. I care about her—I love her. And I let her down."

Dad snorted so loud, we could hear it from the kitchen.

"Ignore him," Mom ordered. Grandma Dorothy's humming increased in volume. "You haven't heard from her?"

"No, and I don't blame her. I should have talked to her about it, but things were going so good I didn't want to ruin them. Then I got denied for the scholarship," I said a little more loudly, "and I had to figure a lot of things out at once. She saw the information on my phone and it just blew up from there."

Silence from the den. *Good.*

Grandma Dorothy continued to hum.

"Poor girl," Mom said as she sat next to me at the table. "She's been through so much. She's probably just scared. She's lost everything. I'm sure she was just afraid of losing you, too."

I hung my head. "I know. I know that more than anyone. I was a fucking idiot."

"Language," Mom admonished. "Just give her time. If you love her, you'll know what to do when the time is right. When you love someone you learn to put up with all of their bull-headed actions!" she shouted toward Dad.

"Thanks, Mom." I leaned over and kissed her cheek. "How are things around here?" I nodded in grandma's direction.

"They'd be better if she could stay home," Dad thundered as he stalked to the fridge for a beer.

Mom gave me a pointed look that said to ignore him, but my blood heated at his words and my brain was screaming at me to engage. This was the fight I'd been spoiling for.

"A nursing home would be more secure. She needs more care then you'll be able to provide," I said.

The beer can hissed as he popped the tab. "We could handle her just fine here if we had you to help out in the fields instead of wasting time at that school."

"Only an idiot would think getting an education was a waste of time," I said through clenched teeth.

Grandma shoved up from the table and began pacing.

"Watch your mouth," Dad barked. "We're a family. You support your family."

I got to my feet. "Support, huh? Where was your support when the first child in the family decided to go to college to get a degree? Where was your support when I needed that scholarship? That goes both ways, *Dad*, in case you didn't know. Now I'm going to graduate in debt, so at least we'll have that in common."

He took a step closer and my mom got to her feet, her chair scraping against the dingy linoleum. "Willy, don't," she warned.

We both ignored her. "You think you know everything. That you can do everything without your family's help. You know nothing, son. You left for school and suddenly you had no responsibilities here. Your sisters, your mother, your grand-mother. They didn't factor in to your big plans. Now everything I've worked for the past forty years is gone."

I flinched. "You want to blame me for it all going to shit, but

I'm not the problem, Dad. The farm was struggling long before I decided I didn't want to go down with it. You just don't want to admit it and now you're punishing me for your failures."

"You think you can just wash your hands of your responsibilities and think it's done. I thought better of you, but I guess I was wrong. I never thought I'd see the day when I was ashamed of my son."

That hurt more than I wanted to admit. "I don't need your approval. I guess I should have known better than to ask you to help me in any way. Consider me dead to you, Dad, since you're so ashamed. You won't ever have to worry about my choices again."

"Willy! Liam! Stop this nonsense," Mom ordered.

I took a step back toward the hall. It had been me who'd instigated the confrontation, hoping it would make the hole in my chest go away, but if anything, it had made it bigger.

When I looked back to Dad, prepared for another verbal assault, he was no longer glaring at me. Instead, his head was on a swivel and he'd lost all color in his face.

"Mom?" His voice broke. "Mom?" He said a little louder.

The humming and pacing had stopped.

And the back door was open.

Gram was gone.

CHAPTER 27
CHARLIE

Things that had once given me pleasure no longer did.

Coffee, even, had failed me.

I stared down at my mug listlessly and then poured it back in the sink. My stomach couldn't handle anything lately, anyway. Apparently a symptom of heartache was constant nausea. Pregnancy had occurred to me, briefly, but my period was regular as always. A baby was the last thing either of us needed. The thought of a mini Liam, however, only made me cry harder in my pillow that night. Maybe it was hormones.

"You seem sad. Problems with your young man again?" Mr. Williams asked as I contemplated my next move.

Sighing, I chose a piece at random and moved it blindly. I almost laughed because that's exactly how I've been feeling since I walked out of Liam's house. Everyone around me seemed to have a plan and I was operating blind, unaware of the rules. In a short time, Liam had managed to redefine all the rules of the game I thought I'd played like a champ.

"You could say that," I said.

He smiled knowingly. "Life's too short. I've told you a thousand times."

Didn't I know it. "You say that, but you've been sweet on Mrs. Agnes for months now and haven't made a move."

"I'm laying the groundwork," he said and captured one of my rooks.

"Sure you are," I replied and smiled for the first time in what felt like weeks as I moved a castle. "Check."

"Think about this question, and then I'll leave it alone. In ten years, when you look back on this moment, will you regret the choices you're making? You'll know the answer then. There are some things we just *know* that no amount of reasoning will explain." Then, he captured my queen and said, "Checkmate."

April was waiting for me a couple hours later when I got off work.

At first, I considered ignoring her completely, but then I decided I was through running. If a tendency to be conflict avoidant was learned, I was going to be the one who unlearned it.

She was dressed in a skirt with matching jacket that was as pristine and polished as fine art. Nothing like the stay-at-home-mom I remembered, now that I studied her long enough to draw comparisons.

"April," I said in a flat, careful voice. "What are you doing here?"

She bit her lip and the action reminded me so much of myself it took my breath away. "I wanted to apologize. I shouldn't—I shouldn't have pushed you the way I did."

I crossed my arms over my chest. "No," I said bluntly, "you shouldn't have."

"I'm sorry, I jumped in too fast. I have no right to butt into your life."

Spotting coworkers down the hall, I nodded to the exit. "Can we do this outside?" I led her to the parking lot where we'd have more privacy. Heat shimmered up from the asphalt, but there was a cool breeze that calmed my frazzled nerves. "No, you don't have a right to butt into my life. Don't get me wrong, I appreciated your help, but you have no idea who I am or who Liam is for that matter."

April nodded. "I agree. I only saw so much of myself in you and I didn't want you to make the same mistakes I did when I was your age. I gave up so much for your father and I lost so much of *me* in the process."

The teeth of my keys bit into my palm. "I'm sure you had your reasons, but if we're going to have any sort of relationship, you need to respect my choices."

"Of course," she said immediately. "It won't happen again."

The coil of nerves in my stomach loosened. "Good. Thank you."

"Would you—I mean, I'm picking up my daughter in a few minutes from school. Would you like to meet her?"

At a loss for words, I could only gape.

"Only if you want to," she hurried to add. "No pressure, I promise."

This was the moment. I could either walk away and continue to let these past wounds fester—on both our parts—or I could stop running.

Thinking about Mr. Williams and Liam, there was no choice. No thinking. No panic.

For the first time in my life, I felt free, a weight lifted off my shoulders.

"I'd love to."

The smile she gave me brought out a mirror grin from me.

I was still laughing as I waved goodbye to April and my half-sister Madison. I had a sister! Grandparents! A mom. I'd lost so much that I didn't quite know what to do with myself as I drove home feeling like I was full up to the brim with happiness.

Except, there was no one for me to share it with.

Well, there was, but I wasn't sure if he'd ever want to speak to me again.

All I wanted to do was take the route that would lead me back to his—our—house and tell him all the things I'd learned today.

Ember and Layla had been begging me to talk to him and work things out, but I hadn't mustered up the nerve. I wasn't sure if I forgave him until I'd been able to forgive my mother. I felt lighter than I had in years. I didn't think I could have gotten this far if it weren't for him.

Acting on instinct, I flipped on my blinker and ignored the resulting angry drivers honking at me as I switched lanes. *Screw it.* I was going to go see him. My heart raced as I navigated my way through the afternoon traffic to Lake Ella and then to Liam's duplex.

I pulled up the drive and slumped in my seat when I noted the absence of his truck. He wasn't home. He was probably working. Feeling a little deflated, I parked and tried to figure out my next move.

My phone rang and figuring it was probably Ember checking in again, I answered it without looking at the caller I.D. "Yes, I'm fine, Em. I'll be back in a little while."

"Charlie? It's Mrs. Walsh."

"Mrs. Walsh. Is Liam okay?" I'd gotten a call like this before. My heart was in my throat along with my breakfast.

"Liam's fine. It's Grandma Dorothy." I stopped breathing, wanted to tell her to stop talking, but she continued. "Oh, honey, I hate to have to tell you this over the phone, but she passed away."

CHAPTER 28

LIAM

'd never forget the smell of the hospital.

I thought Charlie was crazy when she talked about how it smelled like death and antiseptic. But I got it now. The scent was burned into my nose and now every time I thought of Gram, all I'd remember was the smell of the room where they took me to I.D. her body. My mother had been hysterical, and dad hadn't argued when I told him to stay with her and my sisters at home. A testament to his shock, because there hasn't been a day in the past couple years when Dad *didn't* argue with me.

"Mr. Walsh?"

"Yeah?" I lifted my head and found a nurse or assistant or doctor. My eyes were too bloodshot and blurry to even bother trying to read their nametag.

"Is there anyone I can call for you?"

I gave half a thought to calling Charlie, but decided against it. I wouldn't know what to say to her and God, the thought of telling her about Gram had my throat closing in on itself.

"No, thanks." I knew I needed to get back home, so I got to my feet and shoved my hands into my jeans. The nurse nodded and sent me a sad smile before padding back to the nurse's station.

My legs worked well enough to carry me back to my truck, which was parked haphazardly outside the guest entrance to the hospital. I guess a part of me had thought if I got here quick enough maybe I could have saved her. Which didn't make any sense now, but it had then. I'd driven like a maniac with my hazards on, but I was too late.

Looking back so many decisions I'd made were stupid. Unimportant. Reckless.

I drove to my parents on auto-pilot. I'd been up nearly forty-eight hours, but I knew there'd be no sleep for me tonight. There was so much we still needed to do.

My exhaustion and mental and emotional numbness had me staring dumbly at the car next to my parents' vehicles in the driveway. I knew I recognized it, but it took a few minutes for realization to dawn. It was Charlie's car.

Despite how much I wanted her there with me, I took my time getting out of the truck and heading to the front door. I almost didn't want to face what was on the other side. I didn't think I could handle losing both her and Gram at the same time. There's strength and then there's a breaking point and if losing Gram had taught me anything it was my limits. To be humble. That I didn't control everything. Or know everything for that matter.

The soaps Gram used to play non-stop in the front room weren't on, which made the house all too quiet as I made my way back to the kitchen. It hurt to be here. My chest ached with it and my throat was as dry as our fields after a drought.

Sunlight spilled in from the window above the kitchen sink and when I entered the kitchen, it seemed to surround Charlie like a halo. I noticed my parents out of the corner of my eye, but all I could see was Charlie.

She'd been crying and that undid all my self-control. I

crossed the room to her, determined to beg her forgiveness, when she opened her arms and took me into them. I breathed her in, the sweet green apple scent of her washing away the memories of the hospital.

"Liam," she said, her voice full of emotion. "I'm so sorry."

I couldn't even speak, I just nodded even though I'd pressed my face to the curve of her neck. I had to bend my knees since she was so short, but I didn't care. I'd been damn sure I'd never see her again, so a little discomfort was worth having her in my arms. Footsteps scraped against the floor as my parents left, but I didn't let her go to check.

"Let's go to your room," she said as she rubbed my back. I nearly groaned at how good it felt to have her hands on me again. When I wouldn't let her go, she laughed a little. "Okay, big guy," and then maneuvered us out of the kitchen and down the hall with me still clinging to her like a stubborn child.

Charlie frog-marched us down the hall to the spare room that used to be mine when I was younger. My parents had since converted it to a guest room. Clothes and a tangle of cords spewed from the open mouth of the backpack I'd tossed haphazardly on the bed. I was acting like a little bitch, but I could only watch as she carefully cleared off the clutter and turned down the sheets.

"What are you doing here?" My voice sounded like I deep throated a chainsaw. *Christ.*

She nibbled on her lip. "I'm sorry, I should have asked you if it was okay before I came, your mom was just so upset I drove straight over here."

"You don't have to apologize, Charlie. She was yours, too." There was so goddamn much I wanted to say, but I could barely keep my eyes open. My brain had registered Charlie and the bed and all I wanted to do was curl up on it with her, but I didn't dare ask.

"Well, that's a conversation we'll have to have when you

aren't falling asleep on your feet," she said. I thought she might have been smiling, but my vision had blurred until she was nothing but a teal-green blur in her work scrubs. "Let's get you into bed."

I would have cracked a joke if my brain had the ability to form a coherent sentence. All I could manage was falling face-first into the pillows. "Stay with me," I tried to say, but into the pillows, it came out more, "Starlf bith be."

"What?" she asked.

There was enough energy left in me to lift my head. "Stay with me," I repeated. "Please." I'd beg if she wanted me to.

Charlie hesitated in the doorway. "Are you sure?"

I'd never been more certain about anything. "Please."

There was a long pause while she licked her lips and studied me on the bed. For a few thudding heartbeats, I thought she was going to turn me down. Then, she toed off her shoes and stripped off her socks, then walked across the room to climb over me and settle down under the covers. I switched off the light and thanks to the blackout curtains, the room was plunged into immediate darkness.

"I'm sorry," she said again.

"Me, too," I replied, then decided screw it. I wasn't wasting anymore time. "Can I hold you?"

She sniffled. "Please."

I rolled to my side and wrapped my arms around her. She buried her face into my chest and her body began to shake. Time seemed to slow to a stop as losing Gram hit me all at once. I hadn't allowed myself a second to feel it. From the moment we realized she was gone, to getting the call from the police to inform us of her death, to identifying her body, I'd been stoic. Mom had broken down from the stress of me and Dad fighting. Dad had been overrun by guilt. My sisters, when they'd learned about her going missing, had been inconsolable. I'd been the only one to hold them all together.

"This wasn't your fault," she said against my shirt. "It wasn't."

"She left because me and dad were fighting. We'd flustered her. She left and then forgot how to get home. She was wandering around the streets, lost and alone for hours. She died alone. If someone hadn't seen her, we may have never found her. If I hadn't pushed him so hard, she'd still be alive."

She was silent for a while, then she said, "By that reasoning, if I hadn't taken up so much of Dad's time when I was younger, he would have gone to the doctor sooner, caught the cancer sooner. Maybe he'd still be alive."

I shook my head. "It's not the same thing, Charlie."

"It is," she insisted. "Gram was sick. Very sick. I've talked to your mother about it. She didn't have much longer, even with constant care. It was more a matter of making her as comfortable as possible. It was an accident, Liam."

When I didn't respond, she pulled back and as my eyes adjusted to the dark, I met hers as she studied me. "Do you think she'd blame you? Do you think she'd want her only grandson to shoulder that amount of guilt?"

My immediate answer wasn't one I was willing to consider. "Get some sleep, Charlie," I said instead.

Her free arm came around me as her body settled against mine. For the first time in nearly three weeks, I was able to fall into a deep and dreamless sleep.

"Why don't you git and let that young lady have a moment's peace?" My great-aunt Ida told me as she shoved me away from the refreshment buffet set up in our kitchen after Grandma Dorothy's funeral.

Charlie hadn't left my side over the past three days. Through funeral arrangements, receiving out of town guests, and the service itself. When I turned, she was there. After the first night of sharing a bed together, I'd moved to the couch and let her have the bed. She didn't bring up resuming our relationship, and I didn't ask. I was simply grateful she hadn't left.

"He's alright," Charlie told her. "Besides, he gets lonely when I leave him alone."

Aunt Ida eyed me over the tuna casserole. "Well, alright, but you let me know if he starts bothering you."

"Yes, ma'am," I will.

"How is it my family likes you better than me?" I asked as I made up my own plate. I wasn't exactly hungry, but my mom was watching me like a hawk and I knew if I didn't eat she'd beeline over to me in a heartbeat.

"I'm much prettier," Charlie answered and popped a grape into her mouth from the fruit platter.

"And so humble," I teased with a grin that felt like it needed to be oiled.

Charlie's eyes softened, and I realized it was the first time I'd smiled since Grandma Dorothy died. My smile instantly fell, and I took a step toward her, plate of food forgotten on the table. "Charlie, I—"

"Liam, can I talk to you for a minute?" my father interrupted. He stopped short when he realized how close Charlie and I were standing. "It can wait until you're done here."

"No," Charlie said as she pushed me in his direction. "We can talk about this later."

When I opened my mouth to protest, Charlie glared at me. "Fine," I said and followed Dad through the throngs of relatives to the deserted front porch. Good. At least there'd be no witnesses when we had another epic blowout and it devolved to one of us throwing punches. It wouldn't be the first time in the south when fists were raised at a funeral.

I crossed my arms over my chest and leaned against the porch railing. "What did you want to talk about?"

He crumpled onto the porch swing, the metal chains groaning in protest, and buried his head in his hands. "I'm sorry, son. For everything I've said. For what I've done. Mom tried to tell me I was being too hard on you—when she was aware of what was going on. She tried to tell me I was pushing you away, but I didn't listen." He looked up then with a broken smile. "Guess that runs in the family."

I couldn't remember the last time my dad had apologized—to anyone, let alone to me, who'd seemed to disappoint him at every turn. The anger that had seemed to burn a hole in my gut whenever I was in the same room with him had turned to stone. "I'm sorry, too. I got it in my head that I was going to do things my way and I never stopped to consider helping any of you. I thought if I went to school and got my degree I'd be able to make enough money for everyone. Figure we were both equally wrong."

"For what it's worth, I am proud of you, for all you've done. I never could have stuck it out in college and I'm damn proud you're my son."

I looked to my feet, my face heating. "Thanks," I managed to choke out. "That means a lot to me."

"Gram was proud of you, too," he said as he got to his feet and pulled me in for a one-armed hug. "Now let's go find your mom and let her know we made up so she doesn't divorce me. That woman is like your Charlie. I knew I found a good one and didn't give her a second to come to her senses before I chained her down. You'd be wise to do the same."

CHAPTER 29
CHARLIE

"I can't believe you're leaving me. Who is going to spend Taco and Tequila Tuesdays with us now?" Ember threw herself down onto the couch next to me. Layla nodded enthusiastically from her place on the floor where she was sorting through the mountain of things I'd managed to accumulate at her place. I'd only been living at her place a few weeks, but somehow my things had wound up all over her apartment.

I gave them both quelling looks, which they ignored. "I do have a car, you know. I can come see either of you any time. That includes on Taco and Tequila Tuesdays."

Layla sighed heavily as she folded shirts. "It won't be the same with you gone. We won't be able to come over to see you any time we want. You might as well be on the other side of the city!"

I'd given some thought to staying in the building. Now that the semester was ending, there were a lot of openings. Students moving out, graduating. I could have my pick if I wanted. But I couldn't imagine putting up with the landlord again. Besides, my new place was farther from campus, but closer to the hospital where I hoped to apply when I graduated. Call it wishful thinking, but I hoped it would impart good vibes for when I did.

"Who is gonna help me plan to defeat Dash? I just know he's going to plan something horrible for my senior year. I won't make it to graduation if you're not here. I may kill him this time. For real."

My heart squeezed at the thought of missing their fighting, and inevitable making up. Layla may not realize it, but Dash was definitely going to make her life hell—just not for the reasons she thought he was. It almost made me a little misty to think of the wild ride that was in store for my friend. I considered warning her ahead of time but managed to bite my tongue. She'd probably kill me if I ever suggested he only teased her because he wanted to get in her pants.

"Uh, hello!" Ember said, waving a hand around. "I still live here. I can help."

Layla sighed again. "I guess."

Ember threw a pillow at Layla's head. "Jerk."

Liam had been secretive about his plans since the funeral, where we didn't get much chance to talk. I wasn't about to press him for details, not while his family was still grieving. We still chatted and texted constantly, but it wasn't the same. I missed my best friend. I tried to weasel information out of him on the pretense that I'd be willing to adjust my plans for him, but he vehemently rejected that idea. I had to admit, I loved that he wanted me to follow my dreams. Not that I'd ever tell him that.

I'd even grilled his parents for clues, but they were sworn to secrecy. His mother was so overjoyed with the idea that we might get back together that she'd given me one of her rose bushes for my new apartment. "It's tradition," she'd insisted. It was already turning brown, but I didn't have the heart to tell her I was even more hell on plants than she was.

It was late when I finally convinced Layla and Ember I could handle the last load and promised to invite them to my new place as soon as everything was unpacked. I loaded up the rest of the boxes in Liam's truck. I'd let him borrow my car in return as long as I promised him no less than three hundred times that I wouldn't let anything happen to his baby. I drove across town to his duplex where some of my stuff was still stored.

I had to admit as I walked around double-checking drawers and cabinets the emptiness left me feeling a little tender. So much so that when Liam walked through a short while later, I didn't look up from the cabinet I had my head stuck in.

"How'd it go?" I asked from inside, my voice echoing.

"What the hell are you doing?"

"Checking to make sure I didn't leave anything."

"Like a ten-year-old can of tuna?" he asked. I could hear the smile in his voice mocking me, but even that made me want to cry so I kept my head in the cabinet. He'd packed all his things from the duplex the week before. I hadn't realized how much it would affect me until I walked in the living room and found all his furniture gone. It was just another reminder that he could be leaving soon.

For a long time.

Without me.

I had to be strong about it. Liam deserved every chance at a happy future and a good career. As much as I loved him, I loved him enough to set him free if that's what he wanted.

"You never know," I said with forced cheerfulness.

"Can you come out of there for a minute? I have some news."

I froze, half in, half out of the cabinet, my ass probably making a delightful display. I gave a passing thought to staying there and never coming out, but my knees started to ache from kneeling on the tile floor. Standing, I noticed the counter had crumbs on it from God-knows-when and decided to give it a good scrub while I was there.

"Charlie, you and I both know you're not this domestic. Stop procrastinating and get your ass over here before I come over there."

I turned, tossing my hair over one shoulder. "Or what, you'll carry me?"

He leveled me with a look. "If I need to."

There was a moment's pause where I considered defying him, but the edgy look in his eye told me not to push it. Besides, it would be better to go ahead and rip the Band-Aid off so I could deal with the fact that the person I loved most in this world would be halfway across the country for the foreseeable future. Even though I didn't like it, I knew he was right. Whatever he chose, I'd figure out how to deal with it. We'd been just friends before, we could do it again.

"Fine," I said and flounced away, only to realize, too late, that the only piece of furniture we had left in the apartment was his bed. Unwilling to admit defeat, I stomped to his room and plopped down on the bed. If we were going to have this conversation, I'd rather be annoyed than vulnerable. I would be just as unruffled as he was. We were adults with an adult friendship. I could do this.

Except the second I turned to face him and took a steadying breath, my eyes filled with tears. I groaned at my own childishness. This was silly. Even if he did have to move away it wouldn't be forever.

"Aw, sweetheart, don't cry." He pulled me into a hug and pushed my hair away from my face. "This isn't a bad thing."

I sniffled. "I'm not crying. Ignore me."

He wiped away a tear and then settled in to tell me about the new place he was moving to in August. I listened to his voice rumble through his chest and tried to commit it to memory while still paying attention to the actual words. His words tumbled over themselves as he spoke. It sounded like a dream come true. A great city with the best university. Tourist attractions. Nearby beaches. It was everything he'd been hoping for and more because he'd get to do what he loved, finally, with his father's support. I was happy for him, really, I was, but all I wanted to do was cry.

"The best part about it is I won't have to go far away."

"That's good, I'm hap—" I looked up at him, blinking owlishly. "Wait, what?"

His smile was blinding and a little smug. "I decided to enroll at UF instead of taking out loans for California. They offered me a scholarship I couldn't refuse. I know it's not close, but it beats being a continent away."

"You'll be staying in Florida? What? Why?" Maybe I was dreaming.

"You're not dreaming." I must have spoken aloud again. He cupped my cheek with a hand and I closed my eyes, leaning into his touch. Needing it to keep from spinning out of control. "I love it here. I want to be near my family. Near you. It'll allow me to have the best of both worlds."

"But what about the program in California. You were so looking forward to it, I know you were. If this is because of me, then I forbid you from doing it."

He smiled. "You should know by now I do what I want the way I want it. Dad says it's a family trait. I'm sorry, you're stuck with me. If you'll have me."

I didn't know whether I should screech for joy or convince him what a bad idea it was. "Are you sure about this?"

He lifted me to my feet with two hands at my waist, then tipped my chin up to stare deeply into my eyes. "Completely. Tell me I didn't screw things up. Tell me we can work this out over the next couple years. I want to be with you, Charlie. I'll do whatever it takes."

I kissed him, unable to hold back any longer. "You've already got me."

EPILOGUE
CHARLIE

The house was barely bigger than the duplex we shared for those few short months nearly three years ago. It sat on the corner of a heavily shaded road and was flanked by similar homes—though they were in much better repair. When Liam finished school and moved back to Tallahassee to work and I was on my second year as a full-time nurse at the hospital, we'd fallen in love with it, even though it was the first one we'd toured.

"I don't know what you see in this," April said. "There's so much you have to do!"

She wasn't kidding. The crumbling brick structure would need to be repaired, but thankfully, most of the exterior damages were purely cosmetic. Overgrown ivy and bushes blocked most of the view and destroyed whatever curb appeal may be underneath. Inside, we'd need oceans of paint and patience to remove and refinish the walls underneath the acres of faded wallpaper. Underneath a film of dust and neglect lay wide-planked wood floors that I hoped would be as good as new after some refinishing.

Liam wrapped an arm around my waist, his shirt already off

and his hair drenched with sweat. "That's what we love about it. It'll be ours."

April flitted in and out of rooms, her voice echoing off the empty walls and bare floors. "It's so cool!"

Mr. and Mrs. Walsh returned from the back where they'd been scrutinizing the overgrown gardens in the backyard. The scent of damp soil trailed in behind them. The ground was still wet from a violent storm from the day before.

"You're gonna have a hell of a time clearing all that out," Mr. Walsh said with a gleam in his eye.

Liam and I shared a look.

"Actually, I was hoping you'd give us a hand with that," Liam said.

The Walsh's had moved to a smaller house once his sisters had graduated school and moved off to attend college. They kept themselves busy after they retired, but it wasn't a secret that his dad was driving Mrs. Walsh crazy when he was without busywork.

"With the garden?" His eyes brightened.

"Yeah, with Liam starting his new job and me working overtime at the hospital, and now the house, we can use all the extra help we can get. Mom, that means you, too."

April—Mom—jerked as my words sank in. "R-really?"

I smiled warmly and crossed the living space to pull her into a hug. "Really. I hope you'll come by when you can. Madison and your husband, too. You're both welcome."

"Epic," Madison said and we laughed.

"Thank you," Mom said quietly and I squeezed her hand.

"We better get going," Mrs. Walsh said. "We've got a bit of a drive back to Nassau. Why don't we come by this weekend and we'll help the both of you get settled?"

"We'd love that," I told them.

We stood on the porch as Mom and Madison waved their goodbyes and Mr. and Mrs. Walsh honked their horn. The urgency that had always plagued me, always urging me to keep moving so nothing could hurt me was absent. I didn't miss it. In its place was contentment. Peace.

Liam turned to me and tugged me to the steps where we sat and watched the afternoon turn into evening.

"I'm so happy," I said and clasped the hand resting on my thigh.

He lifted the other to brush away a lock of hair from my cheek and cupped my head to bring me in for a soft kiss. "I'm glad, but I'll be reminding you of this when we're knee deep in paint and wood stain."

A contented smile teased at my lips. "You do that."

I leaned my head against his chest and let the sound of his heartbeat fill my ears. Our lives had been intertwined for years. First as friends, then as lovers. Now, we were starting a new life, together, and this house felt like a tangible symbol of the future. A promise. It wouldn't be easy, my own experiences had taught me that, but knowing Liam was there by my side would make whatever curves we had yet to face easier to bear.

With a hand covering my stomach, I stretched up so I could whisper in his ear.

The house wasn't the only symbol of our future together, after all.

Keep reading for a sneak peek at the next book in the series…
Frenemies!

FRENEMIES

NEW YORK TIMES & USA TODAY BESTSELLING AUTHOR
NICOLE BLANCHARD

CHAPTER 1

LAYLA

"What do you mean I have to take another class?" I demanded. "I'm on schedule to graduate in the spring. I've satisfied all the requirements for both my business and art majors."

My advisor, Ms. Jensen, a harried woman in her mid-fifties with her hair in an ever-present bun and her lipstick always smeared, took off her glasses and wiped them with the hem of her wrinkled cardigan. "Ms. Tate, one of the general business classes you took at another facility did not transfer to our institution. It seems previous advisors were not aware, and therefore, you weren't informed. However, if you want to graduate with your degree in business, you'll need to take another business elective and the only one available is Business Ethics. The last available opening is at eight on Monday, Wednesday, and Friday mornings. It'll put you at five classes for the semester, but with your academic record, I don't anticipate it being an issue."

I slumped back in my seat, my brain racing. I'd prepared my schedule with a fastidiousness bordering on obsession over the last three years. I had to if I wanted to graduate on time with my double major and keep my mother off my back.

I didn't just want to graduate this spring—I needed to.

Not only to prove to myself I made the right choice to pursue art in addition to her business degree requirement, but to prove to my mother a menial, low-income position like art was a good career move, even if it didn't feel like it at the moment. If I'd gone into finance like she'd wanted me to, I could have secured an entry-level position making quadruple what I'd make as an artist starting out.

But finance wasn't what got me up in the morning. It wasn't what made my blood pump and my nerves trill as I anticipated the next piece I could tackle or the next aspiring artist I could inspire. In other words—I'd never be my mother—and I'd never be able to make her happy.

Learning I hadn't worked hard enough to be on top of my credits was only going to prove her right and *that* wasn't a conversation I was looking forward to.

"This has to be some sort of mistake. I've triple-checked my credits and degree requirements every year." Was it hot? I was sweating. My legs were sticking to the leather seats.

"I'm sorry, Ms. Tate, but my hands are tied." She reaches across the expanse of the desk between us to hand me a folder fat with paperwork. "This is all the information you'll need to know about the class. Dates, schedules, syllabus. Your first class will be Wednesday morning at eight."

My eyes nearly popped right out of my head. "Ms. Jensen," I glanced at the first sheet, "is there no way to accept the transfer credit? Five classes in addition to my part-time job is a lot to juggle. Is there no way to dispute the ruling?"

Ms. Jensen, who'd lived and breathed administration for the past thirty years merely smiled, getting to her feet. "You're a bright girl, Layla. I'm sure you won't have any problem figuring out the details. If you'll excuse me, I have a ten o'clock."

Thoroughly dismissed, and frankly at a loss for words, I got to my feet and wordlessly shook Ms. Jensen's hand. She was already turning to leaf through paperwork as I drug my feet to the hallway. There wasn't a day during my college career where I'd been as dejected as I was leaving her office. My heart thudded in my chest like it was about to call it quits, my arms hung listless by my side, my fingers barely retaining their grip on the folder. What was the point? It was a stupid thing to be upset over, but I wanted to start the semester on a positive note, and this absolutely wasn't it.

I'd worked so hard, *so hard,* the past few years to do the right things, for my future, and to impress my mother.

I guess I'd have to work a little bit harder.

That Wednesday before my first Business Ethics class, I considered throwing in the towel completely. I could go backpacking. Off the grid. I snorted. It wouldn't matter. My mother would still find me. If I didn't answer my cell phone on her first call, she would just keep calling.

"If you would have listened to me, you'd have a prestigious position at the firm waiting for you in the spring after graduation," she said.

"Uh huh," I answered automatically. I winced at my mother's screech in my ear. Normally, I'd give her an explanation guaranteed to placate her when she worked herself into a state, but I was already late for my first day of the new class, and I didn't have the time to muster up any patience to finesse her into a better mood.

"Are you even listening to me?" Her voice was like nails stabbing into my ears. "I swear you are the most ungrateful child on this earth. I've given you everything: my time, my money, even my body, and this is how you repay me. Your sister never treated me like this. She was always such a good girl."

With the implication being I wasn't.

It wasn't the first time I'd heard how much I'd failed as a Tate. According to my mother, I couldn't do anything right. "I'm listening, Mother," I responded as I hustled my way across campus. Parking was such a joke. It was my senior year and I should have mastered how to find a spot and get to class on time by now. I could only hope the professor didn't have a stick up his ass.

The truth was, I'd let Mom work me up into such a state I missed my entrance to campus and had to double back. Traffic was a nightmare, as it is every morning on Tennessee Street, and it took double the time to turn around and fight my way to the parking garage. A headache had begun to make itself known so I stopped off to Einstein's for a bagel and coffee to ward it off. All the while my mother shrieked in my ear about her favorite topic: how I was a complete and utter failure to her.

"You could have fooled me. I asked you if you'd given any thought to the position I forwarded to your email."

I chugged the coffee and cursed viciously under my breath when some of it splashed on the crisp white button-up shirt I'd bought specifically for my first day of senior year. That's what I got for trying to pretend to be a professional. Unlike my older sister, Delia, I couldn't quite seem to pull off the effortless elegance. I was more a harried homebody.

"I haven't had time to check," I answered, despite knowing that wasn't the response she was looking for. It didn't matter what I said. I could do everything exactly the way she wanted it and she would still find a reason to complain.

"Layla Lucille, the firm is expecting your response." My mother had a habit of emphasizing random words in the middle of a conversation when she was especially incensed by my idiocy. "Please make it a point to respond to the job posting by the end of business today or you will lose this opportunity."

She didn't have to say she'd be disappointed. She was perpetually disappointed. Besides, she made it a point to call me no less than three times a day to check on my progress. Three years ago, I sent her in to apoplectic fits of rage when I changed my major from finance to art with a minor in education. No amount of threats or intimidation could sway me to change my mind. In the end, I compromised and double-majored in business and art to get her off my back. It meant more work for me, but I'm used to work. It also meant less free time, but other than my best friends, Charlie and Ember, I didn't really have many social commitments. Besides, I could use the business side to manage my career in the future.

It still burned my ass that mother got her way in any respect, but I only had one more year to suffer through her meddling, and then I would be free. I'd have my degree, could get a respectable job, and be out from underneath her thumb. May seemed like an eternity from now, but as long as I kept focused, I'd make it through.

"I'll take a look at it after classes," I said. Before she could object, I pushed through the lecture hall doors and added, "Class is about to start. I have to go."

If it was possible to shame someone over the phone, Magdalene Bennett Tate was able to do it. "I expect to hear from you the moment you answer the position posting this evening."

"I'll talk to you later," I said instead of answering. She didn't know it, but I had no intention of applying for the position. I may have been graduating with a degree in business, but I had no desire to join her friend's firm, no matter how many tantrums she threw.

She disconnected without saying another word and in that way, it made her feel like she controlled the conversation.

Stomach full of lead from yet another stress-filled conversation before 9:00 a.m., I could no longer stomach the thought of eating my onion bagel with cream cheese. Full of remorse, I tossed it in the trash can before navigating upstairs to the lecture hall. Business Ethics was one of the last courses I'd need to complete the business degree and was only offered at the earliest slot in the morning. If my mom wasn't trying to kill me, my grueling schedule sure was.

I pushed through the doors to the lecture hall, hoping it will be a relatively easy A. The small group of students turned to face me, and the professor's voice cut off mid-sentence. So much for sneaking in unnoticed. Viscerally aware of their stares, I hurried with my eyes on my shoes to the first available desk at the back of the class. My cheeks began to burn as I pulled out my notebook and pencils. Having always been the perfect student, any sort of infraction made me incredibly uneasy.

"If that's the last interruption," came the professor's smooth, somewhat familiar male voice. He began to go over the syllabus and I followed along with the printed copy I pulled from my carefully organized binder.

My neck ached from the struggle to keep my eyes on my papers. I wanted to glance up to see who it was, since my class list had the space for the professor blank the last time I checked, and I wondered if I'd taken one of their classes before. At the same time, if I knew them, I didn't want the shame of seeing the disappointment on their face, not so soon after the verbal lashing from my mother.

"Why don't we go down the rows and introduce ourselves?" he said, and I mentally groaned. Why teachers thought it was an important part of class, I'd never know.

When it was my turn, I finally looked up and promptly wished I hadn't. I manage to introduce myself, giving my name and major, but I don't know how.

All the while he smirked at me like he was enjoying my discomfort.

He probably was, the immoral, no-good bastard.

My ears burned with indignation and embarrassment. The asshole probably didn't even care I was late, he just wanted to see me squirm. As he went down the line of students, I pulled open my class schedule to confirm my suspicions, and noted the updated listing with growing horror: Business Ethics - D. Hampton, T.A.

Our gazes connected over the heads of the other students and heat crackled between us. It was the heat from fissures in the ground between us, because I must be in hell.

My goal for the past fifteen years of my life, aside from appeasing my mother, has been to annihilate Dashiel "Dash" Hampton. Ever since he humiliated me in front of the entire elementary school during the spelling bee.

I narrowed my eyes at him, thankful no one could see the war waging between us since I was at the back of the room. He merely continued teaching as though my presence didn't bother him. Fine. Two could play that game. If it didn't bother him, then I wouldn't let him see how much it bothered me.

Despite the conscious effort I made to keep my eyes on my paper where I took notes on his expectations for the semester and the timeline of papers and assignments to be due, I couldn't help but glancing back up at him when I didn't think he was looking. Of all the classes—in all the lecture halls—in all the buildings on campus, I got the one where Dash was the T.A. or, as he said in his introduction, "Call me Mr. Hampton." I barely managed to control my responding snort.

Mr. Hampton. I bet he was loving that.

It would be a cold day in hell before I ever called him Mr. Hampton.

Class continued uneventfully, unless I counted the times I glanced up from my notes to find Dash smirking down at me. I ground my teeth and reminded myself I couldn't hit a teacher, even if he was a T.A., and tried to focus on the information he was presenting. It didn't help each time our gazes connected, I was hit with a wave of irritation so strong, I wanted to launch myself from my seat and wipe that smirk off his face.

The moment the hour was up, I thrust myself out of the desk, but not in his direction. In fact, I hustled toward the door like he was my mother trying to set me up with a sweet boy she knew from church.

"Ms. Tate?" I heard him call before I could reach freedom.

I spun around and slammed into a wall of muscled chest.

This couldn't be happening.

Taking a generous step back, I straightened my shoulders and tried to pretend like I was as unaffected as he looked. "Yes?"

He was close enough I could see the flecks of darker green in his mossy colored eyes, and I noted he was weeks overdue for a haircut. As long as I'd known him, he'd been fastidious about his appearance, so I knew the slightly messy, unkempt style must be intentional. Unlike me, Dash looked good no matter what time of the day. I remembered my stained shirt and hugged my books in front of my chest. His plaid button-up was perfectly pressed, and his jeans looked as if they'd just come off the rack.

The silence stretched on, but I refused to meet his gaze. If I was going to survive this semester with him, I was going to have to pretend like his stupid face didn't make me want to plant my fist in it. I'm sure there was something in the code of conduct forbidding assault on a staff member.

As I counseled myself to remember our new dynamic, his scent wrapped around me, catching me unaware and unprepared. Like warm sugar and smooth, dark whiskey it seeped into my system like a drug, and I found myself swaying forward for another taste.

"Ms. Tate?" he repeated, and the amusement in his voice had me snapping out of my stupor.

I looked up and found his smirk had been replaced by a slightly befuddled smile. "I'm sorry," I said, cursing myself for my stupidity. "What?"

"I hope you'll pay better attention in class, but I wanted to remind you class starts at 8:00 am. I know it's early, but I hope you'll be on time in the future."

Oh, he was loving this. He had to be. I couldn't entirely blame him. If I had the chance to be in a position of power, I'd take it out on him, too.

"You bet," I replied through gritted teeth. "I have to get to my next class."

"I look forward to seeing you next time!" he called out to my back.

I made a mental note to check over the attendance policy. I'd never been the type of person to skip a class, but for Dash, I'd be willing to make an exception.

CHAPTER 2

DASH

The long and short of it: I was fucked.

The last person I expected to see walk in to my classroom was the one woman I've wanted as long as I could remember.

It was just too bad she was the only woman who had never wanted me back.

I'd been a couple years ahead of her at the school we both attended, and each time she turned me down, it only made me more interested. I was convinced I'd begun wearing her down—until the day I beat her at the spelling bee.

I gathered my papers up and began readying myself for another class as I recalled the day. I'd been in fifth grade, Layla had been in third. We were both finalists in the spelling bee and even though she was a couple years younger, I'd been drawn to her. Back then it was because she also liked to read comics. Later, I learned it was because she liked the art, but I'd been a kid and knowing a girl who liked comics was out of the realm cool at the time. I only joined the damn spelling bee because I wanted to impress her. When she royally shot me down to share comics the day before, I figured if I couldn't have her, then I'd enjoy pissing her off.

After the spelling bee, there was the honor society elections, then student government, and class ranks. I'd been valedictorian of my graduating class. She made salutatorian. Nothing cheered up my day quite like pissing her off.

Except now she was my student, and there were just some lines I couldn't cross, but damn if I didn't want to toe the fuck out of them.

I made it through my subsequent classes on autopilot and headed straight to the gym to work the thought of Layla Tate out of my mind. Much as I wanted her beneath me, there wasn't anything I could do about it while she was my student. And wasn't that a fucking shame?

She was the type of woman who held everything together, who had her shit together. She didn't care, for the most part, about stuff like status, or money, like most of the women I knew. She cared about books, her art, her future. Stupid as it sounded, she inspired me to be a better person at a time in my life when I had no direction, no positive influence. If it hadn't been for her, who knows what the hell would have happened?

But I knew underneath that carefully buttoned and tightly wound exterior there was an absolute wildcat to be found. She may think we just had a rivalry, but it was so much more than that. She wanted to shove her foot up my ass and I wanted to shove my cock in her mouth.

An hour in the gym did little to help my dilemma, and I knew the past years of antagonization would have nothing on the upcoming months. I just had to keep it together long enough to finish the semester.

Should be easy enough.

Three weeks later and I was losing my mind.

No amount of lifting weights in the gym or throwing myself in my grad work could erase her from my mind as easily as I'd forgotten other women. It's almost as bad as it had been in high school. I get a twenty-four-hour reprieve, forty-eight at the most, and then she was back in my class with those blue eyes on me, and I'd have to start all over again.

She was making me lose my fucking mind.

I'd pulled every trick in my arsenal to get her to see me as anything other than an enemy, but nothing worked. Now that I was her teacher? I might as well kiss any chance with her goodbye.

Women always came easy for me. That was never the problem. It was their motivation and scheming that always bit me in the ass. They were the ones who were only interested in my looks or my bank account. As cliché as it sounded, I wanted someone who didn't give a damn about those things. Someone who saw me for me and not for what they could *get* from me.

With Layla, it was never that easy. She didn't swoon at my looks and she wasn't impressed by my father or my trust fund. When I got a brand-new Camaro for my sixteenth birthday and came to school thinking I was God's gift, she rolled her eyes and disappeared to the library. I'll admit, it could be a little irritating. She thought I was shallow, vain, and an idiot. If I were a smart man, I'd forget her and focus on finishing my MBA without the distractions.

She'd agree, and I was starting to; I was not a smart man.

"People are inherently altruistic," she stated in an argument with another student. "According to research, the human race is a stronger one if we work together to our mutual benefit. Therefore, most businesses are essentially naturally ethical because it's in their best interests to be so."

I turned to her and said, "Then you don't agree with economist, Adam Smith, who stated everyone should pursue their own selfish interests as it works out to the benefit of all as though guided by an invisible hand, Ms. Tate?"

Definitely not a smart man.

She leaned back in her seat, the thrust of her back emphasizing the perfect upturn of her sweet breasts. I was going to hell.

"I do agree with him," she said, her eyes flashing, "because it was also Adam Smith who said human behavior is guided by self-interest as well as empathy. In fact, he believed self-interest was an engine of an economic system, but he also said it was a danger. Therefore, I still believe empathy and ethical behavior are the cornerstones of any economic system or business."

I pushed off my desk at the front of the room. "Can you give me an example from last week's readings of another economist or philosopher with similar ideas?"

Her blue eyes narrowed in my direction, scenting the challenge. Knowing she couldn't resist it, I could only try to hide my smile of satisfaction. "Chinese philosopher Mencius, for example, posited the innate human capacity for altruism in the child in danger scenario. He said, 'Suppose you're walking down the street and you come across the child about to fall into a hole. A human wouldn't worry about the cost of altering their plans for saving the child, they'd just do it automatically.'" Layla eyed me up and down. "Well, most humans."

We locked eyes for a moment, before she lowered hers down to her textbook. She couldn't have made that clearer, and I made it a point to focus on the other students for the remainder of the class. When it was over, I pinned her with my gaze. "Ms. Tate, a word."

The rest of the students filed out as Layla began to stuff her things into her bag. She stalked to my desk at the front.

"What?" she asked.

"I think you mean 'What, Mr. Hampton?'" I corrected.

She scoffed, "Is there something else? I've been on time every day and I haven't missed an assignment, clearly."

"Look, I don't want each class to be like a battlefield. We both have a job to do here, and I don't want this animosity between us to affect your grade." I wasn't thinking of how good she looked, or how much I wished I could bend her over the desk between us.

Layla shifted from foot to foot and tried to look innocent, but her smirk gave her away. "What animosity?"

"Cut the shit," I said, while imagining her ass pink and splotchy from a good spanking. She'd like it. She'd look over her shoulder at me as I spanked her raw and she'd be spitting mad, but she'd egg me on until she was so sensitive, she couldn't sit without the accompanying sting.

Christ. I had to get her to leave my class before I did something stupid.

"All I want to do is finish this class so I can graduate in the spring. As long as you don't give me any trouble, I won't have a problem with my grade."

"Believe it or not, I'm not here to sabotage your grade. No matter what you may think of me, I do want you to pass this class," I said between gritted teeth. If I didn't have her splayed across my lap by the end of this semester, it'd be a miracle.

"Yeah, right. You've had it out for me ever since the fifth grade."

Unable to resist, I said, "Millennium," and watched her face flush with indignation. Of course, I'd rather it flushed for other reasons, but I'd take what I could get...for now.

"I hate you."

"You know what they say about love and hate."

"That it's a thin line between accidental death and premeditated murder," she retorted over her shoulder as she walked away.

I didn't watch her ass, and my mind didn't wander.

Much.

CHAPTER 3

LAYLA

It had only been a month and senior year was ruined.

My resting bitch face game was strong as I pulled into the parking lot of my apartment complex. Before I got out of the car, I was inundated with a wave of loneliness. I hadn't even gotten inside, and it already felt too empty. And it wasn't even because it was the weekend. No, it felt empty because the three amigas were down a number. I was happy for Charlie. She'd snagged a great place across town and closer to work, but that didn't mean it wasn't a punch in the chest each time I thought of running upstairs to the old place she used to rent before it was ruined, and she moved in with Liam.

Sometimes you just needed a shoulder.

I didn't like to show it, but I needed a shoulder today.

Rocky Road ice cream was in order, I decided. Maybe even a full pint instead of the half serving I normally allowed myself. I wasn't overweight, but my body seemed to pack on the pounds at the slightest indulgence. I didn't have a problem with being extra curvy, but in addition to my mother's padded bank account, she also boasted extra padding everywhere else. No amount of money could make that woman say no to extra servings. Finance wasn't the only aspect of her I didn't want to emulate.

I should really stop accepting her calls. They never helped and always left me feeling worse.

The three-story apartment building Charlie, Ember—my other best friend—and I shared was located just off-campus. It had been the perfect place for the three of us during our years at Florida State University, for the first time, it didn't feel like home. I attributed it to lingering discontent from another bad phone call with my mom—certainly not from the constant clashing with Dash—and went straight for the freezer as soon as I got to my apartment.

My place wasn't much to speak of. Two sparse rooms, a bathroom, kitchen and meager living room. The whole square footage didn't amount to much, but it was enough for me, and Mom had offered to cover the rent since I was only working part time. What it lacked in amenities, the location sure made up for. That and the fact for the past couple years, my two best friends had been a couple steps or an elevator ride away.

The reminder of Charlie not being there anymore had me digging into the chocolate-y goodness with renewed vigor. I still had Ember. I was making a bigger deal out of Charlie leaving than I needed to. Everything was just changing, and I didn't do well with changes. I liked consistency. Plans. Outlines. Lists. I still hadn't recovered from learning Dash was my T.A. That was absolutely something I hadn't anticipated.

Then again, Dash always pushed my buttons and disrupted my carefully laid plans.

After I finished with my ice cream, my plan was to go to my favorite place—the library—and figure out my next move. I needed to research the finance firm Mom was so adamant about and figure out if it was even something I was interested in. God knew I loved her, but I didn't want to spend my life in finance. Even though I'd turned her down weeks ago, she wasn't letting up. Maybe if I worked at the firm for a few years, I could use the time to allow my art to get off the ground. Then, I could explain to Mom in concrete examples how I could be successful in such a "useless profession."

With my goal in mind, and as I scooped another spoonful into my mouth, I began writing down a list. By the time I finished, I also polished off the ice cream. Considering that, I added GO TO THE GYM at the bottom and then went to throw out the trash and grab a bottle of water. I changed into a pair of gym sweats, a ratty T-shirt, and some old sneakers. Even if I could afford the tricked-out gym gear, I didn't get the point of dressing up in new clothes if I was just going to be soaked in sweat anyway.

Mood buoyed by the sugar and a loose plan, I practically skipped out into the hallway, where I ran smack dab into the last person in the world I wanted to see.

The world was conspiring against me. That was the only explanation.

Either that or he was stalking me, which had to be against university ethics on some level.

"Hey there, Ms. Tate." His voice was like warm caramel and was as satisfying as slipping into a warm bubble bath.

My eyes narrowed. "Dash."

He smirked. It had only been a month and I was already over being in his class. I couldn't wait until he was no longer my T.A. and I could wipe that smirk off his face. "I thought we agreed you'd call me Mr. Hampton?"

Through gritted teeth, I said, "The only way you'll ever hear me call you, Mr. Hampton, is if I suffer from a stroke," then turned and stalked away. I had to put up with him during class. I didn't have to put up with him outside of it. Then it occurred to me...he didn't live here. I stopped, turned. "What are *you* doing here?"

He lifts a hand to his chest. "Layla, I'm hurt. You sound disappointed to see me."

"I'm always disappointed to see you." Damn, what a waste of ice cream. My sugar high was already disappearing at the mere sight of him. "You didn't answer my question."

Dash, Mr. I'll-Never-Call-Him-Hampton, couldn't look smugger. "You didn't ask nicely, but I'm in a charitable mood." Then he said the words that had my previously buoyed mood plummeting from put-on-big-girl-panties to set-panties-on-fire. "I live here."

My mouth became temporarily glued shut. I might have choked on my own tongue. Some unladylike sounds later, I squawked, "*Live* here. Live where?"

"A room opened up upstairs. New renovation, too. I moved in at the start of the semester. Frankly, I'm hurt you didn't notice. And after we've had such a good time in class."

"You've got to be joking," I blurted. *Why* hadn't Charlie thought to tell me the bane of my existence was moving into her old place?

"'Fraid not, sweet cheeks."

My confusion was obliterated by rage and I saw a mist of red. "Don't call me sweet cheeks. I'm pretty sure that's against code of conduct, *Dash*."

His gaze lingered on my bared skin, which I had to be imagining. The thought of Dash, of all people, ogling me was laughable. He was probably searching for weak spots. "What do I have to do to get you to call me Mr. Hampton, just once?" he asked, and my thoughts were wrenched from his eyes on my skin.

"Drop dead?" I replied with exaggerated sweetness. I resorted to imagining him in various stages of embarrassment and ruin, which always used to cheer me up. Except now that he was in my personal space, my sanctuary, I felt even more exposed and I wished I was wearing something more substantial…like a parka. The way he was looking at me, it was almost like I was naked. Which is absurd. Dash liked to torture me—and not in any pleasurable sort of way.

My brain—probably high on chocolate and his cologne—connected the thought of pleasure with Dash, who was standing way too close for comfort. First, I imagined him running naked through the quad, with the whole campus laughing at him. It would serve him right, the bastard. Except, the image shifted, and then he was naked, and we were alone.

And no one was laughing, least of all me.

As though he could read my mind, Dash chuckled, those clear green eyes crinkling at the corners. His parents must have made a deal with the devil, because there was no way someone could be so perfect and so evil at the same time.

As I was unable to speak, from rage, I assured myself, not the flush of desire, he continued, "First my class, now the same building. I guess we'll be seeing each other a lot."

I was right, I was in hell.

He made a point of scanning my body up and down, which didn't help the tingling sensation I had going on. My breath caught in my throat. What the hell was happening to me?

"I've got to say," he kept going, "in a purely platonic way, I dig the librarian thing you do normally, but this hobo vibe you've got going works, too."

Rage burned away any remnants from whatever stroke I was having. Dash. Desire. Honestly, maybe I shouldn't ever have chocolate again. Clearly it was the devil's work. "Have you ever heard of sexual harassment?" I asked with faux sweetness.

"Trust me, sweet cheeks, no one is harassing you, sexually or otherwise." He walked backward with that damn smirk and winked at me before turning and saying over his shoulder, "I'll see you Monday in class, Lay."

If I wasn't certain there was a rule against maiming a T.A. I would have beaned him with my cell phone right in the center of his big, fat head. Instead, I dialed and put it up to my ear.

"Code Red," I said. "Can you meet in an hour?"

"Here you go," the waitress said, as she placed a big glass of wine in front of me. If I couldn't have chocolate, at least there was wine. "Can I get you ladies anything else?"

Ember smiled and lifted her margarita. "We're good, thanks."

"Put hers on my tab," Charlie added as she gestured to me, then sent me an apologetic look. To me, she said, "It's the least I could do."

Damn right. She owed me a lifetime of wine to make up for this egregious lapse in girl code. I took a deep gulp of wine, then another. "It's a good thing I love you because this is a betrayal of the worst kind. If this didn't taste so good, it would be dumped over your head right about now."

Charlie slumped and gestured to the waitress for another round. Ember giggled, then licked the rim of her glass. "You can't blame her," Ember said after a drink. "She's had her hands full with Liam and starting her new job."

Another gulp. "No excuse." I wondered if I could mainline wine. I would have asked Charlie if there were any wine-IV protocols, but she was on my shit list.

As though her urge to apologize overcame her self-flagellation, Charlie burst out, "I'm *sorry*. I'm so sorry. I had gotten off two twelve-hour doubles and could barely keep my eyes open, let alone process what Liam was yammering on about. Especially when he comes to bed without a shirt on, talking about the cute little animals he's been working on." Her eyes went misty and Ember began to fan herself. "You know how I like it when he is all swoony and half-naked."

"*Please*, continue," Ember said, leaning in. "I've been on a six-month hiatus since Chris went back to Miami. I need *any* form of swoony and half-naked I can get."

"Men are scum," I said firmly before Charlie could go off on a Liam tangent. It was imperative I didn't let any intrusive thoughts of Dash half-naked or otherwise take root or I'd be like Ember, practically panting again. "I hate them all." There, hate was easy. Hate would abolish the image of Dash naked.

"All?" Charlie asked, after sharing a glance with Ember. "Or just one in particular?"

"Don't give me those looks," I warned them. Their tone had me bristling. "You two may have lucked out, but you're not being stalked by Satan."

Ember grinned over her margarita. "C'mon, Lay, he can't be that bad."

I hung my head. "I was wearing my gym clothes and he called me a hobo." It was easier to focus on insults than the real reason why I was so unsettled by Dash's reappearance. It had been easy to focus on rivalry. This…reaction to him? So much worse.

The two of them snorted, and I wondered why I needed friends at all. Clearly the camaraderie we shared had been tainted by Dash's mere presence.

"This isn't funny! It was one thing when he was the idiot upperclassmen who couldn't stop picking on me, but it's entirely another when he's responsible for my grade. Do you realize what it could mean if I fail his class?" Other patrons began to look in my direction as my voice turned shrill. I lowered it to a whisper-shrieked, "Fail!"

Ember put down her glass and leaned forward. "So what? You don't even *want* to get a degree in business."

It was a discussion they'd had with a me a thousand times, and even though I agreed with them, the maternal guilt was strong. "I've come this far, I might as well finish," I argued. It was the same thing I told myself each night as I slogged through business homework I didn't give a damn about instead of following my passion.

"It's just one class," Charlie reasoned. "You're the smartest person I know. All you have to do is make it through one class."

I drank some more. I was going to be an alcoholic by the time the semester was over. "Let's change the subject. I'll survive living in the same building and being his student—somehow, but for now, I want to forget."

"Sure, he's a pain in the ass, but at least he's nice to look at," Ember said.

"Did you hear me?" I asked. I absolutely, positively did not to think about how nice he was to look at.

"If *I* had his class, I'd sure be doing some looking."

My eyes rounded. "Charlie! What about Liam?"

Charlie laughed into her sangria. "What? *Just* looking."

Slumping back in my seat, I studied my friends as they doubled over with laughter, eyes bright from the alcohol. This was exactly what I needed. So, they hadn't been much help taking my mind off of Dash, but they'd loosened the knots in my stomach—at least until I had to see him again on Monday.

CHAPTER 4

DASH

It didn't escape my notice that I was teaching a class about ethics and fantasizing about one of my students. There was just something about the way she'd shoot daggers at me when she thought I wasn't looking that did it for me.

When other students would give me coy looks from underneath their lashes or leaned forward to expose their cleavage, Layla snarled insults under her breath and countered every argument I proposed.

She hated me, that was clear. Maybe I loved antagonizing her so much because a part of me hated her, too. Hated she made me feel, hated she made me want. And I hated I didn't hate her the slightest bit.

As I gave my lecture, I attempted to focus on anyone but her. Except, the more I tried to ignore her, the more she invaded my thoughts.

With my mind half on the discussion, my thoughts drifted to the last time I saw her before my junior year abroad. I'd gone to my younger brother's graduation—they'd been in the same graduating class in high school—and I couldn't resist needling her for being salutatorian instead of valedictorian.

"What is he doing here?" Layla asked my younger brother, Brian, who was already smiling. He got off watching Layla's hatred of me. I had to admit, so did I.

It was so out of the ordinary to have a woman who didn't fall at my feet. It was refreshing. Distracting. And it turned me fucking on.

I should have been focused on my upcoming year abroad, but as I strolled over to where Layla and Brian were standing outside of the auditorium, all I could think about was her.

She wore a snug white dress, fitted to curves she hadn't possessed two years ago when I went off to college. Pale, milky skin filled my vision and her legs went on for miles, accentuated by heels that brought the top of her head almost to my shoulders. She was even more attractive when she turned to me and scowled. It made me grin as wide as I did the first time she didn't fall at my feet. A scowl from Layla Tate was more enticing than a smile from any other woman.

"Come on, Lay, you didn't think I'd miss the big event, now did you? After all, I've been waiting to see you graduate as valedictorian for a long time." Her eyes could have singed me with the force of her glare. "I guess I'll be waiting for a while."

"You're such an asshole." She bared her teeth with the words, her cheeks reddening.

"But you love me," I teased, wondering what it would take to truly push her over the edge.

"I loathe you."

She spun around, her dark, sleek hair fanning out behind her. A part of me was disappointed to watch her leave, but I knew she couldn't stay away for long. Much as I seemed to annoy her, it didn't seem to make her stop from coming back for more.

My brother turned to me, backhanding me on the shoulder. "Dude. Why do you always have to give her such a hard time?"

I threw an arm around his shoulder and tugged him along toward our waiting parents. "She wouldn't put up with me if she didn't like it," I told him.

At least that's what I thought, until I came across her inside the sound booth I'd been asked to manage. She was huddled behind it crying.

"Layla?" I asked before I could think better of it. I didn't know jack shit about handling crying females, let alone one who practically clawed at my throat on a regular basis.

Her red-rimmed eyes shot to mine and her face crumpled when she realized it was me. "What are you doing here? Go away!" Except she could barely speak between sobs.

I knelt down beside her. It was a bad idea, but part of me was concerned I'd made her cry. "Hey," I said, as I scooted closer on my knees. "I didn't mean to make you cry."

Her tears undid me. It was one thing to see her riled up and angry, and quite another to see her hurt and vulnerable.

Even though she was crying, she laughed. "As if I'd care enough to cry over you. Not everything revolves around you. Idiot." She wiped at her nose and kept her eyes downcast.

Bumping shoulders with her, I sat next to her on the floor of the booth. We had some time yet before the ceremony was going to start. I couldn't seem to make myself leave without knowing what had made her cry.

"Then why are you?"

She sniffled, wiping her face with her sleeve again. Her mascara had begun to run, and her porcelain skin was blotchy. "What do you care?"

It hurt me, more than it should, to have her think so terribly of me. For a moment, I wanted to console her. "C'mon, Lay. I should be the only person who gets to pick on you. If someone is infringing on my territory, I want to know so I can kick their ass."

"Oh, please. You're probably loving this." For some reason, that made her cry harder and I panicked.

"Hey, hey. No, I don't. I may be a dick sometimes, but I'm not a monster," I said, except, seeing her cry, it made me sort of feel like one.

"It doesn't matter." She sniffled again, wiped her eyes, then pulled out her phone. At the sight of the time, she squeaked, then opened up the selfie view on her camera to check her face. With a low moan, she began to repair the damage. "You can go now, I'm fine."

My first thought was no, no she's not, but I didn't comment on it. Instead, I said, "Actually, I can't. They needed me to help out with the sound system, the music." When she got up to leave, I blocked her way.

"Don't start," she warned.

"I'm not letting you leave until you tell me why you're so upset."

"It's really none of your business."

"So I'm making it my business."

"Let's not do this right now, Dash. I have to go or I'm going to miss my own graduation."

"Then you'd better get talking, because I'm not letting you out of here until you do."

Her sky-blue eyes lifted and met mine. "If you must know, if you just have to humiliate me one more time on what's supposed to be one of the best days of my life, it's my mother. I didn't make valedictorian like my sister, so she's very embarrassed to be seen with me today. There? Does that make you happy?" She laughed, but it was hollow. "Maybe you should go find her, you can make fun of me together."

Knowing if I sympathized with her it'd only make her angrier, I got to my feet and helped her up. The wary look in her eyes told me she didn't trust me for a second. I didn't blame her. She shouldn't.

It may have been the tears, maybe she was right, and I was a twisted prick. It may have been the warning in her eyes. It was certainly the dress and her go-fuck-yourself sneer.

I think she knew what I was planning before I did, because an instant before my lips touched hers, she opened her mouth to protest. Bad choice on her part, because it gave me the perfect opportunity to see if her feisty mouth tasted as good as it looked.

It didn't. It tasted better.

Later, I'd tell myself it was a one-time thing. Something to distract her from her pain, but it'd be a lie.

She went as still as granite in my arms for a couple long, tension-filled heartbeats and then she melted and gripped my shirt with both *fists. I could taste the salt of tears on her full lips, warring with the sweetness of her mouth.*

It was so Layla I nearly smiled. The contradiction of soft and steel gripped me so hard I lost my hold on sanity.

Turning, I pinned her against the wall of the sound booth. It was dark enough my other senses were heightened. All I could see, smell, taste, or hear was Layla.

She made a sound of pleasure against my lips that shocked me back to reality. I pulled away, and gave myself a moment to savor the look of pure bliss on her face, before I untwined myself.

"Now you've got something to remember me by," I told her.

It took her a moment for her eyes to refocus. When they did, the anguished glaze was gone. Instead, they lit with fire. That I knew how to handle.

"You son of a bitch," she growled.

I couldn't help the smile. "You don't have to be upset, you liked it."

"Liked it?" Her voice was nearly a screech. "You disgust me," she said through clenched teeth and stalked off.

"You and me both," I said to her retreating back. But she didn't hear me.

At least she wasn't crying anymore.

I made it through the lecture, barely, but I made it a point not to draw Layla's attention. Not when the memories of her mouth were so close to the surface. Antagonizing her was one thing, but going down memory lane was another.

That didn't stop me from watching her as she gathered up her books and strode out the door. I was going to hell for loving it was still warm enough for her to wear her go-to sundresses. All I could think about through my next class and lunch was how much I wanted to see what she had on under them.

Thursdays were reserved for dinner with my grandfather and the memory of Layla in that formfitting white dress was all that was going to get me through it.

Edward Hampton was an exacting man with expensive tastes and impossible standards. His expectations of me had been drilled into my every waking moment since I was six. It was a wonder my dad turned out okay, considering who raised him. Dad liked to say it was my mother's softening influence that kept him from turning out like his father.

"You're late," he said, without looking up from the papers on his desk.

"Class ran over," I answered. It hadn't, but we both knew that. I didn't want to spend more time with him than necessary. Sad, when you considered he was family. He and my grandmother had been married forty-three years, but you wouldn't know that by looking at them.

I kissed my grandmother on the head, causing her to frown. Physical affection was rarely tolerated. "Sit down, Dashiel."

"Dash," I corrected because I knew it irritated her. They didn't pull this kind of crap with my younger brother, Brian. He wasn't required to attend meals or check in. He flitted around the world under the guise of finding himself and no one batted an eye. No, I was the first born, the legacy for the Hampton name.

Her mouth puckered and she indicated the food already laid out on the table. "Dinner's already cold. If you'd called to say you were going to be late, I could have held it, but you'll have to make do."

"That's fine," I answered and spooned up roast with potatoes, peas, and carrots. Thursdays were practically the only day I got a well-cooked meal, so it didn't matter to me if it was cold. "So, what was so important?" I asked. Grandmother had called that morning to mention no less than three times I couldn't skip.

"Since this is your last year of graduate school, and you've sown your oats and procrastinated long enough, it's time you accepted your responsibilities as a Hampton."

It's the same speech I'd gotten every year since I was a child. "I'm not ready," I answered as I had every year.

I was going to elaborate, but grandfather didn't give me the chance. Underneath his fake tan and cosmetic surgery, by a confidential and well-paid plastic surgeon, his color heightened. "Elections begin year after next. You'll participate in your father's campaign, network, get your name out there. By the time your thirty-five you'll be the next Hampton in office. Your grandmother and I financed your education. You'll follow the Hampton line just as your father did."

Scoffing inwardly, I stuffed my face with beef and vegetables to keep from saying all the things I wanted to say out loud. Out of respect for my father, I deferred to his parents, but not by choice.

Sensing the growing hostility, grandmother leaned forward, her watery blue eyes bright with excitement. *Shit.*

"We have the most wonderful girl for you to meet. There's a charity function at the end of the month, an auction for the needy we're supporting. You'll meet her there. Her family is very nice. The Martins. Good people. You'll like her."

I nodded because it was easier than arguing. The only person in my life who didn't see me for the stepping-stone, or the legacy, or the pretty face was Layla.

She hated me, but at least it was honest.

I was already looking forward to our next class with renewed enthusiasm.

CHAPTER 5

LAYLA

As I waited for the ancient elevator to creak its way down, I scrolled through Instagram looking for inspiration and stopped when I came to the feed of an artist I'd heard of before, but hadn't paid a whole lot of attention to. Peyton Rhodes. They're portraits, stunning portraits. She painted them in black and white so the only aspect you can see is the pure emotion captured from her subjects.

God, what I wouldn't give to paint like that. I spent more time than I should have looking through her past work. She'd only recently gotten into doing portraits. Her parents had died a couple years ago, and she understandably stuck to landscapes while she worked through her grief. According to an interview, it was love that brought her the wave of inspiration to dive back into portraiture.

I wanted to scoff, but it was undeniable how beautiful her work was. I didn't *not* believe in love, but I also believed in evidence. The only example I had for what a relationship was supposed to be like were my parents. My mother ran roughshod over my father my whole life. Was that love? I didn't think so. I wasn't so sure I wanted to take the leap to figure it out.

It was the perfect time for Tequila Tuesday. I needed the break from work, classes, and the carefully plotted game of chess Dash and I had been playing three days a week. It was exhausting trying to keep up with him all of the time. Exhausting, but I'd started to look forward to it.

Hence the need for tequila. Lots and lots of tequila.

Only three months left.

I climbed into the elevator heading to Ember's apartment, where we decided to host the get-together this week. Ember's twin sisters also stayed with her because instead of overbearing parents like mine, she had a pair who couldn't care less. I wasn't sure which was worse. Her siblings had an afterschool thing, and then a sleepover at her aunt's so we'd have the place all to ourselves.

Ember threw open the door at my knock, her cheeks already red against her Irish-white skin. "*Hola!* I'm so glad you're here," she squealed.

"Someone's already been in the tequila," I commented with a grin.

"I lost one last night. I figured I needed it."

Ember was an EMT part time while she studied to become a paramedic. I didn't know how she and Charlie worked in healthcare. Charlie was an R.N. having recently graduated and landed her first full-time job. They spent their days saving lives, while I drew pictures. Sometimes it felt like my dreams weren't valuable enough compared to theirs. Their jobs *mattered*. They made a difference. But maybe that was my mom's voice in my head. She'd certainly recited the same spiel time and time again.

"Well, let's not disappoint," I said, as I followed her to the kitchen. "You okay?"

She lifted a shoulder. "It comes and it goes. In the moment, it's just about doing what needs to be done next. It's the hours after, when I'm home doing random, ordinary things where it hits me. Sometimes it's not bad. Like if it's an elderly person who has passed due to relatively natural causes. But it's the kids or the parents that get to me."

I saw her eyes flit to the pictures on the wall of her siblings. "Double for you then," I announced to distract her and set my supplies on the counter. Crossing to the tequila station, I whipped up a quick round. "When is Charlie going to get here?"

"You rang?" Charlie said, as she and her best friend and boyfriend, Liam, walked through the door after knocking. "Time to get this party started." She was still in her scrubs, her dirty blonde hair in a messy topknot, but her eyes were bright and full of life.

Smiling, I lined up four shot glasses for all of us and opened a new bottle—Ember had apparently finished off the rest from our last Tequila Tuesday. With an efficiency that spoke to exceptional competence at her job, Ember sliced limes and salted rims.

Liam automatically went for the TV remote and put on some football game. As we readied our shots, he settled into the couch.

"What's Chris doing this weekend?" I asked.

It was a touchy subject. Their on-again-off-again relationship was full of more drama than I could keep up with. But what did I know? I'd barely ever had a boyfriend. Even the thought of bringing someone around made me cringe. Not only would my mother have gone ballistic, I wouldn't know what to do with one if I had one.

Ember rolled her eyes. "No talking about that either. Just drinking."

I couldn't argue with that, but I made a mental note to bring it up later when she wasn't heading toward sloshed and so obviously emotionally raw. I held up my shot glass full to the rim. "What are we toasting?" I asked.

"Knock-knock," interrupted an all too familiar voice.

No.

I almost wished I was hallucinating. It'd be better than the alternative.

I spun around, the tequila sloshing over my fingers, to find Liam letting Tripp and Dash in the front door. He looked so good it made me sick. He'd always looked good, even in high school. Perfect clothes, perfect hair. Expensive watches and a fancy new car when he'd turned sixteen. My mother had provided anything I'd ever wanted, but I never had the knack for labels like Dash. He wore wealth casually, like it was meant for him.

Much as I despised him, maybe it was. He'd changed from what I'd deemed his professorial look—neatly pressed and expertly fitted khaki pants and a button-up shirt rolled at the sleeves and open at the collar—to dark jeans, sneakers so new they were still pristine, and a red T-shirt that fit him like a glove. His green eyes winked and that full, mouth was pulled wide into a knowing smile.

My heart sank. My stomach clenched. I wasn't so sure it was from repulsion, but I'd blame any residual attraction to him to the tequila. How had I forgotten my friends were chummy with Satan himself? I sent them a furious look, but they only giggled at me. The both of them were convinced there was something more between us, aside from complete and utter hatred. No amount of my convincing on girls' night could sway them.

"Are we just letting in anyone off the streets now?" I asked shrilly. Without waiting for their answer, I prepped myself a second shot.

I was going to need it.

"I'm wounded," Dash said and snatched the new shot straight from my hands. "I thought we were getting along so well."

"Oh, I'll wound you all right." I lifted my remaining shot glass and hastily clinked it with Charlie and Ember, who could barely contain themselves. Why I put up with them, I'd never know.

Dash watched with those potent green eyes that haunted my dreams—make that nightmares, I corrected firmly—as I licked the salt from my hand, slung back the shot, then sucked on the lime. I don't know if it was the burning heat from the alcohol, or the flash of something in Dash's eyes, but a wash of pure electricity flooded over me and settled low in my stomach. Good God, did tequila have the same wall-eroding effects that chocolate had? What was going wrong in the world that two of its most delicious substances could fail me so spectacularly?

As the alcohol burned its way down my throat, I coughed and asked, "What are you doing here? Isn't there some sort of rule about fraternizing with students?"

"Hey, we like Dash," Liam interjected.

"Yeah," Tripp added. "He brings the fancy expensive tequila on his nights."

"Sellouts," I muttered. I pointed a finger at Tripp, who sputtered. "See if I bring you donuts to the dugout this year." Tripp played college ball for the university team and was being considered for pro ball. He's had it bad for Ember for years but settled on being her friend when she and Chris hooked up. Why couldn't I have a stalker like Tripp, who was as wholesome and kind as they get? I frowned at him, until Dash shifted and caught my gaze again.

Maybe it's because I'd always had a thing for bad boys. Tripp was nice, maybe a little too safe for me.

While Ember and Charlie were busy making drinks and chatting with Liam and Tripp, Dash ambled closer. "It's not against the code of conduct unless you make a move on me. Then we'd be in some trouble. Why does it matter, Lay?" He leaned onto the counter, his eyes twinkling with mischief. "Thinking about making a move on me?"

"You wish," I hissed. I was comforted to learn he had to keep his distance, but I wasn't sure if it was because I wanted him to —or because I didn't.

"Another!" Ember shouted from across the kitchen, already overcome with giggles. She wouldn't say it, but I knew she was missing Chris. I gave Dash one last scathing look, and then joined my friends.

Dash watched me again, I could practically feel his eyes on me, but I ignored him. Charlie finished prepping mean-ass margaritas and we chose a board game from Ember's stash. They were always missing pieces because of the kids, and some were so worn you couldn't see the boards, but normally we were too shit-faced to care.

A couple hours later, I stumbled my way to the bathroom. Bladder emptied, I splashed some water on my flushed face. The room swam around me pleasantly, and despite Dash's constant comments, I was feeling nice and buzzed. I'd regret it tomorrow when I had to get up early for his class, but for the moment I didn't care.

I stepped out into the hall after drying my hands where Dash was waiting for me.

"I'm going to turn you in for stalking," I said. "First class, then the building, now following me to the bathroom. Those are serious red flags, buddy."

He pushed off the wall and I slipped by him, but in my slightly drunken state, I went the wrong way and he cornered me in Ember's laundry room.

"Running from me now?" he asked.

"No," I said stubbornly.

"Looks like it."

"Then maybe you need to have your eyes checked, Dash."

He made a clicking sound with his tongue. "*Mr.* Hampton," he corrected. "We've talked about this."

I snorted. "In your dreams. Besides we're not in class right now."

I tried to move around him, but he blocked me. My hands bounced off his chest and my body brushed against his. Warning signals went off in my head. A touch of panic mixed in with the tequila and arousal. Dammit, I should have known better than to let him corner me.

"You're right. We're not. Stop trying to get away from me," he said, his tone tinged with frustration. "I'm trying to talk to you."

My hands dropped to my side. "Are you dense? I don't want to talk to you."

He rolled his eyes. "You love talking to me. You just hate that you love it and it pisses you off."

My jaw dropped. "The hell I do."

"Want me to prove it?" he asked, stepping closer.

"I don't want you to prove anything," I said, but the fight had gone from my voice.

The tequila had my muscles feeling loose and warm. The way Dash's body heat began mixing and sparking with mine clouded my head, my judgment. I knew I should get away, but his nearness was more intoxicating than any drug.

"That's because you know I'm right."

Struggling to find a clear thought, I pushed my wild curls out of my face. "You forget, Dash, I've kissed you before and I'm fine never doing it again." There, that ought to shut him up, prove it to him.

But he only smiled. "You think you didn't like it?" he asked.

"The only thing I liked about it was when you finally stopped."

Dash chuckled, lifted a finger to trace a hairsbreadth away from touching my lips. "I think you're lying. You *loved it.*"

"The only thing it made me feel was anger, much like your presence is doing right now." The words were nearly a whisper because I was fairly panting at how close his body was to mine, how much closer I wanted it to be. It was as though we were composed of two volatile chemicals that reacted to each other when we were in close proximity. Instead of a slow burn, it was an explosion.

"You aren't mad because I kissed you at your graduation," he whispered in my ear, causing me to shiver against the nearness of his body. "You're mad because you *liked* it."

I pushed away from him and whirled around, hoping he couldn't see the frenetic beat of my heart in my throat. The hum of Ember's dryer tumbling filled my ears and created a cocoon of sorts in the small space. I struggled to find the right words. "You're so full of yourself, Dash."

He stepped closer and my ragged breaths snagged in my chest. "I don't think so, Lay. Not about this."

"Don't come any closer," I warned with my hands in front of me. "I'm not asking to take a trip down memory lane."

"Why? Afraid you might like it?"

I gulped down air, suddenly finding it impossible to breathe. "No," was all I could manage.

"No, what?"

I didn't know anymore. I had to keep my hands in fists at my side to abstain from touching him, though it was the only thing I wanted to do. The bastard knew it.

He took a step back, looking like he felt none of the things I did. His expression was serious as he studied me. "That's what I thought." A smile ghosted across his lips. "You should get some water to drink, Lay. You look a little flushed."

He turned and ambled away with his hands in his pockets as I fumed with impotent rage behind him.

CHAPTER 6

DASH

It was half of the way through the semester, but it felt like it would never end. Seeing her every day was torture of the most delicious kind. I could look, but not touch. Talk to, but not taste.

If I had been entertained by the constant battle of wills before, now I was tortured by them.

Cornering her at Ember's had been a mistake. One I'd do my best not to repeat. It had been exhilarating being so close to her. Watching those baby blue eyes light with indignation, then with heat. A part of her wanted me on some level, that much was clear.

I almost wished I could turn back time and make different choices. Having the image of her—heavy-lidded and a little blurry around the edges was driving me crazy—she was driving me crazy. All I could think about was how much I wanted to see her with those walls down and how much I wanted to be the guy who scaled them.

It was wrong on so many levels.

Ninety-nine percent of the time, she hated me. But that one percent when she didn't? It consumed me.

In class, we both pretended like the kiss never happened. We were polite and professional. I lectured, she turned in assignments. It was as though we knew if we crossed that line again, there'd be no going back. I was never much for self-control, especially not when it came to getting something I wanted, and wanting Layla was becoming something I *needed*.

Normally, I despised charity functions. Rich people rubbing elbows with other rich people who pretended like the mutual dick-measuring made a difference in the lives of people who needed genuine help. If I hadn't been in such need of a distraction, I would have avoided the fundraiser Grandmother roped me into like the plague. However, because Layla was occupying my thoughts with increasing regularity, I submitted and resigned myself to a night of boring conversations and expensive, tasteless food.

"Thank you for coming tonight without putting up much of a fuss," Grandmother said, as I escorted her from the dining room to the lounge.

Dinner had been plain chicken with overcooked vegetables, and I was looking forward to washing it down with a drink from the open bar. "You bet," I said distractedly.

"Since you've been in such a great mood, let's go to the Martins now before they leave for the night. I've been meaning to talk to Janine about her volunteer work." Code for she wanted to railroad me into talking to their daughter, Jessica, before I turned tail and ran.

"Why don't I meet you there? Do you want me to get you something to drink?" I compromised.

"White wine," she replied and lifted her hand in greeting.

I booked it for the bar before she could rope me into socializing without any alcohol in my system. This semester was going to turn me into a drinker if I made it to the other side alive.

"Whatever white wine you have and a beer, thanks," I said to the bartender. I'd overdone it on the tequila and was going to limit myself tonight, but that didn't mean I had to listen to the inane chatter without the social lubrication.

As I waited, a woman by the bar caught my eye. She was sitting prettily on a barstool observing the crowd and sipping a white wine. Her eyes on the projection show playing on one wall of the lounge. I glanced over to see what had her so entranced. It was a slideshow with information about the charity—arts for youth or something like that.

Of course it was.

I downed half the beer and ordered another. There was no getting away from her. At first it was amusing to run into her in class, at my apartment, now it was my own personal hell.

The woman at the bar sighed and shook her head and the movement was so reminiscent of Layla, I did a double-take. Studying her more closely, I noted the full-length, siren red dress with an objective sort of appreciation. It was formfitting with a slit up the thigh and cut so it emphasized her slim, elegant frame. She turned back to the bar, and her face was in shadow from the moody lighting the event coordinators had rigged to imitate intimacy and draw attention to the projection.

She was literally driving me insane. Seeing her everywhere when she was actually there was one thing, but imagining she was there was another. I finished the beer and started the second. Maybe I'd give that Jessica Martin a chance—anything would be better than this.

Then, the woman at the bar turned and Layla and I stared at each other in shock.

I didn't know whether to laugh or start chugging my beer, so I did both. "Before you accuse me of stalking you, I'm here at my grandmother's invitation," I said once I finished the second beer. The bartender asked if I'd like another, but I declined and switched to water. The last thing I needed was to be drunk around Layla again.

"Sure, you are," she said, her tone scathing.

"What are *you* doing here?" I asked.

"This fundraiser, such as it is, is for the art institute where I work part time. We're trying to raise money to benefit the low-income schools, so their programs don't get cut." She gestured to the slideshow on the projector. "Those are some of my students' projects, not that anyone here seems to care."

"I didn't know you volunteered."

"Contrary to what you may think, you don't know every-thing about me."

And that was where I should leave it. For now, I was her T.A. and I'd already overstepped. I should wish her a good night, tell her I'd see her next class, and walk away.

But I couldn't.

"How long have you been volunteering?" I asked. I was a predator scenting its prey. All I wanted was to gobble up each thing about her like it was my last meal. I was going to hell.

She gave me a look like she couldn't quite figure out what I was up to, then sighed. "I'm not into doing this whole thing tonight. Can I take a rain check?"

"Thing?" I asked.

"C'mon, Dash, I'm serious. Not tonight. I'm tired, my feet are killing me. We're not going to reach our goal and I frankly don't want to argue."

"Who said we had to argue?"

"Dash!" came my grandmother's voice came from behind me. "I have someone I'd like you to meet."

Suddenly the charity had gotten a lot more interesting and it wasn't because of Jessica Martin.

"You should go," Layla said and gestured to the bartender for another drink.

I started to argue, but my grandmother came up behind me and put a proprietary hand on my shoulder. "Dash? I've been calling you. The Martins are waiting." She noticed Layla drinking deeply from her glass and her lip curled. "Who's this?"

"Layla, this is my grandmother, Elizabeth. Layla is affiliated with the organization. She's a tutor and also one of my students."

Ever one to observe social niceties, she took Layla's hand. "A pleasure to meet you. Why don't you join us? I'm sure the Martins would love to meet you and talk about the organization."

"Of course," Layla said, but her smile didn't quite reach her eyes.

I knew she wouldn't take my offer to bow out gracefully, so I didn't try. Instead, I followed the two of them back to the table where Jessica and her parents sat with my grandfather.

"Neil, Laura, this is Layla, I'm sorry, I didn't get your last name," Grandmother said.

"Layla Tate."

Grandmother scenting blood in the water laid a hand on Layla's arm as they took a seat at the table. "You're not Magdalene Tate's daughter, are you?"

"Afraid so," Layla said with a tight smile, reminding me of how I'd found her at her graduation. Because of her mother.

"So wonderful to meet you!" Jessica Martin interjected. Jessica was everything I could have hoped for in a political marriage (if I wanted one) and my grandmother knew it. She was beautiful, charming, elegant, and poised. In fact, she reminded me of a shark, and she was looking at me like I was a tasty baby seal.

My grandparents and Jessica's family began firing questions at Layla about the charity and her involvement. Unfazed, or perhaps bolstered by the topic of conversation, Layla answered them, which gave me time to study her. I could make a career out of looking at her. I'm not sure I'd ever get tired of it.

From my seat next to Jessica, I got an unobstructed view across the table where Layla was seated by my grandfather, who seemed to be as enamored as I was. At least that was one thing we had in common.

As the two of them began their own tangent about the charity, Jessica leaned down to murmur in my ear, "Your friend seems nice. Are the two of you together?"

"No," I answered and sipped my beer. "She's a student in one of the classes I T.A. for."

"A student, hmm? Then you're single?"

"Why do you ask?" We both knew the answer to that question, but I was enjoying the way Layla was glaring at me with Jessica so close. Sue me. She'd been driving me mad the past couple of weeks. The fucked-up part of me was reveling in the chance to do the same to her in return. That almost encounter in the laundry room hadn't been near enough.

As though she knew what I was up to, Layla intentionally turned her attention back to my grandfather. That didn't stop me from catching her gaze when it wandered back to me from time to time. I didn't discourage Jessica from cultivating an intimate conversation, but I didn't encourage it either. I'd let her down gently at the end of the night.

I'd been with women like Jessica before, and as beautiful as they were, they only wanted me for my face or my name. Neither of which had anything whatsoever to do with me as a person. Ironically, they had that in common with my grandparents. According to them, all I needed to succeed in life were my looks and reputation.

All I needed, to be reminded those two things had no real bearing outside of their rich circles, was to look into Layla's eyes and know there was someone out there who saw the real me. Maybe she didn't fall to my feet, but at least it was honest.

It's that thought that had me following her when the evening concluded, and my grandparents were distracted by the Martins and saying their goodnights. I excused myself and followed her to the empty hall outside the ballroom.

"Layla," I said, but she quickened her pace. Damn if I didn't love chasing her. It made me wonder if she liked it as much when I caught her.

"Go back to your family, Dash. It's been a long night and I don't want to fight with you," she said when I did just that.

"Who said I wanted to fight?"

Her hair had started to fall down around her shoulders. Now that there wasn't a crowd around, I let my eyes wander over the deep neckline of her dress and the exposed tops of her breasts. There was just enough creamy flesh exposed to be enticing without being downright X-rated.

"You always want to fight," she said.

"Maybe because you always seem so happy to do it. You especially like arguing with me in class, but that's not what I'm interested in now. Are you okay? You seemed upset."

"You don't have to pretend to be interested." Her shoulders slumped.

"If I wasn't interested, I wouldn't be asking," I replied.

"Fine, but only because I hope my tedious problems will annoy you." She closed her eyes and slumped against the wall. "This benefit was supposed to raise money for low-income schools to support their art programs. I suppose these days, most people seem to think art education isn't relevant, so they're slowly being defunded. We worked so hard with the kids to make their projects for auction and we didn't even make a dent in our goal. Sometimes, when things like this happen, I wonder if maybe my mom is right about art being useless."

"Hey," I said, and leaned next to her. "It isn't useless. The work you're doing matters." She scoffed and I nudged her with my shoulder. "I may joke a lot, but I mean it. Whatever I end up doing with my life won't mean half as much as the time you put in with those kids."

"But my mom—"

"Screw your mom," I cut in and made her laugh.

The moment lengthened, and I became aware of how close we were standing. I turned to face her, studying the genuine smile resting on her lips. I knew I should walk away, but she never looked more beautiful than she did right then.

She had a second of comprehension where her eyes widened, and she brought her arms to my chest before my mouth closed over hers.

CHAPTER 7

LAYLA

His lips hovered over mine like a suggestion and his tongue snuck in like a secret. Dash Hampton was dangerous, lethal even, because one taste made you think the whole ordeal was your idea.

I was being seduced.

I hadn't prepared for it, couldn't protect myself against it. The marginal defenses I had specifically for Dash crumpled as he hooked my chin with his fingers and glued the front of his body to mine.

There was no excuse for it.

No reason.

No plan.

But I melted against him, the heat between us exploding like fireworks on the Fourth of July, and I was powerless against the assault.

I hadn't planned on any of this, certainly not how I responded to him. Not the way I moaned against his full, soft lips or licked at his tongue. My own shameless response would have shocked me on any other occasion, but there simply wasn't a chance. We went from arguing, something we always seemed to do, to kissing with no pause in between.

I pulled away long enough to suck in a steamy breath. "We have to stop," I whispered. The voice inside my head screamed NO, but I could hear the doors to the lounge open and fill with people as the crowd began to spill out into the hallway.

We were going to get caught. Someone affiliated with the school would see, and we'd both be in deep trouble.

Deprived of my mouth, Dash licked and nibbled down my throat to the neckline of my dress. "This spot right here," he paused with his mouth hovering over the swells of my breasts, "this spot has been driving me crazy all night."

I fisted his hair, my body trembling with a mix of nerves and fear. The combination was intoxicating. Something came over me, something dirty and dangerous. Something I'd never felt in all my life at playing it safe, at being the good girl who never crossed the lines.

Freeing one hand from his hair, I tugged at the neckline of the dress, baring the thin silk bra and my pebbling nipple to his gaze. He licked his lips, his breath shuddering out and bathing my fevered skin. His eyes met mine as he lifted a hand to cup and shape my breast and the connection sent sparks of pleasure along my nerve endings.

My eyes began to shutter closed as he peeled back the material of my bra. I felt the quick lash of his tongue against my nipple, then he was reaching up and cupping my head.

"Watch," he said, his voice harsh and low in the relative quiet. When I didn't immediately open my eyes at his command, his hot, wet mouth closed over the peak and his teeth nipped in warning.

I hissed out a breath and my eyes shot open. Seeing him with his mouth on me, feeling his tongue flicking against the bud of my nipple and watching as he sucked and bit, had all the tender muscles inside of me clenching in sweet agony.

At my moan, he surged up and met my mouth again, his hand going to my breast to tease and taunt. For the first time in my life, I didn't think. My brain simply shut off, like he flipped a switch I didn't even know existed.

"Let's go back to my place," he said against my lips. "Hell, your place, I don't fuckin' care. I want you under me in a bed." His fingers worked quickly, baring my other breast and flicking the peak into a hard point. "Any bed. Mine, yours. Whichever one is closer."

"What about—"

"I don't give a damn about anything else. It's just you and me."

He kissed me again and I had never realized it could be so distracting. That's why it took a few long, heated moments for what he said to penetrate. I pressed my hands to his chest and after a moment, he let me free, though we were both struggling to breathe.

"I can't," I said between panting breaths. "We shouldn't."

His lips moved to my ear. "We can and we should. Fuck everything else. Be with me."

"You don't even like me," I tried to reason.

Dash's chuckle was dark and made me shiver against him. His fingers tweaked both nipples and he pressed me tighter against the wall. I could feel him hard and ready against my stomach. My fingers itched to reach down, take him into my hands and explore.

"You want me to tell you what I like?" he asked. His hands lifted and weighed the tender heaviness. "New on my list are these, but I have a feeling they're gonna rocket right to the top." He brought his thumb to my mouth, slipping it between my lips until I tasted the salt of his skin. "This. This mouth, the way it likes to spit fire sometimes, I love that. But I also like when it's sweet. You're a contradiction, sweet cheeks, and I'm finding I like both sides of you." His lips come back to mine and he bites down, just hard enough to have me gasp. "The sass," he said, then licked and soothed. "And the sweet."

I had to admit, I wanted nothing more than to do exactly as he suggested. Nothing else seemed to matter once he got his hands on me, not common sense, not our past, not the future.

It was exactly that lack of steadiness that had me pulling away. "Wait," I said. "Wait a second."

To his credit, he groaned, pressing his mouth to my neck as he soothed with his hands over my back. Then, he fixed my bra, adjusted my dress—though he took his time about it —and I was half delirious by the time he was done.

As the waves of lust cleared, I could hear the low murmur of people not even a few feet away. My cheeks began to burn with shame and surprise. I'd never done anything like it in my life before. Let alone with Dash, who I'd hated for as long as I could remember.

His eyes met mine and were like burning coals in the dark. There was no hate in them, only lust. "Don't," he said before I could start rationalizing everything away. "C'mon, I'll take you home." He began to move with my hand tight in his, then stopped, his lips quirking up. Then he moved back, tugged the clip that kept my hair up in a sleek bun and watched appreciatively as it tumbled over my shoulders. "That's better."

Without giving me time to think, he pulled me forward and I followed because my thoughts were too muddled to make any sense of what had happened. For the moment, I'd do as he said and not think about it. Tomorrow, everything would return to normal, but for now, I let him lead.

I waited by the exit, letting the cool evening air wash over my heated skin as Dash left to find his grandparents and wish them goodnight. Keeping my mind carefully blank, I closed my eyes and steeped in the delicious thrum I still felt all over my body.

Was this what people talked about when they spoke of desire? Lust?

I'd dated around, but I'd never really been so attracted to someone I forgot everything that mattered. Rather than frighten me, it intrigued me. The forbidden aspect excited me. The way he frustrated me now fed into the fire. Would I ever be able to look at him again without remembering the way his mouth felt on me when we were surrounded by shadows and overwhelmed by need?

Another time, I'd agonize over separating the hate from the heat, but as soon as Dash walked around the corner, his hands tucked into the pockets of his tux, his hair still mussed from my fingers, all doubts fled. Except for one.

Was I making a mistake not taking him up on his offer?

"Ready to go?" he asked as he looped an arm around my waist.

For the first time in my whole life, I didn't want to shove him away. Torn, I could only let him lead me around the hotel where the fundraiser had been held, to the parking lot and his car.

He opened the car door for me, shocking me for the second time that night. I folded myself in and the scent of leather, smoke, and something citrus enveloped me. It was like being steeped in him, and I wondered if it was soaking into my pores. If it was, would I ever be able to get it out?

Not knowing what to do with myself, how to act now that things had changed, I kept my hands in my lap and my eyes forward. Dash didn't seem to have the same problem. He reached across and gripped my thigh, leaving his hand there like a brand. When he did, I shifted and finally let my hands flutter down to grip his.

Holding onto him that way kept me from focusing too much on how crazy it was. This was Dash! Not only was he the guy who'd spent the majority of our lives torturing me, but he was also the T.A. for the one class I needed to graduate. But there were other reasons why we couldn't be together.

Reasons I never thought I'd tell him…ever.

I'm not sure if I could.

Despite the muddled state of my thoughts, I relaxed in his car until we pulled up into our parking garage. As he pulled his briefcase from the back of his car, I slipped out of my high heels. I didn't often go for appearance over comfort and when I did, I was always grateful for the time when I could peel myself out of the clothes and shoes and get back into regular clothes.

We walked to the door in silence, and the tension began to build again inside me. This time it wasn't the fun sort clouded by lust. I stopped him at my door with a quick turn and a hand on his arm.

"Wait," I began, but he cut me off.

"No need to give me an excuse. But this is something we'll need to talk about, eventually. It's not a bell we can unring."

"Why not?" I asked.

"Because every time I look at you, all I'm going to be thinking about is how good you taste."

I nearly swallowed my own tongue. "Dash, there's something you need to know."

He lifted a hand. "I don't care about anything that happened before. If you wanna argue with me, I'm fine with that. I like getting you all riled up, but there's more here than that now, and I think you know it."

"That's not it," I said. My heart leapt in my chest. If his kiss hadn't killed me, the nerves might.

"If it's that I'm your T.A. and the rules, then we'll figure that out if it comes to it. You know I sure as hell wouldn't show you any favoritism."

"It's not that, though it does pose its own set of problems."

"Then, what is it?" he asked.

I paused, unsure if I could trust him with such a secret part of me when I hadn't with anyone else. Maybe it was because he'd always treated me without holding anything back. That he pushed me out of my comfort zones that made me say it.

Because it was the biggest comfort zone I had left, and it was now or never.

"I'm a virgin," I said.

CHAPTER 8

DASH

"A virgin," I repeated.

Layla's cheeks burned bright red, but I didn't think it was because she was still turned on.

"That's right," she said. In a move that was entirely Layla, she didn't look away in embarrassment. That color rode high in her cheeks and her eyes were bright with emotion, but she held my gaze as I rolled the new information around in my head.

I settled on, "Thank you for telling me," when I could get my brain and mouth to make a meaningful connection again.

Her lips trembled with humor. "You're welcome?"

I scrubbed a hand through my hair and laughed. "You gotta give me a minute to wrap my head around this."

She shrugged. "There's nothing to wrap your head around. Tonight was a mistake." Turning, she unlocked her door, trying to play it cool, but I didn't miss the way her fingers trembled around the keys.

"Can I come in?" I asked quietly. "I think we should talk."

"There's nothing we need to talk about."

"Bullshit," I replied.

"I don't think so. It was a mistake. Nothing good could come from taking this any further."

"If you truly believe that, then stop me from coming inside."

With my eyes on hers, I reached past her and pushed open her front door. Her arms fell limply to her side. Tension rolled off her in waves, but she didn't stop me as I moved around her and into her apartment.

I knew I shouldn't be there. If I had any sense of self-preservation at all, I'd turn around, tell her we'd keep our relationship strictly professional—aside from the occasional exchange of insults—and never see her again unless it was in a crowded room.

But I didn't.

Instead, I ventured farther into her apartment. Unlike Ember's cluttered chaos, Layla's place was tidy. A small cream sectional framed the living space, draped with a soft, blue blanket and emerald throw pillows—the kind of shit I'd never think to put in my own apartment. Other jewel-toned accents throughout the room made the place homey and attractive. It's must have been her artist's eye that gave her such a knack for color.

I took a seat on the couch and faced Layla, who'd closed the door behind her, but hadn't come any closer. Patting the spot on the couch next to me, I said, "Come here."

She hesitated, her arms crossed around her waist, then joined me, sitting stiffly, but her eyes were on me, which I took as a positive sign.

"Do you want me to resign?" I asked before she could clam up any more than she already had.

Layla's eyes shot to mine. "No!" she exclaimed. "Of course not."

"If it's the conflict of interest you're worried about, I'll figure something out."

"I'd never ask you to do something like that, Dash."

"Then, what is it? Talk to me, sweet cheeks."

The name had her mouth tightening with anger, like I knew it would. I'd much rather have her spitting fire at me than clamming up like she was.

"I don't want you to think of me like a conquest. Just because I'm the only woman who's ever said no to you, doesn't mean I'm going to let you get in my pants so easily."

I nodded. "That's fair. I haven't exactly been the nicest guy in the world to you, but that doesn't mean I'm a complete asshole." She gave me a look and I amended, "Well, not in this situation. C'mon, Lay, give me a break." When she retreated into silence, I said, "Never, though, really?"

I couldn't wrap my head around it. Layla was beautiful, maybe not the smoldering sexuality like Jessica, but she had a quiet, unassuming beauty that you may overlook the first time, but hit you like a freight train the longer you studied her. But it was more than her looks. She had to have had guys flocking after her. I'd seen enough of them panting after her to know that for sure.

"Really."

"Not that it's any of my business, but why?"

She lifted a shoulder. "Just never seemed like the right time, or the right guy, and I didn't want to have sex with someone just to say I did. Call me crazy, but I wanted it to mean something, at least the first time. Sorry if that ruined your plans."

God, she slayed me.

I moved closer to her on the couch and she stiffened at my nearness. Tucking a lock of her hair behind her ear, I said, "You didn't ruin anything. I'm just not sure where you want me to go from here."

"You're not upset?"

"Of course not." I relaxed back against the couch. "I didn't kiss you because I wanted to sleep with you, well, it wasn't the only reason. I kissed you because I wanted to. I've been wanting to do it again for a long time."

She nibbled on one of her nails and adjusted her legs so one was underneath her body, the other dangling off the edge of the couch. "You have?"

Groaning, I closed my eyes and recalled exactly how she tasted, how she felt. "You have no idea."

I heard the shuffle of fabric rustling, then felt the couch shift beneath Layla's weight as she moved closer. "Could I—would you mind if I touched you?" she asked with such plaintive inno-cence, I groaned.

"I'm not sure if you should," I said with brutal honesty.

When I opened my eyes, she was sitting so close I could smell the remnants of her perfume and feel the flutter of her breath against my skin. Maybe coming to her place wasn't such a good idea. We're alone here. No interruptions. It would be so easy to convince her to succumb to me.

But I didn't want that.

I wanted her to be with me of her own volition.

"Why not?" she asked.

"It's one thing to be with me, it's another for it to be your first time. I'm—" the words tangled up in my chest. "I'm not sure I'm a good enough guy for you to share that with."

The tension around her eyes and mouth softened and a little smile tugged at her lips. "You can't be serious."

"Dead serious, sweet cheeks."

The use of the nickname didn't distract her like I'd intended. Instead she shifted closer. I fisted my hands into the couch cush-ions so I wouldn't reach for her.

"Does that mean if I won't have sex with you tonight, we can't do anything else?" she asked solemnly.

"I think we've done enough for now."

"Then why did you come inside?" She'd moved closer and

her lips were at my ear. I shivered and she nuzzled against the skin there.

When I spoke, it was through gritted teeth. "Because I wanted to make sure you were okay."

"I said I was a virgin, Dash, not that I was completely inexperienced."

With that statement, Layla straddled me in one swift movement that had my eyes popping open and my hands settling on her hips. "What are you doing?"

She fitted her mouth to my neck, and I arched back, but there was nowhere to go. "You're crazy if you think you aren't good enough for anyone," she said against my skin.

Sweet mother of God, I could feel the heat of her through my tux pants and the strain of my dick against my zipper was going to send me to an early grave. "That's a veritable compliment coming from you."

"I'm pretty sure it *was* a compliment." Her fingers began mapping my shoulders, tracing my chest, and I wondered if I was in heaven or hell.

"I always knew you were sadistic," I managed to say.

She let out a throaty giggle. "I think you're masochistic because you sure seem to like it."

My hands bit into her hips. "Oh, I like it, but you need to stop."

Layla ground down onto my erection. "Are you sure?"

"Christ, Layla," I bit out, then drove my fingers into her hair. I took her mouth with a violence that shocked the both of us. After a few moments, I broke it off. Breathing hard, I asked, "What do you want from me?" I wanted to tell her, take it, you can have whatever you want, but I didn't think she was ready for that.

"I think I want you, Dash. I don't understand it. It goes against everything I've believed about us for the past...forever, but you make me feel…" Distracted, she rocked back and forth against me. "You make me feel so good."

There was only so much resisting I could do. I tugged her mouth down to mine. Against her lips, I said, "My pants stay on. That's non-negotiable."

She bit my lip. "Are the non-negotiations up for negotiating?"

"Layla," I warned.

Pulling back, she smiled wickedly. "Fine, I accept your terms."

My exhalation rattled out from my lips. Then I reached up and tugged on the sleeves of her dress. It didn't take much to have them sliding down her shoulders, the red material slithering over her skin, silk against silk. She helped push the dress off her arms and down to her waist.

The strapless bra was a thing of wonder. It cupped and lifted her breasts like an offering. I paused to kiss the gentle curves as she arched her back in submission. Fuck everything else, having her in my arms was worth any sacrifice.

When I took my fill, I reached around to unclasp her bra and the anticipation filled me with a tension that threatened to snap my control. She lifted and splayed her hands over my shoulders, letting me take the lead. I flicked the clasp and my eyes were glued to the bra as it tightened temporarily, then released.

With a care I didn't know I possessed, I set the bra aside and feasted my gaze on her bared skin. Her breasts were perfection. They fit in my hands like they were made for me. Her pretty pink-brown nipples tightened in my palms as I cupped her. Her head fell back, her hair dangling in a dark curtain and brushing against my legs. With her neck vulnerable to me, I brushed kisses along the expanse of her skin.

"You're so goddamn beautiful," I whispered against her throat where I felt her purr.

"When your hands are on me, I feel beautiful. I feel—"

Her words cut off as I tweaked one of her nipples with my fingers. The strangled cry had me gripping her more tightly.

"What do you feel?" I asked as she trembled.

"Dirty, but in a good way. You make me want to do things."

It was getting harder to breathe. "What kind of things?" I almost couldn't believe I was here, with her half-naked and spread for me on my lap. I didn't know what I'd done to deserve it, but I wouldn't let it go to waste.

"Everything," she said on a sigh.

I groaned and took her with me as I leaned back against the couch. "Stand up," I said with a tap on her ass. "Let's get you out of that dress."

She shook, either from nerves or excitement as I helped her to her feet. Her movements were jerky and hurried while she shoved the dress the rest of the way down. Inch by inch she revealed more of her body and it was enough to make a grown man beg. Soft, soft skin. Sweetly flared hips and shapely legs. A flimsy excuse for panties that made my mouth water in anticipation.

When she stood before me in just those panties and shifted from foot to foot, I reached for her and gave myself a few long moments to run my hands over her. Beneath them, her muscles quivered, and I pressed open-mouthed kisses to her belly and on each hip bone.

She breathed my name like a prayer and I'd gladly go to hell to have the taste of her on my tongue.

CHAPTER 9

LAYLA

Control was a thing of the past.

There wasn't any room for self-doubt.

All I had was the kaleidoscope of sensations inspired by Dash's touch.

At his urging, I stepped forward, but he didn't pull me back onto his lap, like I expected, instead, he tapped my thigh and slithered down until I was straddling his face instead.

"Dash! W-what are you doing?" Stammering, face on fire, I tried to move, but his grip on my thighs was absolute.

He kissed my inner thigh and wrapped his arms around my legs. "I told you my pants had to stay on, but I didn't say anything about yours."

With his eyes locked on mine, he pulled the crotch of my panties aside, then brushed his fingers over me ever so lightly. My knees buckled, but he didn't seem to mind. In fact, he pulled me closer, replacing his fingers with his mouth.

I cried out, unable to stop myself. His tongue slicked over my clit and I gasped in shock. My whole body clenched at the warm, wet sensation.

Dash pulled away, used his fingers to spread me to his gaze.

"You said you were inexperienced, but have you ever done this before?" When I didn't answer immediately, he latched on to the enflamed flesh of my clit and sucked.

"T-this?" I asked.

"Mmhmm." I could feel the vibrations of it throughout my whole body.

"No. No, I've never done this."

Somehow, I knew it wouldn't have been as good with anyone else.

"Never?"

"N-no."

"I'll make it good for you." His tongue was apparently good at things other than slinging insults, because he was true to his word.

He shifted, adjusted my hips, and his tongue slipped inside me. I didn't have the words to tell him so; I only had thin, soft cries of pleasure.

It was a tease, I knew that much. I'd never wanted to be filled so badly in my life. At the same time, I'd never been so wracked with ecstasy either.

Even more than the swipe of his tongue and the pressure of his fingers, as he began his assault against my clit, was the *sounds* he made. It had never occurred to me a man would make such sounds while he was going down on a woman. He moaned, he hummed. It sounded like he was enjoying the best meal of his life—and maybe he was.

That, along with everything else, is what worked me over the edge. When I attempted to move backward, away from the constant stimulation, he clamped his hands on my thighs and licked harder, faster. The orgasm locked my muscles tight and I fisted his hands, needing the anchor.

Unbidden, my hips rocked against his face and his tongue slicked back and forth from pussy to clit and then back again. I didn't know I could be so blatantly sexual. I never had been before, but I couldn't seem to help myself.

When I began to shake, Dash carefully rearranged my panties, and then held me steady while he shifted so we were lying on our sides on the couch. He took the throw I'd draped over the sofa back, and shook it out over both of us while I shuddered beside him.

Swamped with an emotional response I hadn't anticipated, all I could do was bury my face in his throat and try to fight my way back to a tentative equilibrium. My breathing erratic, I struggled to get myself under control, but it was almost impossible.

Dash tipped my chin up and pressed a soft kiss to my lips. It was a tenderness I hadn't expected from him, one that undid me as much as any orgasm ever could. I could taste the remnants of my release on his lips and I deepened the kiss, unable to contain myself. Lifting my leg, I wrapped it around his waist, but he made chiding sounds and kept me from grinding against him.

"You okay?" he asked.

Self-conscious now, I nodded, not meeting his eyes.

"Don't be shy now, sweet cheeks. That was the sexist thing I've ever seen. Do you always come that hard?"

I shook my head. "No, nowhere near anything like that."

His hand clenched on my ass where he'd been rubbing to soothe me. "Really?"

"You sound surprised," I said dryly. I hoped the easy banter would help turn things back to normal.

"Nah, I just like hearing how much you liked it."

"As if your ego needed any help."

"That's not why I like hearing it."

The closeness was getting to me. I'd already come once, but I wanted more. I guess that's what people meant when they said once you got a taste, you couldn't get enough. It didn't help I could feel the hard ridge of his dick between my legs and the aftershocks still coursed through my body.

Trying to focus on the conversation, I squeezed my eyes shut, but that didn't help. It only intensified the sensations. "Why do you?"

His hand trailed up and down my back. "I like knowing I make you feel good."

"Such a change from pissing me off," I commented. I hadn't known it could be like this. Not only because Dash and I were normally at each other's throats, but because I'd never been able to relax so fully with another man before. Especially not when I was practically naked, and he was still fully dressed. "Are you sure you won't reconsider the pants?"

"Layla," he said in a warning voice.

"I don't—we don't have to have sex, but I want to see you. I want to taste you and make you feel good, too."

And I did, more than anything. I wanted to satisfy my own curiosity, but I wanted to see him unravel, too. The thought of Dash vulnerable and crazy because of me was more than slightly appealing.

"That's not a good idea," he said, but I could feel his chest rise and fall as his breathing accelerated.

Curious, I made enough room between us so I could slip a hand underneath his shirt. Like a shot, his moved to stop me, but I *tsked*. "You said I couldn't take your pants off. You didn't say anything about your shirt."

He let me unbutton the shirt, slip it over his arms, then throw it behind me, but his expression was stormy. "What do you want to do?" he asked.

His skin was tawny and lightly dusted with springy hair that tickled my palms as I explored his chest. Experimentally, I leaned forward and dragged my nipples across his chest, feeling his warm skin against my own. We both moaned in tandem as his hands fisted in my hair and he yanked me forward.

I could get lost in him, I decided as we battled for control of the kiss. It was bruising, punishing, and I couldn't get enough of feeling the rough contrast of hair against the hard tips of my breasts.

"Hmm?" he prompted. His hand dipped between us to find me wet. I mewled in the back of my throat. "You want to come again? Is my girl greedy?"

I gripped his shoulders with both hands, tried, and failed, to focus. "No, Dash, wait." My protests were feeble at best and he knew it, but I wanted him more than I wanted another orgasm.

My hands dove for the clasp on his slacks. I managed to get it undone and unzipped before he could knock my hands away. I took his mouth with my own and had my hand inside his briefs when he cuffed my wrist with his grip.

"What did I say?" he asked darkly.

I couldn't help but grin. "You said they couldn't come off." He was thick and hard in my hands. I stroked once, slowly, and reveled in his groan. "They're not off."

Silence filled the room, broken only by harsh exhalations, soft groans, or the wet, sloppy sounds of his fingers on my pussy or my hand around his cock. I was seconds away from asking—or begging—to fill me up when he brushed my hands away.

"Dash," I started, but then he adjusted my legs and rolled me to my back. I gasped and then parted my knees for him to brace himself above me. "Oh, God," I said thickly.

"This what you wanted?" I didn't have words, so I nodded. "Stay very still," he warned.

I couldn't have moved if I wanted to, not when he pressed the head of his cock to my entrance and rubbed, torturously, back and forth to coat it with my wetness. One flex of my hips and I could have him inside me. I considered it, but he was thick and long and I wasn't even sure how he'd fit.

Then, he shifted my legs to wrap around his waist and began to rub his cock over my clit with long, slow strokes that sent waves of heat all over me. I reached down to feel him, and he groaned as I cupped my hand over his length to press him harder against my clit.

The head of his cock bumped against my palm with each thrust and he began to groan, softly at first, and then deep and long. Distracted, and rapidly becoming obsessed with the sounds of him in ecstasy, I scrabbled for purchase when he moved abruptly, and his head disappeared between my legs.

This time, he allowed no patient buildup. His tongue honed in on my clit with expert precision, and I gasped as his fingers explored my entrance. As the orgasm swelled, then crested, he slipped in one finger. The burn made me suck in a breath, but any twinges of pain were drowned out as another orgasm swept me away.

When I came back down, it was to the vision of him looking up at me from between my legs, his hand swiping at the moisture on his mouth. Without giving him time to protest, I pushed him back until he was splayed on the couch.

This time he didn't say a word as I tugged his briefs down enough for me to reach in and pull him out. The sight of him had my already tender muscles clenching in appreciation. Dicks weren't theoretically supposed to be beautiful, but his was. A fat, pink head flushed with arousal, slightly thicker in the middle and long enough I knew I'd feel every single inch.

He let me explore, stroking his length until he threw back his head, his jaw clenched. I knelt between his legs and dipped down for an experimental lick. At his groan, I swirled my tongue around the head, tasting salt and heat. I sucked softly, then took him deep, as far as he could go, and his thighs shook on either side of me.

"Don't take this the wrong way," he said, his voice strained, "but I'm about to come, baby, and you should stop."

Not a chance in hell. If he got to taste me, then I wanted to taste him. I wanted it more than anything in the world at that moment, so instead, I met his eyes, and continued to stroke him. He groaned again, his eyes rolling back. I felt him get impossibly harder in my hands, heard him moan, then tasted his release as he spilled into my mouth almost faster than I could swallow.

When it became too much, he reached down and stilled my hands. I released him with an audible pop, and he gathered me up onto his lap as we both came down.

I wasn't sure where we went from here—where could we— but I was going to soak up whatever moments we had left until reality came screaming back.

CHAPTER 10

DASH

We must have fallen asleep tangled together, our clothes half off and me still in my shoes, because when I cracked my eyes open, I found myself in an unfamiliar room with Layla curled on my side, snoring softly. Her hair was a knotted mess spilling over my chest and her mascara was smeared under her eyes, but she was the most beautiful woman I'd ever seen.

I gave serious thought to waking her up and taking her right there while she was soft and sleepy. I could imagine it, how silky her skin would be under my roughened palms, how her body would wake to my touch. I'd want her on the brink before her eyes ever opened, then I'd want to push her over just as she came fully awake.

One day, maybe, when things weren't so complicated.

Instead, I gently shifted her to the side and brushed her hair away. "Layla." When she only groaned and batted me away, I smiled. "Hey, sweet cheeks, it's time to get up and stop being lazy."

At that, she cracked open a bloodshot eye and glared at me, which—fucked up as it may be—was almost as satisfying as bringing her to orgasm. She winced and covered her face, then dragged at the blanket covering us to wrap around her body.

As she sat up and stretched, I got to my feet, readjusted my pants, and zipped them. I tried not to think about how it had felt to have her hands and mouth wrapped around me, how her eyes had smoldered when she looked up at me with her mouth full of my cock. Tried and failed.

Clearing my throat, I asked, "You mind if I use your bathroom?"

She shook her head, her eyes wide, and I knew she was wrapping her head around what had happened the night before. I wasn't sure what side of the fence she'd land on, but I figured it was best to give her time to adjust. I used the john, washed my hands, and threw some water on my face.

The bathroom is where the scent of her was strongest. From the shower or the perfume bottles and lotions she had on the counter. It made me think of her naked, lathering on soap or spreading cream on her skin, and my dick decided it fucking loved that thought.

I found her in the kitchen wearing a blue silk robe. It was thin enough I could see the material of her thong at the top of her ass showing through. I could get used to seeing her half-dressed and sleep-mussed, I decided, and ambled up behind her. She'd had enough time to adjust, and I wasn't going to give her any more to decide it had been a mistake.

She stiffened slightly at my touch as I wrapped my arms around her waist and pressed the growing hardness of my dick against her ass. I didn't want to scare her, but I didn't want her to forget what she did to me either, or what I did to her.

"Dash," she began, then choked on her words when I kissed her neck. Her shiver against me sent shocks throughout my own body.

"Don't get bashful on me now," I said, then moved off to pour us both a mug of coffee. "We're both adults."

She flipped the bacon she was crisping in the skillet. "Yeah, but you're also my T.A. and we could both get into a whole heap of trouble. This…we…"

Handing her mug to her, I tipped up her chin to look into her eyes. "We don't know what this is yet, Layla. I'm not going to push you into anything before you're ready, including a relationship, but most especially sex."

Layla choked on the coffee. "Relationship? *You* have relationships?"

I pressed a hand to my heart. "You wound me again, sweet cheeks. Is sex all you want me for? I feel used."

Fighting a smile, she removed the bacon and put it on a paper towel to drain. "You know what I mean. I've never seen you actually date someone before. I thought you were more…"

"Of a manwhore?" I prompted.

Her cheeks burned and she distracted herself by cracking a couple eggs into the grease. "No, more casual, I guess. You seemed to like to play the field in high school."

"Maybe that's because the one person I was interested in couldn't seem to stand being around me."

She spun around. "Don't tease. I'm trying to be honest with you."

I shrugged. "Whose teasing?"

Her mouth dropped open and she gaped. "You can't be serious!"

"For someone who claims to be so smart, you sure can be dense sometimes."

At that, she returned her focus back to the food and was silent as she turned the eggs, then plated them with bacon and toast. I allowed her to stew a little, and finished my coffee as I sat on a stool at the little island bar and watched her. Every now and again, she'd glance back as though to reassure herself I was there, then turn back to her cooking.

When she set a plate in front of me, she said, "What do you want from me?"

"To the point then, huh?"

She shrugged. "I don't like playing games. And you're very good at playing them. This is one area where I'd let you win—because I don't like to gamble—and we've both got a lot to lose."

I considered her as I forked some eggs into my mouth. She ate like she did everything else, purposefully, no doubt with a plan and a checklist. As she carefully cut her eggs into neat little sections, I recalled what it had been like to watch her come apart, to taste her release on my tongue, and know she could break apart because of me.

I wanted that again. Wanted to be inside her when she did and feel her grip me tight as she came. I'd be lying if I wasn't hesitant at the thought of being her first, but at the same time, I wanted to take her and make her mine.

"You're talking about the class?" I said when I could speak again.

She nodded, sipped her coffee. "It's a requirement for me to graduate for the business side of my double major. If we got caught, I'm not sure what the consequences are, but the one thing I am sure of is that it wouldn't be pretty—for either of us."

"I get that. You're not wrong to be cautious. I didn't intend for any of this to happen, but that doesn't mean I regret it either."

"Then we're in agreement that whatever this is, stops now," she said primly and bit into a piece of bacon.

I almost laughed and I could hear it in my voice as I said, "Not a chance."

Her eyes bulged. "Dash, as fun as it was, we both could be damaged by the fallout. You could lose your job. My major. Do you really think some orgasms are worth the risk?"

I polished off the rest of my eggs and bacon, then got to my feet and pressed a kiss to her surprised lips. "No, I don't. But I think you are." When she simply stared in shock, I smiled. "I'll see myself out."

Before I could leave, there was a knock at the door. Eyes wide, Layla bolted to press her eye to the peephole. She spun around with a hand pressed to her stomach. Whoever was on the other side, Layla didn't look happy to see them.

Her face drained of color, she said, "It's my mother."

She didn't need to explain for me to understand. I recalled all too well the way her mother had treated her at graduation. And that had only been one slice of one day of Layla's life. Who knew how she'd been treated behind closed doors?

"Get me a ziplock bag full of coffee grounds," I instructed, as her face showed increasing panic.

"What? How can you want coffee right now? If she sees you here, she's going to go ballistic."

"I'll take care of it."

Layla shook her head, but she was too distraught to argue for once. "I don't see how coffee grounds are going to take care of it, but I'm willing to do anything. She can't know about us. Not that I'm ashamed or whatever, but—"

I came up behind her as she measured out coffee. "I'm aware of what your mother is like, Layla. I'm not afraid of her, but if you need more time, I'll give it to you. Now give me a kiss."

Before she could argue, I took her mouth and kissed her breathless, kissed her boneless. When all the tension had eked from her system, I ran my hands up her back, then down to palm her ass. She moaned against my lips and I eased myself away, leaving her breathing heavily.

"That should relax you enough to deal with her, but don't let her bulldoze you over. Pretend she's me," I added with a wicked grin. "You don't seem to have any problem handling me, do you, sweet cheeks?"

She ran a hand through her mussed hair. "I can't seem to figure you out anymore," she said.

"Good, that'll keep you nice and off-balance. Just the way I like you."

Shaking her head, she led me to the door. Bag of coffee in hand, I pulled it open and found Layla's mother on the other side. The look of surprise was worth the entire experience. To Layla, I said, "Thanks for letting me borrow some coffee. I wouldn't have been able to start my day without it. Hi there, Mrs. Tate. Your daughter is a lifesaver."

Blinking owlishly, Mrs. Tate said, "Is she?" with a little wrinkle between her brows that said she didn't quite understand what was going on.

"Nice to see you, ma'am," I told her, then winked at Layla over her shoulder. "Thanks again for the coffee, Ms. Tate."

"Mom?" I heard Layla say as I made my way down the hall to the elevator. "What are you doing here?"

Layla hustled her mother inside, no doubt to keep her from ogling me and putting two and two together. I wasn't as worried.

The look Mrs. Tate had given me was one I well recognized. First there was shock. Her gaze had shifted between Layla and me. From my powers of observation, I deduced she was surprised as hell to find Layla with company over on a weekend, let alone *male* company. When she'd realized who I was in particular, a *Hampton*, her eyes had glazed over with a look I knew all too well.

It was a combination of greed, envy, and appreciation that made me want to duck and cover. No doubt there wasn't much fooling going on as far as why I was in her daughter's apartment, but I didn't want to give her any excuse to make Layla's day harder than it had to be. It probably didn't help too much, and I cursed Mrs. Tate for her terrible timing.

All the progress I made was about to be undone, and there wasn't a damn thing I could do about it.

CHAPTER 11

LAYLA

I was at Einstein's the following Monday, trying to pretend like everything was normal. But no amount of cream cheese or cappuccinos could erase the memory of the night with Dash from my mind. And I wasn't sure I wanted it to.

My phone rang and I answered it out of habit, not giving a thought to who could be on the other line.

"What were you doing with Dash Hampton Sunday morning?" my mother asked without preamble. Like she'd been asking ever since she ran into him at my apartment.

So much for carbs cheering me up. I paid the cashier and juggled the paperback with my bagel and the to-go cup of sustenance. "He lives in the building and wanted to borrow some coffee. He'd just moved in. Remember?" If it wasn't in Mom's sphere or directly related to her agenda, it was unlikely she paid any attention to it. I had to tell her two and three times before she remembered anything she didn't consider important.

"I don't think it's a good idea for you to associate with him. His family is influential of course, but he'll just distract you from your schoolwork and the position at Kragen's next summer. Just like your father did with me." No doubt she'd given thought to marrying me off like this was some Victorian era deal to be capitalized on. Her distaste for men after my father left her must have soured her on the thought of the Hampton name.

I pulled the phone away from my ear and wondered if I'd fallen into an alternate universe. Putting it back to my ear, I said, "Who I spend my time with is none of your business. Besides, I can't completely avoid him, he's a T.A. for one of my classes. I literally have to see him three times a week. Not to mention he lives in the same building. I can't use the stairs forever."

Her sigh filled the line. That sigh characterized my childhood. It said, 'You'll always disappoint me.' "Then drop the class. He's bad news, Layla."

"If I drop the class, I won't have enough credits to graduate with the business degree, Mom, so unless you want me to lose the opportunity at Kragen's, you'll drop it."

Then, I did something I've never done in my whole life, I hung up on her. She called back three times on my way across campus to Dash's class alone, but for once, I wasn't overcome by anxiety because of it. I had bigger things to worry about.

I pushed into the lecture hall and then the nerves made themselves known. How was I supposed to be in the same room with him after what we'd done, let alone along with thirty or so other students?

Dash was waiting at the front of the room, bent over his laptop, a crease between his brows. He wore a thin navy-blue sweater and dark wash jeans. I'd always known he was attractive, you'd have to be dead not to notice, but now I knew what it was like to feel that body underneath my hands, pressed against my own. It only took looking at him and I was flushed with heat and want.

As though he could sense me, he looked up and I caught him smiling before he smothered it.

Oh, boy, I was in trouble.

"Excuse me," said a petite freshman as she tried to navigate around me.

Ignoring Dash's grin, I took my usual seat in the back of the hall. It used to be because I couldn't stand being so close to Dash for fifty minutes, but now it was because I didn't want to be sitting around any of my classmates while I ogled him and remembered what it felt like when he was hard, hot, and in my hands.

I could barely concentrate as he began his lecture. I was grateful he didn't feel the need to call on me to answer any questions. I couldn't have formed a coherent sentence if I tried. Besides, I didn't want to draw any attention my way. I was already terrified someone could tell things were different between us, even though it had only been one night. *I* felt different. We hadn't even had sex, yet I felt like he was already a part of me, down to my bones.

"Ms. Tate," he called toward the end of class. The way he said my name made my heart flutter.

Then, I smiled a little. Good girl Layla Tate was feeling very bad indeed. "Yes, Mr. Hampton?"

Dash had been leaning across the podium and when his name rolled off my lips, he straightened. There was a lengthy pause and I imagined he was breathing a little harder. I knew exactly how it would sound.

"Can you pass out these assignments for me, please?" I couldn't be imagining the rough edge to his voice, and I could feel his eyes on me as I distributed the papers along the rows of students.

At the end of class, I took my time packing up my stuff and wasn't disappointed when Dash met me at my seat. He leaned over casually, like he was going to talk about the assignment. With heated eyes roaming over me, he said, "I think you need another lesson, Ms. Tate."

I was sure my eyes were sparkling. "Is that so, *Mr. Hampton*?"

"When's your last class?" he asked.

"Cancelled. I'm free the rest of the day. You?"

"Office hours. But I could make myself busy."

I had a feeling I knew how busy he'd like to be. "I'd hate to be the one to interrupt your schedule. Why don't you come over after?"

His smile faded. "Are you sure about that?"

Slinging my backpack over my shoulder, I said, "I guess you'll see when you get there."

"Are you sure you know what you're doing?" Ember asked, as I scurried around my apartment wondering how I could accumulate so much clutter in less than twenty-four hours.

"What are you talking about?" I was nearly out of breath from sweeping and scrubbing down counters.

"I saw the way you and Dash were looking at each other when you were at my place. I'm assuming he's who you're cleaning for."

I stopped scrubbing the island countertops. "What are you talking about?"

"C'mon, Layla, I'm not an idiot." She rolled her eyes. "He's your T.A. though. Isn't that like against the rules?"

"Even if something was happening *which it's not*, I'd be careful."

"Layla!" Ember said in a chiding tone. "I'm shocked. I'm all for you losing your V-card, but is Dash really the one you want to lose it to?"

I began to wipe down the counters again, but my mind was preoccupied. It warred between memories of Dash and his near-constant insults throughout school and how it had felt being in his arms.

Ember whistled low and long. "Girl, you don't even have to answer that question. I can practically read it on your face. He must have been a good kisser." My face flamed and split with a wide smile. At that, Ember laughed. "Oh my God, I wish you could see your face right now. He must have done better than kiss you. I want all the dirty details."

I folded over and beat my head against the counter. "Ember, I don't know what I'm doing. Part of me still hates him for, you know, everything he's ever done to me. Trust me, he's been an absolute dick sometimes, but then, I don't know, there's another side to him. One I can't seem to stop thinking about."

"Is that side located in his pants?" Ember asked, her voice colored with laughter.

"Don't joke. This is serious. I don't know what I'm doing."

Ember padded to the kitchen and pulled me upright. Tucking hair behind my ears, she said, "Honestly, Chris and I have been together a long time and sometimes I think I still don't know anything about love or relationships."

"Is something going on? Why didn't you say anything?"

She lifted a shoulder as I went to get her a beer. Screw the house. Dash could wait.

"This long-distance thing is no joke. Sometimes we have to go a couple days without talking now. If I bring up how much I miss talking to him, he berates me for trying to control all of his time. Do you think it's wrong of me to want to talk to him, not all day, but at least once a day? We only get to see each other a couple times a year."

I wish I had the answers for her. I didn't feel nearly well-equipped enough to handle relationship troubles. But she was my friend and she needed an ear. "I think you deserve to get what you want, within reason, from any relationship. To not consider your needs or to belittle them isn't a sign of a healthy relationship. But what do I know?"

Ember's smile wobbles. "I don't mean to whine."

Waving that away, I pop the tops to our beer. "Don't even think about it. That's what I'm here for. Why don't I text Charlie and see if her shift is over? We can make it a girls' night tonight instead?"

"You don't have to do that. Even though you're denying it, I know you had some sort of plans tonight."

I already had my phone out to text Charlie and Dash an update. "You come first."

Dash replied almost immediately.

> DASH: Still coming over. I don't mind a Netflix and bash man session. I'll bring the wine and chocolate.

Charlie texted a few seconds after that.

> CHARLIE: Wish I could! I'm working a double and won't be off for another ten hours. Tell Ember I'll call her tomorrow to bitch after I get off and give her my love. P.S. Chris is a cocksucker.

Ember settled on the couch while I changed from the cute dress I'd put on for Dash into a pair of sweats and a camisole with a shelf-bra. I doubted Dash would actually stay once he realized what he was getting into.

Ember was staring off into space and occasionally sipping from her beer by the time I returned.

"Charlie can't make it, double shift. She said she'd call you after to talk."

Ember smiled wanly. "I'm sorry for interrupting your plans for my pity party."

"Acctuallyy about that..."

I was interrupted by a knock at the door. With a cross between a grimace and a grin, I answered it with a mouthed "I'm sorry" over my shoulder.

Dash stepped in with a bottle of wine in one hand and a plastic bag full to bursting in the other. "I brought supplies." After placing the wine on the coffee table, he added, "I wasn't sure what kind of chocolate this situation called for so I pretty much got one of everything."

Ember's mouth opened and closed. "I've got nothing. What's going on?"

"Layla told me you were having man troubles. I'm here with wine and chocolate and am offering to prostrate myself on behalf of all the male species. Take your vengeance out on me or beseech my wisdom, whichever you choose."

For the first time since she came over, Ember's smile was genuine. She reached forward and glanced through the bag, studied the label on the wine, and then said, "There may be chick movies and crying."

"I'm not afraid of tears and I love me some Sandra Bullock."

Shaking my head at the two of them, I took the bag of treats into the kitchen along with the wine to pour three glasses. When Dash joined me as Ember flipped through Netflix for a movie, I cornered him where we wouldn't be visible from the living room.

"You didn't have to do this," I told him.

He tugged me closer, kissing me firmly on the lips. After a second, I relaxed against him. "I know I didn't. But you can call it shallow if you like. Maybe it's just the way I'm gonna get in your pants for sure."

I rolled my eyes. "Dream on."

As I spooned up the ice cream, he hovered over my shoulder. "Don't tell me rocky road ice cream doesn't make those panties drop."

I glanced up and met his laughing eyes. Slowly, I put the spoon in my mouth and licked off all the sticky sweet goodness. His gaze turned heated and I grinned.

"Take the wine into Ember, will you?" I asked.

He did and shouted, "Time to get white girl wasted!" along the way and I had to put a hand to my chest.

It wasn't the ice cream, but the man, who'd shown me a side of him I hadn't realized existed, that made my panties want to drop.

CHAPTER 12

DASH

"This is the best movie I've ever seen," I said around a handful of popcorn.

Ember rolled her eyes at me, but she no longer looked like a wounded puppy. "You're only saying that because you get to see women prance around in bikinis."

I grinned. "That, too, but seriously. It's got comedy, action, and bikinis. What's not to like?"

Ember eyed me. "Are you patronizing me because I'm being pitiful?"

I tossed a handful of popcorn at Ember, ignoring the "Hey!" of protest from Layla. "Number one, I wouldn't patronize you. Number two; if I hated the movie I'd tell you straight up. Not likely, though as I've always had a thing for Ms. Bullock."

"I don't know why Layla calls you the spawn of the devil. You're not that bad."

"Spawn of the devil?" I said to Layla. "I thought I was God?" I added with an evil smirk.

Her cheeks turned a beautiful rose and I heard Ember choke on a laugh. "On that note, I'd better get going. I've got an early shift tomorrow."

Layla jumped to her feet and walked Ember to the door. "You're welcome to come hang out any time."

"I'll bring wine!" I shout.

When Ember left, she had a smile on her face, so I considered my mission accomplished.

Layla gathered the bowls and discarded drinks, shooing me away when I tried to help her. "You surprised me tonight," she said as she began to rinse them under the faucet.

"How's that?"

She shrugged. "I didn't figure you for the type who could, I dunno, hang out and cheer up my friend."

"There are a lot of things you don't know about me," I said.

Our eyes caught as she looked back at me. "Will you stay? At least for a few minutes. Let me finish this real quick."

It was a bad idea. She was caught between wanting me and hating me with enough chemistry thrown in to make an already confusing situation even more so. Teasing her, tasting her again was one surefire way to make her virginity go from a sure thing to nonexistent.

I leaned against the counter, watching her as I considered. Water splashed up on her wrists, and her hasty topknot had started to come undone and spilled over her shoulders. I liked her this way, a little roughed up, not quite so put together. Normally, she was meticulous about her appearance, out of habit no doubt caused by her mother, I'd imagine. I liked it even more when she was all mussed-up because of me.

While she cleaned up, I distracted myself walking through her apartment so I didn't drag her down the hall to her bedroom and strip her down. She hadn't begged me to take her...yet, but my control was on a hair trigger, apparently, so it was best for me to keep those impulses locked up tight.

Layla had covered the exposed brick wall with minimalist reproductions of book pages. I moved closer to examine them.

Boring, dry lines from ancient English classics ought to distract me from thoughts of her naked.

Except, the pages weren't lines from sonnets or novels, at least not any old ones. There were passages from Harry Potter, Star Trek scripts, Stephen King, and Dean Koontz books. I stood, slack-jawed and stumped for a few long minutes. Layla wasn't only a bookworm, she was a nerd.

I couldn't say why I found that so endearing, or why it made me want to kiss the hell out of her, but it did.

It also made me to want to explore, to learn more, to find out what other secrets she was hiding behind those pretty eyes of hers.

I should pump the brakes, tell her we should cool it off—at least until the semester was over—and we both weren't in danger of screwing things up. It would kill me to be the reason she tripped up for the first time in her life. She already put too much on her shoulders, much as she tried to hide that, too.

As she finished cleaning up, I found my way back into her bedroom. The scent of her was even stronger here. It surprised me to find Miss-Nothing-Out-of-Place Tate left her bedspread tangled in a heap. Books were stacked three deep on her night-stand. Her closet doors yawned open with clothes exploding out.

I realized my mistake the second I felt her enter the room behind me. Whirling, my heart began a thunderous staccato in my throat. "Finished?" My voice was a croak, my throat unbearably dry.

Layla only seemed amused, if the smile on her lips was anything to go by. "Get lost?" she asked.

I had to shove my hands in my pockets to keep from reaching for her. "No. Being nosy."

Leaning against the doorjamb, she glanced around her room. "And you decided to poke around my bedroom? What did you do—look in my underwear drawer?"

Disappointed the thought hadn't occurred to me, I lifted a

shoulder and nodded toward the hall. "Why don't we go out and watch another Bullock flick?" Anything to get her away from the temptation of her bed.

I tried to squeeze out beside her, but she put a hand to my chest. The subtle contact had me freezing to the spot, all my muscles contracting. "Layla," I warned.

"You didn't have to stay."

"Let's talk about this in the living room," I suggested.

"We can talk about it here." Without giving me a chance to argue, Layla took my arm and led me to the bed. At my panicked look, she laughed. "Don't worry, I'm not planning on making a move on you."

I didn't know whether I should be amused or relieved. "What do you want to talk about?"

She pushed dark tendrils away from her face. "Don't look so serious. I wanted to thank you for staying, for distracting her the way you did. If you're worried, she won't tell anyone."

"I'm not worried," I told her. She nodded, looking at her lap. "I know you are. You're probably confused as hell."

"You're not wrong there. I think what we're doing is crazy. Maybe it's a good thing Ember interrupted tonight. I'm not sure…I'm not sure I would have been able to stop."

She bit her lip, unable to meet my eyes. I wanted to reach out to her, to touch her, but I knew once I got my hands on her, it'd be a slippery slope. "You having second thoughts?"

"I've been having second thoughts the whole time," she admitted. "You know that."

"That's because you think too much."

At my words, she turned to study me. It used to be I knew what she was thinking just from looking at her. Now, her eyes were shuttered.

Then she met my gaze. "Would you stay?" The words were so quiet, I almost believed I imagined them. "Just for tonight. Maybe I don't want to think anymore."

The next day, after a night where we cuddled and fell asleep twined in her bed, Layla found me at my office after class and proceeded to make up for all the kissing I hadn't gotten the night before.

Kissing her was better than screwing any other woman, I was almost sure of it. It wasn't because she was innocent, although there was a certain primal possession, I got from knowing I could be the only one to be with her, it was just *Layla*. Her smart-mouth was even feistier when it pressed up against mine. She battled me as much with words as she did with her kiss and I ate all of it up.

"I have to get to the library. I'm supposed to be tutoring this afternoon." She was giving me excuses, but made no move to leave my arms.

The door was closed. It wasn't locked and that was a bit like tempting fate, but I couldn't find the resolve to move the couple feet to throw the deadbolt. "Okay, then you should get going," I said.

But she deepened the kiss instead. I let her. Delving into her sweet mouth was a level of bliss I wasn't aware even existed. It was a bliss I wasn't wholly sure I deserved.

I carefully disengaged and kept her at arm's length. "Really, Lay, you should get to the library." The throbbing hard-on in my pants disagreed, but now wasn't the time or place.

"You're right," she agreed, her face flushed. She strode to the mirror on the back of my office door and checked her clothes, her hair. The sight of her mussed shirt and smeared gloss made me ache to see her freshly fucked and rumpled in my bed as she woke up still soft and pliant from sleep.

Christ, maybe I was as big of a dick as she thought I was. Only a total asshole would take advantage of a woman like

Layla. She really was one-of-a-kind. Didn't take my bullcrap, smart as all get out, and underneath her sweet, prim exterior, was dynamite just waiting to be lit. God did I want to fucking light her up.

"Do I look okay?" she asked.

I had to force myself to reply with a sarcastic comment to keep from dragging her off to a closet or something. "No worse than usual."

She took it in stride and rolled her eyes before giving me one last kiss that was all too brief. "I'll talk to you later."

I was still frozen minutes later when Jessica strolled through my door without knocking. At first, I looked up with a smile thinking Layla was coming back, but it faded as Jessica's too expensive perfume filled the small space between us.

In order to get away from the cloying scent—and get a safe distance away—I moved to my chair behind the desk. "Jessica. What can I do for you?"

"Isn't she your student? The one who was at the charity dinner?" She asked it in such a way that I knew she was already aware of the answer. It was a leading question, one designed to catch me in a lie. "I saw her leaving your office."

I studied Jessica in her perfectly pressed jeans and meticulously planned coordinating accessories. She looked like the kind of fake-Instagram ready that made me want to close my head in a door. "What she is or isn't is none of your business."

She chuckled, a deep, throaty sound that would have been sexy if it came from any other woman. "That's where you're mistaken, Dash. I know what I want, and I won't hesitate to go after it. And you're what I want."

"I'm flattered, really, but I'm not interested."

Her eyes flashed in warning. "Because you're fucking your student? That's one way to ruin your candidacy before you've even gotten elected."

Hovering between amused and an insulted, I merely leaned

back in my chair. "I'm not interested because of *you*, Jessica. Cold and calculating isn't really my type. Now, if you don't mind, I've got office hours and papers to grade. You can see yourself out."

When she didn't move, I looked back at her. "Is this where you say I'm going to regret this? Because I won't entertain any threats from you."

She smiled, showing off perfect teeth that must have cost a fortune. "Some things don't need to be said. I expect to have an invitation to the gala your grandmother spoke about at the charity function by this weekend, Dash. Give your grandparents my best. Your grandmother has all of the details."

I closed my office door behind her and frowned.

CHAPTER 13

LAYLA

"So, spill," Ember urged, her eyes gleeful over the top of her glass. "What's been going on between you two?"

I took a sip of my own, barely tasting it, as I considered my answer. My friends would understand if I chose to continue my—whatever it was—with Dash, but for some reason, I couldn't bring myself to tell them.

"Nothing." At their disbelieving look, I rolled my eyes. "I'm serious! Besides the fact he's been an absolute douchebag to me for the past however long, he's also my T.A. Even if we were to, hookup or whatever, it would run the risk of us both getting into major shit. You know me better than that." For additional emphasis, I added, "Could you imagine what Mom would say if that happened? I'd be doubly screwed."

"Let me tell you as someone who recently went through this parental bullshit," Charlie began. "Yeah, your parents are important, but you have to realize this is *your* life. You've got to start living it for you. Period."

Ember nodded emphatically.

I pointed to her. "Don't start."

She raised her brows. "What?"

Wanting to change the subject, I gestured with my glass. "Since we're talking about living our lives. What about you?"

Ember sat back in her seat, trying to look innocent. "I don't know what you're talking about."

"Yeah, what's up with Chris?" Charlie asked.

"I thought we were here to figure out the Dash situation."

I made a zipping motion over my lips. "Charlie still hasn't been caught up on everything that happened. Besides, I can handle Dash for now. Even though *nothing* is going on."

"I don't want to talk about Chris," Ember said with a frown. "Talking about him depresses me."

Charlie covered Ember's hand with her own. "That's not a good sign, sweetie. Tell me what happened."

Ember signaled the waitress and ordered another round. With a heavy sigh, she began, "He wants to take a break, which can't mean anything good. He says we need space because it's our senior year and our lives are about to change. I told him I'd support him in whatever he wanted, like I always have, but he said he needed time."

"A break in a relationship is never a good sign. The whole point is to work through problems together," Charlie said wisely.

I had to defer to her limited experience because I had exactly none. I was in over my head with Dash as it was. The only thing I knew was Chris was making my friend unhappy and if anyone deserved happiness, it was Ember. The girl was as selfless as it got.

Ember lifted a shoulder. "I want him to be happy. I don't know. Things have felt off for a while. I guess I haven't wanted to see it."

"What are you going to tell him?" I asked, my heart aching for my friend.

She downed her drink. "I want to tell him if he's that uncertain about me and our relationship, then he can pound sand."

Charlie and I clinked our glasses. "I agree," Charlie said. "You want someone who *wants* to be with you, not someone you have to convince."

I studied the liquid in my glass. Charlie had a good point and I couldn't help but think about her words as they applied to Dash.

Was Dash with me because he wanted to be? Or was it because of the thrill or the challenge? It was something I should definitely figure out before things went too far. We were already flirting with the line. I needed to figure out what he wanted from me, but also what I wanted from him. The attention was nice, the way he made me feel was undeniable…worth the risk? I wasn't sure.

"I know. I know," Ember continued, pulling me from my thoughts. "Intellectually, I realize you're right." She thumped her chest with her fist. "It's my heart that needs to catch up."

I knew that struggle well enough. My heart was telling me to go for it…but my head was saying not so fast.

"We only want you to be happy," I told her.

Charlie nibbled on a pretzel. "Are you?" she asked Ember.

"Am I what? Happy?" She paused after Charlie's nod. "Well, in general…I guess not. I mean, I want to finish school to become a paramedic. I'd like to have time to be a regular college student instead of parents to my kid sisters, and I'd really love it if my parents would stop being such drunks. With Chris? No. Definitely not. I guess that's my answer, huh?"

Feeling the need to lighten the mood, I said, "I guess now you can let Tripp land one."

Charlie snorted, then choked. She tried and failed to stifle her laughter behind one hand.

Ember blushed prettily and shook her head. "Tripp doesn't see me like that. We're just friends."

"Just friends," Charlie said with a knowing smirk. "That's what I used to say about Liam and now look at us."

"Didn't he try to ask you out a couple years ago?" I asked.

"He wasn't serious," Ember insisted. "Besides, he was a huge player back then, going after all the preppy types. We really are just friends now. Besides, I thought we were talking about Layla and Dash."

I gulped down the huge swallow I'd taken, nearly choking myself. "There's nothing to talk about," I replied.

"Sure, you keep telling yourself that," Ember said.

Girls' night always left me feeling replenished, if not more than a little tipsy and lacking some of my usual inhibitions. Which is why, as I stumbled out of the elevator, I screeched to a halt short of my door when I came face-to-face with Dash.

God, he looked good enough to eat.

He hadn't noticed me getting off the elevator as his eyes were glued to his phone. I didn't mind. It gave me time to ogle him before we began our usual battle of wills. Pausing at the entrance to the hall, I did just that.

It wasn't fair that someone so frustrating could be so damn handsome.

It gave me a heavy feeling in my stomach that increased with each step. I wanted him. I wanted him more than I could admit to myself and certainly more than I'd be willing to admit to him. I'd been so certain I was going to tell him to back off, to go back to the way things were, and then I saw him, and rational thought evaporated.

He looked up as I came to a stop in front of him, the dark slash of his hair across his brow. "Hey," he said, but there was a heaviness in his expression that didn't match his carefree smile.

I tried to concentrate through the flush of alcohol. "Hey, were you waiting for me?" I wasn't sure if I wanted him to be or not.

"Yeah, I was. Can we talk?"

"If we do it at your place?"

His eyes crinkled in a real smile. "Mine? Why?"

I lifted a shoulder. "Because you've been in mine. Don't pretend you haven't snooped. If we're going to talk, I figure it would only be fair if you let me snoop around yours."

He shrugged and a flash of skin winked at his midsection. I tried not to stare. "Yeah, all right. But I'm warning you, it's probably a mess compared to yours."

"I don't care."

In fact, I didn't think I cared about anything less. He jerked his chin back to the elevator and we rode the short trip to his floor in charged silence. With each passing second, I knew the likelihood I'd come out of this—whatever it was—unscathed, diminished more and more. Maybe taking a chance on Dash wasn't worth the risk, but what was life without a little risk? I'd been playing it safe for so long, maybe it was time for me to crash and burn.

"You and the girls have fun?" he asked to fill the void.

I thought back to our conversation, or inquisition, rather. "Normally, it is, but we all have a lot going on at the moment. It's nice to have them to talk to, though."

He nodded, then dug a hand in his pocket for his keys, which jingled merrily as he fit them in the lock. My heart pounded in my ears and I swore the combination of alcohol and anticipation had the temperature around me rising like maintenance had decided to bump up the heat to sauna level. To distract myself from the nerves, I peered over Dash's shoulder and into the depths of his apartment.

Would it be like the guys' dorms I'd ventured into to work on projects? Cluttered with yesterday's takeout containers and last week's gym shorts. Or would it be barren, somehow lacking personality and empty? The quintessential bachelor's pad. I'd been in his apartment before, dozens of times when it was Charlie's, but I didn't think he'd be into the cozy, chick vibe she tended to go for.

"Want something to drink?" he asked as he ushered me inside. "Beer or I can make you a drink, whatever you want."

"Beer is fine, whatever you have." More alcohol didn't sound like a good idea, but I needed something, anything, to wet my suddenly desert-dry tongue.

He moved to the kitchen, which gave me time to study his space. The last time I'd seen it, we'd been packing for Charlie to move out. It had been a husk of a place with boxes and the gaping mouths of bare cabinets. In the time since he moved in, he certainly put his mark on it.

Our complex featured a lot of exposed brick and really great hardwood floors, but that's where the similarities between our two places ended. The accent wall in the living room had been painted a slate gray to complement the darker tones of the sectional. A flannel blanket was draped over the foot of the chaise end with a closed MacBook on top. Framed, matted artwork hung behind it. I slipped off my shoes and stepped onto the deep, plush rug in a dark burgundy and wondered if I'd see his bedroom tonight. So far, his apartment was nothing like I'd expected, if I were being honest. The kid who used to tease me in class had grown-up. What else was there about Dash that had changed I didn't know about?

He brought me a beer and I drank thirstily, the cool liquid soothing my dry throat. "Thank you. Nice place you have here." I gestured with my beer bottle to the console table he used for his TV. It was the same dark burgundy as his rug. He was more color-coordinated than I was. "Want to put something on?"

Lifting a shoulder, he said, "I don't have to, but we can if you want."

"I just need something for background noise."

At that, his eyes crinkled. "Feeling nervous, Lay?"

I rolled my eyes. "What did you want to talk about?" I asked instead of answering.

Dash settled on some sort of competitive cooking show, but kept the volume low for background noise. He pulled me to the sectional and ran his free hand through his hair. "I don't know exactly how to say this, so I'm just going to come right out with it."

Oh, God he was going to break it off. Not that there was anything to break off, but I guess if I needed a sign to tell me how I felt, then I got it. I liked Dash. The thought of him breaking it off made my throat sting. I glanced at the door and considered making a run for it, but then he was speaking again, and I was frozen to the spot, the beer turning to acid on my tongue.

"We're playing a dangerous game here, Lay. As your T.A., it's wrong of me to think the things I do, to want the things I want. I could lose my job. You could fail the class. I know how hard you've worked, and it was selfish of me to put that in jeopardy. The last thing I want to do is hurt you, no matter what you may think of me." He said the last statement looking into my eyes. If this was some sort of trick, it was working.

"What are you saying?" I asked once I could unstick my tongue.

"I'm saying..." He trailed off to take a bolstering swallow from his beer, his gaze darting off. He cleared his throat and looked back at me. "I'm saying, we can either keep going as we are and risk it, or we need to end it. I can handle the moral and ethical ramifications. I don't plan on showing you any favor, if anything I'm tougher on you than most, but I don't want to put you in that position. I can handle them, but I don't want you to if you can't."

Whatever I was expecting him to say, it wasn't that. "I could drop the class."

Dash lifted a hand, trailed the back of his hand over my

cheek, then traced his thumb over my bottom lip. "I want you, Layla. But I won't let you risk your education for me. You've worked too hard."

"You're talking about risking your job for me," I pointed out. "There's no use arguing. No matter which way you slice it, furthering our relationship while you're my teacher is wrong."

He nodded, though his expression fell. "You're right. Of course, you're right."

I took his beer in my hand and set it along with mine on the side table. In the process, I scooted closer, put my other hand on his thigh. "Maybe sometimes it's good to be wrong," I said, though it was barely a whisper.

His protests, if there were any, were drowned out by my lips. He let me kiss him for one moment, two, then his hands were at my biceps, pushing me away. "Layla, sweetheart, we can't."

To hell with caution, with overthinking. For once, I was going to leap, to fly. "I want to. Just once. If it's too much, we can call it off. But I want to know, at least one time."

His eyes widened with comprehension and he choked out, "Are you sure?" Then he shook his head, lifted a hand. "Never mind, don't answer that. I don't want you to change your mind. That was the only noble moment you'll probably get from me."

I smiled impishly. "Good, then I know you've gone back to normal."

"Quiet," he ordered and coaxed me forward with a hand on my waist. "C'mere." His lips were cool from the ice-cold beer, but his touch was warm, and his heart thudded underneath my palm where it lay on his chest.

When I pulled back it was to try and catch my breath. My cheeks ached from smiling. If this was what it meant to feel bad, then it didn't feel bad at all. It felt sinful, wicked.

Addictive.

"Show me your room," I said with a voice that sounded nothing like my own.

CHAPTER 14

DASH

One of us was a virgin, and it wasn't me. As I led her down the hallway to my room, I sure as hell felt as nervous as one.

My bed was unmade from that morning. I had clothes strewn all over the floor. If I'd known she'd see it, I would have straightened up my room before inviting her over. I'd planned on warning her, explaining why the two of us were a bad idea, not inviting her to bed.

She deserved so much better than me.

Layla turned and sat on the edge of my bed, not seeming to notice the surrounding mess at all, despite my worries. She only had eyes for me.

Overcome, I stepped forward between her legs and brought her lips up to mine. She was sweet, so sweet. Once I tasted my fill, I said, "You are so beautiful." The words were more serious than I intended. I meant to seduce her, to charm her, but she charmed me.

"I think I remember you saying I looked like a boy in his sister's dress once," she said with a laugh that crinkled the corners of her eyes. Unable to resist, I kissed her there, too. On my gravestone it would say, 'Here lies Dashiel Hampton. He could not resist her.'

"That's only because you'd beaten me at the chess tournament and I was bitter. I got distracted that day because that dress was see-through. I couldn't stop looking at you."

She slapped at my chest. "It was not!"

I nipped at her lips again and inched her backward. "Okay, maybe it wasn't, but I was staring so hard because I hoped it would be."

She stretched out on my bed, as languid and relaxed as a feline, and I crawled in next to her. "If you hadn't been such a dick all this time, maybe this would have happened before."

"No, I'm glad it didn't. I wouldn't have appreciated you then."

"And you appreciate me now?" she asked, her blue eyes twinkling up at me.

Tucking her hair behind her ear, I said, "Why don't I show you?"

Her pupils dilated, and she licked her lips. "Why don't you?"

I meant to go slow, draw it out and make it good for her the way she deserved, but the girl underneath me had zero patience. The girl who'd been so cautious in every other aspect of her life was a woman with no chill in bed. Her hips bucked underneath me and her kiss had an edge of hunger that enticed me to satiate.

Taking her hands, I grinned. "Don't rush me, Ms. Tate."

She threw her head back. "I'm not rushing you," she said. Then, she wrapped her arms around me, tightening her legs around my hips. "You're just going very slow."

I was lost to her. A better man would have told her this wasn't the perfect moment. Then again, a better man wouldn't have pursued her in the first place, wouldn't have driven her to madness, wouldn't have bullied and teased her. A better man would deserve her, but there was no way in hell I'd give anyone else the chance to try.

Maybe that's why I liked to toy with her so much. She was always so damn perfect, so put-together and sure of herself. That's one thing I wasn't. I might act like I had my shit together, like I knew what I was doing, but I had no fucking clue. Then I'd see her, and it was like I was being pulled in her direction. I had to make her look at me, notice me. I'd been willing to do whatever it took to get her attention. Now that I had it, I was afraid the wrong move would make her change her mind.

I wouldn't give her the chance.

She'd had plenty of time to walk away, to come to her senses.

Now, she was mine.

I let her pull me down to her, let her wrap me as tight as she wanted. It was almost as though she was afraid I would leave, but she didn't need to worry. I wasn't going anywhere. She had me, completely. I was over trying to think otherwise.

Her ferocity took me by surprise. She was in the submissive position, but she was the one kissing me. I took a moment to catch up, but then I was with her, battling her like we'd been doing for years. I welcomed her assault, letting her taste and her hands explore. The places where she touched tingled in her wake, although they were perfectly innocuous. Places like the back of my neck where my hair brushed the collar of my shirt. The inside curve of my elbow. The skin exposed by the neck of my button-up shirt.

Our bodies tangled together, and I wasn't sure I wanted to spend another moment any other way. I lifted one of her legs around my hip, the other entwined around my calf. We fought against each other to get closer. The seam of her jeans caught against my belt buckle and I heard her breath catch. It inspired the same effect as if she'd touched me. God, what she could do to me without a word.

Beneath me, she shuddered and gasped, her hips rising to meet me as though from instinct. As I teased her with nips and strokes, she grew restless. I tried to keep my head clear, tried to take my time, but she would dip her fingers beneath my shirt or claw at my belt buckle and I'd lose myself, my head swimming with thoughts of sex, of her naked. I wanted her naked beneath me.

I didn't know if I said the words out loud. I may have, considering feeling her below me was driving me so out of my mind I couldn't think straight. Either way, she shrugged out of her shirt, then undid the clasp of her bra.

Whatever marginal leash I had on my control snapped at the sight of her, bare before me. Her hands tangled in my hair as I dove forward. If I thought I'd lost control before, it was nothing compared to the wildness that came over me as I tasted her skin.

Layla's sighs turned to moans as I teased her and all too soon the little seduction scene I had planned devolved. I panted against her skin and her head twisted back and forth against the pillow. Her hands tugged at my shirt, but I wasn't in a hurry to stop what I was doing.

"Please," Layla whispered. And that was all it took for me to realize there was an ambrosia more alluring than her sounds of pleasure. I could get used to hearing her beg for me. Maybe this was the key to winning our friendly rivalry, making her want me. Except none of it seemed to matter anymore.

The only thing that mattered was her.

I let her peel off my shirt and toss it aside, but only because her pleading took on a frantic edge. Her hands painted designs on my back, carving her desires with her fingernails. I hissed out a breath against her skin as I tried to wrangle back control.

With impossible care, I dragged her jeans down from her hips, revealing inch by inch of passion-pink flesh. I shed my own, but left on my briefs because feeling her completely bare beneath me was a sure-fire way for this to end before it even began.

"I'm sorry," she said abruptly, as I was filling my hands with her soft, feminine curves.

"What's that?" I asked. Her scent was driving me to distraction.

"I'm sorry—you know—for not being as...experienced." She didn't meet my eyes when I lay down beside her. The vulnerability that emanated from her urged a primal instinct inside of me to stroke her, to pet her until she relaxed underneath my hands.

I paused for a second, then gave a mental shrug. She was being as vulnerable as a woman could ever be, maybe more, considering our past. For her to give herself to someone who practically terrorized her must take monumental strength. Maybe I owed her the same. "You don't ever have to apologize."

She smiled. "Are you sure?"

"I've never been more sure." I said.

"Is this what you want, too?"

"For you to be mine?" Even the words caused me to choke up. I wanted them to be real.

Her bravery faltered, as did her gaze. "Yeah," she said, looking down at my chest where my heart was racing wildly.

"Part of me wants that more than anything."

She glanced back up. "And the other?"

"The other part is scared of hurting you."

"You won't hurt me, Dash. You've always been honest, sometimes brutally so. Maybe that's why I'm not scared." She looked up at me from underneath long lashes. "Are you going to make me wait any longer?"

My whole body shuddered. I wrestled myself back under control and arranged her on the bed beneath me. She trembled, but her muscles turned to liquid beneath my hands when I slid down between her legs and tasted her. I groaned against her skin, somehow knowing her flavor would haunt me. Her legs tightened around my head as I carefully worked at her clit. Quick flutters, long licks.

She was like a drug I couldn't seem to stop once I started. All I wanted was another fix.

When she broke, my fingers dug into her hips to keep her from bucking me off. I kissed the inside of her thighs, her stomach. I wanted to kiss her everywhere I could reach.

"Please," she whispered.

"Don't stop saying that," I said, as I moved up her body. "I like hearing it too much."

Her eyes were glassy with desire. "Please," she said again. I brushed back her hair from her face and waited, hovering over her, until they focused on me. She smiled faintly, her arms twining around my neck.

Layla slipped her fingers under the band of my briefs and my brain went blank. Would I ever get used to having her hands on me? She kept going until her fingers were tight around my cock.

"Probably the only time you'll ever hear it," she said and squeezed.

"I don't think I'd mind that so much." It took me a minute to get the full sentence out. She'd worked my briefs down my hips and I toed them off. I'd never be able to see her again without thinking about having her naked and willing.

Naked—willing—and mine.

I could say it a thousand times.

Layla was mine.

Maybe that's why I'd been fighting her for so long. I knew she was meant for me and didn't truly believe I could ever deserve her.

I kissed her slowly, more for my benefit than hers. The second she got her hands on me, it took everything I had not to go off. Not because it had been a while, but because it was her. She'd ruined me.

Maybe I was about to ruin her. Maybe that made me as bad as she'd always thought.

Maybe I didn't care.

She braced her hands on my shoulders, her nails biting into my flesh. I smoothed away the wrinkle in her brow with my lips and said, "Let me get a condom." More to remind myself than inform her. If I didn't stick to a script, I was going to lose it completely before she ever tasted bliss and I couldn't let that happen.

"I want to," she said, and grabbed the condom from my hands after I retrieved it from the nightstand. I didn't have the chance to stop her and had to grit my teeth as she ripped the wrapper with her hers and then slowly worked it over my cock. Sweat beaded at my hairline and prickled along the backs of my knees.

She was going to be the death of me. That was all there was to it. Here I was trying to be a gentleman, trying to keep myself somewhat detached and in one innocent act, she disarmed me completely.

"I'll take it slow," I said when I caught my breath. *Focus, Hampton.*

"I trust you," she said, and I didn't realize I'd been waiting to hear those words until relief coursed through me.

Poised above her, I fitted myself to her entrance and observed her expression to make sure I wouldn't hurt her more than I had to. Her eyes were closed, but she nodded and said, "It's okay. Don't stop," when I paused with the tip of my cock barely inside her. "Please."

Who'd have thought I'd need the encouragement?

Who'd have thought the barest hint of her would have my muscles going lax?

There was no sweeter heaven than being inside her.

"Open your eyes," I said, without thinking, the words ripped from the depth of my chest. I was losing control—or she was taking it. "I want to see you. Wanna watch you."

I saw in her eyes the girl I'd admired, hated, feared, and worshipped. Felt her open and give all she was. She was sweet, tender…and I was going to be her first. I didn't think virginity mattered until I was on the precipice of taking hers.

I groaned as I slipped inside the slightest inch, clenched by the swollen fist of her flesh so tightly I thought I'd be trapped there. I didn't seem to mind the thought. I'd spent so long fighting her, her physical acceptance was the sweetest reward.

"Yes," she sighed as though she was reading my mind. "You feel… God, you make me feel so good."

"Fuck," I said on an exhalation, pulling back to clear my thoughts and realizing it was a mistake. The friction was almost too much to handle, too sweet to resist, just like the woman herself. The push was almost as delicious as the pull.

She shifted, lifted her hips, searching for more. "Please." Hearing her beg only shoved me closer to the edge. Fuck, I was seconds away from begging myself. "More."

Sweat spread over my back and chest at the effort to maintain a tenuous grip on my control.

Who was I kidding? I had no control left where she was concerned.

She bit her lip and arched her neck.

"You alright?" I asked, the words ripped from my throat. I was barely holding on, but all I could focus on was making it good for her.

She was still for a moment before she let out a breath, nodded. Her eyes focused enough to meet mine. I felt the connection of her gaze almost as viscerally as I did being inside her. "Yes, I'm okay. Don't stop now."

"I'm not going to stop."

She shuddered underneath me and I lost her gaze as her eyelids slipped close Her legs viced tight around me and she rocked her hips up. "I want more."

I froze, her movements having caught me off guard. "More?" I choked out. More might kill me.

"Please keep going."

"I said don't rush me. Always ordering me around." My brows furrowed as I tried to concentrate.

She seemed to be having the same problem focusing. "I'm not, I just… please."

"You keep saying that and this'll be over before it starts."

Her head thrashed against the pillow. "Dash, please."

"No, you're going to listen to me for once."

"I am, I promise I am," she whimpered and lifted her hips to meet mine, sending stars shooting across my vision as I slipped deeper inside her.

"Fuck, baby, you can't do that. I'm already a goner here."

I licked my finger, tasting sweat and musk, and reached between us to stroke the stiff bundle of her clit. Her reaction was instantaneous. She clenched even tighter around me, both inside and out, then loosened, her legs lifting, opening. I cursed and buried my face in her hair.

My strokes lengthened until I was plunging nearly all the way inside her. She lifted her hips to meet me, searching for the friction provided by my finger against her clit. With a soft, beseeching cry, she gripped my hips with her hands and pulled me tight to her. One slick thrust, then I was all the way inside, her thighs cradling my hips.

I saw black. Saw stars. Saw heaven and hell. She was my ruination. My salvation. She was everything.

Her moan broke, then held, her head thrown back, mouth wide. I kissed her throat, nipped with my teeth, breathing heavily against the throbbing pulse beating against my lips. I trembled above her to keep still.

"Okay?" I asked again when I could talk.

"No," she answered. "Dash, I don't—" She lifted her hips to finish her thought, searching for fulfillment just out of reach.

"I've got you," I said. I increased pressure with my finger against her clit, then moved slowly, rhythmically. Seducing her to the edge as much as I was myself with quick, hard thrusts, and slow withdrawals. It was a torment and a tease. Like the woman herself.

I wanted to come more than anything, but I wanted to see her first. Wanted to watch the wave of pleasure crash over her, watch her lose it in my arms. My arms shook with the effort to hold my orgasm back, but I kept the pace, studied her reaction until I found the spot that made her writhe beneath me.

She came, wrapped around me like she never wanted to let me go. Like being anchored to me is what allowed her to fly. I watched as her mouth turned into an "O" of surprise and a flush spread over her chest. Her nipples beaded up, and I tasted them, flinging her higher, sending her soaring.

Then, she said my name on a sigh and sent me tumbling after her.

CHAPTER 15

LAYLA

I couldn't stop smiling. It wouldn't take Charlie or Ember long to figure out what had happened, but I didn't care.

Dash was still asleep in front of me and I was wrapped around him like a starfish. It was the weekend, so we didn't have any classes. I was glad to have a few more moments with him where reality didn't intrude. The thought had me hugging him a little tighter until he chuckled and turned around to face me.

"Trying to smother me already?" he asked.

I pressed my face into the warmth of his chest, let the dusting of hair tickle my nose, along with the scent of him, sleepy and warm. "Not today," I answered.

"Sex makes you compliant. Good to know," he said, and I could hear the smile in his voice.

"You're lucky I'm feeling so relaxed or you'd have a fist in your stomach right about now," I replied.

"Did you have anything planned for today?" he asked. His thumb lazily trailed up my wrist, causing me to shiver.

"Nothing important."

"Good, then you're mine for the day." I felt a little thrill at the words "you're mine" but decided not to read too much into them.

"What do you want to do?" I asked.

His hand skimmed playfully down my back to cup my ass. "First, I want to get you in the shower, then it's a surprise."

The wicked glint in his eye was intriguing. No one had ever planned a surprise for me aside from Charlie and Ember. Certainly not family. And definitely not any guy. "What kind of a surprise?"

He flicked my nose then rolled out of bed. "Now, Ms. Tate, it wouldn't be a surprise if I told you, would it?"

I took a moment to watch him walk naked to turn on the shower. There was a reason all the girls had gone for Dash in high school, and part of it most definitely had to do with his body. Well-muscled thighs, tight, round butt. Broad shoulders coupled with strong arms. The tingle between my legs, coupled with a touch of rawness, made me groan. I pressed my thighs together, but the sensation didn't abate. In fact, it made it worse. It was the definition of an ache, but a good one. I'd wanted him before, but it was nothing compared to how much I wanted him now.

Flinging the covers off of me, I padded into the bathroom where Dash was already under the spray. Before joining him in the shower, I quickly brushed my teeth and rinsed with mouthwash. I'd already let him see me at my most vulnerable, but I wasn't ready to subject him to my morning breath.

That finished, I opened the curtain and stepped into the shower. Dash made room for me, cocooning my body underneath the torrent of blessedly warm water. He pressed my body against him and kneaded out the soreness in my arms, back, and even down to my thighs. My sharp inhalation didn't deter him from working out the lingering soreness, and when he finished, my body may as well have been featherlight.

"How are you feeling?" he asked.

"Keep doing that and I'll be perfect."

With care, he squirted a handful of gel into his hands, then spread it over my skin. I made a sound of surprise and squealed, "Boy soap!" but that didn't stop him from covering me with pine-scented suds.

He paid particular attention to my nipples, tweaking them between his thumb and forefinger, which stifled all of my protests. When I ran my hands over his body, he turned me around and pressed my back to his chest, so I couldn't reach him. I groaned in frustration, but I quickly forgot my dismay as his hands wandered down to pay special attention between my legs.

I braced myself against him as he detached his showerhead from the post, surprised when I realized it came in two pieces. With a few adjustments, the stationary head was soon jetting out in sporadic pulses, which made my skin warm, then tingle with awareness. With the extendable showerhead, he set the spray to a single, gentle stream.

He directed the stream of water between my legs where he used it, along with his hands, to soothe any tenderness. The strength of his body kept me from falling into a puddle at his feet. When he deemed me sufficiently clean, he said, "How do you feel now?" in a dark, low voice that made me shiver.

"I want you," I said, and felt as though my words could have dissolved along with the steam.

Dash kissed my throat. "Not yet, you're still too sore, but I will give you something. Does it ache, sweetheart?"

I nodded, unable to form words.

"I'll take care of it."

I don't know how it happened, how he became the one to soothe when he'd always caused so much torment.

He directed the stream of gently pulsing water at my clit and my knees gave way. He braced my body against his chest, otherwise I would have melted to the floor. One hand cupped the tender weight of my breast and the pad of his thumb rasped against the sensitive nipple. My head, too heavy for me to hold upright, relaxed against his shoulder and my eyes fluttered closed. Breathing the steamy air was nearly impossible, but who needed to breathe, anyway?

The spray of water, like his hard body behind me, was impossible to escape. But I liked I had nowhere to go, liked when I strained against him, he held me in place. Possibly, I shouldn't like being restrained. I'm sure there's some feminist part of me that should be outraged at his presumption, but I liked it too much to give a damn.

I was already so sensitized, from the night before, it didn't take me long to reach a fever pitch. My moans echoed off the tile walls and his whispered encouragements tickled my ear. His free hand snaked between us, pausing to cup my ass, then slid between my spread thighs in a rear assault. His fingers probed my entrance and I winced a little at the sensation. It didn't hurt much. I let him trace my opening, loving it with his touch.

"Does it hurt?"

I shook my head against his shoulder. "No, I like it."

He filled me with one finger, enough so I could feel him and not be overwhelmed by the sensation. It stung a little, but I relished the burn. It was the perfect complement to the gentle waves of pleasure from his attention to my clit. But it wasn't either that pushed me over the edge. It was his taunting in my ear. His words. Him.

Maybe it had always been him.

"Dash," I whispered uncertainly as I crested.

His arms tightened around me, like he knew I needed his reassurance. "I'm right here. I've got you. Fuck, I wish I could see your face. I want to fill you up all over again."

My vision dotted with black and my whole body shook. Carefully, he removed his finger, replaced the showerhead, and turned me in his arms to cradle me against his chest until the trembling ceased and my breathing returned to normal.

I reached for him, but he stopped my hand before I could wrap it around his cock. Looking up at him quizzically, I asked, "What's wrong?"

Dash shook his head. "Nothing, but if you touch me, I'm gonna want more and we should wait a while. Don't worry, feeling you come all over my hand was enough for me." His blunt talk made me blush, but it also made me want him more. I must have shown it in my expression because he laughed. "Let's get some clothes on and get somewhere public before my dick overrules my common sense."

"Where are we going?" I asked as we got in the elevator.

After he'd helped me wobble from the shower, then dried me carefully with a fluffy towel, I'd waited for him to dress. Okay, maybe I ogled him as he did. It really wasn't fair. He made jeans and a long-sleeved shirt look attractive and he didn't even have to try!

Once he dressed, he followed me back to my place and I'd tried to convince him to give me a hint about where we were going, but he wouldn't budge. I nixed his suggestion of a little black dress, that barely skimmed my thighs, and chose jeans and a light sweater that complemented my eyes. The jeans may or may not have been skintight. From the look in his eye, they drove him a little crazy, which I felt was appropriate.

Later, I'd think about the consequences from my actions. Later.

Today, I would forget the rules and enjoy.

"For a ride," Dash said mysteriously.

I rolled my eyes. "To where?"

"You let me worry about that," he answered.

He took my hand as we left the elevator and journeyed through the shadowed parking garage to where his Jeep was parked. He unlocked it, opened the door for me, then helped me up into the lifted seat. His hands lingered on my hips, then he gave me a teasing grin and climbed into the driver's seat.

Whatever, if he wants to chauffer me around town, then fine by me. My mother was due for a drop-by soon, especially since I hadn't given her any indication I'd done as she'd asked and applied to Kragen's. I had no urge to be home when she did, which I'd certainly hear about later, but I didn't care. My whole life had been about catering to someone else's whims instead of my own. Today, I would do what I wanted.

It made me want to laugh that what I wanted most of all was to spend it with Dash.

I shook my head at the absurdity as he reversed out of the parking space. How times had changed.

Casually, like he'd been doing it for years, Dash's hand found its way to my thigh as he navigated into traffic. It made my heart skip a beat, then jump into my throat. We'd done far, far more than the simple contact of his hand resting on my skin, but the affection was unexpected.

"Something wrong?" he asked, glancing over at me.

All at once I realized I'd never had affection like this. Not from my mother. Not from Delia. I could barely even remember my father. I didn't even know it was something I'd been missing until Dash did it without a thought.

An ache burned at the back of my throat, but I forced myself to speak normally. The radio was up, so I hoped he couldn't hear the quaver in my voice. "No, everything's great."

He zoomed up and down the hilly terrain and wound his way through traffic, all while touching me. A hand knotted with mine. My fingers pressed to his lips. His grazing my cheek during stoplights. If he was a drug, I was high on him. By the time we pulled to a stop, hunger had extinguished my curiosity. He'd given me a taste and I wanted more.

His eyes were as hot as the fire burning inside me. "Don't you want to know where we are?"

I jumped at the distraction. Breathing heavily, I turned away from the magnetic pull of his gaze and grappled to regain my balance. I recognized the parking lot and the red brick and white columned building. "The library?" I said, my tone laced with bewilderment.

Of all the places I would have guessed he'd take me, the public library hadn't been one. He unbuckled, then rounded the front of the Jeep to open my door. Every time he did something nice for me, it was like a shock of electricity coursed through my body. Not only because he'd always done the opposite, but because I couldn't remember someone, other than my friends, being so thoughtful.

"Do you have something against libraries?" he asked, taking my hand and helping me down.

"No, of course not." It was the middle of the day and the parking lot was nearly empty. It crossed my mind there was a slim possibility we'd run into someone from school, but I didn't want to think about that yet. "What are we doing here?"

"You ask so many questions," was his only answer.

Normally, I valued being in charge. I liked knowing what would happen, when, and how, but I had to admit it gave me a little thrill not knowing what he had planned. I followed as he bounded up the steps and held the door open for me. He made a beeline for the help desk and gave the woman behind it a dazzling smile. I hid my own as he retrieved a handful of scrap paper from a basket on the counter and two stubby pencils. Apparently even married librarians weren't immune to Dash's charm.

He herded me across the room toward the maze of shelves and handed me half the scrap paper and a pencil.

"Okay?" I said with a raised brow. "Don't tell me you brought me here for homework."

"Don't tempt me. No. When I was younger, my mom liked to bring me here. We'd write notes and put them in our favorite books for the next person to read. After they moved to Washington for my dad's campaign, I'd come here whenever I missed them, and I'd look through all her favorite books to see if I could find any notes she'd written. Your mission, should you choose to accept it, is to write notes and leave them in your favorites. Last one finished buys lunch."

"You're crazy," I said with a laugh, then added, "But you're on."

Without waiting for his response, I booked it to the end of the aisle, already hunting for the titles of my favorite books. I'd never known he used to do this with his mother. It humanized him, turned him from the guy who'd been my enemy to something more. What else did I have to learn about him?

I searched through the rows of books, lost for a while in the memories that arose with each one: *Anne of Green Gable, Charlotte's Web, The Secret Garden*. The notes were a combination of life advice and things I'd wish someone had told my younger self, specifically, things I'd wished my own mother had said instead of the constant litany of 'you're not good enough.'

When I finished, I glanced up and didn't see Dash anywhere around. Curious and feeling a little competitive, I snuck around the shelves searching for him. I found him in the chapter book section a couple rows away. He hunched over a battered copy of *Moby Dick*, which made me smile. I could picture him reading it, engrossed. He carefully tucked the slip of paper into the pages and replaced the book on the shelves.

He glanced up and I threw myself behind the shelves, not wanting him to catch me staring at him. I peered above a row of books and watched him amble down the end of the row and out of sight. A few more seconds passed without him returning. Ears straining, I crept down the row to the place where I saw him put the book back and scanned the titles until I came to *Moby Dick* by Herman Melville.

The cracked spine whispered as I opened it. The pages rustled open to Dash's handwriting.

> *"I know not all that may be coming, but be it what it will, I'll go to it laughing."*

I did the same thing when I found him on the next aisle. This time, it was a copy of *Alice in Wonderland*. It's note read:

> *It's no use going back to yesterday, because I was a different person then.*

These words had touched Dash, the guy who'd mercilessly teased me, who'd been the bane of my existence growing up. I couldn't help but feel like they were a message. Maybe I'd been the person who needed to read them.

Competition forgotten, I ambled up and down the aisles, lost in thought, until Dash found me wandering around the picture book section. "There you are!" He spotted the papers in my hand. "Looks like you owe me lunch!"

I gave him a small smile, but I couldn't seem to look him in the eye. "Guess so. Where do you want to go?"

He lifted a shoulder. "Wherever you want. I'm not picky if you're treating."

I made to move past him, but he stopped me. "What?"

"Did it hurt?"

Laughing, I shook my head and stepped away. "Dash, no."

He blocked my exit. "C'mon, sweetheart. Be a good sport."

I turned away so he couldn't see my smile. He didn't need any encouragement. "I don't think so."

Dash nipped at the underside of my jaw, causing my breath to catch. "Pretty please?" His voice was low, intimate. Like it had been last night when he spoke those sweet, sexy words in my ear.

"Fine. Let me guess. When I fell from heaven? I hate to break it to you, Dash, but I'm no angel."

He pressed a kiss to my lips. If it had a taste, it would have been sugar-sweet. "No, did it hurt when you fell for me?"

The denial is immediate and overwhelming, a wave that swelled in my chest and washed away all my thoughts. "Stop it," I said, my voice almost a whisper and smile turning to a frown.

It was too much. I couldn't handle the feelings that had taken root inside of me the night before. Not when he'd charmed his way through my defenses, then completely disarmed me today.

If this was war…he was winning.

"Stop what?"

I squirmed away, but he pulled me right back. Despite everything inside of me telling me to fight, to run, to hit back like I'd always done when it came to him, something stopped me. A part of me wanted to hear what he had to say next. After seeing all the sides of him I'd never known existed, maybe there was a new side of me, too. One that wanted Dash more than it wanted self-preservation. I swallowed hard.

"Teasing me."

"I'm not teasing you." He lowered his voice even more. "You'd know it if I was."

Instead of answering, I reached for him. Took the kiss I'd been craving since we left his apartment. It was a little desperate, yearning. It took the line between love and hate and blurred it until there was nothing left but shadows.

CHAPTER 16

DASH

She pushed against my chest, but it was half-hearted, and her fingers twisted the fabric of my shirt. The distance between us shrank the longer the seconds drug on. I regretted bringing her to a public place. At first, it had been because I knew I needed the buffer. It was too easy to fall into her, too easy to get lost in her. If we'd spent any more time alone together, I would have convinced her to get naked again. Convinced her to let me inside her. She'd given me her virginity, but it felt like she'd taken a part of me instead.

I stared deep into her eyes, the playful smile on my lips disappearing. "What are you doing to me?" I asked, my tone softening from teasing to questioning.

She flinched, then licked her lips. Her voice was breathy when she answered. I imagined her on her knees, licking her lips like that as she held my dick. She was barely touching me, and I wanted her with a fierceness that superseded common sense. "I'm not doing anything."

She was everything.

"I think about you all the time now," I told her, the words wrenched from my chest like she was my absolution. "Used to be it was because I liked getting a rise out of you. I'll admit, arguing with you is fun. Part of it was knowing you'd be thinking about me for hours afterward."

"I don't think about you for hours," she protested.

I studied the flushed swells of her cheeks and thumbed her red lips. "You think about me so much, that's why you're always so fired up when you see me. You think about me so much it pisses you off. You wish you could dismiss me as easily as you claim."

"I can," she says defiantly, tossing back her mane of brown hair. I'd believe her more if her hands weren't roaming over my chest.

"If you could, then what are you doing here with me now?"

Her mouth dropped open and I took advantage of her surprise with a kiss that tempted us both. Lips parted, she moaned against mine, then submitted, her body going lax.

And. I. Fucking. Loved. It.

Watching her fight how much she wanted me, and then succumbing to it, had to be the hottest fucking thing I've ever experienced. Women had wanted me, chased me, fallen for me, but never, not once, have they fought against it. Tried to run. Not like Layla did. For years I'd been trying to catch her. And, God, how I enjoyed the chase.

"Let's get out of here," she whispered against my lips. Her words tasted of desperation. It would have been easier to say yes. "Let's go back to your place. I want you. Please."

"You only say that because you don't want to have to think about what's going on between us. You want to run away from what's happening here, just like you're always running from me. Sex is easy, it's feelings that are hard."

She pulled away. "Why do we have to complicate it? Life is complicated enough as it is."

"The things in life that are most worth it never come easy. Maybe I think you're worth it." My words stole her protests and while she had time to think, I tugged her toward the exit. "Let's get something to eat. Are you hungry?"

"Really, Dash? You're just going to ignore the whole thing? We have to talk about this." I had to be a bastard, because much as I liked her, there was something about hearing the frustration in her voice that brought a satisfied smile to my face. Surprise or disbelief had her pulling away. I glanced back and found her frozen in place.

"I'll buy you ice cream after lunch. Chocolate fudge, whatever you want. C'mon."

She hesitated for a moment on the edge of indecision, then took my hand. "It'd better be a big one."

I took her to the Railroad Square Art District, a little bohemian mecca for occultists and obscure art collectors and distributors. Situated in the heart of Tallahassee, it's nestled on a railroad track and shaded by ancient oaks, like much of the rest of the capital city. Funky little businesses occupy candy-colored storefronts. It has everything from a second-hand store to an herbalist to an eco-tourism place.

When I first came to Florida State as an undergrad, I took advantage of the nightlife. Wasted away thousands of hours trolling the bar scene, the party scene. They didn't call FSU a party school for nothing. Since I've come back, I've spent most of my free time exploring the city for hidden nooks like this one.

"Where are we going?" Layla asked when I came to a stop in a shaded gravel parking area. "Where are we?"

"You're treating me to lunch. Then we'll hunt down some ice cream."

"You act like that's going to solve all of our problems."

I shrugged as I helped her out of my Jeep. "You act like ice cream doesn't solve all problems on a regular basis."

She harrumphed, but followed me down the road nonetheless. When I took her hand, she didn't protest. Baby steps.

"There's a little restaurant just over here. It's actually made from the caboose of a train. I think you're really going to like it. They've got good beer and great sandwiches."

As a plus, the area didn't get much business in the middle of the day, so we were unlikely to be spotted by anyone. Campus may be huge, but my father had campaigned enough that it wasn't out of the norm for me to be recognized. Word traveled quickly when you were named one of Tallahassee's Hottest Bachelors. Even more quickly when you were teaching.

"I'm only going with you because I'm hungry," she said, then gasped as we drew closer to the train car.

It was painted a faded red that drew the eye. We approached from the back where a large sign advertised open spots for entertainers. The entrance was on the short side of the car and facing the front was an outdoor seating area under an open-air structure. A small stage was situated under lights that must be stunning at night all lit up.

"This is beautiful," Layla said with a sigh. "It's so cute!"

I held open the door for her. "I thought you might like it. The meatball sub is especially good."

Small two-person tables lined the wall of windows to the left and a bar flanked our right. Layla took a seat at the bar and studied the menu written in colorful chalk on the wall in front of her.

Needing to touch her, I always seemed to have some part of me connected with her, I laid a hand on her shoulder and stood behind her. She rested her cheek, just for a moment, on my hand, then went back to reading.

This.

This was why I kept coming back to her even though experience, common sense, and even the girl herself kept warning me away.

One touch from her struck me deeper than any other. It meant more, made me feel more, than anything else I'd ever known.

The owner finished with another customer and moved down the bar to take our orders. I thumbed Layla's cheek, loving the texture of her skin under my hands, as she ordered a meatball sub and a bottle of water. I got a brat with cucumber salad and a craft beer. She paid without comment, even though I grinned unabashedly.

"You can wait here or outside, and I'll bring it right out to you," the owner said.

"Lead the way," I said.

The bit of Indian summer we were experiencing had the temperature at a balmy sixty-nine degrees, so Layla didn't hesitate to step through another door and into the outdoor eating area. Benches peppered the space and she chose the one closest to the door. We were the only ones sitting outside and I was grateful for the privacy. I wasn't quite ready to share her yet. I liked having her all to myself.

"Why are you doing this?" Layla asked after taking a sip from her water. She played with the cap as she spoke, twisting the top on and off.

"Feeding you?" I asked. "I've known you long enough to realize you're better when you're fed."

She rolled her eyes. "After we eat, are we going to discuss what we're going to do about this? And don't play dumb. You know what I'm talking about."

I rested my elbows on the picnic table where we were sitting and nodded. "Sure, we can talk about it. We can talk about it all you like. After we eat, and that includes ice cream. I want you in the best possible mood before we have this discussion."

"You just want to tip things in your favor, but I have news for you, Dash, lunch and ice cream isn't going to change our situation."

"You never know," I waggled my eyebrows at her. "You haven't had it yet. Let's make a deal: you drop the discussion talk until after we've eaten and when we're done, we can hash things out. I won't dodge questions, and I'll respect whatever decision you come to in the end."

She pressed her lips together, her posture straightening in interest. "Even if I say we can't see each other anymore? Including get-togethers with my friends and those little verbal sparring matches you seem to like so much?"

I nodded in affirmative. "Whatever you decide, I'll respect. Even if it's not what I want."

She hesitated, lifted a shoulder. "Why do you care so much?"

"Shouldn't I?" That seemed to stump her. I can't say I didn't enjoy watching her struggle for words.

"If you want to talk, I'll be asking the questions."

I gestured for her to go ahead.

"You'll tell me the truth?" she pressed.

"I've never lied to you, Lay, I don't plan on starting now."

"Why didn't you go into politics like your dad?" It was a question I've gotten several times before—from my friends, family, the press. It's one I normally dodged with a joke and a change of subject.

"Getting right to the good stuff."

She sipped her water. "You promised."

"I guess because I wanted to prove I could make it on my own. If I would have followed in the great Hampton footsteps right away, there would have been no way for me to distinguish myself from the name. I wanted to earn what I get on my own terms."

Layla didn't comment, but there was no mistaking the smile on her lips. "If you could be anything in the world, what would it be?"

I could have answered anything, could have made up something that wouldn't have been so embarrassing, but I didn't. I cleared my throat. "A father." My voice didn't tremble, but I could feel my throat flush.

She choked on her water. "What? Really?"

"Why the tone of surprise?" I asked.

"I guess I never thought about it. Why a father?"

I had her whole attention and I couldn't deny having those wide curious eyes wholly devoted to me. I lifted a shoulder. "My grandparents may not be the warmest people in the world, but my parents are wonderful. I had a great childhood growing up. I want what they have. The partnership. The commitment. The family. They only had me, but I think I'd want to have two or three rugrats. What about you?"

"Do I want a family?" She fiddled with the cap of her bottle, readjusted her legs. "I'm not sure, I guess I haven't thought about it much. I've been so focused on school and graduating, there never seemed to be time for anything else."

"I would have thought you'd have it all planned out by now."

She laughed and it lit up her eyes. "Maybe that's the next step after graduation and getting a job. One thing at a time."

"That all you wanted to know?"

"Not even close, Hampton."

CHAPTER 17
LAYLA

A father.

That had been the last answer I'd expected him to give. An entrepreneur, a rock star, an athlete. Those had been the answers I would have thought he'd give. Something with flash and prestige. A career that would put him in the limelight he so clearly deserved. A father had been nowhere on the list. He may as well have said an orangutan.

Once the words came out of his mouth, though, I couldn't stop picturing him toting around babies, joking with smart-mouthed preteens. Kissing a heavily pregnant wife. He'd be a great father. The image shouldn't be so appealing, but it was. I guess that's what people meant when they talked about ovaries exploding.

Family had never equaled happiness to me, not really. It had meant obligation. Guilt. Disappointment. Family had always emphasized the things I lacked.

My sister, Delia, had never experienced the same; she'd always been the Golden Child, She-Who-Could-Do-No-Wrong. She had my mother's unflinching support and praise and didn't seem to understand why I was always so downtrodden.

"Get over it, Layla. Just do what she says, and she'll leave you alone. If you'd stop arguing with her, she wouldn't be so hard on you."

Delia had never gotten the verbal abuse I did. She either didn't care or didn't realize it was wrong because it had been the same all of our lives. Maybe she was just grateful she wasn't on the receiving end of one of Mom's tongue-lashings.

Mom...I'd never felt like family to her. Or she to me. She'd been a dictator, a bully, a drill sergeant, but never what I thought a mother would be. I'd never known any different until I went to school and was exposed to how other mothers treated their daughters.

Seeing other families together had only underscored the notion I was the reason we couldn't have a normal relationship. She'd said as much to me often enough; it didn't take long for me to believe her. After all, she was the authority figure, the adult, my parent. Who was I to know any different?

Dash waved a hand in front of my face. "Did I lose you?"

Before I could answer, the owner came out with two plates full of food. The scent of cheese and sauce made my mouth water. He sat our plates in front of us with a flourish. "Can I get ya'll anything else?"

Dash looked to me and I shook my head. "No thank you," he said. "This looks great."

I took a bite of my sub sandwich and groaned. An explosion of fresh bread, thick sauce, and sharp cheese coated my tongue. "Oh my God," I moaned.

"Good?"

"So good." I took another bite, then a sip of my water. "So, a dad, huh? I can see that." All too clearly. It made what had happened between us last night all the more...real.

He looked up from his plate, "Oh, you could?"

"I mean I don't think you'd let them die or anything," I quickly corrected.

His laugh made his eyes light up. Seeing it made me want to

make him laugh all the time. I liked it almost as much as seeing his expression go stormy with anger or irritation. Maybe there was something to the way he liked to provoke me. Did he feel the same way about me when we were arguing?

"Well, thanks for the vote of confidence." He paused to eat some of the side cucumber salad he'd ordered. "If you could do anything, what would you do?"

I thought about my mom's insistence about the finance job. About the flush of accomplishment and satisfaction I felt during my student teaching hours. There was no comparison. "I'd be a teacher." My mouth moved without conscious thought, and I spoke without hesitation coloring my voice.

"Why do you let your mom push you into the business thing, then, if that's not what you really want?"

Stuffing my face with spicy tomato sauce and well-seasoned meatballs seemed like the best response. He waited patiently, eating his own meal in the meantime. Patience was a quality I'd never considered Dash to possess, but he did in spades. In class, in his personal life, with me.

I ate half my sub before I broke down and answered. "Sometimes it's easier to buckle under and do what she wants, so she'll get off my back. She's paying for my degrees, some of my bills. I don't have much of a choice."

"Do you ever stand up to her?" he asked.

Pointing my drink at him, I said, "I thought this was supposed to be my rodeo. I'll be asking the questions."

He made a 'go-ahead' gesture with his brat, but I knew he wouldn't be dropping the subject, simply filing it away for later.

"Why me?"

The question slipped out, again without thought. It was getting too easy for me to drop all my barriers around him. Too easy to let him see and possess parts of me without my permission.

I shook my head at myself, my tongue tangling. "You don't have to answer that. It was a stupid question."

Dash reached across the table, dwarfed my hand with his. "I'll tell you as many times as you need to hear it. I'll keep answering it until you believe me. It's you because it's always been you, even when I didn't want it to be. It's you because as much as you hate me, I know you like me just as much." At my burning look, he laughed and corrected, "Okay, maybe you hate me a little more."

"What are we going to do about this? We both have a lot to lose."

He turned my hand over in his, twined our fingers together. "I don't know what we're going to do. I don't have the answers here anymore than you do. I can tell you what I want."

I finished my sandwich one-handed, almost afraid of asking, but I did because I had to know. I burned for the answer almost as much as I ached for him the night before. "What do you want?" I was nearly breathless with anticipation.

He had no hesitation and his unflinching gaze was on me. I wasn't at all prepared for what he said. "I want to see where this is going to go. I want to get to know you more. I want to see you. And I'm willing to take that as fast or as slow as you want."

"And if I said I thought we should go back to a professional relationship, at least until the semester was over?"

Dash took my plate and empty water bottle, threw it and his own away in the trash. He helped me up from the table and tucked me into his side. "Then, I'd understand, and I'd be patient. You're worth waiting for."

He seemed to realize I needed time to process, and we walked hand in hand back to his Jeep after finishing our meal. He closed the door behind me, and I buckled myself into the seat as I contemplated his words.

Dashiell Hampton wasn't only the bane of my existence. He was also a talented teacher, a focused student, an aspiring businessman, a loyal son and grandson, and maybe, possibly…the man I was beginning to love.

He was a whirlwind. There was no other way to describe it. I'd coast along, thinking I had everything planned out, every eventuality carefully plotted and decided, and he'd scoop me up like a tornado and drop me miles away from my previous destination.

Dash wasn't anything like I'd planned. He was so much more.

I wasn't entirely sure how I was going to handle it, until I saw his grandmother, her name was Elizabeth, I remembered, standing at my front door. Much like her grandson had been doing not so long ago.

"Mrs. Hampton," I greeted, as I walked across the hall from the elevator. I was all too aware of Dash's taste still lingering on my lips, the ghost of his hands still branding my waist. "Please, come in." Whatever it was, it couldn't be good. The look in her eye wasn't congenial, but I motioned into my apartment after unlocking the door. When we were both inside, I asked, "Would you like something to drink? Water, coffee?"

She clutched her purse and shook her head. "No, thank you, I won't be here long."

Anxiety clutched my belly tight. "Well, what can I do for you, Mrs. Hampton?"

"When I met my Edward, I wasn't much different than you; a reasonably attractive woman, from an acceptable family, attending college for a lucrative degree. I was in law school when we met. Of course, I quit my dream school because I knew what it would take to be a Hampton wife." She pinned me with a hard, unflinching gaze. "Edward's mother, Clarissa, didn't think I had what it took to be a good wife to her son, and if Dashiel's parents weren't so busy on the campaign they'd tell you the same thing. You are not the woman for him, you will never be the woman for him. He needs someone who understands his family, his future, and isn't afraid to go after what she wants, to stand up for herself. You are none of those things."

My back stiffened. Heat painted the base of my neck. "Excuse m-me?" I stammered. "You don't know anything about me." The words barely made their way over my tongue, which had the taste and texture of a baked Nevada highway at noon. The fact she spoke aloud the fears, I didn't even realize I had, made my stomach threaten to reject the delicious lunch Dash had treated me to.

She shook her perfectly coiffed head and smiled knowingly. "I know everything about you, Layla Lucille Tate. I know you're a Business-Art major, which tells me you can't even make up your mind about what you want with your future, let alone give my grandson the attention and dedication he'll need. Before this gets any more difficult, I'm here to advise you to do the right thing and let him go. Let him go before this affects both of your futures."

I was quite simply, without words. She reminded me so much of my mother, the same self-assured singlemindedness. It didn't occur to her, maybe I was the right person for Dash, even if I wouldn't admit it to myself. It didn't occur to her, it wasn't her place to meddle in our lives. Just like my mother, she thought she could dictate to and micromanage those around her without a protest or complaint.

She started for the door, already certain I would comply with her demands. "I trust we have an understanding?" she said over her shoulder.

Before I could so much as reply, she was out of the door and it swung shut with a smart click before I could even unclamp my jaws. I folded limply into a pile on my couch, still staring at the door where Elizabeth Hampton had disappeared, her expensive Chanel perfume still lingering in the air.

I'd barely had time to process the night with Dash, the day, and now this? I couldn't seem to get my head on straight before something crashed in and destroyed what little certainty I'd managed to scrape together. And I couldn't talk to anyone about this.

My friends still didn't know we were together, and I couldn't tell them. Especially not now. Admitting to anyone what had happened would put both of us at risk.

I'd wanted more time to figure things out. To understand how I was feeling.

Time I didn't have.

There wasn't much I thought Dash and I had in common, until now. He'd been born into a sterling family name, the proverbial silver spoon in his mouth. He wouldn't have to fight for what he wanted—it was handed to him. A cushy career in politics, a vast family fortune. Status, wealth, prestige. It didn't hurt that genetics had blessed him with a face fit for a prince. He never wanted for anything. Whereas I had to fight for every-thing. I'd only succeeded so far because I worked for it all. My mmmmother liked to put on a mask that we were upwardly mobile, that we had money and she certainly spent it like we did, but when my father abandoned us, he took his bank account with him. We had our name and little else.

But the one thing Dash and I had in common was apparently the women in our lives, pushing, manipulating, orchestrating. Every moment planned, every step carefully mapped out. I had my mother—he had his grandmother. It made me wonder what other parts of his life had been controlled by his family like mine had.

Needing to think, knowing I couldn't let anyone else make the decision for me, I headed for my bathroom and pulled the shower curtain aside. I set the water to steaming hot and let the bath fill as I poured myself a glass of wine and lit candles. I pushed the dilemma to the back of my mind, as I poured cherry blossom bubble bath in the running water and stripped. It may have been my imagination, but I could still feel Dash's hands on my bare skin.

By the time I stepped into the water, steam was already curling the ends of my hair and I'd come to a decision.

CHAPTER 18

DASH

I f I thought it had been worse before, seeing her in class the following week was something akin to hell.

This time, she didn't spend the whole hour ignoring me, pretending I didn't exist. She studied the text as I lectured, took notes—because who was Layla if not the dutiful student—but in between the notes, her eyes would be on me. They burned with an intensity I'd never seen in her before.

I spent the hour lost in thought, lecturing purely by memory, wondering what was going on behind her stare. Had she decided to walk away? I couldn't necessarily hold it against her if she had. Our timing was shit. Did she blame me? I would. I took advantage of her, in more ways than one. Used our history to get her into bed, risking both of our futures.

There wasn't one good reason she should even consider anything I'd said the day before or my carefully reasoned arguments that had gotten her into bed.

Everything was against us. Hell, even I'd done my best to sabotage us in the beginning.

By the end of class, if I hadn't written the lecture and given it several times, I wouldn't have known what the hell I talked about. I considered dropping to my knees right there in front of God and everyone and begging. Is that what she wanted? For me to beg? I was more than willing.

Without looking up, I packed my things. I was sure if I did, I'd watch her walk away and I didn't want to tempt myself. Layla hated scenes, being the center of attention. By the time I'd carefully stowed away my laptop, phone, pens, and anything else I could think of to give myself more time, I'd at least gotten my hands to stop shaking.

Christ. What was this girl doing to me?

When I couldn't put it off anymore, I looked up.

And there she was.

Layla.

A knowing smile sat on her lips as though she could read my mind.

When had she become the aggressor in this little scenario?

Probably around the time I got my first taste of her, if I were being honest with myself. Maybe even before that. Maybe it had been the first lashing she'd ever given me with that sweet tongue of hers.

My feet drew me toward her without thought. She stood, shouldered her bag, and waited for me.

I stopped when I could scent her. Clean, something simple. Something that invited me closer to find all the places where it lingered on her skin. Oh, how I wanted my mouth on her again. I would have given anything to taste her.

"Mr. Hampton," she greeted soberly.

All I could do was nod.

"Do you have office hours now?" she asked.

I had no idea, but I held out a hand for her to lead the way. If I didn't, I'd cancel whatever class I was supposed to be teaching next.

When I found my voice, I said, "What is it you want to talk about, Ms. Tate?"

I couldn't read her expression. "We can discuss it when we get to your office," was all she'd say.

I followed her out of the lecture hall, through throngs of students, and wondered if I could convince her not to throw us away before we'd even got started. If my friends from high school could see me now, they wouldn't believe the womanizer Dash Hampton was following a woman around like a forlorn puppy dog.

She stood patiently as I unlocked my office door and let her in. It closed behind us with a pronounced thump and I locked it, just in case. With exaggerated care, I placed my bag beside my chair and turned to face her. For the first time, I couldn't read her expression, so I memorized the moment instead.

She was wearing jeans and some sort of sweater combo, one whose neckline dipped just enough to tease at the tops of her breasts and nip in at her waist. Her dark hair tumbled around her shoulders and I wanted to bury my face in her throat where her scent was the strongest.

As I studied her, she sat in the chair across from my desk, crossed her trim legs, and knotted her hands in her lap and simply waited, watching me.

"What is it, Lay?" I asked when the silence great to be unbearable.

Was she enjoying this?

The smile that bloomed on her lips said she was. "I thought we should talk."

I relaxed into my chair, feigning a nonchalance I absolutely did not feel. "About what?"

"Us," she said simply, and rose from her chair to sit on the edge of my desk, bringing her close enough I could feel her soft heat.

"What about us?"

"After you brought me home, I thought a lot about every-thing that's happened." Was I imagining it, or did a shadow cross her expression? I tensed as she continued. "I think if we were to continue our relationship right now, it wouldn't end happily. One of us would get hurt or we'd get caught." I opened my mouth to argue, but she held up one slim finger and I shut it. "What we're doing is risky and would have consequences for both of us if we were seen and someone reported it to your superior." She was basically repeating the argument I'd given her a few days ago.

Although I knew she was right, I couldn't help but protest. "Then we'd be careful."

But she shook her head. "We were already taking a risk yesterday. All it would take is one person. Do you really want to spend the beginning of whatever this is constantly looking over your shoulder, wondering if we're going to get caught?"

What she was saying made sense, hell, I'd told myself the same on several occasions. That didn't mean it didn't suck to hear. Stop being a pussy. "I told you I wouldn't push you into anything, and I won't. Graduating means everything to you, and I understand that."

I sounded like one of her academic advisors.

She nodded. "Good. I'm glad we're on the same page."

I wanted to grab her, so I clenched my hands into fists. "Good. Was there anything else you wanted to talk about?"

"No, that about covers it."

How was this so easy for her? I'd never had much of an explosive temper, but the frustration that rose inside of me at her casual tone made me want to rage.

When I spoke, my voice was as rough as gravel. "Was that all?"

Layla straightened, stepped closer. Christ. "So, we have an agreement?"

I nodded jerkily. "Of course. I'll keep my space. No one has to know what happened. Our relationship from this point on will be purely professional. I should apologize for crossing that line, but I'm not fucking sorry."

"You don't have to apologize. You're not the only one at fault here."

I wished she'd give me some space. There was only a breath of room between us and with her standing in front of me; I was level with her chest, craning my neck to look up at her. "You're my student. I pushed you and you know it."

"Then we'll just have to wait until I'm no longer in your class. Then you won't have any excuses."

My hands unclenched. "No, I was such a—wait, what?"

She smiled. "Until class is over, we won't see each other outside of the lecture hall. We'll keep our relationship completely platonic—at least until the end of the semester." She lifted a shoulder. "This way we can both cool off and decide if what happened was just hormones and lust, or if there's something more there without the risk of putting our futures in jeopardy."

I swallowed and almost choked on my own tongue. "So you aren't breaking things off?'

"Well, sort of. At least until after the semester. No more of those come-fuck-me-looks, no more flirting, no more lingering in the hallway in front of my apartment, and definitely no more kissing."

"No more kissing?" The end of the semester was an eternity away. Four or five weeks at least, if not more. I couldn't think straight. Could I last that long?

She shook her head. "None." Her confident tone and expression faltered. "W-what do you think?"

I reached out, took her hand, and pulled her onto my lap. Her thighs spread over my legs and I was grateful my desk chair had no arms, allowing her to fit close to me.

"I think if we're going to spend the rest of the semester without any kissing, then I'd better get my fill now."

I covered her mouth with my own and she pressed her hands against my chest. When she broke apart, I buried my face in her throat.

"What are you doing?" she asked, and it pleased me to find her breathless.

"Paying you back for torturing me a second ago. I thought you were trying to tell me to get lost."

She made an impatient sound as my lips captured her earlobe. "I am, sort of. We shouldn't be doing t-this here. That was the whole point."

"I locked the door. No one is getting in and my next class doesn't start for an hour. If I can't have you until next semester, then I need one last kiss to hold me over." My mouth traversed a languid path back to hers. "We'd better make it a good one."

She melted over me in the way I liked so much, and her lips softened, opened, over mine. At the submission, my tongue delved into her sweetness, urging hers to battle. I rubbed mine against hers until her hands lifted to grip either side of my face. She took over the kiss, tinder to flame.

"That's enough," I said and pulled away. Too much more and we'd have more reason for the locked door. "You should go now."

But her blue eyes had gone bright with hunger and she shifted restlessly on my lap.

"Maybe you were right, about one more time," she said thoughtfully. Her gaze followed her hand as she toyed with the collar of my shirt, her fingers fluttering over the exposed skin.

"I said one more kiss."

"Are you asking me to stop?" Before I had a second to reply, she was lifting her shirt over her head. All of her carefully reasoned arguments evaporated as creamy flesh filled my vision. The thin bralette she wore underneath did little to hide the flushed rose of her nipples. My mouth watered and shifted to get her off my lap, but she bored down on me, grinding down against the growing hardness.

"Layla," I said between gritted teeth. "You should go." My hands made me a liar as they gripped her hips to work her over my erection. The layers of fabric did nothing to disguise the paradise between her legs. Her heat burned through both our jeans and made my thoughts turn muddled.

"I will," she said and got to her feet. Dual edges of relief and despair had me reaching for her, then rubbing my eyes and wishing for a cold beer.

When I dropped my hands, my spine stiffened. "Layla, what the hell are you doing?"

She didn't answer and didn't need to. The sound of her jeans dropping to the floor was answer enough. I protested and then she tucked her thumbs in the waistband of her panties and pushed them over her hips. The sight made it damn near impossible to breathe, let alone speak. In a few quick movements, the lacy bralette joined the pile of clothes and she was naked in front of me.

A roaring filled my ears and I gave up trying to make her see reason and reached for her instead. I'd been crazy since the moment I saw her, what was wrong with succumbing to the madness a little longer?

Her nimble fingers undid the catch on my jeans and lowered the zipper. All I could do was hold onto her hips. Somehow the student had become the teacher. Her hands found me aching and hard as steel. She bent her knees, but I stopped her.

"No, c'mere." I guided her onto my lap and hissed at the meeting of heated flesh. "This way."

Layla made a sound in the back of her throat as she threw her head back and began working herself onto my cock. She wasn't completely wet, but the friction was glorious. Her thighs trembled as she lifted and seated herself until she engulfed me completely.

"You feel so good inside me," she whispered against the shell of my ear. "I just wanted to feel it one more time."

"Whatever you want," I answered.

Her hips already moved of their own accord. This was something past seduction, past attraction. All I wanted was to rear up and take her, make her mine, but I gripped her hips and let her do the taking. The incredible pleasure in the submission.

She folded her legs, hooking her feet on the seat behind me until she found an angle that made her cry out and her hips buck wildly. Once, the students in the hallway beyond my door shouted, making her pace stumble. At first, I thought it frightened her, and maybe it did, but it also made her slick around me.

"Better be quiet, Layla. They may be able to hear you." Her strangled breathing filled my ears and the fingers gripping my arms would undoubtedly leave bruises. "That lock isn't strong. If someone wanted to get in here they could. It would only take one hard push." She buried her face in my neck and her hips slowed as she tried to control herself. Not a chance. I gripped her hips and resumed the pace. She held onto me for dear life. "They're right there on the other side of the door. Less than five feet away. We're practically surrounded by people."

"Stop, someone might hear us."

"Do you really want me to? You feel so hot and wet around me, Lay. I want to feel you come on me one more time. I want to watch you when you do. Just make sure you don't make a sound." As though to punctuate my words, someone thudded against my office door and laughter burst out.

It shocked Layla so thoroughly; she nearly shot right off my lap. "It's okay," I said in her ear. "They haven't heard you yet. Come on me, Lay, or I'll make you scream so loud the whole building will hear you."

"You're crazy," she panted, but her hips were dancing back and forth like mad. "We're going to get caught."

I got to my feet with her in my lap and her legs twitched

around me and she slapped at my chest. "What are you doing?" she whisper-screeched. "Dash, no."

I flicked off the lights so the most anyone would see through the frosted glass were the hint of shadows. Beyond, bodies moved in the hallway, illuminated by the fluorescent glare from the lights above. It gave the illusion that we were in a room full of people.

"This is so wrong," she said as I pinned her back against the glass. She threw her head back when I lifted her legs over my forearms, and then sucked in a deep breath through her nose. "So wrong."

Her hands gripped my shoulder as I moved in and out of her. She couldn't move, couldn't do anything but take it. Her eyes rolled back behind her lids and she bit her lip so hard it appeared to be bloodless.

"So wrong, but it feels so good, doesn't it?" I said against her throat.

"I hate you," she answered. "Harder."

"Can't," I responded. "Someone might hear. They're so close if we make too much noise, they could hear you."

She sobbed against me, her hips arching to find the angle that would take her to completion, but I held her steady, kept my thrusts paced at the border of being agonizingly slow. She slapped at me until I pinned her arms, too.

"You're...such...a...jerk," Layla said in between pants.

As though to block me out, she turned her head to the side, which made me smile, though she couldn't see it. She was too busy looking at the shadows of the people on the other side of the window. The walls of her pussy clamped around me, and I hissed out a breath.

"Oh, God," she whispered.

Her back arched and I used my weight to press her more firmly against the unforgiving wood. "Better not make a sound," I said again.

"Oh, God, oh God, oh God."

There was nothing like watching her come. Nothing in the world that compared, but I was willing to repeat it a thousand times, a million, to prove myself wrong. It was like watching a storm. Her face clouded over with concentration, the build of the orgasm rumbling just beneath the surface. Then her body drew up tight, her nipples contracted in to hard points, and her mouth opened to a wide "O" of surprise. The calm. She would hold the sweet tension for a few moments suspended in time, then, like thunder and lighting all at once, she'd shake and explode over and around me. Then her muscles would melt, and her body would cover me like soft rain.

Yeah, I could see her come a million times and I'd never get used to it.

I'd always want to make her do it a million more.

CHAPTER 19

LAYLA

Charlie was stuck on a double shift, but made us promise to tell her everything the following day. I couldn't wait for advice, so I invited Ember over to my apartment once the twins were down for the night. She came wearing a pair of yoga pants and a thin sweater over a camisole. In her hands she carried a baby monitor and a bottle of wine.

"I should have an hour or two before one of them wakes up wanting something, and that should be enough time for us to kill this wine. Do you have any glasses?"

I was already pulling glasses out of the cabinet. "Here."

She poured two healthy servings and handed me one. She lifted hers to mine and clinked. "To seeing the end in sight. Graduation can't come soon enough."

"I'll drink to that." The white wine was cool and crisp and just what I needed. It had been a long couple of days.

Ember pulled me to the couch, sat the baby monitor on the coffee table, and tucked her feet beneath her. "Do I have to pull it out of you, or are you going to tell me what's been going on?"

I cupped my wine glass in my palms and studied the liquid inside while I spilled the whole story about what had happened between Dash and me. Eyes bright, Ember listened intently, pausing me only to ask questions or emit shocked gasps. When I finished, she squealed and gripped my hand.

"Lay, I can't believe you've been keeping this a secret. Well, not a good one, because Charlie and I guessed something was going on between you two, I mean no one fights that much and doesn't end up in bed."

I winced. "Well, I hope no one else figured it out. We've been trying to keep a low profile so neither of us gets hurt. But that isn't what I wanted to talk to you about."

Ember took a long sip from her wine and settled more deeply into the couch. "I shouldn't be so excited, because you've clearly been through the wringer, but I've been hip deep in calls. Both the girls just got over the flu so I need the distraction of someone else's life."

I pressed a hand to her knee. "Feel free to indulge in my drama. No judgment. Anyway, so after Dash took me out on the date, he dropped me off at home, and who do I run into but his grandmother."

"No."

Nodding emphatically, I said, "Yes. I invited her inside and she sat down on this couch, all regal like, and warned me away from Dash like this was some soap opera from a million years ago and they're a royal family, which would make me the lowly peasant."

Ember drank deeply, wiped at her lips. "What did you say?"

"I didn't have time to say much of anything. She left before I could even put up an argument, but I was fuming."

"I'll bet you were. Did you tell Dash?"

I shook my head. "I couldn't. He loves his grandparents. He'd be devastated if I told him they were capable of doing something like this. Besides, it'd be my word against hers. He wouldn't believe me."

Ember didn't seem convinced. "I don't know. From what

you've said, he seems to be pretty into you. I think you should tell him what's going on, that way you can work through it together."

"Is that how you and Chris work through your problems?" I was still worried about her. She seemed pretty broken up about how he'd been treating her.

She nodded, then stopped herself. "I mean, it used to be. When things were good we could talk through anything. That's what makes a relationship work more than all of the other stuff. Communication. But this isn't about me and Chris. What happened after you talked to his grandmother? The miserable old hag," she added with another sip of wine.

"Well, I thought about everything for a long time, even though I'd already made up my mind once she tried to convince me otherwise."

"You always have to think things to death," Ember commented.

"I can't help it. I want to make sure I'm making the right choice."

"What did you decide?" she asked. "What did you tell Dash?" There was an edge of impatience in her tone that made me smile.

"I decided, it would be best if we didn't see each other."

Ember deflated a little, composed herself before answering. "Oh, I guess I understand that. He is your T.A. and you fight like cats and dogs."

I held up a finger. "That's not all. I decided it would be best if we didn't see each other...until after the semester. That way neither of us gets in trouble. It'll also give us time to think about things and make sure this is actually something we want to do."

"You can't think yourself out of love," Ember said, and that gave me pause.

"I'm not," but I drank deeply of my own wine, "I want us both to be sensible."

"There is no making sense of it. It happens when it happens. With the right person, there is no right timing."

Ignoring her, I said, "That's my point. If it's right, then it'll work out—after the semester is over."

"So you're going to let the old hag win?" Ember demanded.

"I'm not letting her win. I don't want her to have any ammo, that's all. Once I'm not in his class anymore, she won't have any leverage over me or him. The last thing I'd want to do is risk his career. That's what's most important to me."

"I do understand that, I just think you're trying to control a situation that's uncontrollable."

"I'm not trying to control it. Let's call it stacking the deck in my favor," I amended.

Ember got up from the couch and retrieved the wine from the fridge. After topping off both of our glasses, she said, "Call it whatever you want, but it's still the same thing."

"I don't think so."

"What are you going to do about your mother?"

The buzz from the wine washed away all of my worries. "Why does she have to know?"

Ember clinked her glass against mine. "That's my girl."

The apartment was quiet after Ember left a couple hours later. I ached to go upstairs to Dash's room, could practically feel him despite the floors that separated us, but I knew the separation was for the best. I lay on the couch, still buzzed from the wine and randomly flipping through Netflix, trying to find something to watch, when my phone buzzed on the table beside me.

Noticing my mother's name on the screen, I hit ignore and let it ring to voicemail. I'd pay for it later, I was sure, but I didn't want to talk to her. Especially not when the scent of Dash's grandmother's perfume still lingered on the air. I'd had enough of controlling women for at least a week. Besides, all she was going to do was complain I hadn't reached out about the finance thing, and I really wasn't interested. The closer it got to graduation, the less inclined I was to have anything to do with her plans for me.

I settled on some mindless piece of fluff to distract me from worrying about how bad her meltdown would be when I heard from her next. I'd switched my wine for a ginger ale and sipped as I let my mind wander. Inevitably, it settled on Dash, more specifically, on the encounter in his office.

I couldn't believe I let him do that to me. Couldn't believe the girl, who had always confessed not only to hate his guts—but was a self-proclaimed rule-follower—had not only let him do it, but had enjoyed it. It gave me a little quickening low in my belly every time I thought of how close we'd come to getting caught. And I'd liked it. I'd never come so hard, and even now I could feel him inside me. I could remember the excitement and fear of having someone just on the other side of the thin barrier. Plus it was Dash. Fighting against him, feeling the edge of frustration heightened everything.

From the satisfied grin, when I could open my eyes again, he knew exactly what I was thinking. Perhaps it had been punishment for teasing him, but it had been worth it. He'd had the upper hand for so long, it was nice to be on top so to speak.

When my phone rang again, it took me a second to pull myself from the fantasy. One of these days, he'd let me be the dominant one. Even if he took some convincing, I figured it'd be fun to take our arguing to the bedroom. Maybe the way we clashed was the reason why it felt so explosive with him.

I almost let the phone go to my voicemail again, but something had me glancing at the screen out of habit. Training from my mother, no doubt. But it wasn't her name on the screen. It was Dash's.

"Hello?" I said, hoping my voice didn't sound as desperate as I thought.

His didn't sound breathless at all. It was smooth, confident, and the very same as the one that had been haunting my dreams. "Hey, sweetheart."

That's it. That's all he had to say for me to be right back in his dark office, naked and needy. I swallowed hard.

"You shouldn't be calling me."

Dash chuckled. I remembered how his eyes lit up when he laughed. I ached to see him, to watch that light appear. "This isn't the CIA. They aren't going to track our phone calls."

"What do you want?" I asked.

"I guess phone sex is a no-go?"

My blood heated. "Not funny. Is that why you called?" Just hearing him was enough to have me shifting restlessly on the couch. His voice was like an activator switch. My skin itched to feel his hands. My mouth yearned for his lips.

"No, but if you're ever lonely I'd be happy to serve as your own personal 1-900 number. Just say the word."

"I'm hanging up now," I warned. More to stop myself from begging than from actual irritation.

"You're no fun. I wanted to call to give you a head's up. The woman who was at the benefit will be at a gala my grandparents are a part of. I'm escorting her, but I didn't want you to think it was a date or anything."

I remembered her. Sleek and elegant. The kind of woman his grandmother would be ecstatic for him to be involved with. "Oh?" I said, because what do you say to that?

"If you want me to tell her no, I will. She saw you coming out of my office a while back, and I didn't want her to be suspicious. Since we're laying low for another several weeks, I thought this would be a good time to disprove her suspicions, at least for now. I didn't want you to be caught off guard if it got back to you. I want to be completely honest with you, Lay. That's how much I want this to work."

I muted the TV so I could think. When I didn't speak right away, Dash pressed, "Sweetheart? Say something. I'll do whatever you want me to here."

"I'm not happy, but I understand why you'd do it. As long as it's platonic, like you say, then I guess I'm fine with it. I don't want to put you in an awkward position, and I know how much your family means to you."

That and he had no reason to be suspicious about his family. Knowing what his grandmother thought, and his feelings about honesty made the wine sour in my stomach. I wanted to tell him right then, but I was afraid of how he would handle it. My mother had chosen people over me my whole life. He was very close to his grandparents. Would he choose them over me, too?

I wasn't ready to know the answer.

Not yet, anyway.

I'd always been raised to believe family should be put first. My mother made it clear my whole life that the only opinions that mattered were hers. It made it hard for me to put myself above his grandparents.

"Are you sure? Say the word and I'll tell them no."

I swallowed back the sour taste in my throat. "I'm sure. I trust you. Besides, we're both going to be busy. I don't want you to think you have to check with me about plans. I appreciate it, but you don't owe me anything. Not until after the semester."

"Don't be stupid," he said without heat. "As far as I'm concerned, this is the real thing. I'll check with you about anything I feel will make you uncomfortable. You're important to me, Lay."

"You're important to me, too," I said, my chest flooding with emotion. "But we can't talk like this all the time. It makes it harder."

"Don't worry, sweetheart. You'll be back to arguing with me

in no time. Especially when you consider I'm giving your last paper a B."

With that, the line went dead, and I stared at the phone, steaming.

Like hell that paper deserved a B.

I couldn't wait until I could punish him properly.

CHAPTER 20

DASH

knew the moment we walked into the ballroom, and I saw Jessica standing in a sleek black gown waiting for me, it was a terrible idea to agree to go with her. My grandmother clutched my arm and propelled me forward. Sometimes I was sure she thought I was sixteen instead of an adult.

"There are the Martins," she said with barely disguised glee. "Let's go tell them hello."

Jessica beamed as we crossed the room to their side. I couldn't help but remember the calculating gleam in her eye when she'd confronted me in my office. She latched onto my arm the moment we got close.

"Dash, I'm so glad you could make it."

I removed her talons and forced a smile. "Thank you for inviting me."

She followed my grandparents and her parents to our assigned table. As we walked, she chattered on about the gala, but honestly it went in one ear and out the other. All I wanted was to find a way to escape. Being with her felt wrong down to the bone.

It was going to be a very long night.

I reached for a glass of champagne from a passing waiter along the way and drank deeply. As I was lowering the glass, a couple making their way across the room caught my attention. I sprang to my feet and in three long strides had my arms around the woman of the pair and smiled at the man.

"Mom, Dad. What are you two doing here? I thought you were in Washington."

My mother, Naomi Hampton, barely reached my shoulders. Her strawberry-blonde hair fell in sheets to the middle of her back, a rose-gold waterfall. Green eyes, the same shade as mine peered back at me, alight with excitement. A weight I didn't know I'd been carrying, since I said goodbye to Layla, lightened.

I looked to my father, Peter Hampton, as he spoke, "The holidays are coming up. We thought we'd surprise you. Besides, Mom mentioned you'd met someone, and your mother couldn't contain herself at the thought."

Dad was about my height with dark brown eyes and the same dark hair as mine. Aside from my eyes, I inherited everything else from my father. Mom used to harass me about being his twin after the burden of carrying and delivering me.

I started to mention that Layla wasn't here, but caught myself before I could. Manners ingrained in me since childhood allowed me to introduce Jessica Martin to them without faltering. I guess I'd inherited my father's ease for smoothing over social situations, because no one seemed to notice my pause. Mom looked at me with interest, but that was probably because it had been a while since she'd seen me.

"Peter," Grandmother ordered after the introductions, "come sit. We have to catch up. They're about to serve dinner."

Dutifully, my father took the seat next to her, my mother on the opposite side. I sat next to Mom and Jessica took the open seat to my left.

Drinks were ordered, small talk made. Having my parents in

attendance made the conversation much less stilted. I began to think the night might not be so bad after all.

Until the topic changed to my work and my plans after graduation.

"How is teaching going, Dash? Last I heard you were assigned a business class?"

I felt Jessica tense beside me, even though my gaze was on my mother. "It's going well. Professor Johnson seems pleased."

"I'm happy to hear that, honey," Mom says, patting my arm.

"He's excited to join your campaign in the new year," Grandmother broke in. "I can't wait for the Hampton line to continue. I'm so proud."

I took a sip of my champagne before I responded. "Well, don't get too riled up about it. I haven't decided whether or not I'm going to join him."

Grandmother waved that away. "Don't be silly, Dashiel. Of course you will."

Dad and I shared a look. He'd told me stories about how his mother had pushed him, first into graduating at the top of his class, then into law school after college. Then up the ladder in politics. There hadn't been a moment in his life she didn't orchestrate, at least not until he met my mom. She was the one thing he chose without Grandmother's influence, which—according to family history—she hadn't been thrilled about. My mother hadn't come from a wealthy family. Her parents had been thoroughly middle-class working people, good people, from what I've been told. They both passed away when I was young.

I ignored Grandmother's comment, like I ignored most of her behavior. She was my father's mother and deserved respect, but that didn't mean she was allowed to control my life the way she'd done his. He turned out all right, but that was only because he had Mom, or at least that's what he's told me several times over the years.

"Jessica, why don't we dance?" I suggested after we'd eaten.

Jessica beamed up at me and accepted my hand. I ignored the pleased look on my grandmother's face and led Jessica to the dance floor. She attached herself to me like a burr, but I reasoned it was only one dance. It'd give both of us some space from my family, and I'd have an opportunity to set things straight.

"I love this song," she breathed into my ear.

I didn't even hear it. "Are you having a good time?" I asked politely.

Her claws contracted as thought to prevent as escape. "I'm having a wonderful time. Your grandparents are such wonderful people. I've been dying to meet your father. He's such an inspiration."

As she spoke, recounting the conversation at dinner, I couldn't help but think about Layla. She would have hated the gala, where most of the money went into throwing it rather than supporting the cause. I had a hard time imagining her in this life. She'd never be able to sit on the sidelines, blinded by the glitz and glamour. She'd want to be in the trenches, volunteering, organizing. She was a doer, not a watcher.

"Dash," Jessica prompted. "Did you hear me?"

"I'm sorry," I replied with a kind smile. "What were you saying?"

"I asked if you were having a nice time."

I nodded dispassionately. "Of course. Thank you again for coming."

Her eyes sharpened, and she cocked her head. The look reminded me so much of my grandmother's that I blinked twice. "Are you sure? You don't even seem like you're here. Is something wrong?"

"No, of course not. I'm sorry. You've been wonderful, I'm afraid my heart's just not in it tonight." My only goal as far as she was concerned was to placate her suspicions.

Jessica's lips twisted. "It's that girl, isn't it? That student?

She's the one you're thinking about. Why you've been so distracted all night. Really, Dash? I thought you wanted me here because you'd given up on her."

I shook my head. "It's not about her. Or you. I didn't mean to lead you on, but you should know I have no interest in pursuing a relationship with you. I'm sorry if that hurts your feelings, but—"

She cut me off before I could offer any more platitudes. "She is. You don't have to lie to me. I saw the way you looked at her when she left your office. I'm not stupid. I thought when you invited me here tonight; you'd come to your senses, but apparently not. I won't make a scene tonight, but you should really think about what you're doing. What you're risking. Is she worth it?"

The song ended and Jessica turned and glided back to our table. When she saw it was only my mother reigning, she made a deft turn for the restrooms. That hadn't gone the way I'd expected. I hoped she meant what she said about not making a scene. Not for my sake, for Layla's.

Mom turned as she heard me approach and beamed when she saw me. "Good, you're father's gone schmoozing, and I'm dying to hear more about what's been going on with you. I wish you'd come join us in Washington. I miss you."

"You sound like Grandmother," I said with a teasing smile.

"Blasphemy," she answered with a laugh. "You know better than to compare me with Elizabeth. Now, tell me all about this young lady you brought here tonight. Do you like her?"

"Jessica. She's nice, but it's not what you think."

"Oh," Mom said with a tone of surprise. "Why not?"

I lifted a shoulder and sipped champagne that had gone warm. "I'm not interested in her romantically."

"So who is she?"

"Her parents are friends with Grandmother and Grandfather."

Mom laughed and her eyes twinkled. "I don't mean her, silly goose. I mean the girl you are interested in."

I sputtered slightly, choking on my drink. "What?"

"Don't play dumb. A mother knows when her son likes a woman. If it isn't this Jessica girl, then who is it?"

I thought of Layla with her obsession with books and her love of art. A woman who worked so hard to please everyone she sometimes forgot to please herself.

Mom slapped my shoulder affectionately. "I knew it. I told you. Who is she?"

"She's...complicated," I said slowly. "I'm still trying to figure it out. If something happens, you'll be the first to know, I promise."

"Well, if she can put that look in your eye, I'd say you have it figured out," she teased. "But I'm patient. When it gets uncomplicated, you should bring her to meet us."

Jessica kept her word about not making a scene. At the end of the night, she'd managed to keep the conversation flowing and didn't say another word about the conversation we'd had on the dance floor. She left with her parents after thanking my grandparents and saying what a pleasure it was to meet my mom and dad. Being with someone like her would be so easy in this way. Her family was remarkably like mine. My grandmother certainly liked her.

The problem was she wasn't Layla. And she never would be.

It was as simple and as complicated as that. My parents took a car back to their hotel and my grandfather stayed behind to talk business with some contacts, which left me to drive my grandmother back home.

"That was a lovely evening," she said as she got into the passenger seat.

"It was. Did you have a nice time?" I asked.

"A lovely time. What did you think of Ms. Martin?" She was about as subtle as a rock.

"She seems great, but before you get any ideas, we're just friends. "

"Just friends? Is this a young person thing?"

"No, it's an I'm not interested in her kind of thing." I was thankful it would be a short drive.

Grandmother turned in her seat to face me with the same look in her eye she got when something went wrong in one of my father's carefully coordinated campaigns. "Don't be obtuse, Dashiel. She's a wonderful girl and the two of you make a beautiful suit."

"I'm sorry to disappoint you, Grandmother, but it's not going to happen." I pulled into her driveway and unlocked the doors.

As I helped her out of her seat, she clasped my hands. "Why don't you take some time to think about it? She and her family will be attending Thanksgiving with us, and you'll have more time to get to know one another." With that, she kissed me on the cheek and strode inside.

Now I know how my father must have felt his whole life. It was no wonder he decided to move to Washington as soon as he could.

I gave a passing thought to calling Layla, but decided against it.

As I drove home, I thought of her and mentally calculated the days until I could see her again and make her mine for good.

CHAPTER 21

LAYLA

"**M**s. Tate, Ms. Tate, there's a ghost!"

I smiled at the little boy who was working with pieces of magazine prints to recreate his own picture story as a part of an assignment for one of my education electives. "There's a ghost in your story?"

I would miss them when the class was over. I loved being in the classroom. Answering their questions. Watching a student exploring art was an experience without compare.

The little boy named Tony was a mischief maker, but he did well if he was encouraged to stay on task. He shook his dark brown curls and said, "No, Ms. Tate." Then, he pointed toward the classroom door. "Right there!"

I glanced over his shoulder, prepared to humor him, but found something more horror inducing than a ghost—Mrs. Hampton stood at the door—her pale overly made-up face peering through the keyhole window. I gasped before I could check my response, causing several other students to perk up from their assignments and follow my gaze to the door.

Mrs. Hampton knocked twice in rapid succession, then opened the door before I could get to my feet. She was as intimidating as ever. Not a hair was out of place and her outfit—a sleek, feminine suit—cost more than my entire wardrobe. She took a step inside, pausing by the door.

"Tony, why don't you finish up here while I talk with our visitor?" I replaced the glue I was using and got to my feet.

I trembled with a combination of humiliation and rage, but I tried my best not to let it show. Lifting a hand, I gestured to the hall. "Why don't we talk outside, where there's more privacy?"

With a derisive little sniff, she turned on her heel and I followed her out into the hall.

"What are you doing here?" I asked when we were alone. The hallway was blessedly deserted. It was embarrassing enough being confronted by her again, without having it witnessed by a colleague or student. "This is my job. You shouldn't be here."

"I wouldn't be here if you'd taken my advice from our last conversation."

"What I do or don't do in my personal life is none of your business."

"If it involves my family, it is my business." She reached into her leather bag, dug around, then pulled out a checkbook. She flipped it open with ease, clearly used to spending money like it was water. The gold glint of her pen flashed in the dingy light from the fluorescents overhead. She scribbled in a neat scrawl on a blank check.

I took a step backward, uncomprehending. "I think you should leave," I sputtered before she could say a word. She wasn't doing what I thought she was. People only did that sort of thing in the movies. There was no way this was real life. I glanced back at my classroom to find my students peeking up from their work to see what I was doing. At my glance, they turned their attention back to their desks.

"I'm afraid I can't do that," she said, still writing.

"Don't make me call security," I warned. How had she even

gotten past the front desk? I didn't think she had any kids here at the school.

She gave a mirthless laugh and arched a perfect brow. "Please do," Mrs. Hampton invited. "My family has donated thousands of dollars to the public school system."

I gritted my teeth. It was like dealing with a steel wall. She should have gone into politics instead of her husband. People like her, and my mom, expected others to bow to their will. They saw the world as theirs for the ruling. A migraine pounded behind my eyes.

"Then what do you want?" I asked in a measured tone. The sooner I could get it out of her, the sooner I could make her leave. "Dash and I aren't together, so I'm not sure what you're doing here."

She ripped a check out of her checkbook and snapped it closed. After thrusting it back into her bag, she pursed her lips, then said, "I'm not an idiot, Ms. Tate. Dashiel may have brought Jessica to the gala last night, but a woman knows when a man isn't interested, and his mind was on someone else."

I brushed my hair out of my face, wishing I could feel half as put together as she was. "I'm not sure what you want me to do about that. I can't control how someone feels." Which was an understatement.

She shoved the check under my nose. "That may be so, but you can make sure he has no reason to keep his hopes up."

I glanced at the check. I couldn't help it—it was practically down my throat. There were so many zeroes my eyes crossed. "Is this a joke?" I blurted out. "I'm not taking your money. Are you insane?" My voice rose with each word and I checked myself before someone else could hear.

"Think about it, Ms. Tate. This money could set you up for the next chapter of your life. You've only been with Dashiel for a short time. Is that acquaintance worth passing up such an opportunity?"

Heat flamed across my cheeks and my eyes narrowed. I clenched my hands into fists at my sides. "You must think very little about your grandson," I said, my voice vibrating with fury.

"On the contrary," she said coolly, "I think very highly of my grandson." The disdain for me couldn't have been clearer. "I want what is best for him. I thought I'd been perfectly frank the first time around, but I should have considered you'd need a motivator."

"This conversation is over. I'll do you the favor of never speaking of this to Dash, because it would break his heart, but let me make it clear: whatever I do with Dash is none of your business. I will never take your money. Now you need to leave."

She reached forward, but I was so angry I was frozen to the spot. With a quick movement, she tucked the check into the pocket of my khaki pants. "In case you change your mind." Mrs. Hampton put on a sleek pair of sunglasses, then stopped a few steps away. "I hope I've made myself clear. I wouldn't want something to happen with your education. It would be a shame."

With that parting shot, she waved her fingers in my direction and sauntered off.

I stayed by the door to my classroom. Less than five minutes had passed, but it felt like my whole world was off its center axis. Did that really just happen? It was a complete nightmare.

Before returning to my students, I took some time to calm my emotions. I couldn't let them see me upset. Even though I waited until my breathing calmed and my face cooled off, the moment I walked into the classroom and sat next to Tony, he turned his boyish face up and said, "Is everything okay, Ms. Tate? Do you want a candy? Candy always makes me feel better when I'm upset."

I ruffled his silken hair. "I'm fine, sweetheart, just grown-up stuff. Nothing to worry about. Why don't you show me what you were working on while I was gone?"

All I wanted after my student teaching was done for the day was an hour at the gym to clear my thoughts and a long, steaming hot shower. It had been hours since our confrontation, but I still felt like I was covered in a sticky, slimy residue. It was the same feeling I got after a family vacation with my mother for a week without an escape.

I went home to change into gym clothes and made my way back to campus. The gym was always packed with students, but the equipment was top-of-the-line and free for students, so it was worth the drive. I scanned my I.D. at the sensor and plugged in my headphones, hoping to drown out the booming music and buzz of conversation. All I wanted to do was disappear for a little while.

When I saw Charlie on the treadmill, I had to admit, I wasn't super stoked. I didn't want anyone to see me like this. Didn't want them to read the conflict in my eyes. But I couldn't turn away when she recognized me, brightened, and waved.

I crossed the crowded gym to her side and took out an earbud. "Hey! I didn't expect to see you here."

She bounded off the treadmill, her face pink with exertion. "Layla! I'm so happy to see you. It's been so busy at work, I feel like it's been forever. I don't want to interrupt your workout, but I'd love to catch up with you. It's not the same nice I moved in with Liam."

I shook my head. "Of course. You finished here?" I asked.

"I've got about fifteen more minutes, if you don't mind joining me?" she said.

"Sure." I wrapped my towel around the bar and stepped up to the treadmill beside hers. "How has work been?"

Charlie bumped up her speed and resumed her trot. "Hell, that's why I'm here. Liam got tired of listening to me complain, so he forced me to go to the gym a couple times a week to work off my frustrations."

"That bad, huh?" The brisk pace of my own treadmill caused me to pant a little.

She grimaced. "It's not bad, really. Just a lot of red tape and a lot to learn. I complain about it, but I'm loving it." Charlie shot me a look and swiped at her brow. "But that's not what we were going to talk about. Ember updated me about everything that was going on. I'm sorry I couldn't make it to the last powwow."

"You don't have to apologize. I know you're busy. You don't have to drop everything for me."

Even though she was nearly jogging, Charlie still had energy enough to give me a look that said don't-be-stupid. "I'm not even going to touch on that. From what Ember said, you've had a lot on your plate, too. I just want to be there for you."

"You're always there for me."

"I hate to say this, but you look like you got run over by a truck. Did something else happen? Do I need to kick Dash's ass? You say the word and I'll do it."

I laughed, but it was half-hearted. "Well, I'm assuming Ember told you about what his grandmother did a little while ago?"

"Yeah, the dusty old bitch. Oh my God, did she do something else?" She abruptly turned off her treadmill. "Let's do some weights. I need to be able to focus, and I can't do that when I'm almost out of breath."

"It just happened," I said, following her. "I don't even know what to think."

"Well, spill. I'm happy to commiserate and say some chants to curse her for life. One of my patients in a witch and she's been teaching me some stuff."

Selecting a dumbbell, I sighed. "It's a long story."

"We have time. It'll help you feel better to talk about it. What happened?"

"Fine, but no curses. I don't need the bad karma."

Charlie did a few bicep curls. "I promise."

As we worked through several weight training exercises, I recounted the conversation with Elizabeth Hampton, getting more and more angry and desolate the second time around.

"You have to tell Dash!" Charlie said when I finished.

"I can't. Would you want to hear that?"

It was already bad enough I hadn't mentioned the first conversation to him. The second would kill him. As much as this break was killing me, I was grateful for the time to process what had happened so I could figure out how to handle it.

"I would want to know if my family was scheming behind my back. So would he."

I reverse curled as I considered. "Maybe. I have some time to think about it while we're on this break until the end of the semester. You never know. Maybe he won't even want to get back together, and it won't be an issue."

Charlie just shook her head. "You're being too pessimistic. We've all seen how Dash is around you. You've got it bad for him, too, and you know it. You're just too afraid to admit it to yourself."

"We don't even get along most of the time!" I blurted out. "We argue more often than not. Not to mention his grandmother. There are so many things working against us."

"Then don't make a decision now. Take the break to think about it. But first, you've got to tell me... How much money was it?"

I couldn't help but laugh. "I'm not telling you that. No amount of money could have convinced me to walk away from him."

Charlie just smiled. "I guess that means you have your answer."

CHAPTER 22

DASH

have three missed calls from Jessica and three times as many text messages, but there's nothing from Layla. Not that I was expecting there to be. She made it clear, taking this break meant minimal to no contact and I understood.

That didn't mean I had to like it.

She would have killed me if I took a ride down to her apartment, even though I thought about doing just that dozens of times a day. My sleep was shit because all I could do was remember her in my bed and think about how impossibly close she was. Just an elevator ride away. In less time than it would take to order an espresso, I could have my hands on her, could have her body beneath mine.

The time between now and the end of the semester seemed to multiply with each passing day.

I've kept our relationship as professional as possible, like she requested. I only saw her during class and never showed her any preferential treatment. She sat every Monday, Wednesday, and Friday in the same spot in the lecture hall. I made it a point not to stare, but I'd watch her out of the corner of my eye whenever I gave a reading assignment or when the other students were distracted.

I began searching for her face in the crowds on campus. Even though there were thousands of students, I always seemed to think I recognized her everywhere. It drove me a little crazy.

Sighing, I got to my feet. It had been another sleepless night, and I'd need about two pots of coffee in order to face the day. While it brewed, I took a shower and stroked myself under the hot spray, thinking of Layla's face when she'd come in my office. There was something about pushing her to those limits. Watching her overcome the apprehension and dive into the plea-sure without hesitation. I ached with the need to see her, touch her, taste her again. Hell, another one of our arguments would probably do it for me at this point.

The shower and jerking off didn't help. Thinking about her only made it worse. It had been less than a month since we agreed to take some space; another month was going to kill me.

I thought about visiting my parents for a distraction when I was finished with my own classes for the day but decided against it. When they visited, it almost always ended with my grandmother barging in at some point, and I really didn't want to be poked at any more about what a nice girl Jessica was.

I poured the coffee into a thermos and dressed in loose gym shorts and a light long-sleeved shirt. I had a couple hours before I needed to be in class and a long, exhausting walk sounded like the best way to spend it. As I was locking up, the elevator dinged and drew my eye. Cursing, I jogged to it, hoping to reach it before it shut again.

"Hey, man," Tripp said as I walked into the elevator. He had a bag slung over his shoulder and was wearing a similar getup, track pants and a light long-sleeved shirt.

Relieved at seeing a familiar face, I said, "Hey, what are you doing up so early?"

Tripp also lived in the building and hung out sometimes

during Taco Tuesdays with Ember. An idiot could tell he had a thing for her, but both of them tried to say they were just friends. Not my business.

He adjusted the bag over his shoulder. "Practice, dude. I've got gym for an hour this morning for weight training, then some team drills."

"It's not even season yet, and you have to get up this early to practice?" Sports outside of recreational football, had never really been my thing.

"Year-round, dude. Baseball is life. Where are you going this early?" he asked, as we got off the elevator at the parking garage.

I waved my thermos of coffee around. "I thought about heading out to do some working out of my own."

"Why don't you ride with me to the gym?"

"Are you sure, man? I don't want to get in your way."

"Don't worry about it. It's free training in the off season, so the other guys won't care. We can throw some balls around. Whatever."

"Sure, why not?" I could use the distraction.

"We can take my car. I'll drop you back by here after the gym."

Tripp lead me to a beat-up, old Honda Civic. For some reason, it wasn't the sort of car I imagined the star baseball player would drive, but I didn't comment.

"Haven't seen you around Taco Tuesdays lately," Tripp said as we buckled up.

I shrugged. "I figured I'd give Layla some room."

"Did the two of you have another fight?"

The teasing tone in his voice made me smile a little for the first time in a while. "I guess we aren't very subtle."

"About as subtle as a foul ball to the back of your head."

"We're just taking some space. It's hard being objective when she's one of my students. She takes her education very seriously."

"Ahh, I get it," Tripp said with a sly glance in my direction.

"Get what?"

"You've got a thing for her, right?"

"That obvious?"

Tripp drove lazily with one hand on the wheel and the other on his thigh. I'd never given him much consideration before now because I'd been so focused on Layla, but he wasn't all that bad. I didn't normally hang out with the jock types, but he wasn't in your face about it. In fact, he seemed pretty down to earth.

"Nah, I overheard Ember talking to Charlie about it the other day, when we were studying."

"Oh, studying. Right. Is that what the kids call it now?"

"It's okay, I won't say you're projecting. And I won't tell Lay you've been pining over her."

"You mean like no one has ever told Ember you're into her, too?"

Tripp grinned, surprising me. "That's old news, man. I asked her out once freshman year, but I was a bit of a manwhore back then, and she didn't take me seriously. Blew my chance. Then she hooked up with Chris and the rest is history. We're just friends now."

"You do know she and Chris have been arguing, right?"

"They always argue. Get back together. It's a two-person soap opera."

"So why do you stick around? Star baseball player, self-proclaimed ladies' man and all. Do you enjoy watching her with her boyfriend or something? No judgment if you do, I know some people are into that."

"No worse than you getting off on picking fights with Layla." At my less than amused look, Tripp laughed. "Like I said, we're just friends."

"If you say so."

November. Nearly December.

So close to the finish line, I could taste it.

I packed up my things with lightning speed. It's the only way I've managed to keep myself from watching Layla leave and not feel like a fucking stalker. As a result, my work has never been better, even my grandmother seemed pleased by my participation in planning my father's upcoming year during the recent Thanksgiving break to pass the time. Begrudgingly, I even happened to enjoy it, not that I told her. She would have taken that news and run with it.

Jessica's texts had slowed down to one a day. Despite our conversation at the gala, she still didn't seem to understand I wasn't going to be interested. I wasn't sure why she didn't just give it up, but I had other things on my mind.

Which is why, when I looked up and found Layla standing in front of me waiting patiently, I froze, unsure of what to do. That's what she'd done to me. Turned me into a man who was so completely rocked by a woman, he didn't know which way was up. I could only stare at her as the classroom emptied, leaving us alone.

"Do you have a second?" she asked.

Fuck me, but her voice had me instantly, painfully hard. I'd missed it. I'd deliberately not called on her in class so I wouldn't have to listen to her answer a question. I wasn't sure I could have hidden my response. For this exact reason.

"I don't think that's a good idea," I answered and edged toward the exit. "If you have any questions about the material, you can email them to me, and I'll answer them as soon as possible."

"Dash," she said softly. "Please."

Her hair was up in a messy bun. She wore a slightly wrinkled

FSU hoodie and skinny jeans. Her face was bare of makeup and there were dark smudges under her eyes, like she hadn't been sleeping well.

"What's wrong?" I asked. "Are you okay?"

"Can we talk in your office?" she asked instead of answering.

Considering what had happened there the last time, I wavered before saying, "Sure, of course. I've got a few minutes."

As we walked the short distance, I wondered what the hell made her change her mind about keeping her distance. Then, I worried maybe she'd already made a decision.

I unlocked the door to my office and led her inside, making sure to keep a respectful distance. She sat in the visitor chair at my desk, but I remained standing. My desk chair drew to mind too many erotic visions of her on my lap. I needed to keep a clear mind.

"What's going on?" I asked to fill the silence.

She got back to her feet and began to pace. "I've been thinking about this for a long time and I don't exactly know where to start."

Much as I wanted to tell her to cut the shit and spit it out, I kept silent as she fidgeted and paced.

"I guess I should start at the beginning." She spun around and her eyes flashed. "You're a jerk."

My brows lifted. That certainly wasn't what I was expecting her to say.

"You're a jerk. And you drive me crazy more often than not. I know we spend just as much time arguing as we do having regular conversation. I've never been good at the relationship thing, it's why I've been single most of my life, and why I was a virgin at twenty-two. I've never met a man who made me want to stop being alone. It's safe that way. I know what to expect, how to be. I'm used to control. If my mother isn't dictating how my life should be, then I'm planning every second to death, so I'm not caught off guard."

Her hands fisted at her side, she looked a bit like an avenging angel. "But I didn't plan you. You were unexpected. Every minute I'm with you, I feel alive. Being with you makes me feel explosive. And it was scary at first how strong those feelings were. And a part of me hated you were the one who caused them."

I opened my mouth to protest, but she shot me a look that had me slamming it shut again.

"Aside from Ember and Charlie, you are the only other person in my life who takes my thoughts, dreams, and opinions seriously. I think you push me because you know it's the only time I show you the real me, instead of the person programmed to mimic the viewpoints of everyone else around me."

She took a step closer, her hands coming to my chest. My whole body was wire-tight. "You're a jerk," she said softly, "but I love you, anyway."

Then she kissed me. I was so stunned, all I could do was hold on.

She tasted like salvation, and I was a sinner of the worst sort.

Then my office door flew open and Jessica stood in the doorway behind a gaping Professor Michaels.

CHAPTER 23

LAYLA

I don't know what Dash said to his boss as I waited in the hallway next to the smirking woman. She was lucky I never resorted to physical violence, because I'd never wanted to deck someone so much in my life.

But I knew it wasn't really her fault. Spiteful bitch she may be, but I'd made the choice to see him. If anyone was going to be punished here, it should be me.

There hadn't been a pause for me to speak with Dash, to decide what our story was, how we were going to protect—not only my standing in his class—but his job, too. His reputation.

There hadn't been a moment for me to apologize. This was all my fault. His grandmother had been right about that. If I'd kept my mouth shut, stayed away, none of this would be happening. Part of me knew that wasn't true, but the part that was still the vulnerable girl at graduation was afraid she was right.

Speaking of his grandmother, I still hadn't told him about what happened. How had everything spiraled so fantastically out of control?

I thought I'd been doing the right thing by risking it all and letting him know how I felt.

The thing with risking it all is that you have to be willing to make the gamble…and lose.

I chewed on my thumbnail and watched the shadows on the other side of the misted glass moving around. Above the din of the students milling around the hallway and the riotous conversation, I could hear the professor's raised voice and Dash's calm, soothing baritone.

Had it been worth it?

I could hear my mother's snotty voice in my head, judging me, criticizing as she often did. She'd find out soon enough, but I already knew what she was going to say. That I'd been stupid to bet everything on a man. That my future was worth more than any man, none of them could be trusted, and I was just like every other idiot girl who gave up her life for a roll in the sheets.

For so long, I'd listened to her dictate like she knew what she was talking about. But one thing I'd realized about growing up was, if there was a universal truth, it was that no one knew what they were doing. We were all like balls in an arcade game crashing around, pinging off the walls, hoping we'd win, but not really knowing how.

God, I guess I was more like her than I thought possible. I tried to control everyone in my little circle, as though it had any bearing on the outcome. In my effort to control my relationship with Dash to circumvent getting caught, what had happened?

We'd been caught.

I used to think nothing was worth throwing away my future. Like a bull, I kept my head down, forging a path from grade school to graduation, not letting anything stop me. Stubborn, as Dash would say. Until now, I would have argued with him, naturally, but deep down, I would have known he was right. Like he'd been right about so many things.

The door opened and I straightened, the breath immediately wheezing out of my chest at the sight of Dash appearing in the doorway. Jessica straightened too, and while she'd looked bored and smug while we'd waited, her face brightened when he walked out. He didn't even spare her a glance, which caused her to deflate.

Professor Michaels, a stern man in his mid-fifties with a white fluff of hair and immaculately trimmed goatee, hovered in the doorway. He didn't say anything when Dash came to my side, but there was a disapproving frown on his lips.

That didn't bode well.

"Let's get out of here," Dash said, and took my hand.

We left Jessica and the professor staring after us—or at least —I thought we did.

I didn't look back to find out.

Dash didn't speak all the way back to the apartment. I was too dumbstruck to say anything. My hands were clammy and knotted in my lap the whole drive. Fear clawed at my throat, and a cold sweat dripped down my spine.

The elevator ride up to my floor was silent. Dash seemed to vibrate with tension. I wasn't sure if he was dropping me off, and never going to speak to me again, or if he was just waiting until we had some privacy before giving me a thorough tongue-lashing. I almost wished he would. Part of me felt like I deserved it.

My hands trembled as I unlocked my door and let him inside. It felt like years had passed since we spoke in his office when, after confirming with a glance at the clock on my microwave, it had been a little over an hour.

"Can I use your bathroom?" Dash asked when he'd stepped inside behind me.

"O-of course."

I pushed my hands through my hair and made my way to

the kitchen to make some coffee to give myself something to do to keep busy. As I was pouring two mugs, Dash appeared in the hallway. I froze with the mugs in my hands.

God, why did he have to be so beautiful?

It really wasn't fair.

His hair was slightly messy where he must have run his hands through it a thousand times. He tended to do that when he was deep in thought. His brilliant green eyes were bloodshot, probably from the stress and rubbing them too much. Maybe he was having as much trouble sleeping as I was. He wore a flannel shirt tucked into dark jeans, but he'd missed a button somewhere so it was slightly lopsided, which made me smile. Even that little imperfection didn't take away from how good he looked.

"Coffee?" I asked when the moment stretched on too long.

He nodded. "Thanks."

We sipped in silence until he sighed, "What a day."

"I'll say," I murmured, then mustered up my nerve. "Did he fire you?"

Dash didn't seem shocked by my question. He merely sipped his coffee as he gathered his thoughts. "I'm not sure yet. There's going to be some sort of informal investigation. They're going to interview a couple people, check our correspondence on the university email, your grades, and all that to see if you were given any sort of preferential treatment. They'll probably call you for an interview, too, to make sure I didn't coerce or intimidate you into giving me sexual favors in return for better grades."

I sputtered into my coffee. "Well, I guess they have to be fair. I should have thought of that, though." That made Dash smile, but I still felt lousy. "I'm sorry. I never should have come to you today. It was a bad move on my part. If I'd kept to the plan, none of this would have happened."

Dash sat his empty cup on the countertop and pulled me into

his arms. "I'm glad you did. I was dying not talking to you. Fuck the consequences. We'll deal with them."

I yawned into his chest, soothed by the warm, musky scent of him. "I know we need to talk about this, and there's a lot I still have to say, but I'm pretty worn out and I haven't slept well since you stayed the night here. What do you think about a nap?"

"I'd say you're speaking my language."

I knew it wouldn't take my mother long to stick her nose in my business. I wasn't surprised when, later that night, she knocked twice at my door before inserting the key I certainly didn't authorize her to have and barreling through looking like an Amazon on a mission. Thank God we were both dressed and had fallen asleep on the couch after our short conversation.

"Mom!" I exclaimed as we sat up. Dash stayed close with a hand protectively on my waist. "How did you get in?"

She glared at the space between Dash and me before saying, "I have a key. Are you going to explain why I received a call from Elizabeth Hampton, asking me to control my daughter?"

My face burned. "Why do you have a key to my apartment?"

Mom dismissed my words with a flick of her handbag and scoffed. "I pay for this apartment, in case you've forgotten. Of course I have a key."

"Mom, you can't just burst in here like this. You may be paying for the apartment, but it's my house. You could at least call before you came over."

"Layla Lucille you do not talk to me like that. I knew there was something going on. You haven't been yourself for months. First it was the internship, then it was dodging my calls. It's because of this boy, isn't it?"

"Mrs. Tate, Layla is a great girl she—"

Mom looked at him with a freezing glare that could have flayed skin with its intensity alone. "Don't you tell me about my daughter. Everything was going on just fine until you came along and preyed on her. You should be ashamed of yourself. If your grandmother hadn't already reported you to the Dean, I would have done it myself."

I jumped to my feet. "He didn't prey on me, Mom. In case you've forgotten, I've known Dash my whole life. If anyone preyed on anyone, I preyed on him."

"Don't be ridiculous. I know what his kind is like. Men with power who target young, innocent girls. Your father was the same way, and I refuse to let it happen to you."

"It's not up to you, Mom. Not every man is like Dad. I'm not going to make the same mistakes you made. I'm going to make new ones. Big ones. But it's my life. I should be allowed to make them. I'm tired of you thinking you can control everything about me, down to the career I pick."

"Not this again. I'm just trying to do what's best for you. Teachers make peanuts. Finance is a stable career."

"I don't want to talk about this anymore. I'd like you to leave."

Mom looked like I'd slapped her. "You can't be serious."

"I think we'll talk about this when you're ready to have a mature conversation and treat me like an adult. That includes requesting to speak to me, not barging into my house. It means treating my opinions and desires as equally important. I'm not yours to treat like a puppet, Mom. I'm a person with my own dreams. My own visions for my life. If you can't respect that, then maybe we need to reevaluate our relationship."

There was a long tense silence. Mom's shoulders heaved as she breathed heavily. Her eyes were bright with a fury I'd never seen before. Then again, I'd never stood up to her before, either. For a moment, I was afraid she was going to throw a tantrum like a toddler right there in my living room, but she merely shouldered her bag and gave me a disdainful look. "You are making a mistake. The difference is, I won't be there to correct it when it blows up in your face."

"I'm sorry you feel that way," I said to her retreating back.

"Not as sorry as I am," she said. She took two steps through the doorway, paused, and then turned back. My heart fell to my feet. I braced before she spoke in a low, guttural voice. "I always knew you were a stupid girl, but I tried my hardest to do what I could to make you successful in this world. I gave you every opportunity and in return, you practically spit them back in my face. When I heard Elizabeth Hampton offered you a fortune to walk away for this boy, I thought 'Finally, Layla will see some sense.' Money like that would have taken you much farther than a man ever could. But no. You were too stupid to know a good thing when it hit you in the face."

With that little bomb deployed, she spun around and disappeared through the door.

CHAPTER 24
DASH

It took a few heartrending moments for the gravity of Layla's mother's words to penetrate. 'Offered you a fortune' kept repeating in my head like a battle cry. My grandmother, my family, bribed Layla. I should have been surprised, but the only emotion I could muster was disappointment, which battled with a numbness I couldn't quite shake.

I couldn't look at Layla while the information sank in, afraid to see the expression on her face. Was it true? One glance at her would tell me the answer.

But I didn't even need that.

Her silence told me everything I needed to know.

When I found my voice, I asked, "Is it true?" while staring at the plush rug beneath my feet. My head felt too heavy for my neck to lift. "Is what your mother said—is it true?"

Layla's sniffles were an arrow straight to my heart, but I held myself away from her, afraid if I looked, I'd shatter. After a moment, she sighed heavily, and said, "I was going to tell you."

I surged to my feet, but there was nowhere to go. I rounded on her. "Why didn't you tell me? When did this happen? What exactly did she say to you?"

She studied her feet, the top of her messy bun coming undone, tendrils of hair framing her ghost-white cheeks. "I didn't tell you because I knew it would hurt you. You love your family. I didn't want to be the one to break your heart. I thought—if we didn't work out—it wouldn't matter anyway. You would never find out. If we did, then I'd cross that bridge when I figured out what I was going to do about us."

"When?" I demanded in a bark that caused her to flinch.

"After the gala, I think. She came to me when I was doing my student teaching and pulled me out of class." Layla shuddered as she spoke. It pissed me off that I was too angry to comfort her. It pissed me off that I wanted to comfort her. It pissed me off that so soon after she admitted how she felt, I was being confronted with this shit. "She told me you deserved better and if I knew what was good for me, I'd take the money and keep my mouth shut."

"Why would you tell me you loved me now?" I thought of all the women who'd chased me because of my family. The ones who'd only cared about my money or my looks. Layla wasn't like that. She was headstrong, stubborn as an ox, and the smartest woman I knew. She wouldn't use me that way.

But there was an insidious fear inside of me that slithered and coiled like a snake. It whispered fuel into the doubts that sprang free. If your own family thought they could buy your future, why not the woman who cared about you?

At this, her head snapped up, eyes flashing like lightning. "Because I do love you."

It hurt to hear the words. If my own family could treat me like a commodity, what was stopping her from doing the same thing? "And yet you took the money. How much was I worth to you, Layla?"

My words shocked her to silence and she gaped at me, her previously pale cheeks flooding with color. She jumped to her feet snarling, "How could you ever think I would do something like that?"

"Are you saying you didn't?"

She glared and bared her teeth. "Of course not. What kind of person do you think I am?" She held up a hand to stop my answer. "You know what? Don't answer that. I think it would be insulting to both of us."

"Why didn't you tell me? Were you going to change your mind?" I don't know why I said it, don't know where the words came from, but they were out before I could take them back. It wasn't really her I was angry with, but I didn't want to believe the alternative.

"Now you really are being insulting. You need to go before I say something we'll both regret."

"Layla." I reached out for her, already regretting how badly this had gone, but she brushed my hands away.

"I think now is probably a good time for us to take a breather. We'll deal with the fallout from what happened today and then —I don't—I don't know."

Layla wrapped her arms around her waist, but flinched when I tried to step closer. My hands dropped to my side in defeat. How had we gotten here?

There wasn't anything else I could say.

So I left.

I drove around for an indeterminable amount of time, taking backstreets and cutoffs until I was riding on a red dirt road in the middle of nowhere. I didn't want to go home, it was too close to Layla, too tempting. My temper had already gotten the best of me, and she didn't deserve it. The people who did, I was terrified to confront.

My grandfather, he'd always been a cold, hard man. It was surprising my dad had ever grown up to be the kind, warm man he was with parents like his. I couldn't go to my grandparents' house, not yet. First, I needed to know if my parents had a part in this. Mom never would have gone along with it, but Dad—he didn't really grow a spine until he met her. Had he knuckled under to grandmother's machinations? I didn't want to think so, but I had to know.

Somehow, I made it back to their hotel room. I knocked and Mom answered the door. Her hair was down, her face scrubbed clean. I glanced at my phone and the time illuminated: 8:05. My parents were early to bed, early to rise people, so they were getting ready to go to sleep.

"Do you have a second?" I asked. "I'm sorry it's so late."

Mom gave me a warm smile. "Of course, honey. What's wrong? You look terrible. Are you okay?"

"I'm fine. Is Dad around? I have something to talk to you both about."

"You're scaring me. Peter! Peter, it's Dash. Can you come out here for a second?"

"Naomi, you don't need to shout the whole place down. I'm right here." He came out of the bathroom of their suite, his tie loose around his neck and his suit missing the jacket, which hung around the back of a chair. "Dash, what is it?"

"He said he has to talk to us about something."

"Well, come in. Do you want something to drink?" Dad asked.

"No, thanks. I'm fine."

Mom hovered by the door as I went inside. "What do you need to talk to us about, honey?"

"It's about grandmother. Dad—" My throat constricted on the words. "Dad, did you know anything about her bribing the girl I was seeing to stay away from me? The truth, please."

"Bribing? What the hell are you talking about?" Dad's face flushed with anger. "I don't know anything about bribery."

"Jessica?" Mom asked.

"No, not Jessica. Her name is Layla. She was a student of mine. I went to school with her."

"Was a student?"

"I'll explain," I said to Mom. Then I turned back to Dad. "Did you?"

"Of course not! I haven't heard a word about it, and frankly, I'm insulted you'd believe she'd do such a thing. She loves you."

"Peter," Mom broke in, trying to alleviate the growing tension. "Don't get upset."

"Don't get upset? He's accusing my mother—"

"You say that as though she didn't show up to our wedding, dressed in black like it was a funeral, Peter. This is our son, he deserves our trust." She turned back to me. "Tell us what happened."

I sat on the edge of their bed and told them everything. From meeting Layla at the beginning of the semester, to an abbreviated version of our relationship, and ending with our argument from a few hours before. The longer I talked, the more disgusted I felt with myself.

She'd told me she loved me and the first thing I did was turn her away.

CHAPTER 25
LAYLA

Ms. Jensen looked the same as she did at the beginning of the semester, except this time her lipstick was a bright orange-red to match her festive sweater, instead of the deep pink. Her mousy hair was in its customary bun and there was a pencil tucked behind her ear.

"Well," she said, then paused, sipped coffee that had gone cold. "Well," she said again.

I wondered how many other times she'd have to say it before her vocabulary would expand.

"I must say I didn't think I'd see you again so quickly, and over such unpleasant business." Ms. Jensen clucked her tongue, then shuffled a stack of papers. "I'm sorry to say considering, well, considering, you won't be able to resume the business ethics class for the rest of the semester." She paused, adjusted her glasses and then studied me over the rim. "Of course, when we took into account your grade point average and your academic records, we decided to make an exception on a one-time-only basis."

I straightened in the creaky leather seat. "I'm sorry? What do you mean?"

It had been a week since my blowup with Dash. I hadn't spoken to my mother—who surely thought her silent treatment was punishment rather than the reward it was. My sister spent most of every day alternating between calling, texting, and showing up at my classes. I'd blocked her number and pretended she was a stranger.

According to her, I should forgive my mother for her latest transgression. Mom only called me stupid because she was so upset about the bad decisions I was making. She didn't really mean it.

The one person I hadn't heard from was Dash.

Now that the dust had settled, I didn't know where we stood. I hurt him, that I accepted, but he knew me. He should have trusted me.

Otherwise, everything we went through was for nothing.

I realized Ms. Jensen was speaking, so I pushed Dash from my mind and tried to focus on what she was saying. "If you wanted, that is."

"What?" I said and flushed. "I'm sorry, can you repeat that?"

She smiled. "I said considering your academic record and the fact that there was no proof Mr. Hampton showed you any sort of preference whatsoever—the administration will allow you to repeat the course next semester—with a different professor, naturally."

This should have been good news.

It could have been so much worse.

I could still finish both degrees on time as though nothing had happened. If I so desired, with a little placating, I could even convince my mother everything would be fine. By placating, I meant I'd need to take that finance position she was so all-fired about. Meaning I wouldn't have any time at all to participate in any showings or work on my pieces. It would mean giving up a part of me that felt as vital as breathing.

"No," I said, and it was as though the word unlocked something inside of me. "No, I don't think so."

"No?" Ms. Jensen repeated. "Honey, I understand it's disheartening to have to repeat a course, but if you don't, then you won't be able to complete the requirements for the business portion of your degree."

I already felt lighter. Free. "Be that as it may, I don't wish to repeat the course. I'm still okay to graduate with the degree in art with a minor in education, though, right?"

Ms. Jensen shuffled through her papers, her cheeks a little pink. "Well, of course, I suppose if that's what you want. It just seems silly to have done all that work and not receive credit for it."

"It does, doesn't it? I could have saved us both some time if I'd realized what I wanted in the first place. Excuse me," I said and got to my feet. "There's something else I need to take care of. Have a wonderful break, Ms. Jensen."

A few months ago, I'd walked out of her office with the weight of the world on my shoulders. I'd been pursing a degree I didn't even want, for a mother who only cared how it reflected on her. If I'd told her no years ago, I would have never been in this mess.

Then again, if it weren't for her, I wouldn't have crossed paths, and hypothetical swords, with Dash again.

As I walked to my car from the admin building, I took out my phone and considered calling him. I wanted to apologize, for everything, but I wasn't sure what, exactly, I could say to bridge the gap between everything that had happened.

Instead of reaching out to Dash, my fingers keyed in the number for my mother instead. She'd be overjoyed to hear from me—but only because it meant she'd won—and I'd broken the silence first.

"Hello?"

She answered on the first ring, sounding slightly breathless.

I'd put money on the fact she'd been waiting for my call, and she'd run to her phone the second she heard it ring.

"Hey, Mom," I said. My voice was steady, sure, but I felt more vulnerable than I had in a long time. Vulnerable, but immovable. For so long, I'd tried to be the daughter she wanted. I did everything she asked, even if doing so meant losing parts of myself.

"Layla. To what do I owe the pleasure?" she asked.

I could imagine her in her office, leaned back in her desk chair with a satisfied smile on her face. I'd seen the same smile several times before—it was the one she wore when she got her way. Even thinking about it made my stomach tight with anxiety.

"I wanted to thank you for everything that you've done for me." Her tone of surprised satisfaction made my mouth twist in revulsion. "Thank you for showing me how little I meant to you. Without you, it never would have been so easy to tell you that I no longer need your help. I've dropped the business ethics class, which means I will be ineligible to graduate with the business portion of my degree. I've already informed Kragen's that I'm not interested in the internship. I've also spoken with the financial aid office, and I'll be applying for student loans next semester. So your threat about owning my apartment and essentially my life is now moot."

"After everything I've done for you, how dare you treat me this way?" she screeched in my ear. "You're going to fall flat on your face without my help, and don't you dare come running to me when you do."

At the start of the semester, facing life without my family as a safety net would have terrified me. Defying my mother had been unthinkable. But after everything that had happened, I'd realized life wasn't worth living if you weren't doing what you loved. It may have been selfish to live on my terms, but I'd been selfless long enough.

"If that's how you feel, I understand. I wish you the best and hope you find happiness. I know I will."

My answer was a click. Somehow, I wasn't surprised. Disappointed, a little hollow inside, but not surprised.

I ached a little at the potential loss of my sister. She'd always been my mother's second-in-command, and I'd never really gotten to know her as a sister, just a flying monkey my mother would send when she didn't get me to do something she wanted. I hoped with a little space and time, maybe she would change, but I wasn't holding my breath.

I didn't think about either of them as I drove back to my apartment. With the radio cranked up, I blotted out all of my thoughts by singing along with Miley Cyrus' "Party in the U.S.A."

Ember and Charlie were already waiting for me in my apartment. It wasn't a Tuesday, so they'd brought a couple twelve packs, tape, and boxes.

"I had these extra from my move last year," Charlie said as she handed me an ice-cold beer. "I never got around to throwing them away, but I guess that's a good thing."

"It's not a good thing," Ember complained. "I can't believe both of you are just deserting me. Some friends."

Since my mom was officially no longer footing the bill for my apartment, I had to find somewhere more affordable. I'd applied for a full-time job with the art charity and had my fingers crossed I'd get it. It wouldn't pay much, but what it didn't cover I would supplement with what scholarships I could scrounge up and use student loans as a last resort.

"We see Charlie just as much as we did before she moved out," I reasoned, then laughed as Ember fervently shook her head.

"That's grossly untrue. She works back-to-back shifts all the time. Before we could see her like that," she snapped her fingers for emphasis, "but now we basically have to make an appointment. Mark my words, it'll be the same when you leave. All I'll have left is Tripp." She made a face.

"Oh, that's such a travesty," Charlie said with a giggle. "Truly, it's torture. How many abs does he have? I saw him lift his shirt last year during playoffs, and I swear I counted at least twenty."

Ember threw a towel she'd been folding at Charlie's face. "For the last time, we're just friends. I'm with Chris."

"For now," Charlie and I said at the same time, then shared a smile. These two—they were better than any man.

"Whatever. Are you two going to pack or are you just going to sit there and run your mouths?"

"I think we're going to run our mouths while we watch you pack," I suggested.

"I'll remember this." Ember began throwing towels and washcloths into a bag willy-nilly at Charlie's burst of laughter. "Next year, when it's my turn to move, I'm going to sit back with my feet up, mark my words."

"Sure, sure. I don't think you'll ever leave your apartment." Her face fell a little, and I reminded myself I wasn't the only one with problems. "I think you need another beer as much as I do," I said and grabbed her a fresh one.

"Are you going to tell us what you decided to do about Dash?" Ember said in a clear bid to change the subject.

I sipped my drink and considered. "Maybe… once we finish packing."

They both threw towels at my head.

CHAPTER 26

DASH

"You're a good man, Dash. I'm sorry to have to do this, but it's university policy."

Professor Michaels stood at the door to my office and watched as I packed. Official policy mandated suspension and immediate termination for grad students who fraternized with their students, but as there wasn't concrete evidence my relationship with Layla went beyond one kiss he witnessed, I was given the termination and advised to steer clear of applying for any other T.A. positions.

It could have been worse.

I had one more semester before I graduated, anyway. And I didn't need the money, although the experience was useful.

"Don't sweat it, Professor. I understand. Thank you for going to bat for me. I appreciate it."

"I wish I could do more, but my hands are tied. You'll let me know if you need anything? I'll be in my office."

"Of course, sir. Thanks again."

He nodded, rapped his knuckles on the doorjamb, then left me to my thoughts.

After the conversation with my parents, I'd gone home;

painfully aware of how close it was to Layla's. I was too consumed by guilt and fury to be in the right frame of mind to face her. Especially considering I hadn't figured out how to confront my grandmother.

After I finished packing up my office, I planned to drive over to my grandparents' place on the way home and talk to them. Even if I had no clue what I was going to say.

I worked steadily during the afternoon, clearing out the bookshelves, the mini fridge, and then finally, my desk. It wasn't until I sat down in my chair that I noticed the book sitting on the center of my blotter. I knew what it was the moment I laid eyes on it.

It was a first edition copy of *Dracula*. The cover was bound in a deep crimson with gold foil and filigree. I opened the cover and confirmed the publication date. Inside was a piece of paper. I recognized the handwriting from papers I'd assigned in our class.

In Layla's neat penmanship were the words:

"There are darknesses in life and there are lights, and you are one of the lights, the light of all light." – Bram Stoker

Beneath it, she added:

You are one of my lights.

Before I could jump to my feet to race home to her, there was a knock at my door. For a split second, I was swamped by pure joy thinking it was Layla coming to see my reaction to her gift. I stood, still holding the book, but it wasn't Layla waiting for me.

It was my grandmother.

"Dashiel," she said primly.

My mouth firmed and a white-hot bolt of rage shot through me. "Grandmother," I replied. "What are you doing here?"

She stepped inside, closed the door. "You haven't been answering my calls."

"There was a reason for that."

She lifted a brow. "I assumed so. That's why I came to speak with you in person, like an adult."

I barked out a laugh. "Interesting."

"What?" she asked.

"It's interesting that you're suggesting we should treat each other like adults."

"And what is that supposed to mean?"

I gripped the back of my chair to keep myself focused and to steady my twitching hands. "You know what I'm talking about." Despite my fury, my voice was deadly calm.

"Really, Dash, I don't have time for these games."

"You offered Layla Tate money to stay away from me."

I already knew she wasn't going to cop to what she'd done unless she was confronted directly. It was disappointing to realize how similar she was to Layla's mother. No wonder the two of us got along so well…relatively speaking.

A parade of emotions washed over her face. Shock. Anger. Denial. Then she cleared her expression and affected a mask of sorrow. If I hadn't been watching her so closely, I wouldn't have believed it.

"You'd believe that girl over me?"

"That girl is a beautiful, kind, genuine person. Which you would know if you spent two seconds getting to know her."

"I don't have to get to know her to know who she is. She's exactly like your mother. Money-hungry and only interested in what she can leech from you."

I shook my head. "You're delusional. You'd rather have me with Jessica, who would dance on my grave to inherit my portfolio, than with Layla, who genuinely cares about me. What is wrong with you?" I asked, exasperated.

"The only thing wrong with me is caring too much for my family, which goes unappreciated. I won't speak anymore about this, Dashiel, and if you want to have a place in our lives, you'll stay away from that girl—and understand when I do something —it comes from a place of love, because I care about you."

I almost believed the tears, the watery voice. Except her eyes were completely devoid of emotion. The pulse beating in her throat was steady. She could have been at a spa for all the genuine emotion she showed.

"If you cared about me, you never would have interfered."

The tears dried. Her voice hardened. "You better watch how you speak to me, Dashiel Hampton."

"I don't think I will. The men in this family have let you run over them for far too long, and I won't let you ruin the best thing that's ever happened to me."

This time, the shock in her expression was real. "You'd choose her over your own family?"

I leaned across the desk, pressing my hands into its surface. The gold foil from the book glinted in the corner of my eyes, solidifying my resolve. "When my family lies and manipulates me? I'd choose Layla, fight for her—Every. Time."

Grandmother straightened, looked down her nose. "You're going to regret this. Don't come crawling to me when she uses and discards you, Dash. I won't want to hear it."

She left and shut the door quietly. A Hampton didn't make a scene. It must have really peeved her when news spread about my relationship with Layla. Bad press wasn't acceptable. Apparently, deceit and exploitation were much more tolerable.

I finished packing in the ringing silence of my grandmother's departure with the copy of *The Hobbit* catching my eye every few seconds. It sat in the passenger seat of my car as I drove home.

Without thinking, I took the elevator to Layla's floor and my feet carried me directly to her door. I knocked, but she didn't answer.

I tried knocking again. No answer.

Her phone went straight to voicemail when I tried to call.

After twenty minutes, I gave up. I'd try again in the morning. And the next day, and the next day until she answered.

Because she was right.

We were worth fighting for.

I made my way back to my floor with renewed determination, already coming up with a plan to win her back. I was going to go the whole nine, flowers, chocolates, trips to her favorite art galleries, and enough orgasms to leave her limp and sated for the rest of her life. All she had to do was give me another chance.

I wouldn't fuck it up.

I got out of the elevator on my floor, but I was looking down at my phone, texting Layla for the third time.

So I didn't see her standing at my front door until I nearly bumped into her.

She grabbed onto my arms to keep from being bowled over, but our feet tangled, and we went tumbling down.

"Oof," Layla said as I landed on top of her. "Were you trying to turn me into a pancake?"

I steadied myself, raising up on my forearms to keep my weight from crushing her. "If you'd answer your phone once in a while, I wouldn't have run into you."

"I packed my phone charger, and I don't know which frigging box it's in or I would have answered my phone," she growled.

"Packed away? What do you mean packed away?"

"It's where you put things into boxes to make it easier to move them," she said slowly.

"Why are you packing?"

Layla scowled up at me. "Do we really have to have this

conversation in the middle of the hallway while you're squishing me to death?"

I got to my feet and helped her up. "Now speak."

"I'm not a dog, Dash. Why do you always have to boss me around?"

I nearly growled. *I missed this?*

With exaggerated care, I opened the door to my apartment and waved her inside. "I suppose asking you to sit would be outside of the question?" She sent me a scathing look and spun on her heel to leave. I caught her arm and said, "I'm kidding. Kidding! I promise. No more jokes."

I'd left my box of stuff from the office in my car, but I'd carried the copy of *The Hobbit* upstairs with me. When we'd crashed into each other it had gone flying. While she took a seat on the couch, I retrieved the book from where it had landed by my door.

Holding it up as I went inside, I said, "I guess by fight for me, you really meant fight with me."

"Dash," she said in a warning tone, but there was a hint of a smile shining from her eyes.

I sat beside her on the couch and took her hands in mine. She angled her body to face me, a wave of vulnerability creeping into her expression. "I was just at your apartment to talk to you. I guess we both had the same idea. Why are you packing?"

She looked down at our hands. "I blew my mom off and she basically cut me out of her life. I can't afford to live alone for next semester, so I signed a lease with a couple other roommates until summer when I can figure something else out."

After kissing her fingers and pulling her in for a hug, I said into her hair, "I'm so sorry it came to that, but I'm proud of you. So fucking proud. She didn't deserve you. You're an amazing person, Lay. Right down to the bone. If she couldn't see that, then screw her."

She pulled back, and a tear leaked from her eye. I brushed it away with a knuckle. "Thank you. I know that's true. It's just hard because she's my mom."

"I understand. I wish I didn't, but I do."

"What about your grandmother?" she asked hesitantly.

"Before we get into that, I just want to apologize for the way I reacted. I was wrong. I know you, Layla. I should have trusted you. I will trust you, from now on. For a long time the people around me have used me for their own means, and even though I knew you would never do something like that, it was a knee-jerk reaction. I hope you know I'll spend every day, for as long as you'll let me stay around, making it up to you."

Her hands came to my shoulders and my eyes closed at how good it felt to have her touching me again. How right. "I understand how hard it is to be faced with the truth about your own family. If it weren't for you, I never would have come to realize exactly how bad mine was. I just hate I had to come between you. I hope your parents understood."

The fear in her eyes had me pulling her close. "They did. My dad didn't, at first, but my mom has been putting up with my grandmother for a long time and didn't hesitate to stand up for me. And you didn't come between anyone. My grandmother made her choices. You didn't do anything wrong."

"It feels so good to hear you say that. I was worried you were going to tell me to take a hike." She sighed as she settled into me, and I wondered if there was a more perfect feeling than having her in my arms.

"That wasn't what I was planning on saying," I told her.

"What were you going to say?"

I tipped her chin up with a finger and smiled. "That you're worth fighting for, too."

EPILOGUE

LAYLA

Two years after graduation, I'd never sold a piece at a gallery. I'd never become a household name as an artist. Hell, even my Etsy page did a minimal amount of business. I guess my mother had been right in assuming my art degree would never rake in the bucks.

But I couldn't be happier.

As I tidied the little garden behind the sweet yellow cottage Dash and I rented, I felt full to bursting. Radiant as the sun. If Dash didn't get home soon, I would explode with the news.

Brushing my hands off on the little apron I wore when I puttered around the garden, I surveyed my work with a keen eye. The dainty pansies and perky petunias danced in a gentle spring breeze. Tomorrow, I'd finish the darling little hummingbird feeders I'd been working on, and I'd hang them in the ancient oak that towered over our backyard like a sentinel.

A tortoiseshell cat I'd named Tiger twisted around my ankles as I gathered my supplies and packed them away in the garden shed. When I shooed her away, she scampered off to chase a pair of butterflies flittering around my lantana plants. Dash had surprised me with the kitten after I won an award last year from my employer.

Rookie Teacher of the Year.

I still couldn't believe it.

Not only that I'd found my niche, my passion, but that it hadn't been in the avenue I expected at all. I suppose it was the student teaching I'd been required to do for my education minor. The semester after I dropped my business class, I'd decided to fill the extra time with education courses. I loved them almost as much as I loved art, which had come as a surprise to me.

I never would have considered it if it hadn't been for Dash.

At the sound of the door opening and closing, Tiger's ears perked up and her tail flicked three times in rapid succession. When footsteps echoed, she scrambled out of the lantana bushes, up the back steps, and disappeared into the dining room. Moments later, I could hear the low rumble of Dash's voice greeting her.

Tiger had been a gift for me, but Dash was her true love.

I couldn't blame her.

He was mine, too.

Noting a flower that must have gotten uprooted when Tiger was chasing the butterflies, I squatted down to pack it more securely into the soil. When I finished and looked up, I found Dash sitting on the top step of the deck, the kitten purring contentedly in his arms.

Like he had done almost every day since that fateful day in his class, he simply took my breath away.

Dash was handsome no matter what he wore, but the suits were my favorite. I was ever so thankful he was required to wear one to work Monday through Friday. I liked seeing them on him, but I also enjoyed taking them off him.

Crossing the garden, I bent down and kissed his lips as the kitten settled into his arms. "How was work?" I asked, already feeling a little breathless and wondering how quickly I could convince him to make a detour to the bedroom.

"Dad's on a tear. His opponent is tough this year."

Despite all the protests he'd made, Dash had gone into politics, though not at the pressure of his family. His parents had told him repeatedly—whatever he decided to do—they would support him.

It turned out, without the constant pushing from his grandmother, he actually enjoyed helping with his father's campaign. After completing his MBA, Dash joined his father as a campaign manager, and he never looked back.

It was a side benefit that his grandmother wasn't allowed to attend any events, and she frequently made her displeasure known. Not that anyone cared.

My mother hadn't contacted me since the day she disowned me. She wasn't missed. Delia, on the other hand, had since been to therapy and we're slowly rebuilding our relationship. It was hard and awkward, but she was making the effort, so was I. I was cautiously optimistic, but I kept my ears tuned for any nonsense about mending fences with my mother.

"He'll win. Hamptons always do," I said.

"That's because we have excellent taste," Dash said, drawing me into his lap, displacing a disgruntled Tiger. "I have something for you."

"I have something to tell you, too."

Dash smiled patiently. "You first."

The news burst forth. "Liam and Charlie are having a baby!"

He winced a little at the volume of my voice. "That's wonderful. I bet they're excited."

"She couldn't wait to tell everyone. Now you, what's your news?"

"We may have to wait to tell them so we don't steal their thunder, but maybe you can keep a secret."

He placed a package in my lap, and I tore into it with the enthusiasm of a child.

It was a pristine copy of *Shakespeare's Sonnets*. Inside was a note.

> *"Love is not love which alters when it alteration finds, or bends with the remover to remove: O no; it is an ever-fixed mark, that looks on tempests and is never shaken."*

Below that it said:

> *Layla,*
>
> *There's nothing I would like more than to spend the rest of my life arguing with you.*
>
> *Marry me?*

Attached to the note was a ring.

Keep reading for a sneak peek at the next book in the series...Friends with Benefits!

FRIENDS WITH BENEFITS

NEW YORK TIMES & USA TODAY BESTSELLING AUTHOR

NICOLE BLANCHARD

CHAPTER 1

EMBER

got the text message while I was in the home improvement store trying to figure out which carpet to buy to replace the one my sisters had ruined.

I ignored it for a few minutes as I decided between sandcastle and brilliant beige. The last thing I should be doing is putting more stainable, light-colored carpet in their room, but these were the only two options in my price range, and my budget was already stretched to the max. My parents should be attending to this particular responsibility, but asking them to do anything responsible was like trying to pluck a star from the sky: impossible.

"How much is this one?" I asked, pointing to the beige. The clerk stretched to check the printouts as I dragged out my phone to read the text.

At first, my heart lifted at the From: indicator. It was Chris, my boyfriend, who was away at college in Miami. It had been a couple of days since I had heard from him, and although I wanted to talk to him more often, he'd made it a point to let me know I was smothering him, so I had backed off.

Apparently, I hadn't backed off far enough.

> CHRIS: Hey pretty lady. Wassup?

It should have pleased me to hear from him, but an indescribable weight seemed to take up residence on my shoulders. Anxiety bubbled in my stomach. All I wanted was for us to work out. Our relationship had become more work than anything else, but that's what relationships were—or so I told myself. If I kept working at this, it would pay off.

> ME: Getting carpet for the twins' room. How are you?

Somehow, my relationship with the man who I thought I loved had turned into a carnival reflection of itself. I didn't recognize it when I looked in the mirror. Chris and I had met when we were in high school and then reconnected when we were at the same community college. I had been training to be an EMT; he had been finishing prerequisites to transfer to a four-year university. To be honest, I'd had a crush on him for as long as I could remember, and when he had reciprocated interest, I had thought I was the luckiest girl in the world.

It had been a long time since I thought I was the luckiest girl in the world.

Ever since things had gotten more serious and the time began to draw near for me to either stay in Tallahassee or join him in Miami, he'd begun to retreat. The more I tried to make it work, the more he pulled away. In my heart, I knew what that meant, but I didn't quite know how to give up hope.

It didn't matter. Reading his text told me all I needed to know about our future together. As the words began to sink in, my tongue went as dry as the Mojave, and my thoughts blurred together.

CHRIS: Look, I think I need to be upfront about something with you. I don't want to hurt you, but I've met someone. I thought I should tell you.

My fingers went numb where they clutched at the phone. Even though I had an inkling it was coming, the reality was so much worse than anything I could have dreamt up. My vision went white, and, dramatic though it was, I couldn't seem to catch my breath.

I'd never been the type of girl who went gaga over any guy, but I guess there was a first time for everything.

It shouldn't hurt so much to have my suspicions confirmed. I hadn't wanted to say my fears out loud, afraid that it would make them too real.

But here it was, in black and white. The undeniable truth.

The guy I loved, the one I'd trusted and believed in for so long, wasn't who I thought he was.

The poor clerk who was reading off measurements, colors, and prices gaped after me as I dropped the other supplies I'd been considering in the shopping cart and then abandoned it in the middle of the aisle.

Normally, I loved this store. I loved the possibilities of it. The little apartment I rented for my family wasn't in the best shape, and fixing it up was one of the most rewarding things about my somewhat dismal life. But suddenly the sky-high shelves of paint chips and caulk didn't feel reassuring. Instead, the winding aisles became a maze from which there was no escape.

I texted a response blindly. I was sure to read it back later and regret it, but if the only weapon I had was words, I wanted to aim for his heart and make it hurt.

ME: Then I guess all the promises you made about wanting to be with me forever, all the times you said you loved me meant nothing. All those were just lies? I'm not a perfect person, but I deserve better than this. I shouldn't be as surprised as I am, but I actually believed the bullshit you spun to me about it being us against the world. Lose my number. I don't ever want to hear from you again.

As tears flooded my vision, I blocked his number and navigated through the aisles to the front door. I don't know how I made it back to the apartment complex without wrapping my car around a pole, but I did. Sheer will, I suppose. All those late nights driving an ambulance, high on adrenaline, must have paid off.

An indeterminable amount of time later, I found myself in the shower, the hot spray beating down on my naked body and hot tears streaming down my cheeks. I didn't know a person could hurt so much. It felt like I was dying, except there was nothing I knew in my repertoire of life-saving skills that could resuscitate me.

I don't know how long I sat there, wallowing in self-pity. It could have been minutes, but it felt like years. The water began to run cold, although I could barely feel it. My brain seemed to have disconnected from my body. It was probably a good thing. The flashes of pain that radiated down to the marrow of my bones were almost too much to handle.

I'd never believed in broken hearts. Get over it, I'd think to myself when friends of mine would go through a breakup. Even when Liam and Charlie or Layla and Dash had split, granted it was only for a short time, I didn't think it was so bad. They'd gotten back together, after all. I'd been with Chris so long it had never occurred to me what would happen when we broke up. Not even when things started to get so rocky a couple of months ago.

What a fool I was.

My laugh echoed off the dingy subway tiles, and I peeled myself off of the tub floor to turn off the water. My hair was matted to my head, but I couldn't find the energy to care. Any concern aside from surviving had leaked out of me in the torrent of tears and had seeped down the drain.

The twins still had another couple of hours at school. Mom was probably off with whatever bum she'd hooked up with over the weekend, and my father, who didn't seem to care who she slept with, was no doubt glued to a barstool down the road at his favorite haunt.

I was alone.

I doubled over as the implication stabbed through me.

I was alone.

I had my family, but they were more of a responsibility than a comfort. I'd get through this for them. I had my friends, but they had their own lives, and I didn't want to burden them—not yet. It wasn't in my nature to lean on others. I provided for my family, working myself to the bone without any help from my deadbeat parents. I would survive this, even if it didn't feel like it at the moment.

For now, it felt like the pain encapsulated everything, blotting out my surroundings until it contracted to a dull ache in my chest. I staggered to my bedroom with a towel wrapped loosely around my body and water dripping from my saturated hair onto the worn wood floors. I didn't care. I couldn't scrounge up the energy to do more than throw myself onto the bed and pull the mussed covers around me.

My phone was hauntingly silent, which only made the tears fall harder. There were no social media notifications. No emails. I knew, somewhere deep down in my soul, that he wouldn't try reaching out that way.

He'd found someone else.

I'd supported him through his father's death the year before.

When he didn't think he could pass his finals after the funeral, I stayed up after two double shifts and helping the twins through a stomach virus to quiz him. For his birthday, I'd driven down and taken him to his favorite restaurant, even though I was barely making enough money to pay rent and support my sisters.

I would have done anything for him.

I did do anything for him.

Was that where I went wrong? Had I made it too easy? Was I one of those women who got boring in a relationship because I wasn't exciting or sexy enough?

My thoughts spiraled down a black hole, and I covered my face with a pillow until I'd cried myself dry. I must have dozed off at times because a sudden realization would jerk me awake, and then it would start all over again.

One day, I told myself. I'd give him one day of being upset, and then I'd push it away, bury it deep, and never think of this— or him—again.

It was wishful thinking, considering we'd been together for a long time. But the thought of feeling this way forever, of giving in to the temptation to give way to a despair so all-encompassing, was overpowering. I was afraid I wouldn't survive it.

The front door slammed, and pattering feet bounded into the apartment. The twins were home. I shot to my feet and winced as a headache throbbed insistently behind my eyes.

"Ember!" one of them called.

"Shh!" said the other. "What if she's sleeping?"

The first scoffed. "She's never sleeping."

It made me laugh. They always made me laugh. Raising them never should have fallen on my shoulders, but it had. Even with the burden of taking care of my sisters, they were the lights of my life. The sound of their innocent debate drew me from the shelter of blankets, and I glanced at my phone to find it blinking 3:24 p.m. I must have fallen asleep after my crying jag.

"Do you think we should check on her? What if she's sick?" the second asked.

"Maybe we should get the therbombiter, Tillie." Which meant it was Molly speaking.

"Do you know how to use it?" Molly asked with clear interest.

"Sure. All you do is stick it in her mouth and push the button. I'll get it from the medicine cabinet. You get a glass of water and the throw-up bowl in case she's stomach sick."

Matilda Leanne was the oldest of my twin sisters—by a whole twenty minutes. It may as well have been twenty years for how she bossed around her younger sister, Molly Elizabeth.

The patter of their feet echoed down the hall, and I decided to wait for them to return to see what they would do. Besides, I didn't have the energy to get back to my feet quite yet. As I contemplated getting up, I heard them return.

"You knock, Tillie," Molly said.

"No, you knock," Tillie replied.

"You always tell me what to do," Molly whined, but a rapping sound followed anyway.

"Ember, are you 'kay? It's us."

My face felt like I'd been repeatedly punched as I smiled and raised my voice to say, "Come in." I wiped away any evidence of tears and tried in vain to straighten my hair and look like I hadn't been crying for hours.

Two orange-headed girls of six bounded into my room. Tillie's curls were soft waves that floated around her shoulders. Molly's were tight ringlets that bounced with each step. They were both the terrors and the lights of my life.

"We brought you some water and a therbombiter. Are you sick?" Tillie asked as she sat on the side of the bed. Molly climbed up and around to my other side.

"Just a little tired," I said, edging around the truth. "The water will help."

I took the glass Molly offered, amazed she hadn't spilled it during her climb up. The water was tepid, but wet, and after crying for hours, I felt like a wrung-out rag. I was probably a little dehydrated.

The girls stared at me, expectantly. "Thank you, babies," I said with a squeeze. "This is perfect. Do you have homework?"

Tillie wagged her finger at me, and Molly giggled. "No work until you feel better. You always let us watch TV when we don't feel good."

I didn't have it in me to argue. Homework could wait. I pulled the girls close, sighing as their little bodies fit into my side.

Who needed a man when I had them?

CHAPTER 2

TRIPP

FRESHMEN YEAR

"Hey, hotshot," a voice called out.

Looking up, I glowered at the source and then felt a jolt go through my body. A beat-up sedan was stopped behind the car of the girl I was hitting on. The driver leaned out, her glossy red hair tumbling over her shoulders. Her eyes were spitting fire, even over the short distance. They made me forget my original goal—the pretty little brunette sorority chick I'd been eyeing for weeks.

"There are other people in the world, you know," said the redhead. "Do you mind?"

Red gestured to the sorority girl's car, which was blocking her way in the parking garage.

I straightened and sent Red a winning smile. "Not at all, angel. Why don't you come and join us?"

"In your dreams," Red retorted. "All I want from you is for you to get out of my way. I'm kind of in a hurry here."

"Do you know that chick?" the sorority girl—I think her name was Gemma—asked, attitude on full display.

"Not yet," I said under my breath.

Red must have heard. "Not ever."

I heard a thin wail that sounded familiar, but I couldn't place it. She turned to the backseat, and I saw through the windshield two tall backed car seats strapped in on either side. This caused me to straighten. She was a mother? That certainly made me do a double take. The sound I'd heard was a kid crying.

"Great," I heard Red mutter when the second kid's ear-piercing cry joined in. "You think you could take your seduction routine somewhere else?" she snarled.

"I should get going," Gemma said. "You wanna call me later?"

"Sure," I said absently. My eyes were all for Red, who was still turned around, comforting the writhing bundles in the backseat.

"Don't you need my number?" Gemma asked.

"Right," I answered, shaking my head. I passed her my phone, and she put in her contact info with a sultry smile. Returning it, I winked and watched as she drove off.

"About time," Red said as her car sailed by and pulled into a parking spot.

I jogged to catch up, my leg muscles still loose from afternoon practice. She was unloading the babies from the car by the time I came to a stop by her side. Red looked up and frowned at me. It made me wonder what it would take to make her smile.

"What?" she asked pointedly. She had to raise her voice over the little screaming machines she was now loading into a stroller.

As a freshman athlete, hooking up with a woman who clearly came with strings attached didn't seem like the best idea, yet I couldn't walk away. Not even the squalling kidlets in the back seat could deter me.

"What's your name?" I asked.

She snorted. "That's the best you got? Look, I've had a long night here, and I've got a long morning ahead of me. I honestly don't have time for your bullshit. So, if you don't mind, I'm going home. If you aren't a creep, you won't follow me. Got it?"

Red locked the second kid into the stroller and strode off with a toss of her hair. It must have been the hair that drew my dumb ass after her. I followed it through the parking garage entrance and down the hall to the elevator. When we arrived, she scowled at me.

"I'm not following you. I live here, too. Third floor."

"No, you don't."

I smiled. "Yeah, I do. You just move in? I haven't seen you around here before."

The elevator opened, and she pushed the stroller inside, heaving with the effort from the heavy contraption. Red-faced and with a lung capacity to rival my team's best sprinters, the kids hadn't stopped screaming since they'd woken in the car. I winced a little, but even that didn't dull my curiosity.

I was a goner.

"Are you for real?" she asked. Being so close to her, I could see her eyes were dark, mossy green—the color of leaves deep in the forest where sunlight struggled to reach.

"I seem to be," I answered when I remembered her question.

"I don't really have time right now to entertain whatever delusions are cropping up inside that head of yours."

The elevator dinged, and the sound of the discontented children echoed off the walls in the hall. I hurried after her. When I caught up, she caught sight of me and growled under her breath, causing the twins to jerk in surprise and cut off mid-scream.

"Didn't I tell you not to follow me? I don't have time for this right now. Stop following me!"

At her shout, the twins began screeching again, and I winced.

I pointed to my apartment. "I'm not following you." Well, not really. "That's my place right there." I held out the key and shook it. "I've even got the key if you don't believe me."

Red glanced from me to the door and then back again. Her face crumpled, and she rested her back against the door, crumpling into a heap. I peered around the stroller and found Red's face buried into her knees, her shoulders shaking.

Two kids, I could deal with. After all, kids cry…I wasn't sure much, but I was pretty positive it was often. Not much I could do about that, but a grown woman in a crying fit? Left me feeling like I had two left feet.

I crouched in front of her and placed a hand on her knee. "Hey, I'm sorry. I didn't mean to upset you. Please don't cry."

Patting her back like I would a puppy was about the extent of my soothing abilities. After a second, she blew out a hot breath and looked up at me with bloodshot eyes, her nose running.

She was beautiful.

"You alright?" I asked with half a laugh. Clearly, she wasn't alright, but I was at a loss for words.

Red rolled her eyes. "I'm fine. I was just…overwhelmed for a second."

She accepted my hand to help her back to her feet. The ringing in my ears had me glancing back at the toddlers, who'd cried themselves to sleep. Studying them warily, I asked, "Are they okay?"

"They're just overstimulated. They hate riding in the car seats. Not that I blame them." She placed a hand on each of their chests and gazed at their slumbering faces.

"How old are they?" I asked to fill the silence.

Glancing up at me, she said, "Two years."

"I don't mean this the way it sounds, but you look amazing for having two-year-old twins."

"Am I supposed to take that any other way than how it sounds?"

Thank God she was smiling.

I sputtered to defend myself, but she laughed. "Don't sweat it. I'm not their mom. They're my baby sisters."

"Ah, right. Sorry again."

"Since you're here, you can bring them in for me while I get their snack ready." When I did nothing but stare, she waved me inside. "Come on. They aren't going to bite. If we're going to be neighbors, we might as well get to know each other. Besides, I feel shitty for yelling at you. I'll get you a soda as a friendly gesture."

With exaggerated care, I wheeled the stroller into the apartment as Red bustled around the kitchen, opening cabinets and cutting up bite sized pieces of fruits and veggies, 'cause I had no clue. The toddlers slept in their car seats, but I didn't trust them not to wake up and turn into air raid sirens again, so I didn't make a sound as I waited.

She looked up, and her eyes danced with laughter. "You look like you're going to set off a bomb or something. They aren't going to bite you."

"They might start screaming again," I whispered.

"What's your name?" she asked after shaking her head. "I guess I'd better know it if we're going to be neighbors. This probably won't be the first time you hear them screaming at all hours of the night."

"Tripp. Tripp Wilder."

She paused mixing the bottles. "That can't really be your name."

"It really is."

"Is that short for something?" she asked.

"John Thomas III," I answered. "Tripp, as in triple or the third."

"That makes more sense." She capped the bottles, tucked them under her free arm, and then opened the fridge and got a soda, which she handed to me. "Tripp suits you better than John, that's for sure."

"I get that a lot." It was part of the problem.

"I'm Ember. These little boogers are Matilda, Tillie for short, and Molly."

Ember.

God, her name couldn't have been more perfect. It matched her hair, her fiery attitude, and how her presence seemed to heat me from the inside out.

Ember.

"I'm sorry for being a bit of a bitch earlier. I was in a hurry to get home because these two were fussy, and I knew they'd be hungry soon."

She was a natural with them. I wouldn't have had a clue how to take care of a kid, let alone two at once. But she sat the plates of food on the coffee table, unhooked the car seats, and lifted them out. Once she was settled, she situated one little girl on one side of her and the other in the crook of her arm. It was like some sort of kid-style Tetris. I was fascinated. The girls woke up in increments, but thankfully they didn't start crying again. Food seemed to placate them. I needed to remember that.

"You don't have to apologize," I said. I scrubbed a hand over my neck as one started talking gibberish. "Do you need some help?"

Amusement danced lively in her eyes. "You? You want to help?"

"How hard could it be?"

She shrugged a little and said, "If you want to. Tillie says she wants some juice."

I got up and found some apple juice in the fridge. Two sippy cups were on the counter next to it. I filled them up and brought them back. "You must be Tillie," I said to the little girl, who smiled shyly. "Nice to meet you."

The little girl happily took the sippy cup and babbled something back.

"Are you sure you wouldn't rather be chasing that girl you were talking to?" Ember asked with an amused smile.

I sent her a sly look. "What? Why be with one when I've got three right here?" She tried and failed to hide her smile. "So, where are your parents? Shouldn't they be taking care of the kids?"

Ember merely looked down at the toddler in her arms. Molly was smiling around her sippy cup. "They aren't what you would call involved parents. My dad's at the bar, and who knows where my mom is."

"Don't you have school or a job?" I asked.

"I'm an EMT, but I only work three times a week, so I take care of the babies on my day off."

"I thought this was only university housing?"

"Technically, it is, but I'll keep a secret if you can. I don't think the twins will rat us out."

I could only stare down at Tillie who'd taken a seat next to me, momentarily shaken, when I realized she was staring up at me as she sucked back her juice. She blinked owlishly, and her throaty little grunts made me smile.

"You're pretty good with her," Ember said.

"The ladies love me," I cooed to Tillie.

"Whatever you say, hotshot."

"What's up with the hotshot?"

"You play ball, don't you?" She nodded toward the hoodie wrapped around my waist. "I've gotten used to reading people. You seem like the cocky sports type."

"I can't argue with that. I'm a pitcher."

"Naturally," Ember said, lifting Molly onto her lap for a cuddle. She pulled out baby wipes from a basket under the coffee table and began wiping Molly's sticky hands.

Tillie was already fighting sleep again as I picked her up to do the same. I copied Ember as she patted Molly on the back. Both girls fussed a little, and Ember showed me to her room, which she shared with the twins. She put Molly down in one of the cribs and then Tillie in the other.

"So, your parents live here with you?" I asked as the twins settled into a deep sleep. They were kinda cute when they weren't screaming.

"For the most part. They're rarely here. This used to be my place, but they got kicked out of theirs, and then mom got pregnant. I couldn't exactly leave them on the street." The red tinge of shame colored her cheeks, but I didn't judge her for that.

Ember pulled the door closed on the sleeping girls, and we were alone in the hallway.

The silence closed in around us, and my heart began to thud in my chest. I'd followed her because I couldn't not, but now that I had her alone, I couldn't quite find any words. It was a first —being awkward around a woman.

She raised a hand before I could get them out. "Don't," she said warningly.

"Don't what?"

"You're going to ask me out—and you're cute and everything —but I'm in no place to have a boyfriend. I just started my job at the station, and I've got the twins and my parents. I'm sorry, but I'm not looking for a relationship right now."

I nodded and tried to hide how crestfallen I was. Which didn't make sense. We had just met, and I wasn't looking to get tied down either.

"I understand, but I should get going," I said and made to move toward the front door.

She stopped me with a hand on my arm. "I could use a friend though," she said.

CHAPTER 3

EMBER

"Ember! EMBER! EMBER!"

I struggled to consciousness, slowly at first, and then all at once, snapping awake and jerking to a sitting position. There was a moment where I wasn't sure where I was. Sometimes it was like that at the station when we got a call and I couldn't remember if I was still at home or not. Then my eyes focused on the twins, who'd fallen asleep on my bed again, and I relaxed.

Molly slept with her mouth slightly open to my left. Tillie was curled into a protective ball on my right. We must have fallen asleep watching TV after I had nagged them through our nighttime routine.

There are plenty of college-aged girls who would have resented having to take care of their sisters. I'll admit I'm not perfect, but who could resent such innocent faces? It wasn't their fault they were born to such irresponsible people. They didn't deserve to be punished for my parents' mistakes.

Sure, it was hard giving up most of my free time to care for them. I essentially became a teenage parent at seventeen and have been responsible for them ever since, but I wouldn't have it any other way. They were the lights of my life.

"EMBER!"

My mother's hoarse shout sounded as though she was screaming right in my ear, thanks to the thin walls of the apartment. I scrambled from the bed, careful not to wake the twins. Whatever my mom was screaming about couldn't be anything good. She never paid us any attention unless she wanted something.

I followed the sound of her smoker's cough into the living room, frowning when I discovered her with a lit cigarette clutched in her claw.

"You aren't supposed to be smoking in the apartment, Mom."

She really shouldn't be smoking at all. She was only thirty-nine, but she looked twenty years older. Her skin was like aged leather, and the scent of stale tobacco clung to it like a shadow. No matter how much I urged her not to smoke, there was no point. There was no explaining anything to Jill Stevens.

"That's the first thing you say to me when you wake up? No *good morning, Mom, how was your night?*" Mom snorted and puffed away on the cigarette, the cherry glowing a bright red-orange.

"You called me for something?" I asked instead of rising to her bait. There was no point in that, either. Arguing with her only gave fuel to feed whatever was irritating her.

I checked my watch, noting it was already six-thirty, and the twins had to be at the bus stop by seven to make it to their kindergarten class on time. As mom made discontented sounds behind me, I busied myself with pouring bowls of milk and cereal for the girls and packing their bags. She should have been doing it, of course, but in the six years the twins had been alive, I could count the number of times that she'd been proactive about their care on one hand.

Maybe this was why Chris jumped into another woman's bed so quickly. Was I that much of a drag? Taking care of the twins was second nature to me, but maybe it was more of a hindrance to him than I'd thought. What kind of fresh college grad wants to be saddled with two kids right off the bat?

The train of thought distracted me, and I had made both bowls of cereal and packed the twins' bags before I realized Mom was still speaking.

"Maggie has two tickets, and it's gonna be a great show. Thank you for being there for your family, sweetie."

I tuned back in with a quickness. "What are you talking about?"

Six forty-five. Mom lit another cigarette, her eyes squinting in my direction. Sometimes, I thought she was the child rather than the girls. Clearly, she wanted me to react. But I simply didn't have the time. If she got us kicked out again, I'd take the twins to my next apartment, but she wouldn't be tagging along.

"I said I need you to watch the twins tonight. I've got plans to go to a picture show." She kicked off her house slippers and relaxed into the recliner. Her designated soap operas played on the TV through the smoke-filled room.

"I can't watch them tonight. You know that. I've got a shift."

We went round and round about this at least two or three times a month. Normally, I'd switch a shift with one of the other guys at the station, but there simply wasn't enough time to do that now. She had to know on some level that her request was ridiculous.

She blew out smoke and wrapped her tattered robe more tightly around her midsection. "Then switch shifts with someone."

I shook my head as I placed the bowls of cereal on the island counter. "If you'd given me more notice, I might have been able to, but it's too late now. I've told you that before. You can't just ask me to watch them last minute. Someone has to work to support everyone," I added under my breath as I headed down the hall to wake the twins.

Mom mumbled behind me, but I tuned her out. I didn't have time to deal with her bullshit this morning, and after being through the emotional wringer about Chris the day before, I didn't have the patience. I'd pay for it later, but whatever.

The twins had inched closer to each other in my absence. I paused in the doorway for a second to drink in the sight of them twisted in the sheets together, their little hands intertwined, inseparable even in sleep. It made me a little jealous, I'll admit. They'd always have each other; they'd never be as alone as I felt.

I was reluctant to wake them, but an alarm on my phone alerted me to the fact that we had ten minutes to get them dressed and out the door. After a gentle shake on each of their arms, their eyes began to crack open. Mirror emotions of annoyance and reluctance flared in their eyes.

"Five more minutes," Tillie cried and then flung an arm over her face.

Molly, on the other hand, stood, if a bit slowly. "Can I wear my purple shirt?" she asked after a moment of hesitation.

Despite my confrontation with Mom this morning, this simple request brought a smile to my face. The purple shirt was infamous around our house. If allowed, Molly would wear it every day of the week. I'd managed to convince her to restrict it to twice a week instead, but it had been a battle. Some kids had blankies or stuffies. Molly had her purple shirt.

"It's in the laundry basket on the dryer, but that means you can't wear it again until Monday, okay?"

Molly sighed. "Okay."

I shook Tillie one more time and made sure she was up— grumbling, but up. As the two of them dressed and brushed their teeth, I finished packing their bags, along with mine. After dropping them off at the bus stop, I'd head over to the station to start a twenty-four-hour shift.

Mom was still sitting on the couch, smoking like a steam engine, but I didn't say anything to her. If I kept harping about her smoking, she'd only do it more to needle me, and I simply didn't have time for her crap. Especially not when my alarm sounded the five-minute warning. Besides, she'd probably complain about my not watching the girls, and I really didn't want to go in to work with a headache already brewing.

The twins, dressed and relatively awake, slurped down their breakfast. As they ate, I brushed and styled their hair and gobbled down a cup of coffee and a handful of dry cereal. One day, I'd have myself together and would be able to wake them up and eat breakfast without rushing. But it wasn't today.

As I herded them out the door, I tossed my Mom a, "Have a good day, Mom. They'll be home at three-twenty after school. My shift will be over tomorrow morning around eight if it doesn't hold over."

Mom waved a hand, and we hurried out.

It was the kind of night that never seemed to end.

And that was on a regular shift.

Add in the recent heartbreak, and I wanted to lie down in front of the ambulance and let my partner Josh run me over— then back up and do it again. I huddled in the corner of the station and plugged in my headphones to listen to an audiobook, hoping to pass the time without any more interruptions. There'd been nonstop calls since I had clocked in, but not the exciting, heart-pumping kind. It had been the menial, headache-inducing kind instead.

Not that I minded, really. It was better than being stuck at home with my thoughts.

I was damned if I was home, damned if I wasn't.

Frowning at myself, I tried to focus on the words. Audiobooks helped pass the time when there was nothing else to do. Throughout the night, we'd had several transfers and a couple of regular patients—nursing home residents, elderly people with chest pains, the usual. Now, it was nearing nine at night. I'd finally finished the last transfer and was hoping there wouldn't be any other calls so I could relax for a few hours and maybe catch a good night's sleep before I had to be home with the twins.

Trying to focus was useless.

The voice in my ear was a buzzing drone. I couldn't focus on the words, let alone derive meaning from them. All I could do was check my phone every five minutes, bouncing between hope and sadness. It was pathetic.

Chris was still blocked on my phone and social media. I'd held fast there. But there was a part of me, however small, that thought that he would still reach out. Use someone else's phone and text me. Try messaging me from a dummy Facebook or Instagram account.

Total idiot.

If he'd wanted to be with me, he would have made an effort to reach me.

Hope springs eternal, I guess.

I started to doze off, my half-unconscious dreams plagued by images of Chris alternately apologizing and laughing in my face. When my phone began to ring, I had almost convinced myself it was him calling to apologize.

Except I didn't recognize the number on my display. Rubbing at my eyes, I answered, thinking it was probably Mom calling for some emergency or another.

"Hello?" I winced at the sound of my sleep-rusty voice.

"Hi, is this Ember? Ember Stevens?"

I cleared my throat. "Yes, this is she."

Well, at least it wasn't my mother. Knowing that didn't help the anxiety in my stomach.

"Hi, this is your neighbor from across the hall, Lennox Marquette."

"Hey, Lennox. Is everything okay?"

I'd seen Lennox on occasion in passing. I knew she was working on her master's at FSU and spent most of her time with her nose buried in books. If she was calling, it couldn't be good. The only reason she'd get in touch was if there was some sort of emergency.

"Actually, I hate to call, but I heard crying coming from your apartment. When I went to knock on the door, your sisters answered." I sat straight up, adrenaline pumping through my veins. My first overwhelming thought was that my Mom had had a heart attack and the twins were alone with her dead body. Then Lennox continued, "They told me your mother had left them all alone."

"She what?" I whispered faintly. It should have been a relief that she wasn't dead, but this was somehow worse.

"I'm sorry, Ember, that's what they said. I was able to get your phone number from the contacts list taped to your fridge. I hope you don't mind me going in your apartment."

I pushed a hand through my sleep-matted hair. I could hear the girls chattering in the background. At least they sounded normal. "Of course not. My mother wasn't there?"

Was I hearing her wrong? I knew my mother wasn't the best in the world, but she'd never deliberately put the twins in danger.

"I checked everywhere. They said she told them to watch TV and she'd be back later, but that was hours ago. They got scared when it got dark."

Lennox offered to watch the kids until I could schedule

coverage for work. Thankfully, my captain was understanding and called in a favor. I'd have to work a double shift next week, but I couldn't focus on anything but getting home to the girls.

I tried calling my dad, who was rarely home as it was, but he didn't answer.

The first real threads of fear wove through my chest on the drive back to my apartment.

What if they'd left for good?

CHAPTER 4

TRIPP

This was my last chance and I was going to kick ass.

Or at least that's what I told myself after eight hours of practice and classes.

Muscles sore and protesting, I heaved myself from my car in the parking lot of my apartment complex. With the heavy weight of my gym bag thrown over my shoulder, the trek from my car to the elevator felt like an eternity. All I wanted was a big bottle of ice-cold water, a hot shower, and about a century of sleep.

I aimed to do just that—and I would have if I hadn't heard the quiet sobs coming from behind the apartment door next to mine. It was so out of place that I froze with my key raised to my door. The last time I could remember hearing Ember like this was the day we met when she had the twins. Of course, the twins cried from time to time, but theirs was more of a high-pitched wail than the soft, heart-wrenching cries I heard now.

It had to be Ember.

The thought didn't quite compute. She was a rock. She put up with more than I thought physically possible. I thought I had it hard with my constant practices, workouts, and training, but that was nothing compared to working, going to school, and taking care of two kids with deadbeat parents.

She was like Superwoman.

I knocked on her door after a pause. Maybe she wouldn't want me butting my nose in. She probably wanted to be alone. I would check on her to make sure she was okay, and then I'd bounce if she wanted me to go.

I immediately knew when she opened the door that she wasn't okay.

Not in the slightest.

I had to hold myself back to keep from pulling her into my arms.

It wasn't the red rims around her eyes or the smeared mascara that gave it away—at least not for me. I'd known Ember long enough to get used to her moods. She was either balls-to-the-wall full of energy or she was sleeping. I spent half the time we hung out just trying to keep up with her—and I was supposed to be a star athlete for fuck's sake. It was how wrung-out she looked that clued me in. Like she simply didn't have anything left to give.

After dropping my bag inside her front door, I closed it behind me. She had her arms wrapped around her waist, and, as much as I wanted to pull her close and comfort her, I knew it wasn't the right time. So, I shoved my hands into my pockets instead. "What's wrong? Is it your parents?"

She shook her head but wouldn't meet my eyes as we sat on her worn couch. I tipped her chin up with a finger. "Em, tell me what's wrong, angel."

As long as I'd known her, Ember had been a rock. Immovable. Unbreakable. I'd never seen her crack.

Until now.

And it made me want to do whatever I could to make her feel better.

Tears shimmered in her eyes, and then she cleared her throat, her shoulders lifting as she sucked in a deep breath. "It's everything. My parents, pulling more shit. I had to take off from work when I really needed the hours. Chris broke up with me. He's seeing someone else."

"Broke up?" It didn't quite penetrate. He had Ember. Why would he need anyone else? "You're kidding. What happened with your parents?"

I didn't want to touch the conversation about her boyfriend—ex-boyfriend—with a ten-foot pole. Didn't want to open that can of worms. It had taken a long time to get over her—or at least get to a place where I wasn't thinking about her constantly.

Thankfully, she kept me from making a complete jackass out of myself. She was clearly hurting. Now was not the time to make any sort of move on her. No matter how much I wanted to.

"God, Tripp, I don't mean to blubber all over you like this. I'm sorry. You look exhausted. You should go get some sleep."

She made to move away, but I hooked her arm. "No, c'mon. Tell me what's going on. I've got time." *Time for you* echoed in my head, unsaid.

Ember wiped at her nose. I was a piece of scum for noticing how beautiful her eyes were, even when she was crying. "Are you sure?"

It was the hopeful upturn in her voice that had me nudging her shoulder with my own. "I wouldn't say so if I wasn't."

She sighed heavily, and I was struck, as I always was, by how quiet the apartment was without her mother's soap operas blaring or her father shouting demands from his place on the couch. The twins were mute in comparison to their parents.

Ember started recounting what had happened with Chris. It wasn't the first time I'd heard her complain about him, and I wasn't entirely convinced it would be the last. I'd been keeping my feelings about the asshole to myself as long as they'd been dating. It wasn't my business. She was a big girl and could make her own decisions. But it burned me to hear how easily he'd squandered his chance with her. It only confirmed that he didn't deserve her.

Not that I did, either, but that was beside the point.

"I wouldn't be such a wreck right now if I hadn't gotten a phone call from my neighbor saying Mom had split. I tried getting a hold of her, but her cell is out of service, and Dad is naturally nowhere to be found. She left the twins at home, hysterical and terrified. It took me forever to calm them down. We had a million calls last night, and all I want is a long, hot shower and a four-hour nap, but she dropped this in my lap. Trade parents with me?" she pleaded.

If I could, I would in a heartbeat. My parents were about as boring and kind-hearted as anyone could hope for. They'd supported and encouraged my dream to become a baseball player my whole life. Married for thirty-four years, they were the epitome of stability and understanding. The complete opposite of Ember's.

I couldn't imagine growing up the way she had, essentially raising herself and then caring for twin sisters when she should have been enjoying her life. It made me admire her all the more for her determination and will. Instead of following her own dreams, she'd gotten a job straight out of high school to support her family, first as an aid at the hospital and then working nights while she went to school to become an EMT, all while helping to care for her sisters.

I'd never had to deal with anything like that on my own. My parents were always in my corner, cheering me on and supporting me. Ember, on the other hand, had always had to support herself.

Knowing her kitchen almost as well as my own, I decided it was time for someone to take care of her for a change. "Don't move," I ordered and went to make her a drink. "What about your dad?"

She sighed heavily. "I tried calling him after she hung up on me, but he didn't answer. Naturally. Sometimes I wish they'd disappear. Then, it wouldn't be this constant back-and-forth rollercoaster all the time." Her head drooped, and she studied her hands in her lap. "That's a terrible thing for me to say, I know."

I made a tall glass of iced tea and sat the glass in front of her on the coffee table. "I won't tell anyone. Besides, what they do to you isn't fair. I'd say you're allowed to talk shit every once in a while. What are you going to do?"

With her schedule of a twenty-four-hour shift every third day, Ember normally watched her sisters on her day off, and one of her parents would watch the twins after school on the days that she worked. It hadn't been easy for her to convince them to do that. I remember the blowup. They had wanted her to work, but they hadn't wanted her work to take away from her watching her sisters either. I had been able to hear it all because my apartment was right next to hers. In fact, we shared a bedroom wall. I had heard them yelling at her for hours that night.

With both of her parents gone, it would mean she had no one to watch them on her over-nights.

"What about my parents?" I offered as the thought popped into my head.

My mother was a retired grade-school teacher, and my father owned a home improvement store. We'd been trying to convince him to let someone else take over, but he was determined to work until he had one foot in the grave. These days, my mother spent a lot of her time working with education-based charities or tending her award-winning flower garden.

Ember drained the glass of tea and then shook her head. "No, don't worry about it. I'll figure something out. I can find the money for a babysitter or daycare somewhere. Do they even have those overnight?"

"I'm serious. Mom isn't working. She has a lot of free time.

I'm sure if I asked, she wouldn't mind. In fact, this might be perfect." Before she could object, I said, "At least let me ask her before you say no."

Her eyes were no longer red from tears, but there were dark blue smudges underneath them. Strands of flame-colored hair fluttered around her neck and shoulders where it had come out of her messy bun. The shapeless, almost tactical, pants and faded, dark-blue shirt emblazoned with her station number did nothing to showcase the bombshell figure underneath.

But I'd never found her so sexy.

". . . but I don't want to make it a permanent situation," she was saying. I forced myself to tune back into the conversation. "You can ask them, but don't make them feel obligated. In the meantime, I'll try to make more permanent arrangements."

"I'll call them after I finish practice, but I promise they won't mind. They like you better than they like me, remember?"

This made her laugh. "Shut up. Your parents love you. It's almost hard to watch. Every time you come home, it's like you haven't been home in years. King Tripp," she teased, then glanced at her phone and cursed. "It's so late. I shouldn't have kept you here for so long. You need to sleep. Thank you for helping me, but now you need to get going." Ember got to her feet and pulled me to mine, shoving me to the door.

"Are you sure you're going to be okay? I can call Coach Taylor tomorrow and tell him I'm sick or something. Probably the flu from one of the brats."

Ember laughed. "I'll make sure to tell them you said that."

My heart eased at seeing the smile, however brief, flit across her lips. "I'll stop by after practice tomorrow to check on you guys."

"You don't have to do that. We're fine. My parents have gone on benders before. It was a lot of things at once, and, apparently, I need to take a nap before I break down and cry on anybody else."

I reached up and tugged on a loose lock of her hair, causing her to smack my hand away. "You can cry on me anytime," I said.

I thought about her when I went to sleep in my room that shared a wall with hers. Which wasn't new. I thought about her all the time.

It wasn't really a secret, either.

Which somehow made it even worse.

CHAPTER 5

EMBER

"When is Mommy coming home?" Molly asked.

How was it that children could be so innocent and so intuitive at the same time?

I decided the best course of action was honesty. The girls knew what our parents were like, and I felt that they didn't need another adult in their lives who lied to them. Of course, I didn't know if telling them the truth was the proper course of action, but I was doing my best.

"I don't know, sugar bean. She...had some plans, and they must have taken longer than she anticipated. But don't worry, we'll do something fun today to pass the time."

Explaining it to them when she didn't come back tomorrow or the day after or the day after that would be a little more difficult.

Tillie shared a look with her sister. "What about Daddy? He didn't come home last night either."

They were too smart for their own good. I knew it, and yet sometimes I took how much they absorbed for granted. Kneeling down, I cupped both of their cheeks.

"Babies, this is one time I won't have all of the answers for you. Sometimes grownups make mistakes. Sometimes they disappoint you and do the wrong thing. Mommy and Daddy aren't making very good choices right now, but I don't want you to worry. No matter what happens, I'll always be here for you. You know that, right?"

Their eyes watered, and I pulled them close, my heart aching for them.

"Do they not love us anymore?" Molly asked, her voice wobbly. Tillie sniffled in my ear on the other side.

My heart broke into tiny little pieces. No child should ever have a reason to ask such a question. I held them tighter. "Of course they still love you. Who wouldn't?"

"Then why would they leave us?" Tillie asked. "Were we being bad?"

I would have gladly ripped my parents to shreds as I listened to the twins' questions and allayed their fears. It had never bothered me how inattentive and downright negligent our parents were when I was growing up. I hadn't known any different.

"This isn't about you," I said firmly. "You haven't done anything wrong. I don't want to hear you say that again. You two are perfect. I don't ever want to hear you thinking it's your fault again."

Next time I saw either of my parents, they were going to get an earful. I'd never truly stood up to them before. They somehow always managed to convince me things would change, and nearly a dozen years later, they were the same as they had been when I was the twins' age. It wasn't fair to any of us.

Molly pulled back and clutched her sister's hand. "We're sorry the lady had to call you in from work. We tried to be brave, but it was so dark, and we kept hearing creepy noises, and we got scared."

"You don't have to apologize for calling me, sweetheart. You did the absolute right thing. It's not safe for you two to be home alone. You don't worry about work; that's my job. Now, let's get you two dressed for the day, get some breakfast, and maybe we'll go down to the park?"

Their eyes brightened. "Will you push us on the swings?" Molly asked.

"Of course, sweetheart. Now, do you two want pancakes or scrambled eggs?"

The time at the park helped us all unwind and take some space from the stress. I'd texted and called both of my parents about a dozen times but without any answer aside from the one hangup from my mom. It was a fruitless endeavor, but, for the first time, I wasn't sure what to do.

I didn't want to think about it too directly, but I knew this could be considered child abandonment. Taking custody of the girls had always been at the back of my mind, a seed of doubt I'd never really nurtured. Perhaps it was time to fertilize that seed and put it in some fresh air with a little sunlight. Maybe it would wither and die, but…maybe it would bloom.

It did my heart some good after the stress the night before to see them laughing and playing, seemingly worry-free for now. All I knew was I didn't want them to grow up like I had—too soon. They deserved to have a childhood, to worry about kid issues—not whether we had electricity or hot water or enough money for groceries. Sometimes I felt like I was failing them because supporting the household wasn't without struggle but seeing them laugh and smile made it worth it. I was starting to think that maybe having our parents around them did more harm than good.

Taking legal custody of them had always been a terrifyingly permanent solution, one I wasn't sure I was totally ready for, but maybe it was time. What would happen the next time my parents abandoned them? What if they got hurt, or sick, or—God forbid—died because of their negligence?

I couldn't bear the thought.

For the time being, I pushed it to the back of my mind. Surely, with some time, my parents would be back, and everything would go back to normal. It wasn't a perfect solution, but it was all I knew.

If they didn't come back…well, I'd deal with that when the time came.

I had my plate full enough as it was. Work had given me a couple of days to get my bearings, and I'd emailed my professors, who were being lenient. Things would have to eventually go back to normal—whatever that meant.

The girls were settled in front of the TV watching *Mulan*, which allowed me a moment to rest. It felt like I had been going nonstop ever since I'd gotten the phone call from Lennox. I had my feet propped up on the couch and was considering what I'd make for dinner when I received the first text. My heart spiked for a moment, thinking it could be Chris.

The spike of adrenaline eased somewhat when I saw Tripp's name. Relieved, I unlocked my phone.

TRIPP: How are the monsters?

I smiled at my phone. The one bright spot throughout everything, besides the girls themselves, was Tripp. I didn't know what I'd do without him.

ME: Terrorizing the village. We just got back from the park. Almost time for dinner.

Now that the apartment was relatively silent, it gave me way too much time to think. With the go, go, go of the past twenty-four hours, the breakup with Chris had been pushed to the bottom of my list of worries. As the quiet began to seep into my bones while the girls watched the movie, the self-doubt and sorrow began to creep back in.

Was it wrong of me to lean on Tripp when I was feeling so alone? I wasn't sure. He'd wanted to go out with me when we'd first met, just after the girls were born, but it hadn't been the right time. Besides, what kind of eighteen-year-old would have wanted to be saddled with a girlfriend who had twin babies?

Not that a girlfriend is what hotshot Tripp Wilder would have wanted at the time.

No, he should be with someone who didn't have the strings I did. That's why I had turned him down back then, and it was probably why I was so keen on dating Chris long distance. And look how that turned out.

TRIPP: It's Taco Tuesday!!!

I snorted but didn't immediately reply. Normally, Charlie, Layla, and I got together to unwind with tequila and girl time on Tuesdays. Then Liam had joined. And then Dash. It hadn't even crossed my mind that we would be getting together with everything that had been going on. It reminded me that I would need to update them on my parents, but I wasn't sure how to tell them. They didn't have perfect home lives, but they'd had enough drama of their own for so long that they didn't need mine, too.

ME: I can't leave the kids and I'm not up for a big crowd right now. Sry. Maybe next week.

Plus, I wasn't able to face Charlie and Layla yet. They'd been telling me for a long time that Chris wasn't worth the trouble. I hadn't wanted to listen. The last thing I needed to hear was *I told you so.*

However, a healthy dose of tequila sounded like heaven.

Less than a minute later, I received another text.

> TRIPP: Just you and me and the kids. I'll get the shit for virgin daiquiris for them. You have the stuff for tacos? Participation isn't optional, angel.

Was this taking advantage of him? It felt like I was flirting with the line of propriety. I knew how he felt about me, and I valued him as a friend. Now more than ever, I didn't want to lose him.

I typed out a text to alleviate my guilt somewhat.

> ME: You really don't have to do that.

I was more relieved than I should have been when I got his next text. It was really selfish of me to accept his generosity, but a huge part of me didn't want to be alone now, either. And Tripp was always so good at cheering me up. I'd just need to be careful to make sure we kept everything platonic.

> TRIPP: All I heard was 'Yes Tripp.' I'll see you at six.

I snorted and texted him my excuses again, but he didn't answer—and likely wouldn't. There was no talking Tripp out of something once he'd made up his mind. Locking him out wouldn't work either. He had a key for emergencies.

> ME: Fine. I'll make tacos. But I'm putting guacamole on every single one of them to spite you.

He sent kissy faces in return to let me know he didn't take me seriously. While the girls played quietly—a miracle in and of itself—I pushed myself to my feet and retrieved the things I'd need to make tacos. I always had the ingredients on hand because they were my favorite. I liked to pin it on the girls, but I'd eat them all day every day if it were up to me.

As the meat sizzled in the pan, I grated cheese and chopped up tomatoes, avocados, and lettuce for the toppings. This simple routine, like going to the park, kept me from thinking too deeply about my problems. Tripp's text had come at the perfect time and had kept me from sinking into a world-class sulk.

If my heart thrilled a little when he knocked on the door, it was only because I was excited for tacos, not because I was excited to see him in any way other than as a friend.

Tillie and Molly squealed in excitement, launched themselves from their place on the floor, and threw their arms around Tripp's middle.

"Tripp!" they shouted in unison.

"You'd think I was chopped liver," I muttered as I wiped my hands and joined them in the living room.

"Oh no," Trip said, overhearing my comment. "You've already perfected the art of mom guilt."

"Ha, ha. Very funny. You two go wash your hands. It's time for dinner."

"What are we having?" asked Molly.

"Tacos," I answered.

They shrieked again and ran down the hall, their footsteps echoing behind them.

"They don't take after you at all," Tripp said.

"Shut up. How was practice?"

He brought the bags into the kitchen and started mixing the ingredients for the drinks as I plated the tacos and toppings on the table. Lifting a shoulder, he said, "It wasn't too bad. They released the schedule for this year. First game is in February, a double-header against Maine."

Tripp didn't like to talk about baseball with me too much. I didn't mind. It wasn't exactly my milieu, but I was always a little curious about that side of his life. The side where he traveled across the U.S. pitching for a championship team, being fawned over by stick-thin coeds with lives as apple pie as his.

I knew he went undrafted out of high school, and that he was now one of the top picks for professional ball after graduation. I had to admit it made me a little sad to think of him leaving in a few months for the big time. Not because I was jealous of the fame and fortune, but because I'd grown so accustomed to having him as a part of my life.

I wished it hadn't taken me until now to figure that out. I was quiet during dinner, but Tripp was kept busy enough helping me wrangle the twins.

Yeah, I was going to be sad when he left.

To the rest of the world, he was a nationally ranked baseball superstar, but to me, he was so much more.

CHAPTER 6

TRIPP

I was glad when Ember changed the subject away from practice and ball. I wasn't interested in talking about it. Everyone seemed to want a piece of me when it came to baseball. Ember never did. She always saw me as me. Maybe that's why I couldn't stay away when we first met. She was the only person who ever thought of my "stardom" as a non-issue.

"How are you feeling?" I asked as the twins helped clear off the table. "You hear anything from that douchebag?"

"What's a douchebag?" Molly piped up.

I winced. "Nothing, sweetheart. I made it up."

"Good one," Ember said with a snort.

"I aim to please."

She sighed heavily and lowered her voice so the twins couldn't hear. "I blocked him everywhere. I don't plan on giving him the opportunity."

I bit my tongue, then asked, "What about your parents?"

"Nothing there either. It's not going to give a girl abandonment issues at all."

"Lucky for you, you're never getting rid of me."

"Pfft. You're leaving at the end of the year when you move

on to play pro ball." She shoved my shoulder jokingly, but there was a thread of real concern in her voice. I tried not to read too much into it. She was hurting and probably feeling a little alone.

"Maybe I'll invite you to one of my games when I go pro. You can always come out and watch, you know."

My hope was to be drafted to the Orlando Falcons once I graduated, but I'd be happy anywhere. Except getting drafted to a team across the country would mean leaving my family and Ember. Playing ball was all I had ever wanted, and she was the only person who'd ever made me second-guess my dreams. Though she'd kill me if she ever knew that. She'd given up her aspirations of being a doctor to take care of her family. If she ever thought I'd give up pro ball to be here with her, she'd skin me alive.

"Can we come, too?" Tillie asked, clearly eavesdropping on our conversation.

I lifted her up and spun her around. "Of course you can. I can't play without my favorite cheerleaders."

"Me, too?" Molly asked eagerly. Her wide, innocent eyes were exactly the same color as Ember's.

After ruffling her hair, I knelt down to her level, her sister still on my hip. "Of course, short stuff." I glanced up at Ember, who seemed relaxed for the first time since all that shit had gone down. "All of you."

Ember helped the twins with their nighttime routine after they had thoroughly decimated their tacos and virgin daiquiris— which they called slushies. Their voices trailed from the hallway down to where I was cleaning up in the kitchen, making me smile. I was an only child, and while my parents had been atten- tive and loving, there had never been any other kids to play with when I was younger. My life growing up had often been solitary.

I had to admit it was nice to have their noise and clutter around. It was like a constant hug.

"Tripp!" came a high-pitched call. "Come here."

"Almost done," I answered.

"We want you to read us a story," came another voice.

"I'm sorry," said Ember as she appeared at the end of the hall. "I tried to convince them I was perfectly capable of reading a story, but they want you. According to Molly, you do the voices the best. There wasn't any telling them different."

I dried my hands on a dishtowel and put the leftovers in their Tupperware containers in the fridge. "You don't have to do that. I don't mind at all."

She retrieved her daiquiri and drank deeply despite all the ice being melted. "Proceed at your own risk," she warned. "They seem like they're nice little girls, but they can be pretty demanding."

Ember screeched when I flicked the dishtowel at her legs. "Sounds like they take after their big sister."

"Hey!" she protested behind my back.

I laughed on the way down the hall to the room she shared with the twins. That's another thing I admired about her. She didn't have anything of her own and didn't whine about not having any luxuries. She even shared her room with the twins without complaint.

Somehow, they'd managed to cram a small set of second-hand twin bunk beds in the tiny space along with a large dresser and double bed for Ember. Her bed was technically a mattress on the floor. She'd admitted to me that when the twins outgrew their cribs, she'd sold them and her bed frame in order to get their bunk beds.

"They deserve to have as normal a life as possible," she'd explained when I asked why she was sleeping on a mattress.

It never ceased to amaze me how she did without when other

women her age always seemed to want more—especially from me.

"Tripp!" the twins greeted. They were both snuggled together on the bottom bunk in matching, albeit slightly small, cartoon pajamas.

Molly held out a book. "Here, read this one," she said. *Goodnight Moon.*

My mom had read this to me when I was younger. I wondered who had read it to Ember? Somehow, I couldn't see either of her parents reading her a bedtime story.

The twins made room for me to sit beside them, and damned if it didn't make my heart melt the way they had their arms wrapped around each other. How their parents could fail so spectacularly when they had such wonderful children, I didn't know.

I began to read, and by the end, their eyes were already drooping. "Again!" they demanded. I didn't mind. At the end of the second read through, they were fast asleep. I carefully got to my feet and tucked their blanket around them. They were still snuggled together, inseparable even though they could each have their own bed.

"They do that so easily for you," Ember complained from the doorway. She must have snuck up during the second read-through. "They always fight sleep when it's me."

"It's my charming demeanor," I told her.

"Right," she drawled. "Speaking of, shouldn't you be out somewhere on a date or something?"

"And miss Tequila Tuesday? Not a chance."

"I thought it was Taco Tuesday this time?" she said quizzically.

"That was for the girls. I brought the tequila for grown-up time."

She smiled, but it faltered. "You could always go now," she said softly.

I snorted and went to the counter to make more drinks, this time with margarita mix and a healthy dose of tequila. I thought we both needed it. "There isn't anywhere else I'd rather be," I said.

She shook her head but accepted the drink I handed her. "I don't get you."

"What's there to get? I'm not a complicated man."

A blush painted her cheeks. "Never mind." She drank deeply from her margarita. I tried not to stare at the way her tongue flicked out to lick away the salt on the rim of the glass.

Instead of thinking about it, I mixed up my own and did the same.

Two hours later, I realized my mistake.

I should have left them after dinner, gone back to my apartment, and locked the door behind me. That would have been the smart option. But no, now I was stranded in my own special version of hell.

Ember stripped off the t-shirt she was wearing over a camisole. It wasn't a designer label—Ember dressed more for comfort than for style, but she could have worn a potato sack and looked sexy as hell. I drank thirstily to keep from staring too hard.

"I thought I was a good girlfriend," she was saying. "I helped with his schoolwork. I treated him to dinner when he visited or when I went down to visit him. I took care of presents for his mom and sisters when it was their birthday or his parents' anniversary. I always helped tidy and organize his place when I stayed over. I don't get it. I thought he loved me."

The raw pain in her voice chilled all the heat I'd been stewing in ever since I had made our fourth round of margaritas. I shook my head to clear away the thoughts of her stripping off the rest of her clothes.

Get it together, Wilder.

"You know I've never thought highly of Chris. He was never good enough for you. So take my opinion with a grain of salt. It sounds like you mothered him. Not that it's an excuse for what he did to you. But a man should be able to take care of his own shit, not make you do it."

At my words, she blinked rapidly, and I hoped she wasn't going to cry.

She took another sip, then inhaled deeply. "I can't believe you said that." I opened my mouth to apologize, and she shook her head before I could get the words out. "Don't apologize. You're probably right. You know he never did any of that stuff in return? He wasn't like you. He'd never come over if the twins were here. He'd always make some sort of excuse. If he hadn't dumped me, me having to be here for them 24/7 would have made him bail."

I couldn't say she was wrong, so I didn't say anything.

"I guess deep down, I knew we weren't going to last, but I dunno. I kept holding on because I thought if I was better, then maybe I could change things. Maybe if I was good enough, he would see that and stay." She shook her head. "It sounds stupid."

"You're right; it is stupid. You shouldn't have to change yourself for any man. You're an amazing person. Guys would kill to be with a woman like you. So, fuck him if he didn't realize how good he had it. I can promise you he'll come to his senses. He may not let you know it, but he'll think about you one day and remember what a great thing he had and how he gave it up. He'll regret it."

"You think so?" she asked.

"Oh, I know it," I said, hoping she couldn't hear the gravity in my voice.

A lengthy silence followed, and I was distracted by all of the ways this could have gone differently. If I'd pushed a little harder, made my move after she'd gotten settled with her sisters, maybe I would have had my chance before she'd met Chris. Now, I was so thoroughly in the friend zone, I doubted I'd ever find a way out.

"What if I'm bad in bed?" she blurted, and I choked on a sip of my margarita. The tequila burned my throat as it went down.

"What the hell are you talking about?" I demanded. Maybe I was hearing things because fuck if I was going to have this conversation. I needed to be much, much more wasted to listen to the details of their sex life.

"He met someone else. If he was…satisfied, he wouldn't have been looking." Her cheeks were as red as her hair.

We were having this conversation. Fuck it.

There were things I wanted to say to her that I'd been putting off for way too long.

"Sex is easy to come by—even good sex. It's the people that come along with it that make it interesting. You can have the best sex in the world with someone you don't give a damn about, but when it's with someone you care about, it's different. Better. Easier. You come harder, faster."

"I never came with Chris." She flushed as soon as she'd said the words. "I mean, I did, maybe a quarter of the time. It felt good even when I didn't, but most of the time, it either took too long, and he got frustrated, or he didn't care enough to get me off after he was done."

I pressed a hand to my heart. "Angel, that's a tragedy."

She lifted a shoulder. "I've read that's normal for a lot of women. Sometimes it just doesn't happen."

"That's not what I'm hearing from what you're saying. If he didn't care enough to take care of you, too, then he was a selfish lover, period."

And a fucking idiot.

But we were both fucking idiots. Because as much as I wanted to say something, tell her how much I wanted to be the man to take care of her, I knew I couldn't.

"Maybe."

"Definitely. Any guy would love to be with you, Ember. They'd kill to make you come."

I could think of a thousand ways I wanted to have her screaming for me without trying. But I drank instead and forced myself to change the subject.

There's no way in hell I'd let sex ruin our friendship.

CHAPTER 7
EMBER

A voice cleared, and my eyes cracked open. Tillie and Molly stood in front of me with their identical stuffed puppies clutched in opposite hands. Tillie was smiling knowingly, and Molly's other hand was covering her laughter, though it spilled out in staccato bursts.

"Good morning," they intoned in knowing voices that had alarms sounding in my already-pulsing head.

"Good morning," I croaked. God, it was warm. Was I getting sick? Being sick simply wasn't an option. I couldn't miss any more classes or take any additional time off. I pressed a hand to my head. "Give me a few minutes, and I'll make you breakfast, okay?"

"Why are you and Tripp sleeping together? Are you boyfren / girlfren?" Tillie dragged out the word couple so that it sounded like it was three words instead of one.

I shot up to a sitting position and immediately wished I hadn't. A groan came from behind me—a particularly familiar male groan.

Oh, God.

I turned and found that they weren't kidding. Tripp and I

were sleeping together. At some point, we must have passed out on the couch, and during the night, I'd wrapped around him like ivy on a pole. He still lay on his back with his mouth tipped open. My movement hadn't woken him, and his legs were intertwined tightly around mine.

"Did you break up with Chris?" Tillie asked.

"It's way too early for this conversation," I said as I carefully disentangled myself from Tripp's hold and got to my feet. The heat suffusing my body began to dissipate. "You two go get dressed, and I'll try not to throw up everywhere."

Their giggles followed them down the hallway. I was already doing a bang-up job at this sole guardian thing. I smacked Tripp on the arm. "Wake up," I hissed.

He rolled over and shoved his head into the pillows. The ripple of bare muscle made me realize he wasn't wearing a shirt. My throat went instantly, painfully dry. I'd noticed Tripp was a good-looking guy, I mean I'd have to be dead and buried not to, but it had never hit me so viscerally as it did at that moment.

It actually stole the words from my throat. Made me momentarily forget how bad I felt and the fact that the twins were still in the apartment. The powerful knit of muscle and sinew under his skin was a testament to the hours he spent in the gym each day training. There wasn't an ounce of fat to be found, and I wasn't sure if I should be jealous or appreciative. I settled on trying not to drool.

Then I remembered the conversation from the night before and wished the headache would kill me. I couldn't believe I'd told him those things! I hadn't even told Layla and Charlie about my sex life with Chris, and they were my best friends.

I was never drinking again.

I reached out a hand, and it hovered over Tripp's sleeping body. Where was the most innocuous place I could touch him that wouldn't make me think about how he said a guy would kill to make me come? His shoulder? Except, he had great shoulders. They made me think about what it would be like to grab hold of them with him on top of me. His arm? Nope. He had a pitcher's arms. Strong and heavily-corded with muscles. He was all muscle. Everywhere. My gaze drifted down to his abs. Good God, he had fifty-seven of them.

I settled on poking him in the ribs with my eyes closed.

Super mature.

And also a bad idea.

He turned at my touch, and all those abs came into full view. I swallowed hard. His hair was matted with sleep and stuck out in odd directions. Tripp wasn't brawny like Liam or broad like Dash. He was slimmer, more agile, his build well-defined and sleek. All toned arms and long legs. His hair was more dirty blonde than Liam's and too light to be a true brunette like Dash. He wore it longer on top and in the front. A Japanese-style tattoo sleeve with cherry blossoms and shades of black and gray waves covered his left arm from shoulder to elbow.

How was it that I'd never really looked at him before?

His eyes opened, and I jolted back, surprise mixing with embarrassment for getting caught.

"What are you doing?" he asked while I tried not to stare at the way his stomach contracted as he sat up. His voice was gravelly from sleep, and I felt it touch me in all sorts of delicious new places.

It was like the fusion of alcohol and sleeping together had done something to my brain. There were all sorts of tactile and visual information I'd never paid any attention to before but spending the night next to him had rewired everything. Now I couldn't help but notice everything I'd been hell-bent on ignoring before.

"Ember?" he asked when I didn't respond.

"What?"

"Why are you looking at me like that?" he asked.

Everything seemed to shoot back into focus. "I'm not looking at you like anything. I was trying to wake you up. We fell asleep on the couch, and the twins woke us up."

"That would explain why my back is killing me. Your couch is sized for hobbits."

"It's not my fault you're a giraffe."

"What did you say about the twins?" he asked, rubbing at his eyes.

"They think we're a couple." The horrified tone in my voice was shrill and made my brain pound in protest. "They saw us in here together and woke me up this morning. God, Tripp, what were we thinking?"

Why did I think those last couple of drinks were a good idea?

His smile was way too relaxed. Why wasn't he freaking out? "Well, we did sleep together."

"Yes—literally. As in, just sleeping!" I tried not to remember how good it felt to wake up in his arms.

Tripp cocked his head to the side. "I'm wondering if your horror should insult me."

My brain stuttered. "I—what? No!"

"I enjoyed sleeping with you." He said it so sincerely, I could only blink.

Then I frowned. "You're finding this far too funny, Tripp."

He reached out and twisted a lock of hair around his fingers. "Maybe I'm just flattered."

I pushed his hand away. He was only touching my hair, but I felt the responding tingles shoot up and down my arms. What was happening?

"Don't be stupid. We probably shouldn't drink like that with the girls around. I don't want to confuse them." More like I didn't want to confuse me.

Tripp got to his feet and covered the glory of his bare chest with an FSU baseball shirt. "They're fine. But I'll make sure to tuck you into bed next time."

I decided not to touch that comment with a ten-foot pole. "Don't you have practice this morning?"

He whipped around, muttering under his breath. After a frantic scramble for his phone, he sighed in relief. "I've still got thirty minutes until I have to be at the field. I guess there's a first time for being grateful the monsters get up early."

"I guess we overindulged a bit," I said.

"No such thing, angel."

Giggling sounded from the entrance of the hallway, and we both turned to find the twins watching us with broad smiles. They were haphazardly dressed, with mismatching skirts and shirts, and four different kinds of shoes.

I crossed the room and knelt in front of them. "What are you two laughing at? Did you dress each other?"

"She picked my clothes, and I picked hers," said Molly, and her gaze kept flitting to Tripp, then back to me.

"Don't we look pretty?" Tillie asked.

"Gorgeous," I said. "Do you want me to help you with your shoes?"

They nodded, and I retrieved the correct mates for their shoes and helped them dress. The giggling and looking at Tripp continued until they were properly dressed. He, of course, didn't help matters and kept wiggling his eyebrows and winking at them. I tried giving him stern looks, but that only made the girls laugh harder. Finally, I threw my hands up, got myself dressed, and started a pot of coffee.

The only thing I knew I could do was to keep myself busy and hope whatever weirdness the night before had inspired would disappear. I failed miserably as Tripp appeared out of nowhere behind me and quipped, "Is that coffee?"

I jumped about a mile high and spun around, coffee sloshing everywhere. The screech that burst forth from my chest sounded like a bird on crack.

His eyebrows lifted. "You okay there?"

"Shut up," I snapped, which made him laugh. I made him a cup of coffee in the hopes that it would inspire him to give me some space. I didn't know what had happened, but I couldn't seem to get enough space. "Here."

In return, he handed me a couple of tablets of ibuprofen, and I swallowed them back. Maybe they would magically turn everything back to normal.

"Thanks." My hands were cupped around my mug, which I held in front of me like a shield. "Sorry, this is…"

"Weird," he finished for me.

"A little," I admitted. Keep busy. I retrieved cereal from the cabinet and fixed the twins their bowls at the table. The food distracted them, and they no longer made gooey eyes at Tripp and me.

Thank God for small favors.

"You don't have to look at me any differently, Em. You know how much I care about you, and I'd never do anything to jeopardize that."

If I were the type of girl who cried at the drop of a hat, and if I hadn't already leaked out a river of tears, his comment would have softened that rock-solid place where my heart should have been. "I don't look at you differently," I protested. "It's just a lot of change. I'm being silly."

He rinsed out his cup in the sink and put it on the rack to dry. I tried to remember if Chris had ever done something as simple as rinsing out his own glass. The only memories I could recall involved him asking me to cook for him or me rushing to take care of things for him. It had never been like that with Tripp, who always seemed to come to my rescue instead of the other way around.

"Nah, don't worry about it. We're friends. We can talk about stuff like that. I can keep your secrets," he said with a grin that I felt all the way down to my toes.

I shoved his shoulder instead of responding. "Have a good practice."

Tripp nodded to me, then bent down to kiss both girls on their foreheads. I watched as they smiled, eyes bright with happiness at his attention. He was so good to them that it made my chest ache. So good to me, too, as a matter of fact.

The invitation to dinner hovered on the tip of my tongue. I wanted to pay him back for being there for me, listening to me whine about Chris and rant about my parents, but I knew it was probably the wrong time. It would feel…too intimate after being so close to him all night. I'd wait and offer to cook for him later —when these feelings went away.

"I emailed my mom and dad about watching the girls when you have class or a shift. When I hear from them, I'll give you a shout," he said as he walked to the door. "See you later, monsters," he said to the girls.

I had almost forgotten about his promise to talk to his mother. Yet another way I'd be in his debt.

As soon as he closed the door behind him, the girls turned to me in unison and smiled broadly.

"Oh, finish eating your cereal," I ordered. But I couldn't help it.

I was smiling, too.

CHAPTER 8

TRIPP

I tapped the faded, dirty paint on the wall next to the weight-room entrance. The 1,179 had once been a bright garnet with gold trim, I was sure. Now, it was faded, the paint was worn and ragged, and dirty fingerprints covered a near-perfect oval around it. It gave me a chill damn near every time I saw it. So many of my favorite players had been here and had stood in this very spot. Had touched these numbers.

Now, it was my turn.

The 1,179 signified the 1,179 miles to Omaha, where the College World Series takes place. Every morning when I was up at five thirty, before the rest of the school, those worn numbers reminded me that I do it for a reason. Each workout, each pitch, and each swing got us one step closer on those 1,179 miles to Omaha. One step closer to achieving my dream.

One step closer to pro ball.

I arrived ten minutes early for our five-thirty lift practice with most of the other pitchers. Half split off for bullpens—they'd lift with the rest of the team at the evening practice. The rest of us were in for an hour-long workout. Being late wasn't an option. Coach Rick Taylor deemed anything less than five minutes early as "late." I always aimed for ten, just in case. I didn't want to be the reason the rest of the guys had to run suicides for the duration of practice. Coach Taylor believed the punishment wasn't over until someone was puking.

My best friend Alex sidled up to the weight bench where I was lifting, a mile-wide smile on his face.

"I don't know what you're smiling about," I said as I began with bicep curls. "One minute later, and your ass would have been grass."

Even though we'd been best friends since he joined the team as a freshman the year after I did, we were complete opposites in every way. Where I was lanky and all about precision on the mound, Alex was as solid as a mountain, had at least fifty pounds on me, and was all power, all the time. I was in awe the first time I ever saw him. He grew up in Jersey with a big Italian family and a dozen immediate relatives, whereas it was just my parents and me. He was a diehard Yankee fan, while I lived and breathed the Braves.

Alex waved away the threat with one big paw. "I'm here, aren't I? If anyone is going to get reamed, it's you. You haven't been answering any of my texts. What's up with that?" His northern Jersey accent would have been indecipherable to anyone else. It had taken me years to get used to it. Which was funny because he said the same thing about us Florida natives. He still gave me a hard time for each y'all. I gave him a hard time whenever he shouted, "Yeah, buuudddy," for no reason at all.

I fell silent for several reps. "No reason; just been busy."

"You're a terrible liar, dude." He said liar like "li-uh." "You're still trippin' over that sexy-ass neighbor of yours." He switched to lat raises, shaking his head. "You're hopeless. Why don't you just put the moves on her?"

"I'm not having this discussion." Again.

And especially not now.

"We're gonna keep having it until you give it up. The girl has a boyfriend."

"No, she doesn't," I said before I could think better of it. I winced, even as the words passed my lips. I wished I was a better liar.

His eyes widened. "Dude!"

"Don't read into it," I warned.

"C'mon, bro. This is the last chance you're ever gonna get with this girl. You better hop on that before she's locked down again."

"I can't do that. She's really broken up and shit. She doesn't need me being a douche about it."

"If you say she needs a friend, I'm gonna slug you one."

I focused on my reps for a few. "She does just need a friend."

"That's it; I'm gonna hit you. Someone has to knock some sense into you."

"Not every chick is DTF, man. Even if it was like that, I'm not that kinda guy anymore."

"We're all that kinda guy. You're just stuck on this chick. I don't know what you see in her that's got you so twisted."

"I'm not twisted up about her."

"You're so twisted, you might as well be a fuckin' pretzel. I wish you two would just fuck and get it over with. Then maybe you'd be my wingman again."

"I'm still your wingman," I said indignantly.

He scoffed. "You haven't been my wingman since you laid eyes on that girl."

"Whatever, man."

"I'm telling you," he said as we moved to the benches, "if you'd get her into bed, you'd get her outta your system. Yeah, buddy!"

I was avoiding her.

Call me a dick, but it was best for both of us, especially considering the conversation I'd had with Alex. Spending more time with Ember would only be a bad idea; she had enough on her plate to deal with as it was. Besides, I doubted getting her into bed would get her out of my system.

My phone chimed with a notification as I got on the elevator after a brutal practice. I was sore from my shoulders to my toes, but my throwing arm especially had taken a beating since I had resolved to throw myself into ball to forget all the things I wanted to do to Ember. I unlocked the screen and found an email from my mother. It had been a couple of days, but they didn't often check their email, and Ember had a few more days before she was in desperate straits without a sitter to watch the girls for her shifts.

Tripp,

I'd love to watch the girls for Ember. Does she have a set schedule, or is she on rotating shifts? Why don't you bring them by for dinner tomorrow if they're available, and we'll discuss the details?

Thank you for thinking of me!

Love, Mom

Shit.

It's not that I didn't want to see her. In fact, she occupied most of my thoughts—and even my dreams—at this point. I couldn't seem to get her out of my head. It didn't matter how hard I pushed myself at practice or how many books I tried to bury myself in; the only thing I was able to focus on was Ember.

I blamed Alex for all his shit talking.

All I could think about was getting her outta her clothes and into bed once and for all.

The way her hair had felt, silky and fine against my bare chest, haunted me. I couldn't keep the imprint of her body from haunting my senses like a ghost. I'd wake up in the middle of the night and be disappointed she wasn't there beside me.

They'd let us out of practice and training early today since it was a holiday weekend, and Coach Taylor was going to get reamed if he didn't spend it with his wife. I'd tried to convince them to let me stay and lock up, but no dice.

My plan was to stop by, extend the invitation from my parents, and then get the hell out of there. If I was lucky, the twins would be home from school early, and we'd have chaperones. God knew I needed one whenever Ember was around. Preferably more than one.

That way, I wouldn't be tempted to put my hands on her to see if she felt as good as I remembered.

Maybe she wouldn't even be home, and I'd text her or something instead. Which is what I should have done instead of knocking on her door. But I had promised her that shit wouldn't get weird, and I wouldn't let it.

I could control myself.

At least, that's what I thought until she opened the door in a thin camisole and yoga pants.

Goddamn those yoga pants.

I began to sweat. My tongue stuck to the roof of my mouth, and I forgot what I was going to say. All I could do was stare.

"Hey!" she said cheerfully. "I was just doing some yoga. Pinterest says it's the best way to reduce stress."

"Is it working?" I choked out. Maybe I needed to start yoga. I should talk to Coach about it.

"I guess we'll see." Her skin was covered in a sheen of sweat. I wanted to lick it off her. "Did you need something?"

"What? Oh, yeah. My mom emailed. She said we could have dinner tomorrow and talk about her watching your sisters."

Why was her skin so pink? The flush spread up from her breasts and crept up her neck, a gradient from the lightest red to cream. I wanted to feel the heat of her against my lips. I thought exposure to a stimulant was supposed to make you more resistant. Was I somehow becoming more sensitive to her presence instead?

She made a squeal of surprised delight. "Really? That's such good news. Hey, maybe this yoga stuff does work! Why don't you come in, and you can hang out until the twins get home?"

I hesitated in the doorway. Being alone together didn't seem like a good idea. It was ironic that I'd spent the past few years fantasizing about what I'd like to do with Ember when I got her alone, but now that the opportunity had presented itself, I wanted to run in the opposite direction. Not because I was scared, but because I wasn't altogether certain I could keep myself from doing all the things I'd imagined doing to her over the years.

"Is something wrong?" she asked as she turned back to me. Her short red ponytail bobbed, the tips of her hair brushing against her neck and along the tops of her shoulders. I was mesmerized. "Tripp?" she prompted when I didn't answer.

I shook my head. "No, everything's fine. I've got a load of homework to do, though, so maybe I should head back to my place." The end of my sentence sounded more like a question than a statement.

She scoffed, rolled her eyes, and took my hand, pulling me inside. My feet followed without any encouragement on my part, despite the shouted protests inside my head. I was the one who told her not to make it weird, and here I was, acting like a complete creep.

"You should try yoga, Tripp. You seem stressed enough for the both of us. Practice not going well? How's your shoulder?"

"It's alright," I answered, glossing over the question. "Are you sure you want me to hang around? You're probably busy with the girls."

She shoved my shoulder and said with a laugh, "Don't be silly. Of course I want you to hang around." At my grimace, she gasped. "I'm so sorry. I wasn't thinking. I didn't hurt you, did I?"

The look hadn't been because of my previously injured shoulder. It had been because having her hands on me felt electric—like being struck by lightening.

"No, I'm fine. My shoulder's okay. You seem to be feeling better," I commented as she went to her TV to pause the yoga video. She gestured for me to sit beside her on the couch.

"I dunno, maybe. If you count shoving everything down and trying not to think about it 'better,' then yeah, I'm fabulous."

Her smile was a little too bright, and it was as though her forced cheerfulness would shatter at the slightest touch. It only drove home the feeling that it'd be wrong to make a move on her.

But, God, how I wanted to.

Instead, I nudged her soulder. "Don't bullshit me. What's going on? That dickhead call you again?"

"If I say, 'I'm fine,' are you going to ask if I'm sure?"

I found myself playing with her hair. I always seemed to be touching her hair. It was like candlelight, the way the reds and golds flickered and blended. "Maybe," I answered—when I remembered she'd asked me a question.

Keep your hands to yourself, Wilder.

Easier said than done.

CHAPTER 9

EMBER

Tripp's hands on me after spending the night twisted up with him made me want to shiver, but I locked my muscles and ignored the urge. I had to ignore a lot of urges these days where he was concerned. I knew he was interested, or at least he used to be a couple of years ago, but we were friends now—or so I thought.

I'd specifically told him when we first met that we couldn't be together. I had had too much on my plate. School, work, the kids. My parents. I had told him it would be better if we could just be friends.

Was it the recent heartbreak that had me clinging to Tripp for the attention and affection he so readily gave?

If so, I was being a shitty friend. Sending mixed signals. Being needy and wishy-washy.

"Am I a terrible friend?" I asked.

His fingers drifted from my hair down to squeeze my shoulder. "What makes you say that? Of course not."

I couldn't very well tell him that I was thinking about jumping his bones because I thought it would soothe all the hurt away, so I said, "I've been so selfish recently. I just want to make sure I'm not taking advantage of you."

Was it my imagination—or perhaps desperate hope—or did his grey-blue eyes light up at the thought? My skin prickled with heat, and my nipples beaded under my shirt.

How had I gone all this time and not realized how incredibly kissable his lips were?

He coughed and shifted on the couch. "You're not taking advantage of me, angel." The words were innocent, but my fevered brain wondered if he'd mind if I did take advantage of him.

I needed help. Clearly.

Maybe I was having some sort of mental breakdown.

"You sure? You can tell me if I'm being too crazy or whatever."

"Shut up," he said affectionately. "What kind of friend would I be if I didn't put up with your crazy?

"A sane one," I answered.

"Then I guess we'll be crazy together." He tugged at my hair, then rubbed a hand down my arm. "Since you're keeping me prisoner, wanna watch a game till the twins get home? I know how much you love sports."

I nodded, but I was only half listening.

That's what I liked about him. What I'd liked since we first met. He never backed down when things got too intense. Even when I thought the drama of my life would scare him away, he was always there. Patient. Kind. Unassuming. Totally different from the arrogant jerk I'd initially thought he was.

He settled back into the couch and propped his feet up on the footstool, his arm thrown companionably over the back behind me. It could have been suggestive, but with him, it felt right. It felt natural. There weren't butterflies in my stomach, so to speak.

They were more like fireflies. Lazy, fat, meandering fireflies that emitted a warm, bright glow. The light filled me from the inside out.

"You paying attention, angel? The Falcons are playing. I know how much you can't wait to see me on the field in that uniform."

I smiled at his off-hand comment. Well, he was still an arrogant jerk, but maybe people weren't always so black and white. He could be arrogant, but he could also be spectacularly kind and gentle, especially with the twins.

And—I'll admit—with me.

At first, I thought it was a ploy to get in my pants. It wouldn't have been the first time a guy tried to be nice and considerate only to pull a Dr. Jekyll and Mr. Hyde deal once the sun came up. But even when I had turned him down, even when one year had passed, then two, then three, he was still the same old Tripp. Maybe a little more settled than the skirt-chaser he'd been as a freshman. But he was still Tripp.

Still the boy who'd always made me feel…more right in my own skin.

I couldn't help but compare him to Chris, my one and only long-term relationship.

With Chris, it had been nice, not fireworks like I'd imagined, but I'd liked giving him pleasure. I liked the connection forged during intimacy. But it'd never been…I don't know…entirely comfortable. Now that I thought about it, sex had always been about making sure his needs were met instead of exploring ours together. He'd certainly never made my pleasure a focus.

Not how I was imagining it'd be like with Tripp.

I let my mind wander, letting myself consider being with him in a way I never had before. How gentle he'd be, but at the same time, how thorough and demanding. There's no way he'd ever let me stop without coming first, like he'd said. I could almost see the intensity his expression would hold as he watched me tip over the edge.

It was wrong.

But it felt so right.

I shifted on the couch beside him, glancing to make sure he didn't see how clearly turned on I was becoming. Even in the thin camisole and yoga pants, I was overheating. Thankfully, he was engrossed in the game on the TV and wasn't paying me any mind.

At some point, his arm had drifted down to my shoulder, and he'd begun twirling my hair in his fingers. This time, I couldn't stop the shiver. Automatically, he shifted closer as though to share his warmth to alleviate the chill.

The fireflies in my stomach doubled. No, quadrupled.

Did it make me a terrible person because I wanted to lose myself in him? I wanted those strong arms around me, wanted to wrap myself in the comfort he offered, to blot out everything going wrong in my life. Aside from the twins and my friends, he was the one bright spot. How had I not seen it? Maybe I'd been too afraid to look too closely.

"You're staring at me," he said, and I blinked. At some point, he'd stopped watching the game. Probably around the time I had started fantasizing about him.

My cheeks heated. "I'm sorry. I'm totally zoning out."

"That's alright, angel. You've got a lot on your plate." His trademark Cheshire grin softened, and I made a split decision.

I kissed him.

I blamed the fireflies.

The moment our lips touched, I knew it was a mistake, but that didn't mean I pulled away. No, pulling away was an impossibility. I was helpless to correct it.

I'd be lying if I said I'd never fantasized about kissing Tripp before. Especially in the beginning, when it was harder to resist him after we first met. But this kiss? This kiss…was worse than anything I could have ever imagined.

Because I never wanted to stop.

Tripp, however, didn't have the same problem. His hands, which were buried in my hair, cradled my head as he shifted backward. "Ember?" He opened his mouth, but no other words came out. It was as though he knew if he said anything else, it would break the spell that had surrounded us since our lips touched.

A heartbeat passed, and the sound of it blotted out my sense of reason.

We reached for each other at the same time, a synchronized movement we hadn't planned. Our lips met, needy and inevitable. Desperation superseded finesse, and I climbed into his lap without any thought for grace or seduction.

The announcer on the TV blared in the background, but as Tripp's hands drifted down to dig into my hips, the sound faded into oblivion.

There was only us, and nothing had ever felt so right.

Tripp broke off, breathing heavily. "Wait, stop. What are we doing?"

I tugged him down, twisting so that his weight was on top of me, pressing me into the couch. When he dodged my lips, I made do with his throat. His skin was salty and sweet. Like caramel popcorn. I loved caramel popcorn. I licked up his throat to his ear. When I reached it, I breathed, "Shh. Less talk, more kissing."

"Em, you don't mean that."

My hand found the vulnerable skin at his waist that was bared by his shirt. I slid my hand underneath, my fingers grazing the dusting of hair on his belly that I knew would be golden brown. God help me, but I wanted to nuzzle in it. Lick my way down beneath his jeans. I wondered if the hair there was dirty blonde, too.

"I mean it, probably more than I've meant anything in a long time." His words ended on a harsh inhalation as my hands found his waistband and danced underneath. "You're confused because of Chris. Ember, don't. You're going to regret this tomorrow."

He looked down at me with a stern expression, but I barely heard what he was saying. "I'm not confused about anything," I insisted.

When my hands continued to explore, he growled and pinned them on either side of my head. "Think about it. You're kissing me. You. Kissing me. The one who basically turned me down for years. Years."

"I don't want to think about it. All I do is think. All day, every day. This is the first thing that's felt good in a long time." I strained against him and watched his lashes flutter. "Doesn't it feel good?"

"Hell yes it feels good, but that doesn't mean we should be doing it."

I rolled my eyes. "Isn't that exactly why people do it?"

Tripp laughed and looked annoyed about it. "What's gotten into you today?"

"Apparently, not you."

Fine, if he wouldn't move, I would. I lifted my hips so that he was positioned between them, where I could feel the bulge he couldn't deny was there. He hissed again. "Ember, stop."

"I don't want to stop. That's the point."

"You didn't say that a couple days ago. In fact, for the past few years, you've been putting the brakes on me pretty regularly."

I frowned at him. Since when was he so logical and reasonable? "Do we have to analyze it? Everything in my life is so screwed up. The only thing I know I can count on is you. The only thing that makes me feel good aside from my sisters is you. If you don't want me, then you can say so, and we'll stop right here, right now, and go back to the way things were." I stopped and swallowed hard. I hadn't meant to say that. What if he didn't want me? I wasn't sure I could handle the rejection on top of what had happened with Chris. I was going to say more, but the words wouldn't come.

"You can always count on me," he said.

"Great. Fine." Shame was beginning to heat my cheeks. "Will you let me up now?"

I closed my eyes and waited for him to comply.

Except he didn't move away. I could still feel him everywhere.

"Tripp?"

"I'm thinking."

"Could you think faster before I die of embarrassment?"

"What are you embarrassed about?"

"Can we not have this conversation while you're on top of me? I can still feel your dick."

"You're the one who started it," he said. "In fact, you were pretty persistent."

"Can you not tease me right now?" His hips flexed, and my eyes flew open. "What are you doing?'

"Well, you told me not to tease you." Tripp's fingers linked with mine, his hold gentle. The heat from my face moved between my legs. "And I never leave a woman unsatisfied."

"Tripp…"

"Hush, I'm trying to concentrate now."

His head ducked, and his lips pressed against mine. I thought he'd be eager, dominating, but his lips were gentle, almost nonexistent.

It made me want more.

So much more.

CHAPTER 10

TRIPP

SOPHOMORE YEAR

"C'mon, man," Alex begged. "It's the off-season. Coach Taylor is finally giving us a break. You're killing me." He threw himself onto my couch and gave me a puppy-dog look.

I didn't look up from my homework, although I wasn't taking in any of the words I was reading. My pen tapped repetitively against the desk. "I'm not doing shit to you. I said you should go, so fucking go."

My urging did nothing to thwart Alex's goal. Naturally. "It's my first year in town, and you're supposed to be my role model. Introduce me to all the hot spots. Be my wingman. It goes against the bro code for you to ditch me this way."

"You're a grown-ass man. You can get an Uber. Besides, what happened to all that game you said you had up north? Does that Yankee charm not work here in the South?" I spared a glance at him and grinned good-naturedly. The prick could have anyone he wanted. I didn't know why he was complaining.

Alex wiggled his eyebrows. "Oh, it works just fine. I just don't see how you can waste such a prime opportunity on our first weekend off in months."

Except it didn't feel like a prime opportunity to me. I didn't want to go out barhopping and get smothered by women. The thought would have been appealing a year ago, but now…

"Tripp, did you have a chance to—" Ember's voice cut off as she barged into my apartment toting a twin on each hip. She smiled at Alex, who sent me a knowing smirk. "Sorry, I didn't realize you had company. I can come back," she offered.

Now, this was what I wanted, and hell if I knew why. She was complicated with a capital C, but I couldn't get her out of my head. I'd take her, if she'd let me, complications and all.

Alex launched himself bodily from the couch to schmooze to her side. "Don't apologize, sweetness. We haven't had the pleasure of meeting. I'm Alex Lockwood. I play on the team with Tripp."

The flare of jealousy in my chest had me taking a step back from the two of them. In the year since I'd known Ember, I'd come to terms with the fact that a relationship of any kind was out of the cards. That didn't make seeing her getting hit on any easier. Least of all by my best friend. He knew about her and her about him, but she was so busy with her sisters and him with ball that they hadn't really had the chance to meet.

Ember nodded since her hands were full. "Nice to finally meet you." The twins wriggled and babbled away, fighting to get Ember to release her hold and let them down. "I'm sorry to interrupt. I'll get out of your hair."

"Let's not be hasty," Alex said smoothly. "Why don't you come in?" Deftly, he maneuvered Tillie out of Ember's hands. She watched him with an amused smile—the way she used to watch me. "Hey there, cutie."

Tillie squealed and began to talk my ear off. When Alex

smiled at Molly, Molly grinned, stuck her thumb in her mouth, and hid her face in Ember's hair.

"Hey!" I said to Tillie. "I thought you were my girl!"

Alex heaved a fake sigh and said to Tillie, "Don't worry, all the ladies fall for me eventually. Don't let Tripp bother you."

Tillie giggled, and Ember was beaming. "Don't put any ideas into her head," she warned. "She already thinks she runs the world."

"Naturally," Alex said and bounced Tillie on his hip. Coming from a big family, he was used to having children around. He might put on a big player front, but I always secretly thought the dude wanted the whole wife-and-kids deal more than most of the guys on our team. His parents, like mine, had been together forever. Just because he enjoyed women and partying didn't mean that wasn't his end goal.

Turning to me, Ember said, "I'm sorry for interrupting. I've been running around like a chicken with my head cut off. I'll only be a second, and then I'll get out of your hair."

She didn't know how much I liked having her in my hair. I wished she'd stay there, make a little nest like a bird, and never leave. I cleared my throat. "What's up?"

Molly had come out of hiding and was smiling shyly at Alex. "These two need a zookeeper. I can't get anything done for their birthday party. I was going to ask if you'd had a chance to blow up their balloons, but I can see that you're busy." With the ease of someone who had cared for them their whole lives, Ember scooped Tillie from Alex's grasp and arranged her on her free hip. "You two have fun, and we'll see you later."

Somehow, she managed to open the door and squeeze out before I could even cross the room. For a girl carrying two kids—and they weren't little ones anymore, either—she could certainly move like lightning. She could have given some of the guys on my team a run for their money—literally.

Ignoring a pleading look from Alex, I followed quickly behind her.

"Em, wait up!"

She didn't turn to look at me. "Don't worry about it. You're busy."

"Not too busy for you," I said and squeezed behind her into her apartment before she could shut the door in my face. I didn't know what it was about her, but the more she pushed me away, the more I tried.

"I'm serious. Go enjoy your friend. You've had a long year. You should go enjoy yourself. Besides, what would all your groupies think if you turn into a homebody?"

"My groupies? Really, Em?"

"What else am I supposed to call the chicks who hang around your apartment all the time? On game days, it's like a friggin' mob."

So, she did think about me. "Jealous?" I asked and took Tillie from her arms when she began to wriggle for me. To Tillie, I said, "I think your sister's jealous."

"No," Ember replied vehemently. "I'm not jealous."

"C'mon Ember, be real with me." I thought being on the mound during a championship game was nerve-wracking. It was nothing compared to waiting for her answer. Until that moment, I hadn't realized it meant so much to me.

I was in trouble.

Instead of answering, she changed the subject. I tried not to look too disappointed. "You were going to leave your friends to come to the twins' birthday party, weren't you?" She didn't sound as impressed as I thought she would. "Why would you do that?"

"What do you mean? You told me you needed help, so I'm here, helping." It seemed like an easy conclusion, so I didn't understand why she was looking at me like I had broken her heart.

"You were supposed to go out tonight with Alex, weren't you? That's why he was over at your apartment." Her voice was accusatory, and her hip was cocked like she was spoiling for a fight.

I pushed a hand through my hair. "Yeah, he was going out to the clubs and wanted me to wingman for him. I told him no," I added defensively, but that only seemed to make her even angrier.

Green eyes flashing, she said, "I didn't ask you to do that, Tripp."

"You didn't have to ask me. I wanted to." What the hell was going on here?

I thought it would make her understand, but it only seemed to her piss her off even more as I tried to explain. She shook her head. "That's the problem."

"You're freaking out for no reason. I said I would help you, so that's what I'm planning on doing."

She frowned at me. "Stay here. I'm going to go put the twins down for a nap, and then we'll talk."

That didn't bode well. I could only nod because there was no way I was walking away from her.

I sat on the couch because the recliner smelled like smoke from when her mom was around chain-smoking and watching her soap operas. My parents would have murdered me if they ever knew I had tried a cigarette in the tenth grade. The image of her mom was so outlandish I couldn't wrap my brain around it.

But that didn't scare me away.

I didn't think anything could.

A half-hour later, she emerged, pushing the hair back from her head. I started to get to my feet, but she gestured for me to stay seated and took her place by my side.

"Look," she began wearily, "it's not your responsibility to shape your life around me."

"The hell is that supposed to mean?"

"It means that we can be friends. I like having you in my life. You're an amazing person. But like I told you when we first met, it can't be anything more than that."

Who was she trying to convince? Me...or herself?

"What does that have to do with today?" I asked.

"I want you to go out and have fun," she said firmly.

"But it's their birthday."

"They're going to be three. They'll barely know the difference. We can celebrate together tomorrow or something."

"But I thought you needed help putting the decorations together and picking up the cake."

"I can handle it on my own. That's the point, Tripp. I don't want you to put aside your life because you think there's something going on here." She kept going before I could interrupt. "Please, do this for me. I need for you to go out and have fun. Do it for me, since I can't," she said with a laugh, but it was devoid of humor.

"I don't understand why it's such a big deal to you. I wanted to help you out, as your friend." That was a lie. Maybe she had a point. "But if it means so much to you, I won't come. Even though this sounds backassward. Are you sure you don't need help?"

"Yes," she replied firmly. "I can handle it. I have to be able to do these things on my own. I'm grateful, more than you can even imagine, that you want to help me. But you can't always help me, and I need to be able to stand on my own two feet."

"You already do too much," I said, thinking of her absent parents.

"I'm a big girl."

Stubborn. God, she was stubborn.

Funnily enough, it reminded me of Tillie and the way she tried to do everything herself. I wonder where she got that from?

"Alright, then, I guess." I got to my feet, suddenly ready to be as far away from her apartment as possible. If she wanted me to keep my distance, I guess I needed to be told twice for me to get it through my thick skull. A year of being held at arm's length should have done the trick, but practically forcing me to be with other people worked just as well.

"I'll see you later," I said.

CHAPTER 11

EMBER

Kissing Tripp was unlike anything I'd ever experienced. I thought it was romance novel bullshit. How a connection could be so instantaneous with someone. But when Tripp pressed me deep into the couch and kissed me like I was the best thing he had ever tasted, I thought maybe I was wrong. It had never been like this with Chris.

Effortless.

There was no self-doubt, no self-consciousness.

There was only heat and need.

The more I kissed him, the more I wanted him.

It scared me how much I wanted him.

Hell, he'd scared me since the day I met him.

No matter how hard I pushed him away, he was always there. Unruffled, patient, kind. An unshakeable rock.

"Wait," I said and put a hand on his chest. Somehow, I managed to pull myself away, slip out from underneath him, and put some distance between us. I ended up in the kitchen, but I could have been across the continent, and it wouldn't have been enough.

Whatever wheels I was putting into motion here weren't going to brake as easily as that.

"Tripp, I—"

Tripp held up a hand. "You don't have to say anything. I—you don't have to say anything."

I wanted to pull my hair out. "Stop, just stop. You don't have to be so understanding all the time. It was wrong of me. I never should have crossed that line. Stop being so nice. I'm jerking you around, and we both know it."

I didn't understand how he couldn't see it. I was taking advantage of his kindness. Jerking him around by messing around with him, then telling him there was no chance for a future with me. I was damaged goods. I come with too much baggage. What part of that didn't he understand?

He rose from the couch and herded me with his body toward the kitchen island. "You want me to stop being nice?"

"Yes!" I said, my voice breaking with exasperation. "The things I'm asking of you aren't fair. You have to know that. I'm not in a healthy place right now."

He was so close that I could see the pulse beating in his throat. It was as steady as his gaze, which was locked into mine. "You think I can't handle you?" He smirked a little. "I'm a big boy. I know what I'm doing. But I'm also not an asshole. If all you can handle is friendship, then that's what I'm here for. If you want a little something more, then I'm telling you that I want you."

I placed my hands on his shoulders. "Wait, so what are you saying? Are you saying you want to be…friends…with benefits?" The incredulous tone in my voice cracked a little. We were in college, but we had never entered the world of casual sex. Tripp had flirted, hard, and often, but he'd never been a complete manwhore. And I'd blown off every guy who tried to hit on me but Chris.

"I want you. If that's what you want, I'm willing to give it to you."

"That's not fair to you." I shook my head, trying to clear it of the haze of lust. "No. We can't do that. Situations like that are how people get hurt, and you're the last person I would ever want to hurt. "

He thumbed my cheek and smiled a little. "You don't have to add me to the list of people you take care of."

"I don't want to take care of you," I said hotly, but his words rang with a truth I couldn't ignore. Chris had said something of the sort a time or two.

He clearly wasn't convinced. "You want to take care of everyone. Your patients, your sisters, your parents. Your friends. Who takes care of you, Em?"

"You're starting to piss me off. Give me some space." How the conversation had devolved so completely, I couldn't understand. This was precisely the reason I didn't want to get involved with anyone in the first place. I tried to shove my way around him, but it was like trying to drain the ocean: impossible.

"No, I'm not giving you space. Not this time."

"I take it back. Offer rescinded."

His breath was hot on my lips. I licked mine without conscious thought. "You can't take it back," he said.

I tried to use reason. "We have to leave soon. The twins will be home, and it'll take an hour to get them ready and over to your parents' with rush hour traffic."

Tripp didn't budge. How had I mistaken him for the happy-go-lucky sort? Underneath that puppy dog exterior was a pit bull. "Stop making excuses. Stop trying to think your way through everything. Tell me what you want."

"I think—"

"Not what you think. What do you want?"

"Tripp—"

"What. Do. You. Want?"

His arms were on either side of me, caging me against the island. Our faces were so close I could see the darker striations in his eyes. Dark blue, light grey.

My hands lifted of their own volition, and my gaze followed where they stroked along his strong arms up to his shoulders. I glanced back up and saw his eyelashes flutter closed. The skin at his neck was warm and smooth.

What did I want? I wanted to taste him there again.

So for once, without thinking, I did.

The moment my lips tasted his skin, he abolished the distance between us and pressed me into the island countertop. The edge dug into my back, but all I cared about was the weight of him moving against me. He was so tall, so solid, that he blotted out everything outside of our little bubble. The world shrank to just the two of us, and, for that moment, I didn't need anyone or anything else.

One of his hands lifted to cup my head, his fingers sifting through my hair. I moved to take the kiss deeper, but he broke off. "That's not an answer."

"What do you want from me?"

"I want you to say it."

My cheeks burned. "Tripp," I protested.

"Tell me."

"I want you," I said. "Please."

He seemed to react better when I was kissing him, so I brought my lips to his throat. I seemed to have an obsession with the taste of his skin. I felt his responding groan against my mouth, and his hands dug into my waist.

"Ground rules," he said hoarsely. "We have to have rules."

"Since when does big bad Tripp Wilder care about rules?" I asked and reached up on my tippy toes to tug at his earlobe with my teeth. He groaned and clamped a hand on my head to keep me there. Tripp liked that. I did it again and felt him shudder against me.

"I care about you," he said. "I don't want you to get hurt."

"You wouldn't hurt me." I knew that unequivocally. "I want to know what you meant when you said that sex could be good. I want to enjoy it without worrying too much about feelings."

"You're killing me, angel."

"Good. Let me make it feel better."

I reached between us and quickly undid his pants. I didn't want either of us to have time to come up with excuses. A moment later, before he could dodge me, his cock filled my hands, hot and hard, and at my touch his head dropped back, and he hissed out a breath.

"Fuck," he groaned. "Let's go to your room."

Wishing we had more time, I gripped him tight for a few exploratory strokes. "Can't. We have to be quick. Let's do it here."

"Screw quick. I need at least a few hours."

The desperation in his voice made me smile. "You'll have to up your game, ace. Or is that outside of your expertise?"

"You play dirty," he said. "Fine, but next time I want at least a couple of hours."

Then he spun me around, and I was forced to let go of him. Glancing up, I said, "Next time?"

"That's right. If this goes how I think it will, I'm going to need a next time. And that's the first rule. Now strip."

He pulled off his shirt, and I lost the thread of the conversation. His abs rippled underneath his lightly tanned skin. Just underneath his jeans, I spied his tan line and confirmed a mental theory I'd been courting for a while. Tripp practiced without his shirt on. It's why I rarely went to his practices. Eye candy for days. I wondered if I could now, or was that against the rules?

Which reminded me, "Stripping is the first rule?"

Since I was taking too long to comply, he helped me lift my shirt over my head, and his eyes feasted on my breasts even though they were bound in an unflattering sports bra that did nothing to accentuate them.

When he could speak again, he chuckled darkly, "I won't say no to that, but I meant that we should always talk to each other. Communication is the first rule, so things don't get too complicated."

My nipples beaded underneath the thick material of my sports bra, but it wasn't because it was cool inside the apartment. It was because he couldn't stop looking at me. "I can agree to that. What else?"

He eyed me up and down, then slipped a finger down the front of my bra. "This is next," he said.

I'd never been one to be shy about the naked body—I saw enough of them at work—but I blushed as I contorted to pull off the tight bra, my breasts bouncing free. His hands were there immediately, cupping them, lifting and testing their weight. My nipples were so sensitive that when he thumbed them, the sensation was almost painful.

My voice was thick with lust when I spoke, "I mean, which rule is next?"

Noting my reaction, his thumbs paid intimate attention to my nipples, caressing them in soft swipes that made liquid heat pool low in my stomach. "Honesty. If something changes, if you don't want to do this anymore, then you tell me. I want you to always feel like you can talk to me."

"Same to you," I said, but I was breathing hard. His thumbs were masterful, and when he added his fingers, pinching and squeezing the sensitive buds, I nearly came out of my skin. "Tripp!"

"Shh, I'm trying to focus." He leaned forward and took one of my nipples into his mouth. His tongue flicked, and he sucked deeply, causing me to arch my back against the counter. I wasn't even naked, and I was about to come.

"So am I!" I nearly snarled.

"No one else," he said darkly. "That doesn't make this a relationship, because I know you're not ready for that, but I don't share. And if you find someone else, then you tell me, and we'll call it quits."

"Same for you."

He didn't say anything to that but helped me out of my yoga pants. I wasn't wearing anything underneath, which left me completely bare. I suddenly remembered that I'd just been working out. I hadn't even taken a shower. Oh my God, what if I smelled gross? Shit!

"Tripp, wait, maybe we should take a shower. Clean up first."

"No time," he said, and then he knelt in front of me.

"But wait, I'm probably all sweaty—ahhh!"

I didn't have time to finish my warning. His mouth was already there between my spread legs, which he draped over his shoulders as though I didn't weigh a thing. I threw my head back as his tongue lapped boldly at me. There wasn't time to be self-conscious. Tripp simply didn't allow it. He ate my pussy like he was a starved man, and I was the tastiest thing he'd ever had on his tongue.

There was no hesitation in the way he licked at my clit, no second thoughts. If he had reservations, he didn't show them. The rasp of his stubble rubbed my inner thighs raw, but I didn't care. What he was doing felt too good to worry about anything else.

He pulled away long enough to say, "Last rule is we don't stop until you come."

Based on the way things were going, I didn't think that was going to be a problem—which was something, especially for me.

His hands spread my thighs wide, resulting in the need for me to brace my arms on the countertop behind me. The precariousness of the placement made it impossible for me to find a comfortable position. It kept me on edge, excited, uncertain. I never knew how much of a turn-on being reckless could be.

Normally, when I had sex, it was always in bed, at night, with the lights off. Now, we were in the middle of my apartment, and the sun was blazing through the front windows.

Then, he reached his hands around my hips to spread my pussy apart. The action shocked me so much that I straightened and looked down at him. And that was it. I couldn't look away. His eyes were closed as though in rapture. All I could hear were the wet, slick sounds of his tongue and lips sucking and licking at every part of me.

And the moans, oh, God, the moans.

Except they weren't coming from me.

I mean, they were, but Tripp...he sounded like he was enjoying the hell out of himself. Which had never occurred to me before.

But it was when he opened his eyes and looked up that I truly lost myself in him. His licks slowed as he moved from the sensitive nub of my clit to the place where I wanted him so badly. With his eyes on mine, he thrust his tongue deep inside. It was dirty, so dirty, and felt so good that I cried out, grabbed his hands, and came all over his tongue.

By the time I came back to myself and the haze had faded away from my vision, Tripp was back on his feet. After a moment, I realized it was the sound of his zipper drawing down that had caught my attention. His hands pushed at his jeans, freeing his dick, which glistened at the tip with a drop of precum. I wanted to taste it, but before I could get to my knees, he stopped me.

"You put your mouth on me, angel, and I'll lose it. Next time," he promised.

I meant to argue, really, I did, but he wrapped my thighs around his waist and kissed me. I tasted myself on his tongue. It was something I'd never done before, but damn, I liked it.

Then the thick head of his cock was pressing against me, and the heat that had built while he was going down on me returned with a vengeance. I clung to his shoulders and his neck and threw back my head as he teased my clit back and forth with long, slow strokes. He pushed inside once, and my eyes fluttered close. He was the perfect size. Thick enough to make it hurt in all the best ways, and long enough that he went deep to make me feel like he was a part of me.

He paused, muscles straining. "Fuck me, I didn't bring a condom," he said and sounded like a dying man.

I grabbed at his hips with my thighs, nearly sobbing with frustration. The friction was unbelievable. All of it was other-worldly, and I didn't want him to stop. For the first time in my life, I was willing to say damn the consequences.

"I'm clean. I get screened for work, and I got tested after Chris to be safe. I've got an IUD." It didn't shame me to talk about it. I had never really been shy about my body.

"I get screened for ball. I haven't been with anyone since my last checkup," he admitted, which shocked the hell out of me, considering all of his hangarounds. "But I'll stop if you want me to. I wasn't exactly planning on this."

"No, don't. We should be fine. I trust you."

And I did.

With all of me.

Which is why, when he continued, I relaxed into him, forgetting everything but how he felt.

It was like his hips moved without conscious effort. I could still see remnants of surprise and disbelief on his face, which were soon replaced by rapture. We'd deal with the consequences later. It felt too good to stop.

My arms went around his shoulders, and he twisted to press me against the kitchen wall without me having to say the countertop was digging into my back. The new position made him go deep inside with each thrust, and, with the wall at my back, I had nowhere to go, no place to escape. All I could do was endure.

Strangled, high-pitched sounds that sounded nothing like me came from my throat. It was like he made me lose control. And I liked it.

"That's it," he whispered. "Give it to me, angel. Come on me again."

"Oh, God." I'd never heard Tripp like this before, never dreamed the sweet, gentle baseball star could have such a filthy-talking dirty side.

"Yes, right there," he said, more to himself than me when my moans hitched up an octave. He pinned my hips to the counter and held me in place as he worked a spot inside me that made me see stars relentlessly.

My body tightened all around him, unbidden. I stopped breathing. All of my senses honed in on the point of contact that felt like a spark of stars inside me.

"I'm gonna come again," I warned because it felt like an explosion about to detonate.

"Do it," he ordered. "Now, now, now."

I came on a harsh exhalation, my limbs like vices around him. He continued thrusting until they relaxed, and then his hips pistoned once, twice, three times, and he roared his own release. The heat of him warmed me from the inside out, and as we came down and he put my feet on the floor, I could feel it seep out and down my legs, grounding me a little.

My thighs shook, and Tripp was breathing like he'd run a marathon. "Give me a second," he said. "I think I'm dead." He held me until we both stopped shaking, then said, "We should clean up before they get home. Shower?"

"Yes," I said and followed him to the bathroom.

He turned on the spray and tested the temperature until he deemed it acceptable. It felt so normal to climb in after him, but it was a delicate normality, one I wasn't used to and wanted to savor. Tripp handed me the soap, and I used it to wash his back. He did the same to me, although he paid special attention to his favorite parts on my body. As much as I wanted to linger, the twins were due home, and then we had dinner with his parents.

Oh, God, I had to look his parents in the eye after this.

"Don't," he said before I could begin overthinking it.

"I can't help it."

"Well, try. You've known me forever. Nothing has changed."

I couldn't help but feeling like *everything* had changed.

CHAPTER 12

TRIPP

"You sure you're going to be okay?" I asked.

She gave me a look. "We had sex, Tripp. I'm not damaged. I'll be fine."

"I didn't think—yeah, okay. I'll get changed and then pick you three up."

Her expression faltered. "Is this a good idea? Maybe we should reschedule."

"Never thought you were the shy type, Em. Good to know."

"Shut up, jerk," she said, but she was grinning. "I'll go get the girls. My rule isn't that we can't tell anyone about this. Just not...not now. I know how that sounds, and I don't want to make you feel bad, but there's just so much going on and I can't—"

"You don't have to explain it to me. Hell, I'm the one person you'll never have to explain yourself to."

I'd considered all the consequences of us hooking up years ago. I never thought it'd actually happen, but now that it had, I was faced with what would happen if it all went wrong. While I didn't regret what we had done—and to be frank, I couldn't wait to do it again—those consequences were all too real. If this arrangement went sideways, I risked losing it all. Losing her.

And that scared the shit out of me.

Looking very vulnerable in skinny jeans and a t-shirt, her face bare of makeup, and her hair a deep red from being damp, all I wanted to do was pull her back into my arms.

But I resisted.

"Alright," she said with a shy little smile. "Well, um. I'll be right back then."

"I'll meet you back here after I get changed."

She bit her lip and nodded. "Sounds good."

Leaving was harder than I thought it would be, which didn't bode well for when this arrangement of ours came to an end. Which it would. It couldn't go on forever. She deserved more than just sex, but if that's all she wanted from me, I'd make it the best she'd ever had for as long as she wanted.

Once I changed into a fresh pair of jeans and a shirt, I shot my parents a text telling them we were on our way. After knocking on Ember's door, I waited in the hall. On the other side, I could hear the girls shouting, and I smiled. I really did love those kids. I was an only child, so having them around was fun for me.

Ember threw open the door and said, "Two minutes, promise."

"Take your time," I said.

Tillie and Molly were sitting on the couch watching cartoons, their hair in identical pigtails. Their backpacks and jackets lay in a tumble by the door, the contents spilling out. I said hey to the girls, but they were too engrossed in the TV to respond.

"I'm ready," Ember said in a rush as she hurried down the hallway. I didn't miss that she wouldn't meet my eyes. "C'mon on girls. Time for dinner at the Wilder's house. Let's go."

There was a lot of groaning and "Aw, man", but they did as Ember asked and followed us down to my truck. Ember transferred their booster seats—or car seats or whatever they were called—to the back row and then climbed in. Once she was buckled, we set out.

The ride was long, for the girls at least, but they only asked if we were there yet twenty times, so I considered it a win. Ember kept her hands knotted in her lap, and, as much as I wanted to take one into my own, I gave her space. This wasn't a relationship. I didn't get those kinds of privileges.

Lights were on inside my parents' place as I pulled into the drive. The shadow of my mother flitted around the kitchen as she fixed dinner. She liked to fuss now that she was no longer teaching full time. Which meant she normally fussed about me, but I didn't mind. Especially not when I was reminded what the alternative was every time Ember's mom did something spectacularly fucked-up like abandoning the twins.

"Now, when we go inside, you make sure to tell Mrs. Wilder 'thank you' for inviting us over for dinner. No playing with your food, and play nice, and use your inside voices. Am I clear?" Ember said to the girls over the back of her seat.

"Yes," they both intoned.

"Then let's go get some grub!" I said.

Once Ember unbuckled them, the girls slithered out of their seats faster than a greased pig and darted to the front door where they knocked until my dad answered. I put a hand on Ember's to stop her from jetting out after them.

"I should make sure they behave," she said with a look at my hand.

"Wait," I said.

"Tripp, the kids."

"It'll be fine," I said and lifted my free hand to her cheek. "Don't worry."

She snorted. "Fat chance."

"Well, try not to worry. We'll figure it out."

Her expression turned serious. "Don't be too nice to me, okay? I don't know how to handle it."

"Learn," I said after a moment, then followed the girls inside.

My dad already had them huddled around the train set he'd been building in the den, showing them how to work the controls. He'd slapped a conductors hat on Tillie and was showing Molly how to start and stop the train. He'd been a conductor for twenty years before he retired last fall. Now he spent most of his time making and selling custom train sets like the one he was showing the twins.

One of my earliest memories was going to work with him when they couldn't afford a babysitter. My parents hadn't always had a lot, but despite that I had never wanted for anything. They had always made sure I knew I was loved.

"Hey, slugger," he said as Ember and I walked in. The light glinted in the silver streaks running through his blonde hair. He was only sixty-five, but every time I saw my parents, they looked a little bit older. "Your mom's waiting for you in the kitchen. She's got a pile of food, so I hope you're hungry."

"Starving," said Molly with enthusiasm. Tillie nodded emphatically.

Ember leaned down to kiss them both. "Let me talk with Mrs. Wilder first, and then I'll come get you both to eat. Behave now."

"They'll be fine," my dad told her. To me, he said, "Sneak me one of her stuffed mushrooms if you get the chance."

"I'll try."

"Are you sure it's not a burden to her?" Ember said, tugging on my sleeve before we reached the kitchen. She chewed on a nail and glanced toward the open doorway.

"She wouldn't have offered if it was a burden. They've both got a lot of free time since they retired. Honestly, you're doing me a favor. Having the twins to distract them will get them off my back during the season." At her hesitation, I pulled her into the kitchen. "It's fine. I promise."

Scents of meat and spice wafted from the sizzling pan my

mom was stirring. She looked up and smiled at me, her glasses fogged from the steam. "Tripp!"

"Hey, Mom."

She wrapped her arms around me, still holding the spatula. "It's so good to see you. I'm so glad you came."

"You, too. Mom, you remember Ember."

"Of course!"

Ember looked at me with wild eyes when my mom pulled her into a hug. "Thank you for having us, Mrs. Wilder."

"Janet, please."

Ember smiled. "Janet. Something smells great!"

"Sure does. I'm starving," I said.

"Perfect. The pork chops are almost done, and we've got green beans and mashed potatoes on the side." She went back to stirring the pot of potatoes and said, "If you're going to take one of the stuffed mushrooms to your father, he likes the ones with the cheese," without looking over her shoulder.

I laughed and said, "I don't know how she does that," to Ember before bringing my dad a couple of the stuffed mushrooms on a plate. I added a couple extra for the twins, who were hesitant at first, but each took one when my dad did.

"—you enough for offering to watch the girls. I'll admit I've been panicking. I'll pay you, of course."

"Whatever you feel comfortable doing. I'm happy to help out. To tell you the truth, I've been sort of at loose ends lately since I retired, and consulting work hasn't been as lucrative as I thought it would be. So, Tripp saying you needed help really came at the perfect time."

"And you don't mind watching them overnight a couple of times a week? My shifts are twenty-four hours long every third day."

Mom began scooping up heaping spoonfuls of mashed potatoes and green beans on the plates she had on the counter. "Of course not. They're sweet girls. I just worry about the transition for them. Perhaps we should let them visit for a couple of days before your next shift? Just so they get used to being around the house here before they sleep over."

"I don't want to impose," Ember said and brushed her hair behind her ears with a trembling hand. I wanted to take it in mine. What the hell was with my impulse to hold her hand? Christ.

"Oh, it's not an imposition at all. I'm happy to help." I could tell my mom wanted to say more, but she stopped herself. Ember was protective about her family, and I was sure she didn't want too much sympathy. God, I loved my parents. "I'd love to hear more about the girls' schedule."

Relief made Ember's shoulders sag as she relayed where the girls went to school, what times they had to be dropped off and picked up from the bus, and other crap I didn't really listen to. I couldn't stop staring at Ember, who seemed relaxed for the first time since her life blew up. I liked seeing her this way.

I wanted to keep her smiling and, if being her friend-with-benefits was how I made that happen, then so fucking be it.

The girls were asleep by the time we made it back to the apartment complex. Ember wasn't far behind them, considering her eyes were closed and her forehead was leaning against the glass as I pulled into the parking structure. I shook her gently awake and thought about how much I wanted to kiss her.

"We're here," I said. "I'll get Tillie if you'll get Molly."

She nodded and stifled a yawn. "Remind me to thank your mom again for all the leftovers. She really didn't need to do that."

I chuckled as I lifted a sleeping Tillie into my arms. She

grumbled a little, then went lax in my arms as she settled back into sleep. "I told you she liked to fuss."

"Hmm, I guess you're right. My mom has never done anything like that."

I wanted to tell her how sorry I was that she lost the genetic lottery, but I kept my mouth shut. She didn't need to hear that shit. Saying sorry wouldn't change anything. All I could do was what I'd been doing. Ember could handle her own shit.

I waited in their living room as Ember got the girls changed and into bed, and a thought occurred to me. "Why don't you move them into your parents' room?" I asked when she was done.

She pushed a hand through her hair, and her brow creased as she considered my suggestion. "I don't know. I never thought about it. They've always been there. I guess I could since they both ran out on us."

"You all deserve your own space. But that's not the only thing. You should talk to my mom next time about making an appointment with a lawyer to see what your rights are." Before Ember could argue, I said, "You owe it to the girls. You have to protect them now. You may as well make it legal."

"I'll think about it," she said with a yawn. "But I need to get some sleep. It's been a long day."

Before she could object, I crossed the room and took her into my arms. "I've been wanting to do this all night."

Then I kissed her.

She tasted like sugar, and her hands went to my chest. It wasn't urgent and powerful like it had been before. It was sleepy and sweet. I wanted nothing more than to take her to bed and make love to her until she was too exhausted to move, but I made myself slow the kiss and pull away.

"Good night, Ember."

"Good night."

CHAPTER 13

EMBER

"Do we have to go to the babysitter's after school?" Tillie whined the next morning. "I'm tired. You snored."

Molly nodded emphatically, her thumb stuck in her mouth. She hadn't done that since she was two. I rubbed a hand over the throbbing that was beginning to demand attention behind my right eye. It's okay. I've got this. It wasn't often the twins were whiney and uncooperative, but when they were, I was outnumbered, which made it all the harder.

"I don't snore," I said defensively. At least, I didn't think I did.

"Do, too," Tillie retorted.

"I'm sorry, my sweet babies. I'll try to see what I can do so that I don't keep you awake again. We'll talk about it more after school, but we have to get moving. I have an early shift this morning, and we still have to drive out of town to Tripp's parents' house."

"Are you sure we have to go?" Tillie blinked up at me with owlish eyes. Guilt swamped me for having to leave them overnight with Tripp's parents. I wished I didn't have to work or go to school at all, but someone had to earn a paycheck to keep them clothed and fed and pay for doctor's visits and whatever else. "What if I can't go to sleep at their house? Or what if they leave us alone like Mommy did?"

My heart squeezed inside my chest. I knelt down at their level and laid a hand on each of their shoulders. "Tripp's parents are good people." I winced internally when I realized the statement could be interpreted to mean our parents weren't, but the twins didn't notice. "They have the number at the station and my cell phone. I'll call you when you get off school and again before bed."

"Will you call in the morning when you're on your way to pick us up?" Molly asked, hopefully.

I traced her nose with a finger. "Of course I can. And they won't leave you alone. I made them pinky promise."

The twins shared a glance. "Really?" Tillie asked.

"Of course. I wouldn't leave you with just anyone without a pinky promise."

"Do you think Mrs. Wilder will read us a bedtime story?"

"I'm sure she will if you ask, sweetheart. Now let's get going before we're all late."

I made a mental note to call Tripp's mother and request that she read them a bedtime story. Then I hoped for a miracle shift because the twins weren't the only ones who were tired. I hadn't been able to sleep properly since...well, Tripp. I couldn't stop thinking about him.

"C'mon, Emmy. I thought we were going to be late," Molly said, pulling her thumb from her mouth.

They were so dang cute with their shouldered mini backpacks. Their hair was thrown up in identical ponytails, and their matching green eyes twinkled up at me. I grabbed my overnight bag that contained sleeping clothes for work, headphones, a tablet, chargers, and a change of clothes, along with the girl's overnight bags containing about the same.

I was going to be on edge the whole night wondering how they were doing, so I wouldn't be getting any sleep, but we didn't have a choice. I couldn't afford daycare for both of them, and I trusted Tripp's parents more than anyone else. I'd seen how they were at his games over the years and how they'd responded when he got injured. They would be good to my sisters.

Probably better than our own mother, who I still hadn't heard from. She didn't even care enough to check on the kids she had abandoned.

"Alright, twinkies, let's hit the road."

Whatever fears they had abated by the time we arrived at Tripp's parents' house, thank goodness. They were all smiles as I herded them up the drive to ring the doorbell, which they argued over. Finally, they settled on ringing it together.

Mrs. Wilder—Janet, I corrected myself—answered the door. If I could have dreamt up what a mom should be, by all appearances, Janet would be it. She wore a pair of khakis with a soft pink sweater. Her hair was styled in a sleek bob, and her makeup was subtle and classic. The scent of bacon and eggs wafted through the open door. I couldn't recall a time my mom had ever made breakfast, let alone worn something that wasn't stained or reeking of cigarette smoke. And when it came to makeup, subtlety wasn't exactly her strong suit.

"Good morning," Janet said cheerfully. "I hope you're hungry."

The twins shared a look before nodding enthusiastically. They barely waited for me to give them a hug and kiss goodbye before they dashed inside.

"Thank you again for all of this. I don't know what I would have done without you."

"Don't you worry about it. We're going to have a great time."

Already, I could hear the girls giggling inside, and the knots in my stomach loosened a little. Maybe everything would be okay.

"I'll be back tomorrow morning around the same time." I handed her their overnight bags and school stuff. "This should be everything they need. I'll text you a list of emergency contacts, my boss, the station, and all that. If you can't reach me, Tripp should know where I am, but I'll have my cell on me at all times."

"Sounds perfect. I'll call you around 7:30 tonight for them to say good night."

"Right. Yeah, that'll be great." I checked the time and added, "I'd better get going. Thank you again!"

It was easier leaving them than I thought it would be. Janet couldn't be farther from my mother, and I knew that while the twins were with them, they'd be perfectly safe. Not all parents were neglectful and malicious.

Hours later, I finally had time to settle, and time to think, between a couple of calls. My assigned chores had all been completed, and the other team of EMTs and paramedics were up for the next call.

I secluded myself in the bunkroom where we normally napped and plugged my ears with headphones so I wasn't disturbed. Selecting a podcast at random, I closed my eyes and threw an arm over them for good measure. The low, measured voices from the podcast filled my ears, but I couldn't hear them. All I could hear was the memory of Tripp's voice.

What had I done?

My cheeks burned, though there was no one to see my embarrassment. I pressed the backs of the fingers from my free hand to them. Never in my life had I ever slept around for the fun of it. My mom used to do that during the times she and my father were separated, and I had made it a point once I did have sex to only do it with people I truly cared about.

That included Tripp, didn't it? I cared about him. Aside from Charlie and Layla, he was one of my closest friends.

The truth was, I didn't have any answers. I liked to think I made mature decisions when it came to my life, the kids, and my job, but I didn't know what the hell I was doing half the time. Clearly. The only thing I did a really good job at was pretending.

Pretending to have it all together.

Pretending not to care that my mother abandoned us.

Pretending I didn't like Tripp as more than a friend.

The smart thing to do would be to tell Tripp we couldn't do it again, but, oh, God, how I wanted to. I don't think anyone had ever made me feel so good, which, for some reason, made me feel guilty because not being with Chris was still so new. New, but it already felt like it had been a long time.

In fact, my sisters aside, I was considerably less stressed without him in my life. I didn't worry about how he'd react to me having even less time to be with him or his judgments about my mother leaving. Now that I was thinking about it, he never would have been as understanding as Tripp had been. Judgmental was the word I'd use to describe him. Aloof.

Maybe that's why I'd been drawn to Chris in the first place, back when Tripp had been so overtly interested in being more than friends. Maybe a part of me had known, even then, that we weren't going to work out. Chris was safe because I knew it would never lead anywhere. That didn't mean I didn't care about him. Of course I did, and maybe it made me a little heartless for moving on so quickly. But we were never going to make it. Maybe it hurt so much in the beginning because he was my comfort zone. As long as I was with him, I knew what to expect. I could control the outcome.

Controlling the outcome with Tripp…was impossible.

I fell asleep pondering my next move and listening to the podcast. When I woke up as the tones dropped, I came to the conclusion that maybe I shouldn't fight it. Maybe the best thing to do with Tripp…was to enjoy it.

As I got ready, my phone beeped with a text message.

JANET: We'll be in town this morning. I'll drop the girls off at your apartment, if that's okay.

I texted her that it would be wonderful before I headed out with my partner on the call.

When I got home a couple of hours later, Tripp was already there, fixing our leaky sink. I paused in the doorway to watch him, admiring the sliver of his abdomen bared by his shirt. The muscles contracted as he grunted and reached higher under the sink, metal clanging against metal.

Is there anything sexier than a man fixing something? I don't think so.

He peered out at the sound of the door closing and smiled when his eyes found me. "Hey, you."

I leaned against the kitchen island, my eyes tired from lack of sleep but hungry for him, nonetheless. "Hey. Did you all of a sudden acquire a thirst for being a handyman?"

"I've got skills you've never seen," he said with a wink, then turned his attention back to the sink. "I've also got a rare day off from practice. I figured we could move the twins' room around if you're up to it."

I couldn't deny the thought had crossed my mind. They deserved their own space, and I could use a little more privacy, come to think of it. We'd shared a room since they were brought home from the hospital.

"Your mom is bringing them by in a while. Maybe we could surprise them."

He looked back at me, surprise lining his face, which was

quickly chased by wariness. "Really? I didn't think you'd agree with me so easily. I expected more of a fight."

"Maybe I could use some more privacy," I teased.

That made him choke a little. "Well, alright then," he answered.

Much as I wanted to drag him naked to my bed, or anywhere, I knew the girls would be back soon, and if we were going to get their stuff moved to my parent's room, we had a lot of work to do. Maybe this was the friend part of friends with benefits. He had no other excuse for wanting to help me all the time the way he did.

In the end, we managed to clear out my mom and dad's room. I packed away their things into boxes I'd nabbed from the grocery store. Tripp and I lugged their bed and dresser to the dump. Both had an oily residue and smelled strongly of cigarettes. It occurred to me that their carpets were probably cigarette soaked, too, so I moved my things into my parents' room instead of moving the twins into the room.

I was used to the smell of smoke anyway, and my lungs weren't nearly as sensitive as theirs.

Most of my stuff I stacked on my bed until I could reorganize it later. The most important thing was to make sure the girls' room was straightened and pretty. I wanted them to feel secure and at home. They'd had enough change, and I wanted to give them something that would make them happy.

Tripp maneuvered their bunk beds onto the wall where my bed had been. I brought in a bookcase from the living room and gave it a good scrubbing before filling it with their little things and books. In the end, it wasn't half bad, I had to admit. Eventually, I would like to get them more decorations and knick-knacks to really make it their own, but for now, this was more than they'd ever had, and it felt good. Really good.

Mine, on the other hand, was a bit more run-down. Years of smoke had stained the once cream-colored walls and ceiling. The floor was worn bare from overuse, but it was spacious without the girls' furniture, and the door was solid. It was mine. It was warm. I couldn't ask for much more.

I turned to Tripp, who was securing my dresser. "How can I repay you?"

I expected him to joke, but his eyes heated. "I can think of a few ways."

CHAPTER 14

TRIPP

Weeks had passed, and we had fallen into a routine. One I couldn't say I didn't enjoy for my own selfish reasons. I'd been waiting a long time for Ember Stevens, and I was going to enjoy every single second while she was mine.

Even if it was only for a little while.

She didn't want the twins more involved than they already were, so on the nights I stayed over, I'd get up extra early to sneak out before they woke up. There was never any PDA around them, and I made sure to keep Ember as quiet as possible. I didn't mind that part, though. Her muffled little screams were what made it all worth it. Her ex was a grade-A dipshit for giving her up.

His loss, my gain.

He never seemed like the bright sort anyway.

"Don't go," she whispered in the dark one frosty November morning, causing me to pause with my shirt halfway on. Her words stroked down my spine like a caress, and I was already halfway hard from waking up beside her. Her sexy voice, rough from sleep, pushed me the rest of the way.

I finished pulling on my shirt and sat next to her. Her flame-bright hair fanned over her pillow. I brushed it back to reveal her face and kissed her soft, pink lips. "I have to. The girls will be up soon, and I have practice."

"Play hooky and get back into bed with me." Her hand dipped under my shirt, her nails scratching lightly up and down my back, making me groan, and testing my resolve.

Maybe it had occurred to me on at least one occasion that the friends-with-benefits gig was good for me, too. A girlfriend during the most crucial season of my life would complicate things, and distract me from my ultimate goal. And Ember Stevens was, if nothing else, the sexiest kind of distraction.

"I wish I could, angel. But unless you ever want to see me again, I should probably go. Coach will make me run bleachers for days if my ass is a minute late again." My body heated as I recalled a moment last month when I'd slept in barely ten minutes because I'd woken up to my alarm and wanted to spend a few more moments with her. My legs had been sore for a week because of all the running.

"I'll give you a deep tissue massage if he makes you run. I know you like those."

I let her draw me down for another kiss, despite my better judgment. Common sense didn't seem to work quite right when it came to her. Heat licked along my nerves, settled low in my gut. I gave serious consideration to calling in sick—a little running never killed anybody.

She shifted, and the sheet slipped down her body acciden-tally-on-purpose. My muscles went tight at the sight of her pert, rose-tipped breasts and flat belly. I wanted my head in between her shapely thighs and my mouth on her heat until she was as wound up as she constantly made me.

I couldn't remember a time since we'd been neighbors when I hadn't wanted to be right where I was now. Couldn't remember a time when I hadn't wanted her.

Which is exactly why I pulled back, letting the cool air chilling the room rush between us. Get it together, Wilder. Keep your game face on.

She doesn't need the pressure. Keep it light, simple. Focus.

"Next time," I promised.

Her sigh was petulant, but she said, "Alright. See you Wednesday?"

That should give me enough time to clear my head and give me some perspective. Her classes and twenty-four-hour shifts were honestly a godsend. Spending too much time in her bed, wrapped up in her, made me think stupid things. Like wondering what it'd be like to have something more.

Clarity and space. That's what I needed. Not another morning waking up next to the woman who made me think I could find a woman who'd make me as happy as my parents were.

"See you Wednesday," I repeated.

I was already looking forward to it.

The door closed behind me with a soft click, and I padded down the short hallway to the living room, where I stumbled to a halt. The twins were perched on the couch, their faces ablaze in a glow of bright pink as they stared, rapt, at *My Little Pony* on the television. They both glanced over at the same time, noted my presence like it was a daily occurrence, then turned back to the TV. I mean, it was practically a daily occurrence, but they weren't supposed to know that.

My huff of indignation caught in my throat. We thought we were so clever, having me sneak in after they went to sleep and slip out before they woke up. Clearly, our best-laid plans had been stymied by a pair of munchkins. They didn't seem to be as caught off guard and continued watching TV while I wondered if I should wake Ember up or not.

"Morning," Tillie said before I came up with an answer. She yawned and glanced over at me as the show moved to a commercial. Molly merely smiled, then shoved her face in her sister's arm.

They were too precious for words sometimes. Ember had done such a good job protecting them from her parents' bullshit. "What are you doing up?" I asked and crossed to ruffle their silken hair.

"Waiting for Emmy."

"Do me a favor?" I asked. Tillie nodded, and Molly peered out with interest. "Don't tell your sister you saw me."

"Like a secret?" Tillie asked. At my nod, she said, "We're not supposed to keep secrets."

Too damn smart. "Well, I won't get you in trouble. Don't go too hard on your sister today."

"'Kay. We won't."

I'd have to talk to her about them later. They saw us sleeping together that one time before, but I knew Ember didn't want them to jump to the wrong conclusions. She'd done her best to shield them both from her mom and dad, and she didn't want to fuck it all up now that they were finally settling into their new routine.

I kissed both of their heads. Ember was going to ream me when she found out they saw me leaving after all our careful planning, but we'd handle it. I had no doubt she would try to pump the brakes on our little arrangement, but that wasn't gonna happen either.

She might be a distraction, but maybe, for once in my life, a distraction was what I needed.

"You okay?"

I hated that question with an intensity that couldn't be described.

That's all anyone asked me last year.

Coaches.

Teammates.

Doctors.

Physical therapists.

My parents.

My recruiters.

The answer to that question—if it ever needed to be asked—was an unequivocal no.

No one would ever be okay watching their dreams swirl down the drain. No one would ever be okay watching all their hard work turn into a big, fat fucking waste. I sure as hell wasn't.

But that wasn't going to happen to me again.

I had worked too hard.

I had wanted it too much.

But that didn't mean I could fully ignore the pain in my shoulder when it seared through me like an arrow. I could barely contain the grimace as I tried to control my breathing and moderate my expression so no one could read it. It didn't fool Alex, who jogged to the mound after my wild pitch. Alex, the one man who knew my game better than I did.

I glanced around to the coaches, who were too busy discussing batting strategy to notice one practice pitch gone awry. If they heard one whisper of an injury, they'd be on my case for more physical therapy, and I wasn't fucking gonna let that happen. Physical therapy equaled bench time. And my ass has seen enough bench time to last me the rest of my career.

I belonged on the mound, and I wasn't going to let anything stop me from making sure I stayed there.

Alex stopped when he got close enough to whisper. "Is it your arm?"

The arm in question ached from somewhere deep inside like it did when I had worked it for too long. Fatigue and overuse roused a ghost pain from the torn tissue, but that was all. I simply hadn't stretched enough.

I leveled Alex with a look that had him lifting his hands in a defensive position. "I'm fine. If you fuckin' ask me that again, though, you won't be. I'm gonna warm up some more and send in McGuire to practice for a bit."

Alex nodded, but I could feel his gaze on me from time to time as I threw practice pitches with a freshman catcher and then did some deep stretching exercises I'd learned from my physical therapist, a big, brawny guy named Ted who used to be a big, badass Army Ranger once upon a time.

After a half-hour, my arm felt loose enough to throw again, and I returned to the mound. I practiced the rest of the day without any complications, but Alex's concern was infectious. Dammit, this is why I didn't like anyone asking me if I was okay. People start asking it enough, and you start wondering if maybe you're not.

After practice, I gave myself time in the jetted tub and alternated soaking my shoulder and icing it with a big-ass bag of ice from the machines in the locker rooms specifically for injuries. The shoulder didn't bother me aside from the one throw, but I didn't want to take any chances. There was too much riding on this season.

Like my life.

"Wilder!" Coach Taylor yelled.

"Yeah, Coach, in here."

He rounded the corner, jerking to a stop when he found me in the tub. "Good. You should keep resting that shoulder when you're not practicing. We don't want you to strain it any more than you have to."

"Alright, Coach."

"You were looking good out there today. I just wanted to tell you to keep it up. Although, if you're ever late to a practice again, I won't be pleased."

"No, Coach."

"I know women can be a pretty temptation, but I want you to keep focused until the end of the season. March is going to come quickly, and you don't need any distractions. You hear me?"

Sometimes, I wondered if the man had a sixth sense. Then again, he spent most of his waking hours living and breathing the game, coaching, and coaxing his players to their best. It was no wonder he knew us better than we knew ourselves.

"You got it, Coach."

He narrowed his eyes at my words. "Don't bullshit a bullshitter, kid. I know you've got that girl of yours."

See? Knows everything, I swear. Alex once said he thought Coach Taylor might have bugged our cribs and shit with cameras and tapped our phones, but I had brushed him off at the time. Now that I came to think of it, though, there was no other explanation.

"I'm not going to tell you how to live your life," he continued, "but this is the most important season of your career. I need you focused to win, but you need to focus to succeed. You understand?"

"Yeah, Coach, I understand."

He narrowed his eyes even further. Sometimes, I thought they'd up and disappear into his skull. "I mean it. I'm not distracted. I'm focused one-hundred percent."

There was a pause while he studied my face. Seeming to be satisfied with whatever truth he divined from my expression, he gave a decisive nod. "Well, alright, then. I'll see you at weight training this afternoon. And don't be late."

It was almost comforting how predictable he could be, even when his mind-reading crap creeped the shit out of me.

But he wasn't wrong. I couldn't afford to be distracted, much as I liked the woman doing the distracting.

CHAPTER 15

EMBER

"But I don't want to go to the grocey store," Tillie complained, dragging her feet and making me grit my teeth. "I want to stay home and watch princess movies."

I gave myself three long, deep breaths before I answered. After a long shift and an even longer day of classes, the last thing I wanted to do was drag the girls to a busy store and spend another endless hour slogging through the aisles with them running around me like a pack of snarling werewolves. But our pantry was looking sparse, and the social worker was due for a visit, so I had no other choice.

"Grocery store," I corrected. Feeling calmer, I brushed her hair away from her face. "I would rather watch princess movies, too, sweetheart. But if we don't get groceries, we're gonna have to eat your sister for dinner." I dug my finger into Tillie's neck and was rewarded with a giggle.

"We can't eat Molly," Tillie protested once her giggles subsided. "She wouldn't taste very good. Besides, I'd rather have beef stew."

Taking both of their hands, I said, "Beef stew sounds good, but let's see how it goes."

"Beef stew, beef stew, beef stew," they chanted as I guided them inside the sliding doors. Their laughter was a welcome respite from the cranky mess they'd both been in since I had picked them up from Tripp's mother's house. I couldn't blame them. I'd been cranky, too.

My mother's voice had been in my head all day during classes. Telling me how irresponsible I was being, giving up being with the girls to further my education. I could be working to provide them with a better life instead of wasting time at school. It didn't make sense, I knew that intellectually, but the guilt was very real. It had been a tight ball in my stomach each day I left the girls.

The only time I could ignore it was when I was with Tripp.

Hell.

Nothing about my life was simple right now.

Nothing about my life made sense.

Except the girls.

And…perhaps not so surprisingly, Tripp, in a weird way.

But maybe weird was exactly what I needed when everything was going down the drain.

Maybe he was exactly what I needed.

I shook my head and focused on gathering the items on my shopping list. Milk, eggs, bread. The basics. I couldn't afford much more, at least not until the social worker came through with the government assistance I had been able to apply for—at least temporarily—until we got everything sorted legally. Which was another thing on my never-ending to-do list.

The thought of getting food stamps and WIC didn't fill me with pride, but there was nothing I wouldn't do for my sisters, and we had to eat. As soon as I finished my paramedic's program in May, I'd be able to apply for the paramedic's position at work, which would nearly double my salary and give the girls and me some cushion room instead of working paycheck-to-paycheck, like I was right now. Maybe if I also applied for custody, there'd be some sort of benefits, but I didn't want to think about that too closely either.

The thought of being the twinkies' legal guardian scared the crap out of me. For one thing, it was a lifetime commitment in a way that being their sister wasn't. For another, it meant choosing to kick my mom out of my life—and by extension theirs—in a more permanent way than I'd ever done.

Change might be necessary, but it didn't come easy.

I filled my basket with the necessities and caved on the beef stew for dinner to appease the monsters. As I was weighing my options for the meat selection, I sighed and chose the more expensive one. The girls needed to eat, and I needed leftovers for lunches. I'd simply have to ask work for more hours or find another area to skimp on.

I placed the stew meat in the buggy and looked up. There was nothing in sight save for the small pile of groceries, which I hoped would stretch to last a few days, maybe even until my next paycheck. The girls weren't hovering by the cart where I'd left them.

They were nowhere to be found.

I didn't panic—at first. I generally didn't panic when it came to emergency situations. You'd think I would because of the sheer amount of anxiety that plagued me on a day-to-day basis, but when it mattered, really mattered, my brain hyper-focused on everything around me. It almost slowed the world down so that I could process the information I was receiving.

The meat aisle was barren except for me. It was a weekday afternoon, so most people were probably still at work or school. There were no displays in the aisle for them to hide behind, and the only door was to the butcher, which only opened from the inside.

"Girls?" I called out, almost hesitantly at first. Afraid that if I voiced my fears, it would breathe life to them. "Molly? Tillie?"

When they didn't appear, I felt the first whispers of panic. Surely, they were just playing hide-and-seek. If I wasn't so freaking worried, I'd be annoyed. Except the girls knew better than to run off when we were in public. We'd had the stranger-danger conversation on more than one occasion.

I couldn't breathe. The thought of them being taken…No. I wasn't going to think about that. Images of my mother stalking us and taking the twins out of spite ran through my head as I abandoned the cart and began dashing to each aisle, finding each one empty.

"Molly! Tillie!"

I heard a giggle and thought I had imagined it. Spinning around, I followed the sound to the dairy aisle, where the girls were hiding behind a stack of milk crates. My brain didn't process their mischievous grins or cheeks pink with laughter.

"Ta-da!" Tillie shouted. "You found us. We were playing hide-and-seek."

I fell to my knees in front of them, my heart in my throat. It would make sense to yell at them and berate them for running off in a public place, but I couldn't bring myself to do it. I was so grateful they were safe that it obliterated any anger I may have felt that they were playing games.

"Emmy?" Molly asked. "Why are you crying?"

"You scared me. I thought you were lost." Or worse. But I didn't say that out loud for fear of scaring them, too. "Haven't I told you not to run off when we're in the grocery store? It's not safe."

"We wanted to make you laugh. You've been so busy lately that we thought you'd think it was fun," Tillie said, tears in her eyes.

"Oh, babies," I choked out. God, sometimes it felt like I couldn't ever do anything right. Was it even fair to them to keep them with me? Would they be better off with a real family, even if that meant they weren't with me?

One thing at a time.

At the moment, that was all I could handle.

"I'm hungry," Molly whispered, her lips wobbling. "Can we go home?"

Swallowing hard, I took their hands in mine and led them back to our buggy. "Sure, we can. Let's finish shopping, and we'll go home, and I'll make my favorite sisters some beef stew. Deal?"

The two of them climbed up in the buggy and stared up at me with identical smiles. "Deal," they both said at the same time.

I finished my shopping with their chatter in the background. Having them back didn't assuage the fear clutching my heart.

Because I realized how easy it would be to lose them.

While the twins played in the bath, I tidied up from dinner, moving on autopilot. I packed away the leftovers into containers for their lunches, loaded the dishwasher, and wiped down the counters. *Big Bang Theory* played in the background, even though I'd watched all the episodes at least a thousand times. I didn't care how many times Charlie and Layla made fun of me for watching the same movies and shows over and over: it was one of the only things that gave me comfort.

At least the people in the shows never let me down. Sure, one may get canceled, or an actor or actress might leave, but I could roll back to season one at any time and relive all of my favorite memories. They didn't abandon or neglect me as my family did.

After I got Tillie and Molly home, they helped me make the beef stew and gobbled up two bowls each before I herded them to the bath. They were old enough to take care of themselves while they bathed, for the most part, which allowed me some time to clean up and maybe even do a little homework, but not much.

Sheldon and Leonard were arguing as I worked on a few notes that I was required to make. Next semester, there wouldn't be so much bookwork, but for now, they were dumping as much information on us as they could. It was almost as though they wanted to see which students got overwhelmed and, I had to admit, I was getting close.

Not because of the work—because I could do the work. It was everything else.

The twins.

Work.

School.

Chris.

…Tripp.

Maybe it was too much.

It took being scared half to death when the twins ran off at the grocery store for me to take a step back. I couldn't let this thing with Tripp distract me. The next time I saw him, I'd have to reiterate the whole casual aspect of the friends-with-benefits thing. Just to make sure we were clear.

I was packing my bag for the next day when there was a soft knock at the door. Despite my firm resolve to keep things casual, heat washed over me at the mere thought of it being Tripp on the other side. Apparently, my body didn't care about keeping it casual.

"Hey," he said when I opened the door. "Can I come in?"

"Of course."

When his body brushed against mine, the heat concentrated in my sex, and I gulped. No matter how much I tried to tell myself we needed to talk, I couldn't seem to make the words come out of my suddenly-dry mouth.

"Emmy," came a call from the bathroom. "We're done."

"Do you mind?" I asked.

"No, of course not. Take your time."

"Make yourself at home."

The girls were covered head to toe in bubbles—and so was the floor—but I couldn't find the energy to be mad. They were safe. Tripp was here. I'd figure the rest of it out.

I always did.

"Is Tripp here?" Tillie asked as I helped the two of them get dressed and ready for bed.

The scent of the lavender baby soap I'd been using since they were babies wafted up from their skin and downy hair. They endured me sniffing their heads and giving them a tight hug as they both climbed into the bottom bunk for their story and settled underneath the blankets.

I decided not to lie to them. They were too smart for me, anyway. "He came by to talk."

"After the story, will he tell us good night?"

At this, I hesitated. It was such a fine line between benefits and family where they were concerned. But Tripp was Tripp, and he'd known these girls practically their whole lives. "Of course, sweeties."

He could be a part of our lives as long as I was crystal clear on which parts.

CHAPTER 16

TRIPP

JUNIOR YEAR

The stadium was packed with people, their screams and cheers filling the air. The sun beamed down, relentless and bright. The sky was as blue as I'd ever seen it, without a single cloud marring its surface. I couldn't have asked for better weather.

I should have been excited.

This was the moment I'd been working for my whole life. Countless weeks of nonstop practice. Giving up opportunities to be with my friends in order to play travel ball. Missing milestones like my sixteenth birthday to play away games. Having a normal life—whatever that was—to devote it to living my dream.

After today, either I'd move on to the next level of the game, or I wouldn't.

Either prospect was terrifying.

Alex swung an arm around my shoulder and joined me at the entrance to the field. We were still in the shadows, so the fans in the stadium couldn't see us from their vantage point.

"Don't you love it? They're here for us, man."

"Showboater," I said automatically. Alex always got off on the spectacle of it all. He loved being in the spotlight. He was the type of player who enjoyed being a player. Alex ate up all the attention from the fans—the female fans in particular.

"You know it," he answered. "You ready for this?"

"Born ready."

Alex whooped and punched me in the arm. "Let's do this!"

By this time, the rest of our team had joined us. We were about to run out on the field for warmups. It was the first game of the year, and spirits were high. Our summer practices had been rigorous, but we were more prepared than ever. This was what I'd been waiting for.

The din of the crowd kicked up several notches as we ran out on the field and took our places to warm up. I'd thrown some to warm up, but I always liked to get a feel for the mound before we started the game. All eyes were on me, but my focus was solely for our catcher and the plate.

We were going to dominate.

It was the bottom of the sixth. We were up by two and had one on second. I wasn't a genius at bat, but I was competent. While I was on deck, I took a moment to scan the crowds, looking for my parents. The game had been head-to-head until now, so I hadn't had the chance before.

I found them behind third, a few rows up. They both waved enthusiastically when I lifted a hand in greeting. Then my gaze found Ember, who was sitting in the row immediately behind them. She had her friends, Layla and Charlie, next to her, each with a twin on her lap. They were about to turn five, and no doubt Em needed her friends to help wrangle them because they'd taken the "eff you fours" to the next level.

The three girls waved, and the twins copied them. I saw their mouths move as they cupped their hands and shouted. They were too far away for me to hear what they were saying, but I didn't need to hear it. The twins were holding a sign that said, "WE <3 #9!"

I pointed my bat at the lot of them, and the twins began jumping up and down. With a grin, I turned to do some practice swings while our shortstop was up at bat. He hit a single, and I brought them both in with a triple. The next person up at bat struck out, which ended the inning and put us back on the field.

I walked the first two, and the second got a single to right field. Sweat poured down my face, and my uniform was already soaked. My focus was so absolute it was as though no one else in the stadium existed but the players on the field.

Alex signaled a fastball, and I nodded. I wound up, and the ball torpedoed past the player at bat. Strike. Once I got the ball back, I checked the players on either base out of the corner of my eye. Their coach liked to play it safe, but it didn't hurt to make sure neither was trying to pull anything.

The second fastball made my shoulder twinge a little. It wasn't out of the ordinary, so I rolled it and gave my arms a quick stretch to shake it off. It wasn't abnormal to experience some muscle exhaustion this far into the game, so I didn't think much of it.

Stress on the muscles and ligaments is why we did so much conditioning and strengthening. It's also why Coach Taylor wanted us to give a sign if we were reaching the point of putting ourselves through too much. Injuries could end a career.

A curveball took out the player at bat, and I gave my shoulders another roll as we set up for the next one. A quick glance at the coach showed him focused on the player at bat. We only needed two more outs. I could get through them, no problem.

It was when the final player came up to bat that I realized the pain in my shoulder wasn't merely soreness from routine throwing. It had increased from a normal ache to a persistent burn. I was going to have to ice down for hours once the game was over.

The first fastball tore through my arm like a hot knife stabbing into my shoulder and ripping through my bicep and down to my wrist. I stumbled a little off the mound and had to breathe heavily in my mouth and through my nose to deal with the searing pain.

It wasn't the first time I had had shoulder pain—it was common among most pitchers. The repetitive strain of throwing over and over again caused wear and tear in the muscles that attached the arm to the socket. I'd had my fair deal of sore muscles, but I'd never felt anything like this.

I gave a passing thought to signal Coach, but then I remembered my family in the stands, and the potential employers watching. Giving up now would mean losing so much. I could make it through the rest of the game and get it looked at after.

Alex signaled for another fastball, but I shook him off. I'd have to play it safe, but smart, for the rest of the game. The change-up that got the last player on base gave me a twinge that I ignored. Since I hadn't struck him out, it brought another player to bat with one on first.

I threw a curveball, and the moment my arm reached the follow-through and released the ball, I knew I'd fucked up. White pain tore through me with violent intensity. I let out a hoarse cry, and then the pain reached a peak so intense that my arm went numb. Black flashed in front of my eyes, and white noise blotted out the screams and cheers from the crowd.

Once I could hear again, I heard Coach calling for a time out. I didn't know who was on base or what happened to the ball after the batter had made connection. Sweat poured down my face, and my cheeks were twitching from the intensity of my grimace.

"Get Collins," Coach shouted when he reached my side. I barely paid any attention as the backup pitcher took my place and Coach herded me back to the dugout. "Take him to the team doc and get him checked out."

Someone guided me to the locker rooms where our field medic was waiting. "Can you lift your arm for me?" he asked. I couldn't remember the dude's name.

I did as he asked but could barely lift it over shoulder-height. He repeated the directions, asking me to turn my arm wrist-up and move my arm back and forth, but I couldn't fully do as he asked. He palpated the shoulder, and I nearly punched him in his face.

Sometime later, one of the assistant coaches loaded me up in their sedan and took me to the hospital. I could barely pay any attention. It wasn't so much the pain as the growing realization of what that one mistake could mean for my future.

I was numb through the initial assessment. They did an ultrasound and had me move my arm again as they looked at different ligaments and tendons. I knew it was for-real serious when they recommended me for an MRI. It couldn't merely be a pulled muscle. My spirits sank. The expression on the assistant coach's face—or rather the lack of one—told me all I needed to know.

A pounding came at the door.

"Open the door, Tripp. I know you're in there."

I glanced up from the movie playing on the TV and considered getting up to open the door. In the past week, I hadn't moved from the couch other than to get more food from the kitchen or use the bathroom. There wasn't much need to. I was on leave from school until after my surgery, and I didn't have practice to go to anymore, so what was the point?

"You have three seconds!" came Ember's voice through the door.

Frankly, I was surprised she hadn't shown up sooner. She'd texted to check on me at least once a day, but I hadn't known what to say to her, so I hadn't answered.

The ice pack on my shoulder had turned to water, so I got up to refill it. Keeping my shoulder iced or under a heating pad were the only ways to stave off the ache that never seemed to go away. Sometimes, I could swear I felt it in my dreams.

"One! Two! Three!"

What was she going to do? Breath through the door? I doubted it. She might be a force of nature, but a linebacker she was not.

A little too late, I remembered that I'd given her a key in case I locked myself out. Cursing, I shuffled awkwardly to the door, but she had it open and was slipping through before I could latch the chain lock.

"Really, Tripp? Can't answer a text?" Her green eyes were bright as emeralds. Nose wrinkling, she looked around me. "Good God, it smells like a frat house in here."

"If you're not going to clean, then get out."

Turning away from her, I went back to exchanging my mushy ice pack for a fresh one. I slapped it on my shoulder and reclined back on my nest on the sectional couch, which was now covered in dirty clothes, old takeout containers, and a remote…somewhere in the cushions.

"Tripp," she said, and her voice was so full of compassion that it made me want to hurt things.

"Don't start."

"Please talk to me." She sat down on the couch next to me

despite the junk covering every available surface. "I want to help you."

I scoffed. "What are you gonna do? Fix my shoulder? Go back and win the game for us? C'mon, Em, there's nothing you can do to help me. Just leave."

"I'm not going anywhere. If cleaning is what you need, then I'll clean."

I didn't answer that. She could do whatever the hell she liked. I wasn't going to stop her.

We ignored each other while she picked up trash and dirty clothes. I pretended not to notice her and closed my eyes in protest. If she wanted to waste her time, whatever. I wasn't her daddy.

When she was done, she sat down beside me, but I didn't acknowledge her. I knew that if I did, I'd break.

Another knock came at the door, and I cracked open an eye. It was some guy I didn't recognize. "Hey," he said to Ember. "I was at your place, but your friend Charlie said you were over here." His eyes darted to me. "Are you ready?"

"I can't go out tonight. I'm sorry. I meant to text you." She lowered her voice. "He's still a little down. Raincheck?"

"For you, anything. I'll text you."

"Okay, bye," she answered, but I could hear the smile in her voice.

Since when did she have a boyfriend?

CHAPTER 17
EMBER

The twins fell asleep with surprising ease. They weren't even awake long enough for Tripp to wish them good night. The one night when I could use their bedtime to clear my head and organize my thoughts, and their lights were out in less than ten minutes. Why do they always do the exact opposite of what I want them to? It's a conspiracy. It's like they know.

My heart was thundering as I closed the door to their room and headed back down the hall. This wasn't going to be easy, but it was necessary. Doing the right thing had allowed me to survive thus far. And cutting things off before they got too complicated was the right thing.

Wasn't it?

I reached the end of the hallway. "We have to talk," I said clearly, though inside I was shaking.

Tripp got to his feet from where he was reclining on the couch. "Uh-oh, that sounds ominous. Come here. The twins get to sleep okay?"

Why did he have to be so damn nice? I went to him, taking a

seat by his side. I hoped he couldn't tell how nervous I was. "Sorry, I didn't mean it like that." Even though I kinda did.

"I know what you meant." He held up a finger to my lips before I could respond. It stopped me short—like it always did when he touched me. It only made me want him to touch me more. "I bet I can guess what you're going to say."

Bewildered, but at the same time not really surprised, I blew out a breath. He always seemed to know what I was thinking before I thought it. It was unnatural. "You do?"

He nudged my shoulder and said with patient exasperation, "C'mon, Em, how long have we been friends?"

To be honest, it felt like forever. "A long time."

"I bet you're thinking we were crazy for sleeping together. That a friends-with-benefits relationship could never work between us. That you're worried it'll mess everything up. The twins should be your priority. Am I wrong?"

He wasn't, which was what made it so infuriating. Was I really that easy to read? Apparently, not for him. "No," I admitted. "But you can't say you don't understand where I'm coming from."

Instead of answering, he gripped me by the arm and guided me to my new room. I could have stopped him if I wanted, but I offered no resistance. Carefully, he shut the door behind us. The click of it closing made my heart stutter. This was why I had avoided being alone with Tripp for all those years. It was easier to deny his effect on me when it was dulled by having other people around.

Funny how I'd never actually been able to admit that to myself before now.

In my distracted state, Tripp was able to maneuver me to the bed. But I couldn't let the growing sense of intimacy deter me. This thing between us had to stop.

I managed to say as much out loud.

Or, at least, I thought I did.

"I understand where you're coming from."

Tripp nudged my shoulder, pressing me inexorably back on the bed. He stretched out beside me, his long, lean body blocking out the yellow light from the bedside table. Shadows painted his face, accentuating his cheekbones and sending thrills down my spine. He stole the fright right out of me.

"You do?" Well, shit, that breathless note in my voice didn't help my argument. "You know I have to think about what's best for the girls." My protests were weak.

He scribbled secrets on my skin with the tips of his fingers, drawing gooseflesh to the surface. He knew my body as well as my mind. And just like that, all the thoughts flew out of my head. I let him lift my lips to his with the slightest pressure from a hooked finger. His mouth brushed over mine with easy comfort and the devastation of a natural disaster.

The contrast of his implacable body to his soft lips made me forget myself. His mouth nibbled at mine—no hesitation, no self-doubt. His focus was one hundred percent on me. Tripp's confidence had always astounded me. What must it feel like to always know exactly what you want?

Even more, how did a girl react when that certainty was focused entirely on her?

Sweat gathered in the deep of my lower back as his tongue enticed my lips to part. With light, easy pressure, it rubbed against mine. I couldn't help it. I moaned into his mouth, the sound needy and urgent, even to my ears.

One kiss wouldn't hurt.

Would it?

And I let him. God help me, but no one kissed like Tripp Wilder. He made me feel like I was the only woman in the world.

I deepened the kiss, letting him slide a muscled thigh between my legs. The weight of him came over me slightly, a welcome shelter. I wanted more. That was the problem. I wanted too much.

I'd talk to him.

I would.

I just wanted to be with him for a little longer. It seemed that when it came to Tripp, I'd always want more.

And that was terrifying.

I broke away, exhaling heavily, and already missing his lips on mine. "Tripp, wait."

His lips moved to my neck, biting softly, and then moving to my ear. My weak spot. Was there a link between that spot and my G-spot? It certainly felt like it. Maybe Tripp just knew all my spots.

He stopped. It shouldn't surprise me that he did. Tripp was nothing if not kind and considerate. I hated to think about Chris at a time like this, but he wouldn't have taken me pumping the brakes so well. I should have realized it back then—I had wanted to please him so much that I hadn't given myself enough respect.

Tripp didn't ever make me question myself. He respected me enough for the both of us. This friends-with-benefits arrangement was for my comfort. I was fully aware that he would have been all-in ages ago if it weren't for my own reservations.

He tucked me close to his side. "Talk to me."

"I'm…I…" Words failed me.

Noticing my struggle, he said, "How about I talk, then? And you can tell me if I'm off base or not."

I unstuck my tongue long enough to mumble, "Okay."

"I know you're worried about your sisters. We wouldn't be friends if you weren't the caring, slightly neurotic person you are. I'm guessing something happened today?"

I shouldn't be surprised. He always knew. "Doesn't this break the rules? Emotional chats aren't exactly one of the benefits in our rules."

"Friends come before the benefits," he answered without hesitation.

If hearts were made to beat, mine was beginning to feel like it was meant to beat for him.

I couldn't meet his eyes, especially not after that revelation. "I lost the twins at the grocery store today." Even saying it out loud made my stomach tie itself in knots. "For a second, I thought my mom had found them and taken them. It made me realize how vulnerable they are right now. I can't afford to be selfish."

"And I make you selfish."

It wasn't a question, but I answered anyway. "You make me feel a lot of things." There. That was neutral.

His mouth moved to my ear again. "Do I make you feel good?"

Was I imagining it, or was my temperature legit rising from his words alone? "Yes," was the most articulate response I could formulate.

"Hmm," Tripp murmured, licking my ear again. He eased back, and I caught myself reaching for him.

"How are they?"

My brain ground slowly as I tried to remember how to string words together. "Honestly, they were mostly fine after I found them. They thought it was like hide-and-seek, I think. They were more upset that I was so upset."

"Scared the shit out of you, huh?" His hand rubbed up and down my back. The tension that had filled me while I had been thinking of losing the twins melted away.

"Totally. But it made me think…what if I'm not ready for this? I don't know what the hell I'm doing."

"I've never known anyone more ready. You're incredible, and you don't even see it. I think you can handle anything."

He sounded so sure of himself. Of me. "I wish I had that much confidence in myself."

"I'd be worried if you weren't more concerned. It's a big deal, I won't deny that. But I think you're doing a better job than you give yourself credit for."

"Thanks."

"Is that what you wanted to talk to me about, angel?"

"Basically."

"Let me guess. You wanted to punish yourself for making a mistake. A mistake most all parents make at one time or another. You thought you didn't deserve something good in your life as a result."

That couldn't be right. He was making it sound like I was some sort of martyr.

But I wasn't, was I?

"I've been watching you—in a non-creepy way, I promise—for as long as we've been friends. You always put other people before yourself. Your friends. Chris. The girls. Your parents. It's admirable, don't get me wrong. But you also deserve to pursue your own happiness, too. That's all I'm saying. So, I guess the question is, what makes you happy?"

There was a long, tense silence as his words echoed throughout the room.

When I didn't answer, he said, "If I'm one of the things that makes you happy, Em, for once in your life, be selfish." He continued after a breathless pause, "Do you want me to beg?"

Tripp Wilder.

Begging.

For me.

Was this real life?

I imagined it for a moment, him kneeling in front of me. The image wasn't completely unbearable. But I'd never make him do that. "No, I don't want you to beg. And you shouldn't have to keep having these talks with me."

"What are friends for? Besides, everyone needs a shoulder every now and then. Even you."

"Especially me, these days."

"You aren't infallible, Ember."

"You are," I said, finally lifting my eyes to meet his. "You always seem to have an answer." I squinted my eyes in false accusation. "The right answer. Are you a mind reader? In all seriousness, thank you for being so understanding."

"Listening and communicating are parts of the rules," he said sagely, crawling over me like a cat, all lazy and utterly confident, the ruler of me, if not everything else. His knee nudged mine open, and in one fluid movement, he was on top of me, settled between my legs like he belonged there.

And maybe he did?

That was almost as frightening as my parents abandoning us. What if Tripp wanted to be there for me? Maybe that's why I never let him.

Pushing the thought away, I said, "I don't remember the listening part. You should remind me." My hands lifted to his muscled shoulders, stroked over them, then pulled him fully over me. There was nothing as delicious as his weight pressing me into the bed.

He kissed me leisurely until my head began to swim. "Then we'll have to add it to the rules."

I almost said, "What rules?"

"Change the rules? Is that allowed?"

"For you? Always." His gaze was too serious to be teasing. I knew without equivocation that he was serious. He may have been a flirt, but when he said something like that, something that had *meaning*, he meant it to the core of his being.

Unable to help myself any longer, I brought my mouth to his. Going too long without kissing him was a deprivation I wasn't prepared to combat. He sank into me, mouth and body, and it felt so right that I didn't care if it was wrong or selfish. Any lingering doubts I may have had were obliterated.

If he asked me again what made me happy…

The answer would be him…without question.

CHAPTER 18

TRIPP

A red haze filled my vision, and I blinked several times, confused.

I didn't think I'd gone to a party with Alex. Coach forbade any sort of drinking during the season. The punishment was worse than the worst hangover, and no player on the team would risk the wrath of the others if caught. Mostly, they tried not to get caught, but this year, I knew I had to play it safe.

Which made waking up in a strange room all the more perplexing.

I shifted, and soft, full curves filled my free hand. The memory of the previous night returned with them. Ember.

It shouldn't have been physically possible for me to get hard. We couldn't have gotten more than a couple of hours sleep, and my body had reached a level of exhaustion I'd only felt during the worst days of summer conditioning.

Regardless, my dick didn't care. Ember was my little spoon, and there wasn't a breath of space between us. My legs tangled with hers, which meant my dick was pressed firmly against her ass and happy about it. Those curves? My free hand was full of them.

Sweet Christ.

My hand contracted reflexively, and I froze. Her nipple had beaded up against my palm. This was foreign territory. Much as I'd like to tease Ember awake, then fuck her senseless despite how bone-deep tired I was, this wasn't a boundary we'd discussed in our brief but satisfying arrangement. The hell was a guy supposed to do?

She shifted, and her ass brushed against my dick, which didn't need any encouragement, for fuck's sake. The scent of her hair filled my nose. Her nipple teased my palm. The things I wanted to do to her…

It didn't take a fucking genius to figure out that her shit-bag ex had left her with hang-ups about sex. The idiot must not have known what a clit was to save his life. I didn't have that problem. I could spend the rest of my life happily buried between her legs. He didn't know what the hell he was missing out on.

That's why this had to be some sort of test.

And I was gonna fail so fucking hard.

Inhaling deeply through my nose, I counted to three. I'd get up, and I'd get dressed. The twins were probably still asleep, so I could sneak back to my apartment without making a spectacle. I'd text Em and tell her I'd gone back to my place and that I'd see her later.

Only, when I went to move, Ember shifted again, scooting back against me. The head of my dick teased at the crease of her ass, then pointed down to spear between the crevice of her thighs, like it had a mind of its own. It was paradise and damnation all at once.

Shit.

My breath rattled out, and I moved to extricate myself from around her. I ached like a sonofabitch, but maybe when she was awake, I could convince her to come over the next time she had a free minute. Even then, I wasn't sure I'd ever have enough of her, but I'd take what I could get.

Her hand clamped down on my hand that was on her chest, and I froze again. Her head angled back so that she could see me. "Wait."

"I thought you were asleep," I said. "I was trying not to wake you."

She wriggled back against me, and I strangled a groan. "You think I could sleep with this teasing me all morning?"

"Teasing you?"

"It woke me up. I've been debating whether I should wake you up the same way or not."

"For the record, you can wake me up any way you like."

She relaxed back down on the bed and pulled me against her. I was thinking about getting my mouth on her pussy again, but instead, Ember reached between her legs and stroked my cock, coaxing it between her thighs. All the oxygen in my lungs seemed to evaporate. She was already wet for me, the skin of her inner thighs slick with her arousal.

"Why didn't you?" she asked.

I couldn't help it. Once her thighs closed over the head of my dick, I thrust my hips forward and pressed my forehead against hers. I angled up so that I was brushing against her wet folds, teasing us both. Sweat broke out all over my skin.

"Didn't I what?" What the hell were we talking about?

"Why didn't you wake me up any way you liked?"

She tensed the muscles in her thighs, and I was this close to begging her to let me in. "It wasn't something we'd talked about. I didn't want to cross any boundaries you might have that I didn't know about."

For a second, I thought I had pissed her off because she didn't say anything in response. Then, she lifted her top leg and rested it over my thigh. She reached down again and angled my cock toward her opening. I sucked in a breath as she adjusted her body until I slid in with ease.

"Next time, you can wake me up if you want," she said. "I don't mind."

I was trying to keep a clear head, but it was impossible. She was so warm and wet it was killing me. My voice was hoarse when I spoke. "I'll try to remember that."

We had to be quiet, so I fucked her soft and slow, listening to the sounds of her breathing change, and adjusting the depth and speed of my thrusts. When she was moaning into the pillow she had pressed against her face, I moved my hand from her breast with reluctance to her swollen, sensitive clit. I'd spent the previous night learning everything there was to know about what got her off. I had made her come so many times she'd been begging me to stop in the end.

Ember's fingers clamped down on my wrist as I began to draw circles over her responsive flesh. Her hips bucked, urging me to go faster, but I wanted to take it slow and make it last. We both had a busy couple of weeks coming up, and we might not get a chance to be together for a while. I wasn't going to rush her over the edge if I could help it.

She began to writhe against me, trying to get herself off with my dick. I chuckled darkly and said, "Someone's greedy this morning."

Practically growling, she replied, "Tripp, please fuck me."

Goddamn, I liked it when she was bossy.

Turning, I adjusted her body until she was lying on her side somewhat, belly to the bed. I straddled her bottom leg and angled the top over my arm. When I drove into her, it was long and deep and slow. She stopped breathing for a second, her eyes rolling to the back of her head and all of her muscles tensing when I bottomed out inside her.

She liked this position, I had learned. Her thighs were quivering within seconds, and sounds came out of her throat I'd never heard her make before. If it weren't for the pillow she kept pressed against her mouth, the whole apartment complex would have heard her moaning for me. I kept my slow and steady pace and teased at her clit until she was so wet that I could feel the moisture transfer to my thighs.

When her hips went crazy, I knew she was close. She liked to fight her orgasm, and I had to keep hold of her leg, or she would have bucked me off. In the end, I had her damn near pinned to the bed, playing furiously at her clit as she sobbed out her release into the pillow. I could wake up every morning like this, imagining new ways to make her scream.

She lay there for a while until the aftershocks abated. When she could move, I climbed off her and threw myself onto my back. My dick was still rock-hard, but all I wanted was to make her come again, so I was thoroughly satisfied.

I was only half aware of what she was doing as she slid down my body. Then I felt her hand wrap around my dick and stroke it. I made a strangled sound in the back of my throat.

"Em…" I groaned when she began to lick up and down the length of me. I'd spend so much time making sure she was always thoroughly taken care of that, in the few minutes we managed to steal together now and then, I hadn't let her reciprocate very much. If the devious look on her face was anything to go by, she was going to pay me back in full.

Her heated breath bathed my thighs. "Don't move," she ordered huskily, her hand stroking again.

I could only hold my head up long enough for the vision of her kneeling beside my legs to burn itself into my brain. Her short red hair tumbled around her shoulders. Her chest flushed pink, and her nipples were like pretty little raspberries. I wanted to paint my cum all over those tits, and the thought made me weak all over, and I dropped back against the pillows.

Comprehension was slow, my brain muggy with sleep and the musk of sex. When I realized what she was doing, I fisted the sheets at my side. Certainly, there was no way in hell she was going to—fuck. And then her mouth slicked over the head of my cock. She crouched beside me, her thick ass swaying in the air as she bobbed over me. I reached out a hand and clamped on the flare of her hip to steady myself.

I sputtered, not necessarily in objection, but because I didn't want her to feel obligated to do anything she didn't want to do. Naturally, she ignored me and merely splayed a hand over my abs and applied gentle pressure, pushing me back onto the bed as she licked the taste of her orgasm off my cock.

Was there a more beautiful sight? I didn't fucking think so.

None that I could call to mind, anyway.

While she bobbed up and down over me, I shifted enough to play with her pussy, which was still wet and so pretty pink it was irresistible. Without a second thought, I pulled her hips and helped her straddle my chest so I could get a taste of her while her mouth was wrapped around me.

She kept herself shaved except for a thatch of hair in a neat little triangle at the top that had the same red color as her hair. I didn't care what she looked like, but I couldn't deny hers was the prettiest pussy I'd ever seen, simply because it was hers. She moaned around my dick as I teased her clit. She was so tender that I did little more than lap at the engorged flesh.

To be honest, I could barely concentrate on doing much more than lick at her. She didn't mind. She swayed her hips back and forth over me. Then she took my cock deep in her throat, and it flipped a switch inside me. I wrapped my arms around her waist and fused my mouth to her wet cunt. My tongue found her opening and speared in, causing her to choke on my cock. I probably liked that more than I should have.

The combination of her taking me deep into her throat and the taste of her on my tongue was something that would haunt me...probably forever. She tasted so fucking good, I couldn't get enough. When she readjusted to take the heavy globes between my legs into her hand to squeeze gently and fondle, while simultaneously taking me as deeply as she could, I pulled away, saying, "Fuck, angel, I'm gonna come."

"I'm not going anywhere," she said.

I should have known she'd give as good as she got. She took me deeply again, and I barely had enough time to warn her with a tap on her ass before I was coming down the back of her throat. I moaned against her pussy, inhaling her scent as the orgasm washed over my nerve endings.

She moved to get up once I stopped, but I kept my arms wrapped around her hips and gave her a second orgasm with my mouth, thinking she was the best breakfast I'd ever had.

When we were done, and I'd gotten a cloth to clean us both up, she curled next to my side, and I was so relaxed I drifted in and out of sleep. I liked having her next to me, soft and warm from sleep and sex.

A guy could get used to it.

A door slammed in the hallway, and we both jumped a little. "Guess that's our alarm," she said sleepily.

"We should probably get up," I answered, but neither of us moved.

"In a minute." She yawned, then stretched. "I haven't felt this good in such a long time. I'm glad you stayed."

"Me, too, but I better get my ass to practice, or it'll belong to Coach."

"When can I see you again?" she asked. "I have to work tomorrow, but maybe the day after? You could come after the twins fall asleep."

I punctuated my promise with a kiss. "Looking forward to it."

She went out first, herding the twins back to their room to get dressed, while I snuck out the front door to go back to my apartment.

I was already thinking about when I'd get to see her again.

CHAPTER 19

EMBER

t was April.

If there was ever an end date for my relationship with Tripp, it was the end of the school year, when he'd go off to play professional ball, and we'd have to go back to being friends. I didn't want to think about it, but there was no denying the date on the calendar.

"One more month!" the twins screamed while running around in circles. "One more month!"

I winced and stared at the coffee maker, hoping it would sputter out it's steaming brew more quickly.

"What's all the yelling about?" Tripp asked, coming down the hallway in a pair of low-slung basketball shorts and a tank-top still wrinkled from where I'd thrown it on the floor the night before.

"ONE MORE MONTH!"

"Let me guess. One more month until they go deaf from all the screaming?" he asked as he pulled coffee cups down from the cabinet for the both of us. He was always doing thoughtful things like that. Making me a bath after a long shift at work.

Doing the girl's bedtime routine with them without them having to beg. Cooking for all of us, even after day-long practices.

And that didn't include everything he did for me in bed.

I'd never in my life been with anyone so flat-out generous in all ways. He was mine for a short while longer, and I was going to keep him satisfied while I had him.

"Until they're done with school. They're excited to stay with your mom during the summer while I'm at work. I heard a rumor she was getting passes to the public pool for the three of them."

The twins changed their shouted chorus to, "Pool! Pool! Pool!" as they laughed and screeched around the dining room table.

It didn't even phase Tripp, who was pouring us both a cup of coffee, adding more sugar than should be humanly possible to consume to mine and drinking his with a touch of vanilla creamer. He passed my cup to me and leaned forward to give me a kiss. I let him because the girls had long since caught us making out from time-to-time. They liked to tease us and pretend to be grossed out, but I knew they liked Tripp almost as much as I did. Probably more than they liked me, if I was being honest.

"I'll tell you who is really excited. My dad. He can't stop talking my ear off about how much free time he has to do all the projects he loves now that mom isn't occupying every spare minute with her honey-do list. I swear, if he weren't head-over-heels for her, he'd kiss you for it."

I made eyes at him over the rim of my steaming coffee cup. "You're kidding."

"Well, maybe about the kissing part. But he might build you a really nice spice rack or something as a thanks. I think he really loves it when the girls come over, though. They love it when he does his magic tricks for them."

"How did your parents make it together so long?" The

concept—a happy marriage—was so foreign to me. The example I'd seen for so long told me the only happy relationship was the one in the rearview mirror. Was that why I'd clung to Chris for so long? Was I afraid of turning out like my parents, so I had stayed in an unhappy relationship? Which had ended up becoming like theirs in the end, anyway.

We took our coffee to the living room, sitting on the new couch I'd bought from the online classifieds. It was well-worn and smelled faintly like fish sticks, but at least it wasn't riddled with cigarette burns and stale beer stains. Tripp pulled me into his side, and I settled there, content. The girls had finally calmed down long enough to inhale a banana and a Pop-Tart each before they dashed off to pick out their clothes for school.

"I've never really thought about it. They've always sort of been each other's best friend, I guess. Comfortable with each other."

"He's always touching her. Have you noticed that? Maybe not, because you're used to it. Maybe he doesn't even notice he's doing it." I sipped from my coffee contemplatively.

"What do you mean?" Trip asked.

"Hugging her or kissing her on the forehead. She also does this thing where she'll put her feet in his lap, and he'll automatically start rubbing them. Little habits, I guess."

He didn't have to ask if my parents had ever done that. I wasn't even sure I'd ever heard them say a kind word to each other, let alone show any sort of affection. They were the definition of a toxic, codependent relationship.

I finished my coffee to fill the void in the conversation. Too sensitive a topic. I didn't know why, but thinking about it made me sad. I glanced at my watch. "We'd better get a move on, or we'll be late. Especially you."

Tripp wrapped a hand around my waist. "Hold on there, angel." He tugged me back into his lap. "Is this you saying you want me to be more affectionate? Should I add that to the rules?"

I laughed and tried to push him away. "Don't be silly. C'mon, we've got to go."

"We've got enough time for this."

He arranged me comfortably over his legs and brought my mouth to his. My hand held his wrist as though I was afraid to have him too close. I was, I'd admit it. Thinking about the differences between our parents made my heart ache with an emotion that was a little too close to the surface. I wanted what his parents had, but I thought a part of me was afraid I'd sour it simply because of where I'd come from.

I didn't know how to have a happy relationship. I'd simply never seen one. All I knew was fighting and manipulation and pain. How would that ever translate to a fiftieth wedding anniversary, unless it was one steeped in unhappiness?

Sorrow pricked inside me. That's why this arrangement with Tripp was so perfect. It kept me safe. Protected. But more than that, it kept Tripp safe. I couldn't break his heart if there were no feelings involved. I wouldn't have to show him the real me, the true me, if what we had wasn't serious. Sure, he saw my crazy, fucked-up life, but he didn't see how twisted it made me inside.

"Where'd you go?" he asked, pulling back a little and searching my eyes for an answer.

"Nowhere," I lied. "I'm right here."

He didn't seem convinced, and he could probably tell I was lying. Thankfully, he didn't push it. The alarm that signaled five minutes until the bus blared on my phone, but I let him kiss me, erasing my worries.

My next twenty-four-hour shift was a mentally exhausting rigamarole of drama and heartbreak. A family had argued for forty-five minutes about riding in the ambulance with their pregnant relative, despite the fact that she was half-naked in the back of the truck, screaming through contractions. Finally, I had to slam the doors, nearly taking off a finger of the concerned auntie, and signal for my partner to hit the road.

Then we'd had back-to-back transfers and emergency calls throughout the night. I didn't think we had more than an hour of sleep the whole night. At three in the morning, we had been called to the apartment of a family whose two-week-old baby was blue and unresponsive. We had taken them to the nearest NICU, but the baby never came back. All I could think of was the twins and how they'd been born prematurely because my mother had smoked a pack a day.

To say I was thankful to be home and looking forward to seeing the girls was an understatement. I was tired, but I needed to see them. To play dolls and a million games of Candyland, even though it was the most boring board game ever created. They were due any minute from the bus, and no doubt they'd have stories from their latest stay with Tripp's parents. They were like the grandparents they never had.

A knock came at the door, and I opened it, expecting to see Timothy, the young boy who sometimes helped the girls into the apartment after they got off the school bus. Instead, my mother stood there, one hand on her hip and a cigarette clamped in her red-slicked lips. She wore a pair of jeans newer than anything I'd ever owned, and there was a new Birkin bag at her shoulder. She'd either used her five-finger discount or was deep in the throes of love with a new boyfriend who had money to burn.

The sight of her shocked me so much that I didn't have words. I'd fully expected never to see her again. Once one month had turned into two, then two into three, and three into four, I'd written her off. As far as I'd been concerned, she was no longer a part of my life—let alone my mother—and I couldn't care less if I ever saw her again.

I crossed my arms over my chest. "What are you doing here?"

My mom tipped down her sunglasses. God only knew why she was wearing them inside. "I live here."

She tried to shoulder her way inside, but I wedged my foot in the bottom of the door so it wouldn't budge. "What are you doing?" she demanded. The scent of stale cigarette smoke wafted from her stick-thin form.

My heart hammered in my chest. Confrontation with her was never my strongest suit, but I had the girls to think of. If they saw her when they got home from school, they'd flip. Guaranteed. She couldn't keep flitting in and out of their lives like this without facing the consequences. If she wasn't going to protect them, I was.

With a steadying breath, I said, "I'm trying to figure out what you think *you're* doing. You can't barge your way into our lives whenever it suits you. Do you realize what could have happened to Matilda and Molly when you *left them here alone*?"

Did she care? Even after more than twenty years of neglect, I still couldn't figure it. She kept us around, but she also so easily walked away. How could someone who cared about you just walk away?

She started with a placating tone—one I'd heard a thousand times before. "Well, they're fine, aren't they? You're a fancy medic. You can fix them up if something happens." She rolled her eyes and tried shoving her way in again.

She rolled her eyes.

Something inside me snapped.

"You're not coming in here," I said, a steel edge to my voice.

I didn't know if it was my bald refusal or my tone, but it caused her to take a step back.

She flipped her hair. "What did you say to me?"

My heart was beating so fast it felt as though it weren't beating at all.

"I said you're not coming in here. The twins will be home from school soon and seeing you would only upset them again. They only recently got used to you not being around. If you want to see them again, then I'll talk to them and explain things, and we'll meet somewhere for you to have lunch or something."

Over my dead body. But I felt I at least owed it to them to give their mother a chance to be…well, a mother. Besides, when I had googled custody situations like this, the websites had said it was important to offer a chance at visitation. If we could show that my mom had been offered the opportunity to see the kids and had refused, then maybe I'd have a better standing. It was worth a shot. Fuck, I needed to see a lawyer and make this official so she couldn't try and take the girls ever again.

"You're going to tell me what to do with my kids?" she demanded, her eyes flashing in a way that reminded me all too much of myself. It made me a little sick to think that we could have something in common. The difference was, I'd never play games with another person simply to feel more in control.

"I'm going to tell you what to do with *my* sisters. I'm the one who's always here for them. I pay for the roof over their heads. I have never, and I will never, abandon them. I am nothing like you." My voice shook, but my hold on the door was resolute. She wasn't coming in, not ever again, unless she proved that she could be the mother that the girls—that I—deserved.

My mother smirked, but it was shaky around the edges, like she was barely holding it together. "You're more like me than you think."

"You should leave," I said without taking her bait. But God knew I wanted to. "If you want to see them, then we can schedule a time that works best for them. You're never going to hurt them again, not if I have anything to say about it."

She shouldered her purse, her knuckles white from how she gripped the straps. "You'll hear from me real soon," she said with dark promise.

She was gone by the time I could unstick my tongue from the roof of my mouth. It was ridiculous that I could deal with life-threatening emergencies on a day-to-day basis at work but confronting either one of my parents scared me to death. They disappointed me on a regular basis, but God forbid I ever disappoint them.

With a deep breath, I glanced at my watch and cursed under my breath. Timothy was late. It must mean the bus was a bit behind. On the way down the elevator, I worked on calming down my breathing. The last thing I wanted was for the twins to know something was wrong.

When I got down to the street-side of the apartment complex, the bus was already waiting at the bus stop, but there was no sign of the twins or Timothy. I waited under the awning until the last child got off.

"I'm sorry, but I don't see my sisters, Molly and Matilda Stevens. Are they still on the bus?" I asked the bus driver.

He was an older man with a silver beard and an old military ball cap. "Their mother picked them up," he said and snapped his bubblegum.

Instant anger, fiery and destructive, bubbled up in my stomach and threatened to spew from my mouth. With exaggerated calm, I said, "Their mother is not on the list of people allowed to pick them up. In fact, I filled out paperwork with the school to ensure that I was the only one allowed to pick them up."

The bus driver, clearly in a hurry to move on and not interested in any of my drama, snapped his gum again. "I haven't heard anything about that. The girls seemed to know her and said she was their mother. Listen, I have a whole other bus of kids to take home."

"Taking care of children while they're in your care and ensuring they get home to their proper guardians *is your job*." I boarded the bus, and his eyes sparked, but I took out my phone, despite his cursing to do otherwise, and took a photo of his identification, his face, and the contact number listed on the sticker by his seat. "I'll be in contact with your supervisors."

"You do that," he grunted and slammed the doors shut behind me.

I walked blindly around the apartment courtyard after getting off the bus. It was so stupid of me to think that my mom would have gone off quietly into the night after being turned away. Now, she'd taken the twins God-only-knows-where in retaliation. When my senses returned, I called the non-emergency police line and learned that, apparently, a child's mother could take them wherever the hell they chose. And since I didn't have an official custody arrangement yet, there wasn't shit I could do about it. I didn't know whether to cry or scream. I wanted to do both simultaneously, but it wouldn't solve anything.

"Thank you for all of your help, you fuck-shit," I snarled, then threw myself onto a bench and buried my face in my hands. I'd dealt a lot with the police when running calls, but I didn't see them as the professionals who couldn't help but do their job. For the moment, they were the people who were supposed to help me but were saying their hands were tied.

Without any other options, I returned to the apartment and began to pace. Finally, I texted my mom at her last known number, praying it was back in service.

> ME: Please bring the girls back.

I waited for fifteen tense minutes, checking my phone multiple times for a response. What if she didn't ever bring them back? What if she disappeared, and I never saw them again? Guilt drove over me in crushing waves. I'd been so negative the past few weeks, so hard on them. I thought back to how harsh I'd been with Molly when she'd walked off in the grocery store. What if she took them, and I never got to tell them how much I loved them?

> MOM: I'll bring them back if and when I'm good and ready. I'm their mother, not you.

I dissolved into a puddle on the couch, dropping my phone to the floor. I never cried, but it was too much. First Chris, then my parents, Tripp, and raising the twins. Plus school and back-to-back difficult shifts at work. It was too much for one person.

Tripp. I could go to Tripp. He'd be home from practice in a couple of hours. He'd know what to do. If nothing else, he was always the perfect shoulder to lean on. But he had his own problems with practice and games. He already did enough to help me as it was.

And things had gotten so complicated.

No, I'd deal with this on my own for once. I'd have to.

I should have been studying, but I couldn't concentrate on my notes if I tried. All I could do was picture the girls crying because my mother had abandoned them somewhere. I pictured my buddies at work getting a call and arriving at a scene, with my twins as the victims. Countless scenarios raced through my mind, each worse than the last.

It was midnight before I came to the conclusion that my mother wasn't bringing the twins back that night. Wherever she was staying, she was keeping the twins to sleep over. Without any other option to turn to, I felt hopeless, listless. There was nothing I could do but wait to hear back from them or my mom. I just hoped it would be soon.

I threw myself into my bed and tried not to think about how theirs were empty down the hall. I almost wished I hadn't moved them out of my room. Maybe they wouldn't feel so far away.

My phone chimed with a notification. Hoping it was my mom, I sat bolt upright and turned on my bedside light. My stomach sank when I realized it was only a notification from an app. I almost turned my phone back off until I realized which application it was. It was the app I used to track my cycle. The one that told me when my period was due.

I unlocked my phone to go to the app when I realized what it was saying. I double-checked the dates and then checked them again because it couldn't be right. There was no way.

But it was there.

I was late.

It had to be stress. Or the IUD I got before Chris and I broke up. According to my doctor, my cycle could be wonky for a few months. That was all. Maybe I'd gotten lucky like a lot of women and wouldn't have a period at all.

Knowing I wouldn't get any sleep until I had more information, I went to the bathroom where I kept a lone pregnancy test from a scare when Chris and I had first started having sex and before I got on the IUD. The minutes I waited after taking the test were almost as excruciating as waiting for news from my mom.

The timer I set on my phone dinged, and I picked up the test, my chest full of apprehension.

The digital readout said *positive*.

My knees simply gave out, and I fell to my butt right there on the bathroom floor. When I could breathe again, I checked the screen once more, and the word *positive* was still there. It was the same on the two other tests I ran out to get. I had all the time in the world to watch my life go down the drain. If there was an upside, it was that my panic about the girls was obliterated—if only for a moment.

I was in too much shock to feel anything other than stunned disbelief.

No matter how much I didn't want to believe it, there was no denying the results.

I was pregnant.

Fuck.

CHAPTER 20

TRIPP

Ember didn't answer her phone after I got out of practice, which didn't concern me at first. We played when I came over by ear, so I didn't really think anything of it. Much of our relationship—or lack thereof—consisted of ignoring how much of a relationship we actually had. I spent more time at her apartment than mine. We didn't date or sleep with other people. When she wasn't working, I was normally in her bed after the twins went to sleep.

Which made my apartment feel as quiet as a tomb in comparison. I knew she thought the girls were too much to handle, and they certainly were a handful, but that didn't mean I didn't enjoy them. They were two of the sweetest kids I'd ever known, and, having been in their lives since they were babies, I felt an incredible kinship toward them. Like a mixture between uncle and older brother. I couldn't imagine a future without them in it.

These thoughts and more revolved around my thoughts as I heated up a frozen dinner instead of making myself a meal. I didn't really see the point when there was no one else to enjoy it. My mother had instilled in me a love of cooking, and one of my favorite things was to cook meals for my own personal judgment panel, but it simply wasn't the same without my girls.

That's what the three of them were.

My girls.

And I wouldn't be giving them up without a fight.

I finished my pitiful frozen dinner and daydreamed it was the filet mignon we'd grilled at my parents' house during spring break. While the rest of my classmates headed down to the beach to exchange saliva and STDs, we'd taken the girls to a water park and ate too much pizza. The weekend before school was back in session, we'd packed up the girls and hauled them to my parents' house for the weekend. Ember grilled steaks and made baked potatoes and a salad. My mom gave her tomatoes and cucumbers from their backyard garden. They'd talked for hours while the girls, my dad, and I had taken turns jumping through a beach ball with a built-in sprinkler.

My dad surprised us all with baseball gloves for the girls. Call me a fucking chick, but it made my chest hurt to see them throwing a ball around with him. Molly could only make it halfway to him, but she caught like a champ. Tillie, however, might have a little Wilder in her because she could throw the ball with a bit of heat behind it. My dad and I had shared a glance. Maybe I could talk Ember into signing her up for ball next season. The girls could use more extracurriculars, and they'd liked playing catch.

I fell asleep on the couch, daydreaming about teaching them how to play.

I still hadn't heard from Ember.

It was lunchtime the next day when I finally gave up waiting on her to text me back or answer my calls. It wasn't like her to ignore a message, which could only mean that something was wrong. I wasn't the kind of guy who had to be involved in absolutely everything. I didn't like to be smothered, either, but I also knew Ember, and this wasn't like her.

I gave her until after I'd cleaned up the kitchen from the night before, eaten breakfast, and taken a shower before I grabbed the spare key she'd given me and used it to let myself into her apartment. It was dark as night, so I flicked on the lamp by the sofa.

"Ember?" I called. It was possible she'd passed out after her shift, but even then, she'd normally text me before bed to come over or to tell me good night.

No one answered.

The apartment was dead silent. The twins must have already gone to school. The kitchen and hall bath were empty. I poked my head in the girls' room, but they weren't there. Ember's was the last on the right, and I pushed the door in to find it as dark as the living room. Using my phone as a guiding light, I picked my way to the bed.

The lump in my chest eased as the halo of light from my phone showed her bundled under the comforter on the bed. Setting the phone on the nightstand on what I considered my side of the bed, I slipped out of my shirt, toed off my shoes, and climbed into bed next to her. From her breathing, I could tell she wasn't asleep, but I'd already barged into her apartment, so I wasn't going to demand she tell me what was wrong, too.

Eventually, she relaxed against me. We dozed in and out for a while, with her as my little spoon. At some point, she must have grabbed my hand because I woke up with our fingers locked together. I liked it. More than I should. It didn't terrify me to be linked to her. In fact, it wouldn't bother me to be linked with her for the foreseeable future. But this wasn't the time or place to renegotiate our rules.

"They're gone."

I almost couldn't hear her because her voice was so low.

"Who's gone?"

"The girls."

I didn't understand. "Are they at school?" I asked.

"Mom took them." Her voice was dead. Like there was no emotion or even the energy to infuse it with life.

"The hell do you mean your mom took them?" I urged her to turn to face me, even though I could barely see her through the shadows. "Talk to me, angel. What happened? Where are they?"

She sighed so heavily I could almost feel the weight on her shoulders on my own. "She came over yesterday, expecting me to let her just take the girls on a playdate like nothing had ever happened. Like she didn't just walk out on them like they didn't matter. She had on fancy jeans that must have cost a hundred dollars or more and a designer handbag that could have fed the girls for *weeks*. I mean, I haven't had new clothes in *years*. When everyone else was going apeshit over labels and having fun with their friends, I was buying diapers and formula. But do you think she gave a shit?"

Ember was trembling in my arms. Not with anguish, but with fury. I let her keep going because I wanted to keep my head where it was.

"She thought she could waltz back into their lives without repercussions for her actions. I told her there was no way in hell she'd see the girls. Not until she got her act together and started acting like their mother. I thought I'd done the right thing."

"You don't have to feel bad for that," I said.

As though she didn't hear me, Ember continued, "I went to go get the girls from the bus stop, but the driver said their *mom* had come and got them, despite the fact that no one but me was supposed to be able to pick them up."

I tried to keep calm. It wouldn't help anyone for me to get all worked up, even though I entertained some very vivid fantasies about lighting that woman on fire with her own cigarettes. "Have you heard from her since then?"

Thankfully, Ember let me gather her up in my arms and pull

her close. I couldn't fix everything, but I could do this for her. "I texted her old number, hoping it had been reactivated. She basically told me to go fuck myself."

I refrained from calling her mother some choice names. She might be a piece of shit, but she was still Ember's mother. "Did you call the police?"

"That was the first thing I did. They told me that because she was the girls' mother, she was allowed to watch her own children. I've never wanted to murder anyone until that moment. If Mom had been anywhere near me, I'm afraid that I would have killed her."

I had no doubt about it from the ferocity in her words. Except, she was wrong. That woman wasn't their mother. No decent person would put their children through what she had. Ember had always been—and always would be—the twin's *real* mother as far as I was concerned.

"Let's go." I sat up and tugged her along with me.

"What? Where are we going?" she asked groggily, still wrapped up in her fury.

I was already tugging my clothes back on, lacing up my shoes. I flicked on the lamp again so I could see where I had put my phone. My mind raced, trying to think of all the places she'd ever mentioned that her mother liked to visit. "We're going to every place you can think of that your mother liked to visit. Friends. Bars. Hotels. We'll find those girls, Ember. I promise you."

She paused in pulling on a pair of my favorite yoga pants, and I frowned as her creamy legs disappeared behind the fabric. "You don't have to do that."

"Shut up."

We were at the door, and I was making a list on my phone of places to track down, when Ember's phone rang. Her face drained of all color when she saw the number on the screen. She practically collapsed to the couch. Her hands were visibly shaking as she brought the phone to her ear.

"Hello?" She bit her lip. "Yes, this is Ember Stevens." I went to her side and took her free hand in mine. She clenched onto my fingers like they were a lifeline. "You do? Oh, my God. Yes, I'm home. That's correct. Thank you, Officer. Thank you so much. I'll be here." She ended the call, and her hand fell to her lap. When she looked at me, a kaleidoscope of emotions raced across her face: anger, fear, relief. "They were found at a restaurant in the mall. They said Mom told them I was going to pick them up. What a fucking bitch."

"They're bringing them here?"

"Yes. I don't want to cry. I've been crying so much lately."

"Baby, you don't have to be afraid to cry on me." I pulled her onto my lap. "You don't ever have to be afraid of that. At the center of everything, you're my best friend, Em. I'll always be here for you, whatever you need. Tears, orgasms, tacos. I've got you, babe."

That made her laugh, and then I just held her. When the officer arrived to take Ember's statement, I held the twins. After the officer left with a promise to send social services for a checkup, I held all three of them. Then they all curled up on the couch together while I made them canned chicken noodle soup and grilled cheese. We ate it while watching the first *Harry Potter* movie. The only thing that was missing was a big old fluffy puppy at our feet and a cranky cat on the back of the sofa.

Ember fell asleep first, and I told the girls how glad I was that they were okay. They cried some more, and then they snuggled up on either side of Ember and fell asleep holding hands. I was pinned to the couch by the three of them. I couldn't have imagined a better place to be.

It wasn't lost on me how different my last night had been, and even though today had been rough on us all, I couldn't help but think these girls made it all worth it.

CHAPTER 21

EMBER

"Mm hmm, look at all those big…bats," Charlie said with a wicked grin. Her dirty-blonde hair whipped in the humid air. She was effortlessly beautiful in a dark t-shirt and skinny jeans kind of way. One black Chuck-covered foot was propped on her knee. She'd say she was a tomboy, but I always thought she was simply comfortable in her own skin.

She'd become even more so now that she and her best friend, Liam, had stopped dancing around each other and had started dating and living together. It was like he gave her the space to comfortably be herself. Truth be told, I envied them.

Layla giggled and smacked her on the arm, causing Charlie's drink to wobble precariously in her hands. "You have a boyfriend!"

"So do you," Charlie retorted. "Besides, it doesn't hurt to look. Liam doesn't care what I do as long as I bring it back to him at the end of the day." She tilted her head, studying the away team as they swung their bats at the plate, readying for some practice hits. "Do you think if I got him a pair of baseball pants, he'd dress up for me?"

"Dash had a kilt from Halloween a couple of years ago. When I found it, he let me talk him into wearing it. I never knew a man in a skirt could be so sexy."

Despite my preoccupation with what I needed to tell Tripp, my head jerked in Layla's direction. Layla, the one who'd been a virgin up until the year before. Layla, the studious bookworm who never put a toe out of line. Dash must have changed her in more ways than one. Charlie and I shared a look. It was sweet of them to try and distract me from thinking about how much of a complete and utter piece of crap my mom was. They'd voted to put a hit out on her, but I'd convinced them putting a curse on her was enough.

"What?" Charlie shrieked. "Dash wore a kilt?! How did you not tell us about this?" Her voice took on a high-pitched tone. "When your boyfriend wears a kilt, you should be taking pictures. For…bribery purposes. And research. But mostly to share with your best friends!"

Layla's smile turned mischievous. "I was too busy doing other things to take pictures."

That stunned the indignation right out of Charlie's expression. When she could speak, she said, "It's like I don't even know you. Who are you, and what did you do with our friend?" Charlie demanded.

Layla blushed prettily and sipped her beer with an elegance I never seemed to be able to imitate. "My lips are sealed," she said.

"Ohh, no, you don't. You can't say something like that and then not give us the juicy details. Spill."

Their banter faded into the background as our team swarmed the field, their garnet practice jerseys drawing my eye. I drank thirstily from my soda, suddenly parched. I wished it was a beer, then remembered I couldn't have those, which only made my stomach churn more. I found Tripp almost immediately, his number three like a beacon. My heart sped up at the sight of his dirty blonde hair glinting in the bright afternoon sunlight. Charlie wasn't wrong. The sight of him in baseball pants wasn't one to be ignored.

Not that I'd been able to ignore him at all lately.

"—and then he did this sexy little dance, and I jumped him," Layla was saying when I could focus back in on their conversation. I was being an awful friend, but I couldn't seem to think of anything other than the positive pregnancy test I had hidden under the sink in my bathroom.

"You dirty bitch!" Charlie exclaimed with bright eyes. "You've been holding out on us. Em, can you believe it? Our little girl is growing up."

Layla rolled her eyes, then glanced at me. "What's up with you? You've been very quiet. Is everything okay?"

I was too hollow to cry and too tired to lie, so I settled for something sort of in between. "Nothing I can't handle."

Charlie sobered, her gaze sharpening as she studied my face. "Whoa, whoa, whoa. I thought you and Tripp were great. 'Having fun' is what you said. Did he fuck something up? I'll kick his ass."

"No, he didn't do anything." He found me from his place on the pitcher's mound and lifted his hand in a wave. For some reason, I felt the gesture deep inside my chest. I waved in return. "He's been great. Much better than I deserve."

"Oh, shut up. You deserve the best. And if he isn't giving it to you, well, then we need to have a talk with him."

"Yeah," Charlie agreed. "Or we'll kick his ass."

"No need to kick his ass, he hasn't done anything wrong at all."

"It's like pulling teeth," Charlie said to Layla. "C'mon now, are we your best friends or what? Why do you look like your favorite pet was just run over? Is it your mom?"

"Not at the moment. Okay, there is something, but I need to talk to Tripp about it first. I promise as soon as I do, I'll explain."

"Cryptic," Layla said.

"Agreed. But if you aren't ready to talk about it, you know we'll be here whenever you need us. It's not anything else about your mom, right?"

"No, I haven't heard from her since she took the twins. DCF came by to start a report and take a tour of the apartment. They said they'll be in touch, though."

They really were the best friends anyone could have, and I knew they'd be there for me if and when I was ready to talk about it all. Like they had been there for me when Chris and my parents left. And again when I had called them about what my mom had done.

"I'm sure it will turn out fine," Layla offered.

"Damn right it will," Charlie said.

"Thanks, guys. For now, I want to forget about it for a little while, if that's okay."

Layla gave me a sidearm hug. "Of course, it's okay. We'll look at hot guys in tight pants with you any day."

They spent the rest of the practice game huddled close to me on either side, and I felt their concern and love wrapped around me like a hug. It helped dull the panic and shock to a bearable amount—at least until the game ended, and I was faced with telling Tripp about the baby. It had been a couple of weeks since my mom had taken the girls. Enough time for them to settle back into a routine. Now there was no more putting off telling him the truth.

I could tell he was excited about their win, but it was bittersweet for me. A pregnancy would ruin all of his plans. Those dreams to play pro ball? Up in smoke. Sure, people would say we could make it work, but I'd already been there. Not that I regretted taking care of the twins, but children change lives, and although they're precious, it wasn't always for the better.

They require sacrifice, and I would never want Tripp to have to sacrifice the dream he'd worked so hard to achieve. He'd already nearly lost it once. I couldn't make him face that possibility again.

Tripp wasn't the type to run from his problems, though. No, he was responsible, dependable. He'd want to do the right thing. Because of that, it was tempting not to tell him.

But he deserved to know, and I couldn't live with myself if I didn't. I was used to shouldering my burdens alone, but this one was too heavy for me to carry.

We pulled to a stop in the parking garage, and Tripp got out of the car, still humming happily. Meanwhile, dread began to pool in my stomach, causing the hot dog and soda I'd had at the game to churn unpleasantly. Tripp took my hand, and that was it.

The doors to the elevator closed behind us, and the dam broke. I began to cry, silently at first, then full-out sobbing.

Tripp, who'd been in such a cheerful mood, froze, then wrapped his arms around me. The comforting scent of his cologne filled my nose, and even though everything else seemed to make me nauseous, I was thankful this didn't.

"Hey, what the hell?" He was so bemused that it only made me cry harder. "Okay, angel, I won't make you go to any more of my games, I promise, but you don't have to cry."

"That—that—that's not it!" I wailed. Keening sounds emitted from my chest, and I tried to stifle them, which only made me cry harder.

"Okay, baby. Let's get you inside, and then we can talk about it. We have some time before my parents are supposed to bring the twins back home."

Oh, God. How was I supposed to support three kids? This was madness. I was barely keeping the twins and me afloat.

How would we survive with another life thrown into the mix? I'd have to take off school. I wouldn't be able to work for a while. Tripp was supposed to have his big break this year. He couldn't do that with the weight of me and the girls around his neck. And now a baby. What in the hell had I been thinking?

Sex was never simple.

Relationships were never simple.

Life as a whole was complicated and messy and unexpected. Nothing about mine had ever gone to plan, no matter how much I tried to make it fit. I had wanted to go to college after high school but had only done my EMT certification. I had wanted to get married and have a family the normal way, but Chris had dumped all over that. I had wanted to make a good life for the girls and me, and now I'd ruined that.

I didn't want to ruin my friendship with Tripp, too, but I wasn't sure it would survive this.

The thought only made me cry harder. It didn't faze him, though. Apparently, these months with us had made him immune to female tears. Poor guy. I was sure this wasn't what he had signed up for.

Friends with benefits…that was the arrangement.

Sex without complications.

It was now a whole lot more complicated than either of us could have imagined.

While I freaked out internally, Tripp led me to my apartment, unlocked it, and shuffled me to the couch. It only made my cry harder. He was too nice to me. Too understanding. He was going to take this so well, and it would only make me feel worse.

I wanted him to scream and rage at me. Treat me like crap. Because that's what I felt I deserved. A baby would take away his choices and his future because he wouldn't see it any other way. He was a good guy, as evidenced by how amazing he'd been throughout everything.

He brought me a glass of tea, and I gulped it down to soothe my raw throat. When I was done, he passed me a handful of crumpled tissues. Not caring how I looked—or maybe I was just comfortable with him after everything—I blew my nose and dried my face.

"Feel better?" he asked.

Not at all. I made a noncommittal noise, wiped my nose again, and pulled up my big girl panties. I wasn't going to cry anymore, and I wasn't going to continue with the woe-is-me bullshit. I had made the choice to have sex, and this was one of the potential eventualities. I was an adult. I would have to deal with it like one.

"Tripp," my voice petered out, and I took another sip of tea to steady myself and come up with the words to say. How did one go about potentially changing someone's life forever? "Tripp, I don't know how to tell you this, and I just want you to know before I go on how much you mean to me. I couldn't have been through this without you. I hope you understand that."

He nodded and relaxed into the couch, making sure to tuck me into his side. It was a casual movement. One I wasn't really sure he even realized he did. "You don't owe me anything, babe. I've been happy to help."

"I don't only mean with the twins and everything. I mean, after Chris left me, I don't think I'd ever been so low, and I'm not the type who gives a damn what a man thinks about me."

"Especially not a chump like him."

"We never talked about us, like where we were going to go after the benefits ended."

At my words, he straightened, his concerned gaze sharpening. "You want to end things?" he asked. Was I imagining things, or was there hurt in his words?

My tongue tied itself into knots. "No, I mean, if you want to, but—"

"What would make you think I want to?" His brows pushed

together, and his full, kissable lips folded into a frown. I was going to miss those lips.

Things were so much easier when the focus was on sex. I should have never agreed to this. I knew when I met him, when the twins were little, that taking this too far would be a bad idea. Maybe I was more like my mom than I thought.

Selfish. Reckless. Careless.

Doomed to repeat her mistakes.

My hand pressed against my stomach. I didn't know if it was all the crying or the hormones, but I felt sick.

"Ember?" he prompted.

"I'm pregnant," I blurted. Or I think I did. The ringing was so loud in my ears that I couldn't be sure.

The hand he had resting on the back of the couch dropped to his lap. His face went lax in surprise.

"You're pregnant?" I heard over the ringing in my ears. I nodded, but it made me dizzy, so I clutched the back of the couch to ground me.

"I'm so sorry. I know this isn't what you had planned. I thought maybe it was from stress, but I took a test, well, I took several, and they were all positive. I can't believe I'm doing this to you when you're about to start your senior year of ball and you've got so much going on. I thought about not telling you, but that didn't seem—"

His big arms wrapped around me, squeezing so tight he cut off the rest of my apology. Maybe I was selfish because I soaked up the comfort he provided without hesitation. My tears dried, my thundering heart slowed, and by the time he pulled away, I was somehow in his lap and much more steady.

"You don't have anything to apologize for, angel. Nothing at all. You hear me?"

"I thought you'd be upset." His measured reaction had my brows pulling together.

"I don't know what I am, but it's as much my responsibility

as it is yours, Em." Which is exactly what I had expected him to say.

My voice was tiny when I responded. "I'm scared. This is going to change everything. Your career...the twins."

He pulled me close and kissed the top of my hair. "I know you are, baby. This wasn't exactly part of the plan, but you know I'll be here for you. Whatever you decide. And whatever it is, we'll face it. Together."

CHAPTER 22

TRIPP

There was one qualifying game left in the season. One last chance to prove to myself, to Coach Taylor, to my advisors, and to the world at large that this was what I was meant to do. When I wasn't at Ember's apartment, I was training. I ran three miles a day, lifted weights until all my muscles shook, and pitched until my arm went numb. I was ready.

It should have been the only thing on my mind, but it wasn't. I was at the last practice before our last game, and all I could think about was Ember. The baby. *Our* baby. We were going to be parents.

It wasn't exactly how I'd planned for things to go down, but I wasn't upset. Far from it. Now that I'd had a little while to wrap my head around the idea, I liked the thought of Ember having my baby. I fucking loved it. I knew it wasn't going to be easy. In fact, I was pretty sure it was going to be damn hard. But it would be a piece of the two of us, and I couldn't imagine a better mom for my child.

"Yo! Are you paying attention? I said a fastball, not a curve-ball!" Alex shouted from home plate where he was practicing with me. He jogged to where I was standing at the pitcher's mound and tossed the ball. "You've been off all afternoon. You doin' okay, man? The pressure getting to you?"

It would have on any other day, but for the first time in my life, I had bigger things to worry about than baseball. "I'm alright."

"You don't seem alright. You better get it off your chest before Coach comes over here and tears you a new one. It's that chick, isn't it? Man, how many times do I have to tell you, women are fun to play with, but during the season, you should put a moratorium on pussy."

"You're so fucking stupid. That's not it, either."

"The hell it isn't. You've got puppy dog eyes. I know what that means."

I didn't think he did.

"You're in love with her, aren't you? Shit. I told you she was trouble."

My gaze jerked to his. In love with her? I tossed the ball from hand to hand as my mind raced. Was I in love with Ember?

I was.

It felt like I couldn't breathe. The ball fell from my glove to the mound and rolled a couple of yards away, but I didn't pay it any mind. Alex cursed when I didn't immediately go get it.

What I felt for her seemed too big to be so simple. It was holding her when she was upset. It was teasing her when she was frustrated. It was reading the girls a bedtime story and giving them a kiss on the forehead goodnight. It was putting together furniture and laughing when she couldn't do it by herself. It was seeing her in the stands at my game cheering me on. It was watching her be a mother to her sisters, even when she had to give up most things girls her age wanted.

It was life with her.

That's what I wanted.

I wanted to spend my life with her. To grow with her and

face all of our challenges together. I wanted to see the girls grow up, to give them away at their weddings. The life we'd made together, I wanted that with her, too.

It was messy, inconvenient, scary, and complicated.

I loved her.

"Dude, are you okay? Are you having a nervous breakdown or something? Shit, I mean, do you need a hug?"

A smile broke out over my face. What the hell? I pulled him in for a hug and clapped him hard on the back. He hesitated for a second, then did the same. "Are you sure you're okay?" he asked.

"Never been better. You're right. I do love her. We're having a baby."

I hadn't said the words out loud until now. I was afraid what it would mean if I did. But I wasn't terrified like I was worried I'd be. I wasn't going to desert Ember like her father had.

"For real?"

I nodded. "For real."

"That's crazy. Congratudolences?" At my exasperated look, he said, "What?! Don't look at me like that. You're having a baby! My whole life, I've tried *not* to have babies. Don't give me any crap. I'm happy for you, my guy, but I wouldn't wanna be you."

"Does this mean you don't want to be Uncle Alex?"

His expression melted. I knew that would get him. He might act all hard, but he was a family guy at heart. All you had to do was see him talk about his mother, Angelina, one time, and you'd know he was a big 'ole softy.

"You want me to be her godfather?"

I thought about it for a second. I didn't think Ember would have a problem with it, so I said, "Pending her approval, fuck yeah, I want you to be her godfather."

He nodded. Then he gave me another hug. "Congratulations, Tripp. Thank you. I'd be honored."

"If you two don't stop making out, I'm gonna make you run laps," Coach Taylor shouted.

We didn't end up having to run laps, but by the time I got back to Ember's apartment, it sure as hell felt like we had. You'd think the coaches would go easy on us, considering it was the end of the season, but that wasn't the case. We were expected to be in top form until the ump blew his whistle on the last game. I didn't care. I was more pumped than ever to take us to Omaha.

I unlocked the door with my key and walked in without announcing myself. I barely even went to my own apartment anymore. I couldn't tell you the last time I'd slept there. Ember was in the kitchen making something that smelled like heaven. The twins were on the floor with newspaper spread beneath them, playing with what looked like a science experiment from hell populating half a dozen bowls.

"Are you guys making dinner?" I asked. "It smells good."

Tillie giggled. "No, silly."

"We're making slime!" Molly exclaimed and dug into a bowl with both hands, pulling out a huge pile of neon blue goop.

I dumped my bag of gear by the front door and knelt down next to them to give them a squeeze. "Looks delicious," I said, causing them to giggle.

Ember lifted her cheek for a kiss next. I obliged her. "You look delicious, too."

She was in a pair of sweats and a baggy t-shirt. She wasn't wearing any makeup, and her hair was thrown up in a messy bun. "I think you're full of it," she whispered back.

"How about later I let you know how delicious I think you are?"

She blushed and turned back to the chicken and rice she had been stirring in a pot. "Really?"

"Really, what?" I wrapped my arms around her from behind, my hands going to her flat stomach.

"You still want to?"

"Why don't I show you how much I still want to when the twins go to bed?"

I did just that a couple of hours later, once the twins were clean and snuggled up and Ember and I were alone in her room. I had her lay down, and I stripped her bare, starting at her toes and worshiping on my way up. She stopped me just before, even though she was slippery wet and shaking with need.

"You sure? You're not weirded out?" she asked.

I kissed her navel. And lingered. "What about this would weird me out?"

She shrugged, and her breath hitched when she spoke. "I dunno. Some guys get freaked out about sex and pregnancy. My dad did."

I winced. "Let's not talk about your dad right now. All I want is you. Nothing about you could ever weird me out."

I pushed up to kiss her and took my time there until her hands kneaded my shoulders, insistent.

She tore away and said, "You shouldn't. You have practice in the morning, and it's almost midnight."

Patiently, I peeled her hands away and pressed them to the bed. I knew her mind must be going a mile a minute, trying to solve every problem before it came up. Especially now. I simply couldn't give her time to think, or she'd rationalize to death all the good things we had.

So I pinned her hands above her head with one hand. She

could have gotten away if she wanted to, but she let me do it while watching me with feverish eyes. I gripped my cock with my other hand and wet the head with her juices. Her breath caught again as I slipped inside in one long, slow stroke.

She liked it when I was relentless, when I gave her what she wanted, but slowly. Carving away at her need like a river carved a canyon.

"You think I don't know these things? I knew when we made this arrangement what the deal was. What the risks were. I've never given up on anything in my life, and I'm not going to start now. No matter what, we'll make it work. I'm showing up. I'm showing up for you and the girls. For our baby."

She lifted her hips to meet me, her eyelids fluttering as she tried to stay focused. "Then you have to promise me you're not going to give up on your life either. No more late nights, no more skipping studying or practices. I care about you and want you to succeed, no matter what."

"But the baby?"

She blushed. "It's the size of a pea. It doesn't need anything right now."

"And you?"

"I can take care of myself."

"Try again," I suggested.

"Tripp, I'm serious."

"So am I." I spread her legs over my forearms and fucked her deep.

"That's not a part of the rules," she insisted breathlessly.

"Then I'm making it a part of the rules. From now on, you won't fight me when I try to help with you or the girls. I want to be in this with you. You just have to let me." She nodded, and that was all I needed. "Deal."

CHAPTER 23

EMBER

He was right. I wanted to let him in, to truly accept that he'd be there for us, no matter what. People had made promises like that to me my whole life, but no one had ever stuck to them. Tripp didn't need to make promises. He showed how he felt with actions.

"I know you want to come. But you have to get ready for your game tomorrow. I'll be fine, I promise. Besides, you're coming with me to your parents' after."

He sulked about it for a while but finally agreed to let me go to the first doctor's appointment the next day alone. I knew he wanted to be there like he said, but I was adamant he not jeopardize his future. Besides, it was just a blood test to confirm the pregnancy and then remove my IUD. I could handle that. The important part was that he understood I wanted him to be there and that I'd let him take care of me when it mattered.

I was used to hospitals, doctors, and the scent of bleach and antibacterial spray. I'd spent about a quarter of my life in hospitals, sometimes with patients who were so close to death it was like I could feel death's presence hovering over my shoulder, daring me to fail at my job. But when it was me as the patient?

Hell no. I'd rather be on my deathbed at home, please and thank you.

The nurse walked me back to the room and had me change into a paper gown. They took urine and blood samples to confirm the pregnancy and asked details about my last period and history. Pretty standard routine, like I'd expected.

They explained the risks associated with the IUD removal, which I already knew. But the risks of keeping the IUD in were worse. The experience was a little painful, but not as bad as I'd anticipated.

"Take it easy for a few days," they advised. "And come in if you experience any significant pain or prolonged bleeding."

I was in and out in a little over an hour and felt immediately relieved when it was all over. Everything was going to be okay. Like the life blooming inside me, I allowed a little bit of hope to take root that everything would be okay.

I wondered if he could tell that things had changed between us. The words were on the tip of my tongue. I kept telling myself just to spit them out, but they wouldn't come. What if my feelings were only because of hormones? I wanted to be certain before I said them to him.

Or maybe I wanted him to say them to me first so I wouldn't look like a total fool if he didn't reciprocate. Maybe I just needed to find it inside me to be brave. I had to be brave, take a chance.

He held my hand all the way from the hospital to his parents, who were watching the girls while I was at the appointment and Tripp was at practice. I didn't think I'd ever be able to repay the Wilder family for their generosity.

"You feeling okay?" he asked.

"A little achy, but otherwise, I'm fine. Like I was five minutes ago." I squeezed his hand to show I was teasing. It was honestly cute how concerned he was. He would be a good dad. My heart twinged, imagining him holding a tiny newborn. Damn hormones. If I wasn't already pregnant, I sure as hell would enjoy trying to get that way.

"When do you think we should tell my parents?"

My smile fell a little. That was something I'd been worrying over. I knew they'd be ecstatic, but there was still a little part of me that was worried they wouldn't approve of me as "the one" for their son. He was so wonderful in every way, and I was just...me. I wasn't going to be a big star. I didn't have huge plans with my life other than surviving day-to-day. Tripp should be with someone as special as he was.

"Let's tell them once we're past the first trimester," I said. Maybe by then, I'd come to terms with how much everything had changed. Maybe by then, I'd have the courage to tell him I loved him.

"Sounds good to me. They're going to be so excited."

"You think so?"

"I know so. They love you, and they already consider Molly and Tillie to be their granddaughters. They'll be ecstatic to add another to the brood."

"They won't be disappointed? Like, we're not really in a relationship, and we're not married or settled. I'm almost done with my paramedic certification, but you're just starting your career."

He put his finger over my lips after he parked in their driveway. "Labels don't matter to me, but I know they do to you. I was afraid you'd walk away if I pushed, and I know what I stand to lose, but one of our rules is honesty, and I will always be honest with you." My heart began to thud heavily in my chest. His blue-grey eyes bore into mine, and he took both of my hands in his. "I love you, Ember. I've loved you for years. I think you've known for a while now. Your girls are like my family. *You* are like my family. The only thing I want is to make you happy.

Whether that's as your boyfriend or, in the future, as your husband. I want to do this with you."

"Really?"

"Really."

"I love you, too, Tripp. I was just too scared to say it. I want to be with you, too. Friends and benefits and all."

"Then, c'mon, because Mom and I have a surprise for you."

Another surprise? I didn't think my emotions could take more happiness, but I followed him inside. Molly and Tillie were building an intricate structure out of Legos with Tripp's father. We waved as Tripp pulled me into the kitchen, where his mother was baking something that smelled divine.

He gave his mom a kiss. "I told her we had a surprise for her."

"Did you?" his mom said with a smile. "Well, I'd rather not keep you in suspense. Tripp's father and I were talking, and we'd like to help you get custody of the girls. We know a family lawyer who is willing to help, and we'd like to pay their retainer."

My mouth dropped open. I could barely breathe. "You can't be serious."

Tripp's mother smiled. "Totally serious. We want to do this for you, and you know we adore the girls."

"It's—it's too much. I can't accept it. Thank you, but I can't."

"I told you she'd say that," Tripp said to his mother. "We've been working on her accepting help from others, but she's hardheaded."

I smacked his arm. "It's too much," I repeated, unable to form coherent words. "I—I don't know what to say."

Things like this simply didn't happen to me. I wasn't a perpetual victim, but life had always been hard. I'd always had to fight for everything I wanted. Fight my parents to take care of me simply to survive. Fight them to go to school, then college. Fight them to do what was best for the girls. To have someone be so effortlessly generous...it simply didn't compute. Was that why I'd given Tripp such a hard time for so long?

"Say you'll at least think about it. We want to do this for you. If it makes you feel any better, you can consider it a loan and pay us back when you're able, but you don't have to."

Mrs. Wilder punctuated her offer with a soft smile. Her salt-and-pepper hair was as perfect as ever, falling to her shoulders in a sleek, straight cascade. She looked as opposite of my mother as possible, and I ached for the loss of not having someone like her in my life—in the twins' lives. Would I be depriving them of a mother like Mrs. Wilder if I did pursue custody? I had to admit, even if it was only to myself, the worry plagued me.

"I'll think about it," I told them, and they shared a smile. "I'll have to talk to the girls because I think they should have a say."

"Whatever you think is best, angel. We only want to help," Tripp said.

Mrs. Wilder organized a consultation with a family attorney the following week. I switched shifts with another EMT so I could have a couple of days as a buffer to focus my thoughts. Butterflies took up permanent residence in my stomach, and they dove and swooped so often and so violently that I thought my ribs would crack from the pressure.

I was scared.

Ever since my parents had disappeared, I'd been running on instinct and fumes. Tripp had helped to distract me from the true force of my worries, but I couldn't hide from my problems forever. And the twins deserved to have normalcy and security in their lives now more than ever. If I was so adamant that they have both, then I needed to put on my big girl panties and face it.

I wouldn't become my mother. And the twins hadn't hesitated in saying they wanted me to be their guardian when I talked to them about it.

That was the driving force behind agreeing to let Mr. and

Mrs. Wilder front the retainer for the family lawyer. It would help secure their future, and that was all that mattered. If I needed to bear the brunt of my mother's ire when she was served the papers, then so be it. I was done cowing to her demands. I had not only the twins but a baby to think about. None of us needed that toxicity in our lives.

The secretary led us back to a conference room after a short waiting period where my heart beat double-time, and Tripp had to hold my hand to keep me from flying out of the seat. I hadn't yet started to experience morning sickness, but I was definitely feeling queasy from the nerves. The lawyer had a small practice that had a homey feeling, located in an historic-looking house, with the first floor serving as offices. After gesturing us into the conference room, the secretary left us to wait for another short period.

After a time, a woman in her mid-to-late forties appeared, her hands full of manila folders. "Good morning! My name is Tara Shultz," she said brightly, shuffling the folders to shake our hands. "Thank you so much for your patience."

She took a seat behind her desk, opened a file, and perched a pair of thin, wire-rimmed glasses on her nose. "Now, we're here today to discuss custody of Matilda and Molly Stevens, aged six." She glanced over her glasses to me. "You'd be their older sister, Ember?"

"Yes, I am," I answered, my voice shaky. Tripp gripped my hand more tightly in his.

"Tell me about your parents. How long have they been gone?"

Then everything sort of seemed to spill forth—their negligence when I was growing up, how I'd supported the twins and my parents, and how they'd abandoned the girls.

"And have you spoken with your mother or father since they left?" she asked.

"I spoke to my mother the day she left. And she came back a

few weeks ago and took the girls without warning. They were found abandoned at the mall the next day. The police took a report."

Ms. Shultz took down the information and promised to get a copy of the police report. She explained that in order to receive custody, we'd have to prove both parents were unfit for custody in some way or have them waive their rights. It wouldn't be hard to convince my father. He didn't give a shit either way. It was my mother I was worried about. She was spiteful and vindictive and would fight 'till the end simply because she could. The thought made my stomach ache.

After the visit to the lawyer, Tripp drove to pick up the girls, and we went home and watched cartoons until they passed out. The next morning was Tripp's last game of the season—the one that would determine if they went to the championships or not.

He left before we woke up to head over to the field for warmups. I'd planned on getting the girls awake and dressed so we could go cheer him on, but all that changed in an instant.

CHAPTER 24

TRIPP

S weat dripped down my brow, and I wiped it away with the back of my wrist. This was the last game of my senior year. My last chance to impress—shit, I didn't even know who anymore. My last chance to wipe away the memory of my injury. We were playing a killer game and were in the lead 10-0, but I knew better than anyone that it could change in an instant. So I played hard, like my heart and life were on the line.

And maybe they were.

"Good fucking game, man," Alex said, clapping me on the back as we entered the dugout.

"It's not over yet." I squirted water from my bottle over my head, but it didn't do much to cool me down. The Florida heat was relentless. I could already feel a sunburn turning the skin at my neck tight and splotchy.

"The hell it isn't. You haven't given them a break all day. Your arm is on fire. I've never seen you pitch better."

"I don't think I've ever heard you give so many compliments in a row."

"Call me sentimental," he answered, his eyes on our short-stop, who was at bat. "It's our last game together. When I get signed next year, we could be playing on opposite sides of the country. We could even be playing against each other."

"Scared? It's okay. I'll make sure I kick your ass quickly so it doesn't sting so much to lose."

He punched me in the arm, tossed his dark hair back, and slid his baseball cap over it. It always made the chicks who came to the games go crazy. "You wish. Don't think I'll take it easy on you if that day ever comes."

"It will. Believe it. You're almost as good as I am."

"Asshole," he said without heat. "Where's your girl? I thought she was coming?"

Thinking the same thing, I scanned the crowd again for her face in the family seats. She and the girls weren't in their normal spot next to my parents, and neither were Liam and Dash. I figured something must have come up with the girls, but a niggle of doubt and worry wormed itself into my stomach.

"I'm not sure. She was supposed to be here, but she may have had to take care of her sisters or something."

We cheered as our shortstop hit a double, batting in the player on third and scoring us another point. "What's going on with that?"

I lifted a shoulder. "It's complicated."

"You sound like a chick."

"At least I'm getting laid," I said, making him scowl.

"Douchebag."

One of the assistant coaches came out of the hallway that led to the locker rooms. He made a beeline for Coach Taylor, who listened with an impassive expression as he observed the next player up at bat. His body went still as the assistant coach kept talking, gesturing wildly. Then Taylor's gaze moved to me, and I stiffened.

Coach Taylor murmured to the assistant, his eyes still on me. The assistant coach nodded, and Coach Taylor started to cross the dugout to me. Whatever it was, it couldn't be good. Coach Taylor was always focused on the game. Especially a game as important as the one that would lead us to the championships in Omaha.

"Wilder. A word?" I nodded and followed him to the hallway where the assistant had come from. "Listen, I'll get straight to the point. Are you involved with a young woman named Ember Stevens?"

"Yes, sir," I answered, fighting to keep my voice steady. Coach Taylor wouldn't interrupt a game for any reason other than an emergency.

"There's a Miss Charlie St. James here who says you need to go with her immediately. Ms. Stevens is in the hospital."

My heart dropped to my feet along with my stomach. "The hospital," I repeated faintly. The baby. Fuck. Something was wrong with the baby. I had to get to her. "I have to go to her. She's pregnant," I said without thinking.

Coach Taylor's expression didn't change, but the words that came out of his mouth were the last ones I expected. "Of course you do. Miss St. James is waiting at the ticket gate to take you to the hospital."

"I'll make sure he gets there," Alex said. I hadn't even realized he'd come with me.

"What about the game?" I asked, more out of habit than anything. I didn't really give a fuck about the game.

"Go be with your girlfriend." I didn't correct him. "You're young, but you'll realize there's more to life than baseball." I never thought I'd hear him say those words. "Get going. You need to be with her."

When I didn't move, Alex took me by the arm and hauled me through the locker rooms and up the stairs to the main level of the complex where the concession stands, and ticket booths were located. It wasn't as packed as it usually was before a game, but there were still people milling around getting refills on their sodas and popcorn who stopped and pointed at us as Alex propelled me toward the ticket booth. Charlie was there, pacing back and forth, still in her pale blue scrubs.

She turned toward us when she looked up, and I noticed, almost emotionlessly, that her face was bleached of color. She rushed forward. "I'm sorry for interrupting your game, but she's asking for you, and I didn't know what else to do."

"It's alright." To Alex, I said, "Thanks, man. You should get back."

He started backing away, and his normal easy-going expression was grave. "Call me. Whatever time. I'll be there."

"I know. Go win for us."

"You got it."

Somehow, he must have grabbed my bag with my change of clothes from my locker when we went through the locker room because I found myself hauling it out of the complex to Charlie's car. As I tossed it in the back seat, I managed to spit out the words I didn't want to voice aloud for fear that it would make my worries an actuality. "What happened?"

The keys in Charlie's hand rattled as she put them in the ignition. "The doctors think she's having a miscarriage."

"Is she alone?" I asked.

"Layla was with her. I volunteered to come get you."

"How was she?"

Charlie swallowed hard. "She was in pain. They gave her some medication to help the pain and help her rest. They want to keep her overnight for observation. I got here as quick as I could."

"Thank you."

I was quiet for the rest of the drive to the hospital. The baby had only been alive for a few short weeks. I hadn't even had time to properly wrap my thoughts around their existence. It didn't seem fair for their life to end so suddenly. It hadn't been planned, but they had been wanted, and they were already loved.

Charlie drove into the emergency room parking lot at the hospital and stopped under the awning for me to get out of the car while she parked. I signed in at the front desk and followed one of the nurses back into the maternity ward on autopilot. When they stopped at her room, it took me a minute to work up the nerve to open the door, afraid of what I'd find on the other side.

Layla looked up from where she was sitting beside the hospital bed. Both of her hands were wrapped around one of Ember's. The other was hooked up to a bunch of wires and tubes. She looked incredibly small in the large bed. Her eyes were closed, and her chest rose rhythmically in sleep.

I crossed to the bed, my eyes on her face, afraid I'd see her slip away right in front of me. "How is she?" I asked Layla. I studied the dark smudges under her eyes and the hollows in her cheeks I hadn't noticed before.

"Hey, Tripp. She's okay now that she's resting. The doctor says she can go home tomorrow if there are no complications."

I swallowed hard. "Thanks for being here for her."

Layla got up and pushed her hair away from her face. Her eyes were red. She must have been crying. "Of course. She'll be glad to see you're here when she wakes up. I'll give you two some time. Please call Charlie or me if there's anything you need."

"I will. Thanks again."

Layla paused after putting her purse over her shoulder. Then she moved forward and wrapped me in a hug. "I'm so sorry, Tripp."

A tide of sorrow welled up inside me. "Me, too," I said.

There was nothing else to add, so Layla left. I dumped my

duffle on the small couch in the room, then took Layla's place in the chair by the hospital bed. Ember's hand looked so limp and pale when I took it into my own. She was the strongest woman I knew, but in the bed, hooked up to a half-dozen machines, she seemed fragile. The fear that I could have lost her at any moment, too, was overpowering.

CHAPTER 25

EMBER

"Are you sure you don't mind having a girl's night while we pack up? I hope I'm not killing your fun."

Charlie lifted a beer. "You provided sustenance. It doesn't matter where we're at, as long as we're together."

"Don't make me cry," Layla said, then hefted the box she was carrying onto a stack of them at the front door. "I can't believe we're all leaving this place. It won't be the same."

Charlie nodded. "It was fun while it lasted."

It was, I thought, as I looked around the apartment, which was in various stages of disarray. I'd had a lot of hard times here, but there were a lot of good times, too. The girls had lived here their whole lives. They'd said their first words and taken their first steps here. It was bittersweet, but time for a change.

In the weeks since my stay at the hospital, I'd recovered. It hadn't been easy, but Layla and Charlie had helped. Charlie had taken time off work to be my own personal nurse for a few days. Layla had stopped by after school to take care of the girls when Tripp's parents weren't watching them. School and my own work had been understanding. Within two weeks, I had been back in the swing of things. It was almost like it had never happened.

Except it had, and I was forever changed.

"End of an era," Layla agreed. "How is the new place? Do the girls like it?"

Since I was finishing the program at school and was going to be making more money, I thought it was time we left the apartment for something with a little more room to grow. The girls needed something closer to school, and they needed their own rooms. While I had been taking it easy on bed rest, I had scanned the classifieds and found a nice, albeit older, three-bedroom, two-bathroom home with a bit of land and a fenced-in backyard. It was on the girls' school route, so they could get on the bus right in front of the house. What they loved most of all was that they got their own space. Of course, more often than not, I found them curled up asleep together, but they were happy, and that was all that mattered.

"They love it. They're trying to convince me to get a puppy now that we have a backyard."

"A puppy!" Layla squealed. "I want a puppy."

"Don't gang up with them. It's already hard enough to resist their charms. They've been doing all sorts of extra chores all week trying to get in my good graces."

"It's working, isn't it?" Charlie asked with a big grin. She shoved back the dirty blonde hair that was falling out of her long braid.

I groaned and grabbed my own beer. I'd provided a couple of six-packs and snacks in exchange for their help. "Yes. They've even made their own chore chart of how they'd divvy up the extra chores for a puppy. Down to who will walk it on which day and whose room it gets to sleep in. That one caused a bit of an argument."

Layla munched on a handful of chips and salsa before asking, "Have you heard from Tripp at all?"

The smile fell from my face. I sucked down half of my beer before I answered. "He texts every now and then when he can. He's been practicing nonstop and traveling to games. The hope is he can still participate in this year's draft, but we won't know until August for sure."

To think of Tripp not playing ball...the thought simply didn't compute. He was meant to play. I couldn't picture him doing anything else. God knows, he must be feeling horrible. I couldn't even imagine. Having him show up at the hospital during the most important game of his life to be with me was exactly what I was afraid he'd do. Give up his dreams for me. I wouldn't allow him to make the same mistake twice.

Charlie grunted, her eyes on the dishes she was packing into a box. "I'm just saying, if he was willing to leave that game to be with you, girl, he's a keeper."

"Let's not talk about it for a while. Thinking about it too much makes my heart hurt."

Which was exactly my problem. This whole arrangement was supposed to be so that feelings *didn't* get involved. We were supposed to come out on the other side unscathed, without any strings. Somehow everything had gotten so tangled that we were both at risk for getting hurt.

They were both annoyed with me but acquiesced to my request. For the next few hours, we finished boxing up the rest of the kitchen and moved to the bedrooms. By the time the moon was high in the sky, we were all a little dusty, drunk, and exhausted, but the apartment was finally all in boxes. There were surprisingly few of them, considering the four years I'd lived there.

Charlie and Layla tried to convince me to let them stay, but I shooed them away. The weeks after the miscarriage had been hard, and I found that I often needed space to deal with my feelings. Tripp had stayed with me in the hospital until I was released forty-eight hours later. To be honest, I wouldn't have made it without him. He hadn't pushed, hadn't demanded. He had simply been there to help. When I had learned that he'd left the game for me, I'd been furious, but he'd stubbornly insisted I was more important.

I hadn't known whether to be flattered or supremely pissed off. Anger was easier, so I had gone with that. While I had healed, he had given me space to work through my feelings. Which had only pissed me off more. I hated that he knew what I wanted without me even having to request it. Who was he to think he knew what I needed?

That's why, when he knocked on my door after the girls left, I was fuming. If it weren't for the glass of wine I'd been refilling after we ran out of beer, I'd have answered the door with shouts. Instead, I opened it and lifted a brow.

He looked good. Too good. He must have flown in straight after the championship game on a red-eye instead of staying with the team. I'd already heard from various sources on social media that they'd won.

"Hey, Ember," he said and shifted from foot to foot. He was still carrying his backpack and luggage, so he hadn't even gone back to his own apartment yet. I refused to let that soften me toward him.

I took a long swallow of wine for courage. It hurt so good to see him. If he'd wanted to prove how much I needed him in my life, he'd done a damn good job of it. That didn't mean I had to be happy about any of it.

"Glad to see you made it back," I said.

He nodded. His expression was so downtrodden it made me want to take him into my arms. "I wanted to come see you."

"Now you've seen me," I said.

"Can I come in?"

If I were a stronger person, I would have said no. But I missed him, so I moved back so he could come inside. "I was just about to go to bed," I said.

"I understand. I just wanted to see how you were doing. Make sure you're okay."

Dammit.

Why did he have to be so nice? "I'm fine."

He sat on the couch next to me, but he could have been back in Omaha for how uncomfortable it felt. Why was this so weird and awkward? Could we get back to the place we were in before we lost the baby? Did he want to? I didn't know.

But I wasn't going to be a coward about it anymore. If I'd learned anything through this experience, it was that life was short, and it was important to nurture the good things while you had them because they could be taken from you at any moment. Before Tripp, I'd resisted enjoying those things simply because they could leave. But now, I knew it was better to fall and fall hard because that's what made life worth living.

I choked back my stubborn defenses and let go of my anger. "Tripp, I've spent this time apart thinking about all the things you ever said to me. While you were gone, I got to experience what life was like without you, and I didn't like it. You make me happy, even when you're pissing me off. You're my best friend, and I don't want to be apart anymore."

He pulled me into his arms. "It was killing me not having you there. We won, and I didn't even care. All I could think about was getting back to you."

I punched him in the stomach. "Next time, don't make me stay away."

"You won't get a chance. You're obligated to go to all of my games for the rest of your life."

"Does that mean we're done with this whole space thing? 'Cause, honestly, it sucked. I'm not a fan."

"Totally done. I was a shit for thinking I knew what was best for you."

"You're forgiven as long as it never happens again." I let

myself relax and enjoy the feel of him around me again. I wasn't going to cry. I wasn't going to cry.

When I'd had my fill, I got back to my feet. "Be right back." I went to my room and retrieved a small bag from one of the boxes. "I wanted you to have this."

"Em," his voice cut off as he dug inside the gift bag and pulled out a little onesie. It was a Florida Falcons jersey for a newborn with WILDER stitched on the back.

"I thought you would think it was a cute way to tell your parents."

"You— When did you get this?"

I lifted a shoulder. "When I first found out. I meant to give it to you when I told you, but I was so emotional about the twins that I completely forgot. You don't have to keep it if you don't want to."

"No, I want it." His voice sounded like it had been mixed with gravel. He tugged me down so that I straddled his lap. For a moment, all he could do was hold me. "I want it more now than I've ever wanted anything. Will you be with me? I don't want to spend any more time apart."

"Yes," I said without hesitation. "Yes, that's what I want."

"Then, you're stuck with me."

"Is that a rule?" I asked with a smile.

He kissed me. "That's the only rule."

EPILOGUE

THREE YEARS LATER

They won.

I couldn't believe it.

I'd never seen a real-life demonstration of the phrase, "the crowd went wild," until that moment. Cheers erupted so loudly that it made my head ring. Popcorn was tossed into the air like confetti. Sprays of soda and beer poured down like droplets of rain, soaking my navy and gold Florida Falcon's jersey with the name WILDER embroidered carefully between my shoulder blades.

Tillie and Molly jumped up and down beside me. They were older now and understood more of the game, but they were mostly excited because everyone else was.

"He did it!" Tillie shouted. "Tripp won!"

"Can we go see him?" Molly asked. "We should tell him congratulations."

I thought about saying no, that it might be too crowded to navigate down to the field, but Layla motioned for me and said, "Go for it. Everyone else is." Dash was by her side, clean-cut in a pair of slacks and a partially unbuttoned collared shirt, uncaring that he was covered in beer and greasy popcorn.

"Get your man," Charlie shouted, then whooped. Liam scooped her into a crushing hug and spun her around.

They were right, of course. I should go get my man.

"We want to go," Molly said.

"Yeah, he's ours, too."

I couldn't refute that. From the moment he'd moved in with us, they'd staked a claim as good as my own. Sometimes, even better. To say they had him wrapped around their little fingers was an understatement. He was a slave to those girls. I loved him a little more every time I saw them together playing tea, or playing with our new Boston Terrier, Frank, or the three of them all piled up on the couch passed out after a long day of playing on the Slip 'N Slide in the tiny patch of grass in our fenced in backyard.

Each girl grabbed hold of one of my hands, and I hollered above the din for them to stay behind me. Like I did when I got to a particularly crowded scene at work, I barreled through the crush of people like I was a two-ton elephant instead of a 5'6" woman. The girls pressed close to my back, and I kept a stranglehold on their little hands.

We made it to the railing where fans were simply jumping off straight onto the field and flooding around the players near the home plate. I paused for a moment, considering, then decided, what the hell. You only live once. Picking my way to an empty section at the railing, I scoured around me for the perfect spot where the girls and I could access the field without breaking our legs from the significant drop to the grass.

Fortunately, a compassionate person had somehow gotten a gate open with access, and I made a beeline for it before we could get swamped with more people. Once on the field, the girls and I made a break for it, sprinting along with dozens of others toward the diamond. The players stood out in a mass of navy, several being thrown up on shoulders and toted around.

Camera flashes damn near blinded me, but I didn't lose focus. I had eyes only for Tripp.

The crowd began to part when I was within a few feet, and Tripp appeared on its edge. I don't know if it was the sudden chill around the stadium or a sense of foreboding, but I slowed to a walk as I came closer. His teammates ringed around him in a half-circle. The hell?

Tillie and Molly were giggling and ran to Alex, who was on the opposite team. I'd asked Tripp what it was like playing against his friend once, and he had said they had a hell of a good time playing up the friendly rivalry. Off the field, they were still as thick as thieves when they weren't working. Alex scooped up the twins, one in each hand, and smiled at a couple of blondes nearby. He loved the girls, but he also loved that they were a chick magnet. Naturally. Three years and he hadn't changed, but I wouldn't have it any other way.

My eyes went back to Tripp, who'd made it to me, finally. He hadn't even said a word yet, and I was already near tears, dammit. "I'm so proud of you," I choked out.

He pulled me into his arms, and I pressed my face into the humid material of his jersey. I didn't care. I loved him when he was all dressed up, and when he was a sweaty mess. I loved him, no matter what.

"Thanks, baby." He pulled back and cupped my cheek with a hand. "I'm so glad you're here."

"Of course. I wouldn't be anywhere else." I tugged his head down so he could hear me over the shouting and screaming. "Congratulations."

He kissed my cheek. "I couldn't have done it without you."

"Lies," I said, but I was laughing as I kissed him.

The crowd around us muted to a barely-noticeable buzz. He deepened the kiss for one hot, furious moment, and when he released me, my head was buzzing, too. His hands dropped to mine.

A hush descended, and the contrast to moments before was almost deafening. My heart tripped. I glanced around nervously and found the twins grinning from ear-to-ear. "What's going on?"

Tripp squeezed my hands reassuringly.

Then, he got down to one knee.

A quick bark of high-pitched laughter burst from my lips. Then I snapped my jaws closed, closed my eyes, and took a deep breath. When I cracked them open again, he was still there, kneeling before me.

"What's happening?" I whispered. My heart thundered so hard that I could feel it beating in the tips of my fingers and throughout my chest. He wasn't... No, he couldn't be.

Tripp merely smiled. "Ember. I promise to follow our rules for the rest of our lives together. Plus, one more. I promise to communicate with you, even when it's hard. I promise to be honest at all times, even if it hurts. I promise that our family—you, me, the girls—and the lives we make together will always be my priority. I promise to love you for as much time as we have together on this earth. And finally, I promise to make each day better than the last...if you'll have me."

A box appeared in his hand. I may have blacked out for a second, so I wasn't sure where it came from. He let go of my hand to open it, revealing a beautiful halo-cut engagement ring.

"Holy shit," I whispered, struck dumb. Those around me who were close enough to hear my surprised exclamation laughed.

He was shaking when he took my hand with his free one. Looking into my eyes, his bright with unshed emotion, he said, "Ember, will you marry me?"

I was crying. Dashing the tears away with my fingers, I tried to say yes, but the words wouldn't come around the lump in my throat. My feet bounced because I couldn't stay still, and I was trembling as much as, if not more than, Tripp. All I could do was nod.

The world erupted into cheers again, and Tripp surged to his feet to take me into his arms. Over the crowd, which now pressed in around us, I could hear Tillie and Molly screaming and cheering. I saw flashes of faces, Layla and Dash, Charlie and Liam. Tripp's parents. Phones winked and flashed as people revolved around me.

Tripp set me down on my feet amongst the crowd, which was still in a crazy mass around us. "You aren't saying that because I put you in a tough spot in front of everyone, are you?'

I laughed and wrapped my arms around his neck. "That would have been bad if I said no. But for you, it's yes. It'll always be yes."

"You promise?" he asked softly.

"You were the best risk I've ever taken. I promise."

ABOUT THE AUTHOR

Nicole Blanchard is the New York Times and USA Today bestselling author of dangerous romance from antiheroes to aliens. She and her family reside in the Sunshine State along with their menagerie of animals. Nicole is represented by Katie Monson at SBR Media.

Visit her website www.authornicoleblanchard.com for more information or to subscribe to her newsletter for updates on sales and new releases.

facebook.com/authornicoleblanchard

x.com/blanchardbooks

instagram.com/authornicoleblanchard

amazon.com/Nicole-Blanchard

bookbub.com/authors/nicole-blanchard

goodreads.com/nicole_blanchard

pinterest.com/blanchardbooks

tiktok.com/@authornicoleblanchard

threads.net/@authornicoleblanchard

ALSO BY NICOLE BLANCHARD

Battleboro Fire & Rescue Series

Storming His Heart

Shielding His Heart

Saving His Heart

First to Fight Series

Anchor

Warrior

Valor

Box Set: Books 1-3

Survivor

Savior

Honor

Box Set: Books 4-6

Traitor

Operator

Aviator

Captor

Protector

Armor

A Salvation Society Crossover: Reckless

Friend Zone Series

Friend Zone

Frenemies

Friends with Benefits

Box Set

The Lost Planet Series

The Forgotten Commander

The Vanished Specialist

The Mad Lieutenant

Journey to the Lost Planet (Books 1-3)

The Uncertain Scientist

The Lonely Orphan

The Rogue Captain

Return to the Lost Planet (Books 4-6)

The Determined Hero

The Arrogant Genius

The Runaway Alien

Saving the Lost Planet (Books 7-9)

Dark Romance

Toxic

An Immortal Fairy Tale Series

Deal with the Dragon

Vow to the Vampire

Kiss from the King

Standalone Novellas

Bear with Me

Darkest Desires

Mechanical Hearts

www.ingramcontent.com/pod-product-compliance
Lightning Source LLC
Chambersburg PA
CBHW070358310726

48977CB00003B/491